Cheryl Lucas

Hidden
in
Crete

Published by Kingsway Publishing, Bath in association with Cheryl Lucas

ISBN: Paperback 978-0-9931312-2-6
eBook-Kindle 978-0-9931312-3-3

First published in 2015

Kingsway Publishing, Bath
3 Kingsway, Bath, BA2 2NH, UK
KingswayPubBath@aol.com

Hidden in Crete

Cheryl Lucas

Abandoned and alone in a foreign land, John Lancaster has to survive or die. War has shattered the island, but the courageous Cretans refuse to give in. John is hidden in a mountain village. He learns the language and the customs – and how to survive.

His grandson, Alex, finds his wartime diary hidden away in an attic and decides to fly to Crete and retrace his grandfather's footsteps. Once there he unravels a story of intrigue, jealousy, courage and love – and secrets that have remained hidden in Crete for over fifty years.

PART ONE

CHAPTER 1

1941

I was blown into oblivion.

Heat and dust rushed into my face. Dust clogged my nose suffocating me. I opened my mouth to take a gulp of air and it choked me. It filled my ears and blotted out the roaring in my eardrums. A cloud of molten air and smoke smothered me. My body tumbled downwards uncontrollably. Branches whipped my body. Thorns scratched the unprotected skin of my face. My thigh smashed into a rock. I grunted with pain. I heard the fabric of my uniform rip. I felt my body scorching. I seemed to be melting into vapour. Then the ground erupted suddenly. I rolled as I had been trained to do. I must have hit my head then. I did not open my eyes for by then I had blacked out.

The spring saved my life. I woke from a dream that I was drowning. But it was the slow drip of water on my face that brought me to consciousness. I could see nothing. Was I blind? All around me was dark.

I lay there letting my disconnected thoughts collect, giving my mind time to reassemble itself, allowing myself to make sense of where I was: to listen, to smell, to feel.

I could feel and hear the drip, and taste the water of the spring as drops fell on my head.

There was no roar of battle, no thud of mortars, and no crackle of guns. No voices, no tramping feet, no choking smell of gun smoke. As my senses gathered, I became aware of the silence. I have no memory of leaving the battlefield. I have no memory of reaching the lip of the cave and the source of the spring. I have no memory of how long I lay there. Safety, it would seem was in my grasp.

I didn't know if I was injured. I began a careful and cautious examination of my limbs. Yes, my ankles rotated, my feet flexed, my knees lifted. I tentatively raised an arm and then the other. So far, so good. I moved my head and felt a sharp pain, but the movement had brought my skull into contact with a rock. My skull itself, as far as I could gather, seemed intact and was not fractured. I guessed that my uniform was covered in dust and blood, but in the dark I could not tell if it was the dust of battle or if the blood was my own. I shifted my head cautiously to the left and found that in that position I was able to place my mouth underneath the drips to take in some water. A few gulps revived me. I gradually raised myself into a sitting position and, as my eyes became accustomed to the dark, I could just see that I was in the mouth of a small cleft in the rock. I must have rolled there after I fell. Water spilled from the rock in a steady trickle. It had fallen on my face and the sharp cold of it and the wet had revived me.

The sky, now that I had my night vision, was a dark indigo blue. There were no clouds and I could see myriads of twinkling stars. I think there was a moon that night but it was hidden behind the mountain. For me this was a bonus. The dark protected me. I slithered into the cleft, tried to clear my head and assessed my position.

I listened carefully, but I had no sense that there was anyone nearby searching for me. I guessed that the Germans must be swarming all over the area, rounding up any stragglers they could find. Logic and good sense told me that I must move and move away quickly. The explosion, an odd kind of luck, had brought me this far, but I was far too close to the danger of capture to remain safe where I was. I decided to rest for a short while longer to give my brain a chance to clear and then, while it was still dark, I would make a move to rejoin my comrades in arms. I realised that I needed to travel in the dark in order to avoid the German patrols that would be searching the area as soon as dawn broke. I decided that I needed to travel south. This would take me away from the invading force, but closer to my retreating comrades. I hoped to reach the southern coast and find a ship to take me from Crete to Africa. How naïve I was!

I woke with a sudden start. I had drifted once more into unconsciousness and had slept longer than I intended. It had rained while I slept and I was soaked to the skin.

Out of the drizzle a man's face appeared. I rolled over to pull my pistol from its holster, but he was too fast for me. Before I had even snapped the button of the holster, a rifle barrel rested against my cheek. I nearly had a heart attack then. To have come so far and to lose everything now seemed a cruel fate.

'English,' I said, and raised my hands in the age-old gesture of surrender.

It was a young shepherd wrapped in a woollen cloak. A kind of turban was wrapped around his head; his face was almost completely obscured by a bushy beard and wayward black hair. But he was flashing a smile.

'*Kala*,' he said. I did not know what the word meant, but, as he did not shoot me, it seemed a positive sign.

'*Ela*,' he said, and beckoned to me. I guessed that he meant I should come, and so I followed him.

***

2001

I had collected five eggs that sultry afternoon. The sun had been relentless all day, as hot as the *fourno* where we bake the bread and with much humidity in the air. Summer had arrived in May. At my age I find this very tiring. My ankles swell and my head aches. The doctor – and I do not trust doctors – says that I have high blood pressure and must rest more. Then he gives me a paper for expensive medicine and charges me many drachmas for his time. Take it easy he says. *Panegyri!* How can I take it easy when I am all alone, with all my work to do, and when I have no one to help me?

The brown eggs nestle in my basket on a few vine leaves. I know from experience that my six hens are good layers and that their eggs often produce double yolks. After all, I have been caring for hens since I was a small child. My big sisters showed me what to do when I was just five years of age. That was the year the Germans invaded. *Panegyri*, so many years ago.

The thought of an egg fried in sizzling olive oil and laid gently on a bed of green *horta* makes my mouth water. It was my Vassili's favourite. Ah, Vassili. But *Deo. Deo.* God's will be done.

I miss my dear Vassili very much, but no prayers or candles or gifts to the Holy Mother and no yearning on my part will return my dear Vassili to my arms. The emptiness and the ache remain after all these years and if I am honest the desire also. What can I do? Nothing. *Katholu.*

These are sad thoughts. I must push them to the back of my mind. Let me bend – and this is not so easy these days – and scrabble among the straw and twigs and leaves where the chickens lay their eggs to see if I can find more treasure. But nothing. *Katholu.* I heave myself jerkily, and not without pain I must admit, from off my knees and onto my feet. Despite my age, I can still move gracefully, once I am on my feet, and I can occasionally swing my hips like the young girl I was many years ago. I pine to dance, too. I loved the *glendi* and the weddings and the festivals when the entire village gathered together to feast and dance. We dressed in our best and let the notes of the lyra and violin tell our feet what to do. I remember the steps quite clearly. Ah, yes, I love to dance, but it would not be proper for a widow so to do.

I think the eggs will do for the foreigner when he arrives. A welcome gift, that's what they can be and maybe, yes maybe, I will give him a plastic water bottle filled with my best raki.

I frequently find myself sighing – I who used to be so giggly, so full of merriment, so vivacious. Is this what it means to be an old widow? I am surrounded by houses and by people, but I am lonely without a husband to keep me warm at night.

Ela na sup o, the work is hard too, with the chickens to feed, the goats to milk twice a day, the yoghurt and the soft cheese to make to sell to the tavernas along the promenade, not to mention the watering of the tomatoes, potatoes, cucumbers and aubergines every morning and evening. And then, water is always in such short supply from the month of June. Sometimes, in the villages, it is rationed to three hours a week. If I am lucky and God wills it, the water will splash down the conduit onto my orange trees, and roses and into the olive grove – such a happy tuneful sound – and also here in my *kipo* curling round the roots of my vine and finally splashing into my black plastic pipe and into the terracotta storage urns. Water bringing life ... but not an end to my loneliness. Ah yes, lonely and hard: that sums up my life.

Adoni comes to visit me sometimes. He has respect. Last week, for example, we shared some cheese and he drank a small raki.

'*Kalliopi mou*, you make the best cheese in Crete,' he said, wiping his moustaches and licking his fingers.

He spent all the morning clearing out the tiny cottage across the road. It belonged to his cousin. She was a pitiful woman, God rest her soul – a miserable, critical, judgemental woman who was always dissatisfied and displeased and unhappy with her life. I expect she is complaining to the Good Lord in Heaven even now. Or perhaps she is in the other place – shall I allow myself a small chuckle – arguing with the Devil himself!

Adoni took away much of the furniture: a carved sofa, a

table, and some upright rush-seated chairs. One of them was broken, I noticed. He left the bed for later on, but took most of the crockery and glasses, which I expect he will sell although he doesn't need the money. Not much really after eighty years of a life of hard struggle. But then that rascal of a husband of hers spent what money he had on gambling in the *kafeneion* and at the lottery shop. His olives did not give good oil, but then he was lazy and did not pay them respect and attention, and his goats, poor skinny creatures, did not thrive.

Ela na sup o, Adoni, of course, is cut from another cloth. He is shrewd and far-sighted, intelligent and as cunning as a politician, never short of schemes to make him money or the energy to pursue them. Already he has persuaded an innocent foreigner, a *turista*, with little sense and much money to rent this cottage of his cousin's, no doubt for thousands of drachmas. That's Adoni! Never misses a trick.

He loaded all the things onto his pickup with just me for an audience. Afterwards, he came to my cool kitchen across the way and I poured him a large raki from my best bottle and placed a spoon and a saucer of my soft, creamy misithra cheese, which I know is his favourite, to eat with it. We sat for an hour, it could have been more, elbows resting on the table, while we talked of the past, remembering the dead. Were the old times better, I wonder, or am I just being a sentimental old woman? The past seems just like yesterday. But now I must think of the present.

The foreigner will arrive later today.

***

2001

It was an unremarkable notebook, grubby, dog-eared and well thumbed. The kind of notebook with thick, but frayed, cardboard covers you were given at school. The pages were largely written on in fading pencil. It fell open at random when, without curiosity, I picked it up. I had found it in a shoe box, along with a sheaf of papers held together by a rusting paper clip, which had been pushed into the far corner of the eaves.

I almost overlooked it.

We had been clearing the house all day. I was tired and hot and dusty from the effort. So I sat down on a rafter opened the book and began to read because I was glad of the rest.

I looked at the page that had fallen open. It was near the middle, and it soon became clear that I was reading a diary. There were four entries on that page for the month of August. Brief notes and jottings for the most part, scribbles and crossings out. It all meant little to me at that moment, but I was inquisitive and slightly intrigued. Where had it come from? Who wrote it? For whom was it meant? Was it hidden in the roof deliberately, or just slung in there and forgotten, like most of the junk I had been clearing out all day? Was it meant for anyone? Was it meant for me?

Because of this discovery I would begin a journey that would take me across half the world and in search of a past life.

My Grandfather's death had not moved me. I am ashamed to say that I did not force back the tears at the funeral or choke on the funeral baked meats. He had been ill for some time, so the moment of death was not a shock. In life he had been tough, demanding, manipulative and often angry. As men went, he was cussed. He never took advice. He was scornful of those who did. He constantly sneered at his children and criticised their achievements.

Nothing they ever did was good enough. I know that my Mother often felt much rejected, despite her loyalty and best efforts towards him. He was indifferent to his grandchildren and paid us scant attention. We accepted that that was how he was. It never occurred to me to wonder why he was hard, quick to anger and not so easy to love. I admired him for his achievements certainly. It was generally agreed that he had been a success in business. He worked hard, often alongside his men, and he was a hard task master. He demanded absolute loyalty and dedication to the job, or you took your wages at the end of the week and slung your hook.

'I don't ask anyone to do what I won't do myself,' he had declared.

He paid well. He was ruthless, but fair. He was respected, but not loved. He built up the vineyard from nothing and made it one of the most prosperous and highly regarded in the Moutere Hills and arguably in the whole of New Zealand. His Pinot Noir won prizes and medals. I respected him for his achievements, but love was another matter. Love was not offered and love was not required by him. He failed to see life from another man's perspective. He was self-absorbed and to an extent self-satisfied. He had no time for those who analysed their emotions. Business was all to him – and making money.

My Mother was as regretful at his death as she would have been at anyone's – but she was not sad either. This was natural and I understood it. He had not shown her much love or attention as a young girl and he showed little interest in her adult life, in her hopes, her ambitions or her fears. That was the lack of empathy in him. Her achievements meant nothing to him, even though she had tried to please him and impress him, and I know how much that disappointed her. As his only grandchild, he regarded me as his heir and assessed me rather as he assessed the quality of his vines. I expect he found me wanting, but in my case he never mentioned it.

It was to help and support my Mother that I was up among the dust, cobwebs and spiders of the old man's ranch, undertaking the task of sorting and clearing out the last of his boxes, bits of furniture – a stool, a brass bedstead in several pieces – various clocks which had long seized up, boxes of books, the remains of a life about which I knew very little at a deeper personal level.

And there was the shoe box, the grubby notebook and the sheaf of papers.

At sundown, I joined my mother for a beer on the verandah.

'That's about the last of it,' I said, as I flopped into the wicker chair. 'I found this.' I passed over the box. 'Have you seen this before?'

She lifted the lid cautiously, almost with suspicion as if she were expecting a spider or even a snake to jump out and bite her. She looked at the contents for a long time before she lifted out the notebook, and turned it over carefully in her hands, opened it and flipped over some pages.

'It looks like it could be Pa's War Diary, I think. How strange. He never mentioned it.'

'Did he talk to you about the war – his war?' I asked.

'No. Not much. Not really. Do any of them?'

'I suppose there are a few who claim to have had a good war after a few jars,' I replied, taking a long gulp of a jar of my own. She cradled the diary in her hands as if it were a fragile artefact in a museum, which in a way I suppose it was.

'Have you read any of it?' she asked.

'No. Not really. It was practically the last thing I found. It was tucked away in the eaves out of sight.'

'I don't want it,' she said abruptly. 'No I don't want it.' She put the notebook back in the box and thrust it at me. 'You have it, Alex. Take it away.'

I was surprised at the strength of her reaction, but, after

the stress of my grandfather's death, the funeral and the wake, I decided that it was a perfectly understandable reaction and I brushed the thought aside.

'How about another beer, Alex?' she suggested. 'Or shall I open one of the old man's wines – the Pinot Noir'

I felt that the subject had been deliberately changed.

I was very busy at that time, with a big shipment of wine to deal with. I left the ranch almost immediately, dropped my Ma at her house and spent the next week working late in the office. I took away some items for auction at her request and the box came too. It was some weeks before I thought about looking at the notebook again.

CHAPTER 2

1941

The shepherd was called Mikailis. He told me by pointing a finger at his chest and saying Mikailis. I did the same in reply and said John.

'John Lancaster.'

Mikailis was festooned with weapons – a bandolier hung cross-wise over his chest, a pistol and several knives were thrust through his belt and he carried a rifle as if it were a third arm. A black fringed scarf was wrapped round his head and another of dark red around his waist under the belt. Beneath the cloak, he wore a heavily embroidered, but very grubby, faded, blue waistcoat over a cotton shirt, and below, instead of trousers, he was dressed in voluminous pantaloons, tucked into knee-high leather boots.

Mikailis led me away from the cave and down a treacherous, rock-strewn slope, until we reached a donkey path. The track was no wider than a yard and was sliced into the side of the cliff face. We marched silently through the dark. I say 'marched', but I stumbled and scrambled and lost my footing all the time, while Mikailis was as nimble as a goat and as graceful as any ballet dancer. I trudged behind him with heavy feet, almost in a trance, like a sleepwalker, and in places where it was pitch black I was hardly able to distinguish the track beneath my boots. Several times I missed my footing and fell painfully on my hip or my knees. The earth was very unstable after the rain. Rocks and stones rolled away underfoot when I least expected it, upsetting my balance and sending me tumbling. Where olive nets remained uncollected from the winter harvest, they were as treacherous and slippery as ice and trapped my feet in their folds, causing me to trip or turning my ankle. I strained my eyes trying to penetrate the dark, to locate the narrow track and distinguish the edge of the precipice. When you concentrate on that, you miss the branches that whip you in the face and the briars that claw into your clothes. I stumbled many times and once fell badly, but Mikailis caught my arm before I slid over the edge of the precipice and into oblivion. I wondered then how I had survived my first fall.

We reached a gully near a frothing stream, flanked by oleander bushes, small oak trees and low herb bushes. On three sides, almost sheer cliffs soared upwards. Here we rested for a while. I knelt by the stream cupped my hands and gulped some of the pure water. It was very cold, but sweet and clear. I washed the grime and sweat off my face. The cold revived me a bit, but I felt exhausted. I ached all over. I could tell that my feet were raw with blisters. My head pounded and somewhere in my side I could feel the incessant tug of a pulled muscle. I had a strong urge to lie down and sleep, but Mikailis's hand tapped my shoulder.

He pointed to a shadow above us. At first, I couldn't make out its significance, but then I realised that it was the entrance to a small cave, partially screened behind shrubs and bracken and almost invisible to the naked eye.

'*Epano*,' he said and pointed. I realised that he intended us to climb up to it and take shelter. I did not think I could do it. I was too exhausted and in pain, but Mikailis set off at once and so I followed. It took over an hour of hot, hard struggle, and without Mikailis's strength, hauling me up behind him, and his determination I would not have made it. I crawled behind him through the narrow entrance and came into a wide circular cavern which appeared to contain some stores or provisions. Exhausted almost beyond reason, I collapsed on my stomach and lay there panting. Then I fell asleep among the sacks of beans and the barrels of olives and oil.

Gunfire from the valley!

I woke in a flash. Mikailis lifted a warning hand.

'*Germania!*' he said.

As I moved a stabbing pain shot through my ribs from the pulled muscle. With difficulty, I slithered on my stomach to the mouth of the cave. The sun blinded me at first. I blinked a bit and when my sight readjusted I could see nothing at all; no movement. But the gunfire had been real alright and there was no doubt that German patrols were scouring the mountains, searching for any of us who were on the retreat from the battlefield.

Mikailis and I waited all day. We ate a few olives and Mikailis produced some very dry bread and a small bottle of yellowy oil from his shoulder sack. We soaked the bread in the oil and ate it with lumps of hard cheese which Mikailis cut with one of the piratical knives in his belt and we washed it down with some fiery spirit which I came to know well as raki. The first mouthful bloody nearly choked me it was so strong, but it sure settled the stomach.

We heard sporadic gunfire and occasionally voices echoing up from the valley. The acoustics were amazing. And we waited. The German patrols did not appear to leave the donkey tracks as the slope was far too steep and far too dangerous for anything but goats – and us! When I looked at how far and how steeply we had climbed, I could not believe how I had done it. After a while, we heard the roar of motorbike engines fading away and guessed and hoped that the patrols had given up for now.

At dusk, we left the cave and set off towards the south, along yet another narrow track, passing through rock outcrops and slipping and sliding over scree. We were buffeted by a biting wind which roared around us in unpredictable gusts, strong enough to blow you over. I felt as if my head was being bludgeoned by hammer. Clouds enveloped us in a mist and drizzling rain soaked my clothes which hung heavy, making each step doubly hard. Every muscle screamed with pain.

Finally, we came to a circular stone hut. Inside, it smelt strongly of goats. But any port in a storm.

The interior of the hut was lined with stone shelves upon which were stacked rows of round cheeses. On the bottom ledge, I saw fleeces and coarse, woollen blankets. Exhausted, I collapsed onto one of them. Mikailis disappeared. He returned with an armful of grey-leaved shrubs which he piled into a pyramid and set alight. Soon, a fire was blazing in the middle of the floor. I sat as close as I dared and in next to no time my wet clothes were steaming. Mikailis took down a cheese from the shelf, cut it open with a knife and we ate a hunk each, washed down with raki. Then Mikailis disappeared outside again, but he soon rejoined me with his herd of goats which he preceded to milk. He offered me a mug and it was frothy, thick and warm. He spent the next few hours making cheese. I was amazed at his stamina after hours of strenuous mountaineering in foul weather. Eventually, he wrapped himself in his cloak and lay on the ground before the dying fire. I wrapped myself in one of the sheep's fleeces and a blanket and did the same.

When I woke it was dawn and Mikailis had gone. I was on my own again. I had no idea where I was. But the sun rises in the east. I wanted to go south. I waited for the sun to appear from behind the mountain and using it, together with my compass, I set off again.

**

2001

It was several weeks before I had the time or the inclination to return to the shoe box and read the contents. I began with no real expectations of finding much in it beyond a few bare facts and some boring details. But the pale pencil entries in the notebook revealed an increasingly engrossing tale of danger, determination and heroism. The Cretan characters sprang to life with such vigour from the page that I spent a whole evening totally absorbed in their stories and I had drunk two bottles of Grandfather's excellent Pinot Noir before I put down the book and the sheaf of pages.

Each time I re-read the memoir, I became more and more intrigued with the story that unfolded. It was clear that my Grandfather had been involved in the Battle for Crete in 1941 as part of the New Zealand forces, although I didn't know where. What does a wine maker from South Island in New Zealand know about Crete except that it's on the other side of the world and a day's flight by aeroplane?

A few nights later, I was sitting on a wooden jetty overlooking the serene waters of the inlet at Mapua at one of those popular and fashionable eateries where you can eat fresh fish and drink Sauvignon Blanc (or Sav as we prefer to call it). My drinking companion was my oldest mate, Marty Henrickson, or Hennery as we call him for short. We do this catch up regularly and before long I was telling him all about the diary.

'Great stuff,' he enthused. 'So the old man was like a fugitive? Like in that TV series, except that he was escaping the Germans, right? So what yer gonna do, man?' he asked. 'You gotta do something, ain't you?' Hennery regularly talks like this, even though he has a better university degree than I do. It's a posture he adopted when he became a student. He believes that his language and his clothes make him the individual he is. I can't dispute that and I wouldn't have him any other way. That night he was wearing an Iron Maiden T, camouflage shorts – and wellies.

I had not formulated a plan of any sort until that moment, but Hennery's question focused my mind.

'You know what, Hennery? You are right. Definitely right. What do you think I should do?'

'Go to Crete, man. No sweat. Find that village. Find

those people.'

'It's sixty years since my grandfather was in Crete.'

'Stands to reason someone will remember, man. Some of those folk got long memories, ain't they? Can't they recite all of Homer? Family gotta be alive, I guess.' Hennery emptied the bottle and started the second. We always order two bottles to start with: it saves time. He plunged his fork into the plump John Dory and munched while he thought.

'Take the diary; follow in the old man's footsteps across the island. Ask questions!'

'Easier said than done, Hennery. There won't be signposts saying "Lancaster was here", you know.' I joked.

'Fair do's. Tell you what, I'll do some research on the internet see what I can find about the war stuff. You can book some vacation. Shouldn't be a problem as you are the boss!' He laughed. 'Unlike some of us poor exploited workers!'

This was a joke too, as Hennery did complicated things with computers which mystified me. He got up when he felt like it, which meant late, worked flexi-time which often meant far into the night, and was his own boss too. And I suspect he didn't earn peanuts in such a growth industry. In fact, I guessed he was well on his way to his first million and I don't mean New Zealand dollars.

'Get yourself a flight to Crete, man, and it's as good as.' announced Hennery, demolishing a large portion of fish.

'I don't know anyone in Crete. I can't speak Greek.' I said, spearing a fat prawn.

Hennery wiped his mouth on the back of his hand and slopped some more wine into our glasses. I noticed that he had recently tattooed his left-hand knuckles with signs of the zodiac.

'Stop hitting me with those negative waves, man.' he retorted quoting from his favourite movie *Kelly's Heroes* and doing a passable imitation of Donald Sutherland at his most sublime.' You get yourself on one of those speed-learning language courses. You'll speak Greek in a week!'

'I'll drink to your unfounded confidence,' I said emptying the second bottle myself and we planned the campaign.

First of all I bribed Jade in the office with extra pay – and a case of Sav – not something we produced at our vineyard – to type up a transcript of the diary for me which made it easier for me to read. I put the original carefully away in the office safe.

I rang my Ma and asked her if she knew any more about the old man's war, but she couldn't help or didn't want to.

'It was all so long ago, Alex,' she said in her soft drawl, 'and the past is the past. Best forgotten, I say.'

I trawled through the diary again looking for clues. The original book with cardboard covers consisted mainly of brief notes as if my grandfather were rushing to get everything on paper while the memory was still fresh and, indeed, some of it seemed very vivid and alive to me. It was written in pencil, pens and ink not being available, and had the biro been invented by then? I was not sure. The notes were possibly even copied from cigarette packets and small scraps of paper, at the time and on the move, and in fact I found one or two examples of each slipped between pages. The sheaf of papers was produced on an old typewriter with indistinct keys and a letter 't' that regularly rose above the line. They appeared to be an enlarged and improved account of events that he had written up afterwards. It seemed to me that he was capable of writing observant, perceptive and even dramatic prose and, when he was in the mood, he enjoyed playing with words. Then I recalled that Ma had said that he had wanted to be a journalist and, though thwarted in that ambition by the demands of the emerging vineyard which he had set up on the family farm, he had regularly written pieces for the local paper.

Hennery called me two days later demanding to meet.

'As soon as,' he ordered.

Hennery turned up wearing acid green shorts, a Rolling Stones Sticky Fingers Tour T and the ubiquitous wellies. We sat at the same table at the Jetty Bar and he plonked a file of paper on the table in front of me.

'The result of a lot of midnight oil, mate. You owe me.' he said, and I noticed that the tattoos had disappeared. 'Order the bottles! Here's all you need to know about Crete and the battle in 1941. It seems the Germans took everyone by surprise. The Allied top brass thought that the invasion would come from the sea. They weren't expecting parachutists!'

'Why not?'

'Never been used before. Hard to believe, nowadays, ain't it? It's ironic too that one Allied general had a German name: Freiburg. He got a VC in World War One and was a Kiwi to boot, but I would say that he was past his sell-by date in 1941. It seems that the Allied generals were at each other's throats as well: disagreed all the time. It didn't help!'

'So what happened?'

'Germans invaded and caused chaos. Not without heavy losses though. Then the Allies had to get the hell out of there. The British Navy had to evacuate as many soldiers as they could as quickly as possible off this tiny beach at a place called Hora Sfakion on the south coast of Crete and that included Kiwis, Aussies, Maoris, British and even some foreign refugees.

'Why did they choose the south coast? Wasn't the fighting in the North?'

'Yeah, I wondered that, so I checked. The Germans got control of the ports of Chania and Heraklion in the north pretty quickly. So the troops were ordered south. Crete is at its narrowest point just there – 35 miles I think: it's in the notes – so they chose Hora and sent destroyers from Africa across the Libyan sea. The Germans attacked them nonstop. It was like the Cretan Dunkirk or the Anzac Gallipoli. And you should know that Sfakia was a very remote and very mountainous region and very dangerous! The locals were totally lawless, rather like cowboys in the American Wild West, notorious for sheep stealing and abducting women, knifing Turks, that sort of thing. A normal day at the office! They just loved a vendetta. Apparently, that's some sort of blood feud which went on between families from generation to generation and which spread death and destruction all across the region. No sweat'

'You're kidding!'

'Honest, no sweat, it's all in there,' he said, tapping his pile of papers and slurping his wine with relish. I was just about to ask him about the tattoos when he continued, 'So where was your old man in all this? Do you know?'

'Some. The Old Man doesn't mention many place names. I think that was to protect the villagers or perhaps because he didn't know the names in the first place, but he talked of going south.'

'So he reached this place Hora Sfakion?'

'There was a lot of panic and confusion after the battle and during the retreat, he says, but apparently my Grandfather did get to Hora Sfakion – but he missed the boat – quite literally'.

'No sweat! It says here that lots of troops were left behind.'

'He was one of them. The Old Man must have been involved in one of the battles on the north coast either at Platanias or to defend Maleme airdrome. After the battle he was ordered to march south but a shell or something exploded near him and he was knocked unconscious and then he got lost and detached from his regiment. The Cretans hid him. He stresses over and over again their bravery and kindness towards him.'

'Yeah, but does he say where he was hidden? I can check that out for you as well if you give me some place names.'

'I can't. That's the problem. Perhaps he didn't know the names or perhaps he was being cautious, but I have made a list of what I found in the diary.' And I handed over the names I had found.

'Right. I'll get on with the background search. Have you got yerself organised on a language course yet, man?'

'I certainly have! I start next Monday. It's a bloody difficult language.'

'I'll drink to that!' laughed Hennery. 'And they don't even use our alphabet!'

The course was difficult and it took all my determination to keep going, but at the end of it I had just about conquered the complexities of the Greek language, and let me tell you that it was not easy, for Greek is fiendishly difficult to master, but I think I was a driven man! By the end I felt that I could just about hold my own in a simple conversation, but I was never going to be able to debate anything philosophical.

I rang my mother to tell her of my plans and was surprised that she was so downbeat. I was enthusiastic and she was, well, off-hand, muted and subdued.

'Why do you want to waste all that time and money on a road to nowhere,' she said in an uncharacteristically critical tone, sounding uncannily like my Grandfather, when I sketched out my plans to her. 'What good does it do?'

I told her that I wanted to satisfy my curiosity, find out about the Old Man's journey, experience the island, the customs, the atmosphere.

'If all else fails I can see the old ruins of Athens and a bit of the Mediterranean.'

She remained unimpressed and I was not able to win her over to my way of thinking. All she said before I hung up was: 'Well, you do what you must – and have a safe journey, Alex.'

CHAPTER 3

1941

Fleas bloody fleas. I've been bitten to buggery by the bastards. Must've been feasting on me all night. It was after I covered myself in that fleece in Mikailis's hut. Trying not to scratch, but itching is purgatory. Legs and arms are covered in large red swellings as well as purple bruises. Depression brought on by exhaustion, strain and anxiety.

What was it the officer said on the training course? Defeat is in the mind. Do not give in. So I shook myself mentally, plodded on, slipping and sliding and occasionally tumbling when a loose boulder dislodged under my foot

In the late morning, a sharp cold wind began. It soon turned into a gale and blew straight into my face, battering my skull and tugging at my clothes. I was glad I had taken the blanket which I wrapped even tighter around me. Each step forward became a struggle against a mighty force of nature.

In late afternoon, I ran into a flock of sheep which had been obscured from view by an outcrop of rocks and scrubby trees. They began bleating piteously and skittered away down the slope. The shepherd appeared, waving his crook menacingly and yelling at me in a harsh voice. I stood paralysed for a moment as he marched briskly towards me, and just as I was preparing to run for it he smiled and beckoned me with a horny hand to follow him.

I hesitated, suspecting a trap, but he nodded again and seemed friendly enough, so I thought: OK, mate, give it a go, and followed him at a cautious distance until I saw that he was making for a hut which had been hidden on the other side of a stand of trees. Like Mikailis's hut, it was a small stone building with a wooden roof.

Inside it was a relief to be out of the buffeting wind and in some sort of shelter from the biting cold. We sat on the stone ledge against the wall and the shepherd poured some warm milk from a pitcher into a grubby tumbler. He took out a monstrous curved knife from his belt and rose to his feet. I held my breath and braced myself for him to cut my throat, but he merely used it to hack some thick pieces of soft cheese from one of the many dripping baskets hanging from the wood and cane-lined ceiling. We ate it with the warm milk and a glass of raki. When I had rested a bit I thanked him and went on my way.

Dogs, bloody dogs! Each time I came near any habitation the bloody dogs started barking. What alerted them – my smell? The sound of my boots? I don't know, but they started their infernal and relentless yapping and barking as soon as they sensed my presence. They were a bloody menace. They alerted the whole countryside. First one dog picked up my scent and barked, then the next would pick up the sound and start too and soon they alerted all the dogs in the whole countryside. If I glimpsed a dog, it would be jumping up and down furiously, jerking its rope or chain taut, and snarling ferociously, saliva or even foam dripping from its jaws, and soon the whole mountain was echoing like a bad choir.

It was worse in the afternoon when folk returned to their homes to take a nap because the cacophony would have woken up the unconscious. I soon learned to skirt any villages I saw which put paid to any ideas I had of scrounging food or a bed for the night. I kept an alert eye open for a wisp of smoke which might indicate an isolated farmhouse so that I could give it a wide berth.

This added to my problems and I soon realised that Mikailis had been right: that it was better to travel at night. Easy for him, with his detailed knowledge of the terrain – bad for me, blundering about uselessly and blind at night. I wished he was still beside me as my guide.

Mind over matter, the officer had said. Survival is all in the mind. But hunger and exhaustion always take over in the end. I had to stop. I found a small gully to rest in for the night. I tucked myself into the scant protection of some saplings and scrubby bushes and tried to sleep. When I woke at dawn, I was enveloped in a chill, grey cocoon. The cloud base had dropped so low that the mist almost eddied round my ankles. The clouds brought with them a steady drizzle which soon turned into pouring rain as the wind strengthened. It rained incessantly all morning.

The vegetation cut out some of the wind, but did not protect me from the rain. My boots filled with water, my beret wilted, my uniform became waterlogged. My stomach knotted into cramps as hunger gnawed at me. I was chilled to the bone. I was invisible from view and the low cloud must have put an end to the German patrols or the reconnaissance aircraft, but the shelter was inadequate to say the least. I regretted that I had not stolen some cheese from Mikailis's hut and my mouth watered as I recalled the taste of its rich sour tang and its texture of clotted cream. And for warmth, I longed for a slug of raki. My luck had run out, I thought.

By late afternoon, the rain had ceased and miraculously the sun had come out. It was surprisingly hot so I removed most of my uniform and watched it steam as I attempted to dry out. Then I re-dressed, curled up and slept again, letting the sun warm me through to the bone. At nightfall I rose and resumed my march.

***

2001

Maleme airdrome is off limits these days. No photos allowed. I drove the hire car from Chania airport directly west along an interminable coastal strip of hotels, tavernas and bars. Instead of the aroma the guide books had led me to expect of roasting lamb and wild thyme, the smell of onions and burgers hung heavy in the evening air. Gifts shops, each one bedecked with beach towels in garish colours, straggled endlessly along the roadside, strung out like the beads of a necklace. Lilos were stacked in rows and sunglasses glinted in the sunset. I expected to see *Kiss Me Quick* hats. Shrieking advertising signs fought for space and were even festooned across the road like bunting: *Funky Fish, Golfland, Strapless Clothes Shop, Speed Wheel, Club Tropicana.* All in English. To my right lapped an exquisite turquoise sea; to my left, rows of concrete hotels and villas to house the tourists. Only the purple and scarlet bougainvillea which scrambled up in huge branches over walls and parapets, saved the coast from disaster. Maleme had been developed for sun seekers.

Maleme was a supreme disappointment.

I parked the hire car on a slip road beside the bank of the river at Tavronitis. The river bed was wide and dry, sandy and strangely forsaken. Scrubby bushes and waving bamboo grew randomly among the boulders and tumbling stones. A slick of dirty, reddish water meandered sluggishly down the centre of the river bed. Here and there I could pick out an unkempt olive tree.

There are three bridges now at Tavronitis. One carries the National Road, which must be one of the prettiest motorways in the world, fringed as it is on either side with white, pink and red oleander bushes. They flower for three quarters of the year and also hide the paper bags, cola cans and empty water bottles which travellers throw from their cars. The second bridge takes the old main road along which I had been travelling from the tourist strip I had just passed through to the large town of Kissamos. Finally, almost concealed near the sea shore, and running parallel to the main road was a small bridge of girders boarded with planks. Two huge rocket shells guard it. Nearby is the remains of a bailey bridge and beyond it, next door to the Municipal Gymnasium and football pitch, is a Nissen Hut. In the far distance I could see Hill 107, the scene of so much bloody fighting.

Here I was, almost sixty years later, in this barren and abandoned place where I believe my grandfather had taken part in the fierce battle to save the airdrome of Maleme in May 1941. His diary does not mention any part he played in the fighting there. It's possible that he suffered some sort of amnesia because his account begins with the explosion which catapulted him over a cliff and into a ravine. He says nothing about what occurred before that moment, but I know that for over four days, from May 21 to May 26, New Zealand troops fought, with enormous bravery, a losing battle against the ineptitude, misleading orders and indecision of their own leaders and against a sky suddenly full of unexpected German paratroops. They fought unrelentingly to hold Hill 107, to hang on to the airdrome. They lost. There was nothing on the bridge to commemorate their heroism. The bridge told me nothing.

I found a room for the night, ate an indifferent meal and drank a local beer called Virgin. Next day, I decided to travel south to look for the resort of Paleohora which my grandfather had mentioned from time to time in his diary and to start my search from there.

As you drive inland from Tavronitis, the mountain road snakes and curves round rocky cliffs tinted silver, green, and purple. The mountain is slashed by deep gorges. Here, in winter, I could imagine the water tumbling fast as an arrow, over the rocks, spurting wild foam on its headlong descent to the sea. In the summer these self-same gorges are arid and still. The torrent becomes a tiny trickle, barely enough to irrigate the roots of the pink and white oleander trees which flourish there on the rocky river bed.

You can see narrow donkey paths hugging the edge of

the sheer precipices. They twist and turn between the terraces, just as my grandfather described, and pass among clumps of tough, grey-leaved, scrubby undergrowth which the locals call *garigue* and we would call maquis. The air is filled with the acrid, pungent aroma of oregano, rosemary, fennel and thyme and in May you can inhale, as I did, the intense perfume of the wild flowers. When you switch off the car engine, open the door and sit still all you can hear is the drone of the bees as they search steadily for nectar.

The day was dull and cool, promising rain, as it had been when my grandfather marched this way, any sign of a blue sky wiped out by gloomy clouds, but I could imagine the white, limestone rock shimmering on a hot day. Everywhere I looked, the olives swayed and undulated in the breeze like a silver-green ocean, mesmerising, calming and tranquil. The road rose steadily higher and higher until I reached a plateau with towering cliffs on one side and a sheer drop on the other. This was the terrain that my grandfather had encountered as he had taken his long march from the battlefield.

I stopped the car to look around me and suddenly saw the eagles. I later learned that they were actually buzzards but to me they will always be eagles. They took my breath away. There were a pair of them, mates perhaps, wheeling and gliding, twisting and twirling with lazy and elegant grace. The larger one dipped and dived as the thermals pitched and tossed him, sending him in dizzying spirals down to the mouth of the valley towards the twinkling sea. The tips of his wide wings looked like feather fingers and must have been over a metre wide.

The Lammergeier or Bearded Vulture, the native Greek eagle, has a wing span of as much as two and a half metres. With his red feathered chest, he resembles a large predatory robin. And he has the charming habit of dropping the bones of his prey on the rocks below to smash them in order to get at the marrow on which he feeds. But this wasn't a

Lammergeier. He is now hardly seen in Crete except, perhaps, in spring in the Samaria Gorge, and rarely there. He has been the victim of Cretan sharp shooters.

The sight of buzzards always fills me with pleasure, because a buzzard represents freedom to me: the freedom to be free. It is what my grandfather and all his allied compatriots were fighting for in May 1941

After the plateau, the road began to descend in spirals, rather like the buzzard on the thermal, through little villages of white painted cottages until, at last, between a distant cleft in the mountains, I caught a glimpse of Homer's wine dark sea, although it was more of an ultramarine blue. I had reached the southern coast, the Libyan sea and the resort of Paleohora.

***

1941

Rosy dawn. Blue sky. No wind. Very hungry. Heard a plane. Kept out of sight. It was a reconnaissance plane flying low. It hovered a bit like a buzzard as it made a slow sweep along the valley. I could almost make out the silhouette of the pilot. It continued its long, unhurried, microscopic search of the area for more than an hour before it gave up and spiralled away. It had been a long and exhausting night's march and I needed to rest. I remained hidden in the bushes watching it and I waited a long time after it had disappeared before I dared to make a move.

The gnawing pain of hunger gripped my stomach like a vice and it was the overwhelming craving for food that impelled me to emerge from my hiding place and set off once more. I came to the outskirts of a village by mid afternoon. Progress had been slow. I felt weak from lack of food, my whole body ached from bruises and knocks, my cuts were sore and bleeding and my feet had blistered so badly that each step was like being cut by knives.

There was an unusual silence after the rain of the previous day. My footsteps sounded hollow and echoed as if I were walking, not on solid ground, but on a thin crust of earth which might break and crumble at any minute. I moved as silently as my damaged body would allow, wary of disturbing the inevitable dogs, but they were soon alerted by my scent or my footsteps and began their incessant barking.

I hoped that the occupants of the village would be inside their houses and taking their afternoon sleep and that this would give me the opportunity to make a reconnoitre and pinch some food. No doors were open, no voices echoed, there was no laughter or chatter that I could hear. The houses were silent.

I crept over to an outhouse and tried the door gently. It was unlocked and inside I found some tall, clay urns big enough to hide Ali Baba and all his forty thieves. The pots stored nuts and olives. I gobbled some there and then and thrust handfuls into my pockets for later. I left as silently as I had come. I skirted the edge of a vegetable garden and picked some broad beans which I quickly shelled and ate raw. They had a nutty flavour. I walked through an orange grove and found some ripe oranges which I picked and kept for later when I couldn't find water. I followed a narrow path until I came to a small, white-painted chapel topped with a tiny bell tower and a terracotta tiled roof. I eased open the door. It was dark inside and smelled of incense and damp. But it offered a safe hideaway. I crept up the short aisle and slid behind the tall, carved wooden screen which divided the altar from the nave and rolled under the white cotton cloth which hung down over the altar table. I lay on the cold, tiled floor, ate some of my food and then slept.

I dreamed once more that I was drowning and

suffocating. My face was wet and I could not breathe through my nose. I gulped for breath and struggled to liberate my limbs from whatever was clamping me down, but my body was restrained by a heavy weight and my limbs seemed paralysed. I thrashed about me, but the weight pinned me down and I could not free myself. My lungs were being squeezed relentlessly and I had no air with which to breathe. I was dying after all. Then, consciousness returned and my brain cleared. I realised that my body was trapped by the massive torso of a huge, slathering, but enthusiastic bloody dog that was licking my face and nose with a large slobbering tongue and whose immense body pinioned mine to the floor. He was black, bulky and powerfully built with well developed muscles.

'Get off, you bloody hound,' I hissed, as I wrestled with paws the size of tea plates in a futile effort to free myself. He growled menacingly. I stopped struggling.

'Mavro,' called a voice from beyond the screen. I froze and wriggled as far as I could back under the altar table. 'Mavro, *pou ise*?'

A female voice.

Some relief, but not much. Next question. Should I go for my gun or should I wait and hope that the dog would answer her command, release me and go to her? Maybe she would not find me.

Mavro barked sharply.

I waited, every muscle tensed, ready for action, willing myself to be invisible.

The dog shook its head, spattering me with saliva, wriggled to its feet, snorted a bit and loped off.

What to do now? Had I been discovered? Or had I had a lucky escape from immediate capture? Could I make my getaway if I waited for some time to elapse? I weighed the options: to stay hidden or make a break for it and maybe get shot in the attempt.

I waited.

I strained my ears for the sound of voices or the approach of tramping feet.

Nothing.

After what seemed a long time, I decided that the coast was clear. I untangled my stiff limbs from beneath the altar cloth and made for the chapel door.

I emerged into the sunlight … and into the guns.

CHAPTER 4

2001

'You want to rent house?'

A man in black materialised suddenly beside my table, rather like the demon king in a pantomime. One minute there was no-one there and in a split second he appeared. I could almost see the puff of smoke and smell the acrid odour of sulphur and I nearly dropped my glass of retsina!

I had already found, in actual fact, a simple room for rent in Paleohora as soon as I arrived. Then I lunched on fried squid and a Greek salad of tomatoes, olives and cucumber topped with a slab of feta cheese in a taverna on the promenade and spent the afternoon driving around the villages, along narrow, snaking, treacherous roads trying to get my bearings.

It was late afternoon, still bright and sunny and the air was warm enough for me to choose a seat outside one of the many bars which lined the main street. My retsina was served in a stout glass tumbler and I watched idly as the evening promenade began. Tourist couples ambled slowly, arm in arm, laughing and joking, relaxed and happy, in the mood for a drink before dinner, checking the menus displayed outside the tavernas, or gazing merrily into the windows of the gift and jewellery shops.

The locals were more purposeful: walking to work, acknowledging friends with a greeting, popping into the shop that sold lottery tickets, hoping perhaps for that elusive win of millions which would mean that they would never have to work again. Some were carrying a bag of bread from the bakery for the next day's breakfast.

'You want to rent house?' he repeated, in heavily accented English. 'I am called Adoni.' The hand that he offered me was as gnarled as the trunk of an olive. He flashed a wolfish smile which did not quite reach his raisin-coloured eyes. 'I can show you house. Good house.'

He dripped gold. As he raised his cigarette to his lips, gold flashed from the fillings in his white teeth and gold flashed on his fingers in the shape of several, large knuckle-duster rings.

'I rent you house.'

Like the persuasive merchants of an oriental bazaar who cling to your sleeve and follow you from one end of the souk to the other, Adoni was out to do a deal.

'I join you,' he stated and before I answered he drew back a rush chair to sit down. Unabashed and extremely determined, he made himself comfortable.

'What you want to drink? More retsina?' Adoni took immediate control and barked a volley of orders at the young bar girl in the tight top and mini skirt.

'*Yammas*!' he toasted, when the pale yellow wine arrived, slamming the tumbler on the table

'*Yammas*,' I replied, and took a sip.

I admit it, I was intrigued. And I was also willing to be drawn into a conversation with this singular man. I also responded to a certain charm he had, despite his pushiness. I had come to the south of Crete on a mission, driven by the discovery of my grandfather's diary. I needed to be here. I needed a guide and Adoni seemed to be heaven-sent for that purpose – although I wasn't going to let him know that.

'You speak good English. Where did you learn?'

'For many years I live in America.'

'Where?'

'San Francisco'

'How long were you there – in America?'

'Maybe twenty years.'

'Why did you come back to Crete?'

'Family reasons. I own this bar. It was my ambition. In America I make much money and so I return and buy this bar. *Lipon*,' he continued not wishing to be diverted by my questions, and returning to the matter in hand. 'You want to rent house here in town or you want to rent house in mountain?'

He leaned forward towards me conspiratorially as he muttered the sales patter out of the side of his mouth, cigarette dangling from his lip. 'I know very nice place.' His iron grey hair curled in greasy, sweat-ridden coils across his forehead in a style which reminded me of the ancient carved statues of Persian princes.

'Very nice house, you can look at sea.'

I was tempted, I suppose, by the adventurous notion that I could experience the Cretan life more realistically if I took him up on his suggestion than if I stayed in my current room or indeed a hotel. I cannot think of any other reason except that I must have been intoxicated by the retsina following a day in the sun.

'Come, my friend, I can show you a small house. It is not far.' He stubbed out his cigarette and twirled his bushy grey moustache. 'Finish your drink and come, come with me.'

I gave in easily and weakly and reached for my wallet to pay, but he stayed my hand.

'No, no, my friend, this is my bar and you are my guest. There is no charge.' But suddenly there was an obligation....

Adoni led me through the town and away from the shops, from the noise and bustle of the bars and the bright lights of the tavernas, past a walled garden fringed with pollarded trees and into tangle of tiny lanes. They were narrow, sometimes cobbled and sometimes cracked, unpaved, crumbling and dusty, and they meandered and criss-crossed like the famous Cretan labyrinth among low, closely packed, whitewashed cottages.

Bright red and fuchsia pink geraniums, intense orange marigolds, tall cream lilies and bushy green basil were planted in rusty, square olive oil tins. They added flashes of colour and stood like sentries on a doorstep or lined the walls that faced the alleys.

I was completely lost by the time Adoni halted in front of a rough stone wall into which was cut a door. To its left was a pair of closed shutters. Both had been painted green but that was long ago and now the paint was flaking or had disappeared altogether.

Adoni rummaged in his trouser pocket and retrieved a large iron key which he fitted into the lock of the door. The door was metal and contained a small window at head height protected by a grill of wrought iron curlicues. The lock seemed well oiled and the door opened easily. Adoni led me inside.

It was dark, but once he had opened the shutters the bright light burst in and I could see a single, square room, sparsely furnished with a bedstead which was bare except for some ferocious looking springs, a single rush-seated chair and an old wooden trunk. There was a rudimentary kitchen unit of the type common in Greek rental rooms consisting of a sink, drainer and double electric burner over a fridge and a small cupboard for utensils, pots and pans. In the corner recess a shower, basin and toilet were hidden away.

'Good room,' he said, grinning and flashing gold.

I did not actually agree with him. Taking my hesitation for uncertainty, Adoni launched into another persuasive speech. He described the wrecks in mountain villages, houses I would never want to rent, the abandoned, the exposed, the truly uninhabitable; he had a salesman's patter for each one. I couldn't get a word in edgeways and, to be honest, I was both intrigued and amused. So I sat back in my not so comfortable rush seat and let him rattle on. He told me that one had no water, that another was torn apart by the ferocious winds, that in third a jealous husband had cut his wife to pieces, that another had no land at all. I would not like any of these, he said. 'No good, no good at all.'

He warned me off them all. But *his* house was a good house 'Just look' he swept his hands around the room 'It has water; it is beside the sea – listen you can hear the waves. The old town is sheltered from the winds.'

It had belonged to his cousin, he told me, and there was a good woman close by who would cook and clean and look after me. I could stay as long as I liked and the rent, he added, twirling those magnificent moustaches, was very cheap. Very cheap.

I looked out of the window across the lane to the little white-washed cottage facing me. There was a garden sandwiched between two small houses. A door was open. I could smell the aroma of a stew. Washing was hanging from a balcony. I heard chickens clucking. A lazy cat stretched on the wall in the last of the sun. A vine struggled up some poles to provide a canopy of green leaves. Roses and geraniums, thyme, basil and cactus in pots edged the path and a vivid purple bougainvillea scrambled up the wall. In the distance a dog barked. I could hear voices. It could have been the radio or the TV or it could have been women chattering on the corner. I soon learned that Cretans always talk at the top of their voices even about the most private of affairs.

And I could hear the waves breaking on the rocks as Adoni said I could. The sunshine played on the walls, deep, cool shadows gave relief from the heat of the sun: a secret life could be lived here among the mysterious lanes and alleys.

The old town was the real Crete, not tourist Crete.

And what was the alternative? A safe, modern, well-furnished room on the sea front, right in the centre of the action, close to the tavernas and bars – and the noise of cars, canned music, motorbikes and chattering tourists.

I gambled. I took the plunge recklessly. I took it because it was old, and Cretan, and because it was tempting to resist all those modern comforts .... Why?

In order to experience the real Crete?

Because we had nothing like this in New Zealand, except maybe an up-country bach?

To try to grasp something of the life my grandfather had lived? This shabby, basic one-roomed cottage would have seemed like the Ritz to him.

Foolish perhaps, but part of the adventure.

I agreed Adoni's terms. He shook my hand vigorously and passed me the key. 'Tomorrow you come. All will be ready,' he assured me. 'Now we go to celebrate with food and raki!'

We sealed the deal with many glasses of raki and plate after plate of goat and greens, octopus, lamb chops, spicy sausages, salad, cheese pies as well as many carafes of both retsina and rough country red wine which tasted like sherry. A large number of Adoni's friends joined us and the party lasted until the small hours.

***

1941

There were four men with rifles trained on the door and at me. I had no doubt at all that not one of them would miss if they fired. Curved daggers were pushed into the sashes around their waists and bandoliers of bullets were slung diagonally over their chests. They looked grim and fierce. They meant business.

Each one wore what I guessed to be Cretan costume consisting of a blue felt waistcoat over a linen shirt and a pair of baggy pantaloons held in place by a sash wound round the waist. Each man was turbaned and all four had black bushy beards which covered most of their faces. They looked wild and dangerous.

'English,' I croaked and raised my hands.

No one said anything but I was roughly seized, my arms were roped and I was marched without any word being said through the groves of olives and oranges until we came to the outskirts of the village where I had stolen the nuts and olives. I was prodded into a narrow alley and along a small cobbled path which wound between low houses and eventually pushed through the open door way of one of these small buildings. I was thrust roughly onto the floor. When I had recovered from my fall and my eyes had accustomed themselves to the gloom I could see that the room was already occupied by a number of other men, also in khaki, their arms roped behind them.

Two of the Cretans checked my bindings while the other two guarded the door. Then all four abruptly left without saying a word. The door was slammed shut and I could hear it being barred.

We prisoners eyed one another warily. Finally, a man with a bandaged head spoke.

'English?' he said addressing me.

'No. New Zealand.' Keep it short, the training officer had instructed. Say no more than name, rank, and number. Don't trust anyone. Careless talk costs lives. You may be among spies or agent provocateurs.

'Maleme Airdrome?' he persisted.

'Yeah. A real mess, mate.'

'Galatas, me.' This speaker had red hair standing up on end like a fox's brush. 'O'Brien's the name.'

'Chania, me. I'm Cooper.' He had a boxer's face and a voice like sandpaper.

'What are they going to do with us?' I asked. 'Are they going to kill us?'

'Maybe. Maybe not.' said bandaged head. 'My name's Titheridge, old chap.' he added, extending a hand.

'Thought the Cretans were on our side, so I did,' said fox's brush.

We lapsed into an exhausted and despondent silence

while we considered what might happen to us. Would the Cretans help us or kill us?

An hour, maybe two, elapsed before we heard the clatter of hobnails on the cobbles outside.

'They're coming for us,' yelped O'Brien, cringing into the deep shadow.

I sat up straight. If this was my last moment I had no intention of letting the bastards see me looking afraid.

We waited apprehensively, silent, trussed up and hungry, our thoughts dwelling inevitably on what would happen to us next. Nothing occurred. The footsteps died away and we subsided into that lethargy that comes as a reaction after the exertion of great effort and retreated into our own thoughts.

Some time later, around dusk, the four Cretans returned with a fifth man. He was dressed much like Mikailis my first guide. A scarf tied round his head controlled wild hair with a life of its own. He had the face of an eagle with a beak-like nose, high cheek bones, ferocious round eyesand large curly moustaches which seemed to be the fashion among mountain men. His outfit was dilapidated and shabby, but worn with dash and spirit. He wore black boots to the knee, a baggy set of pleated pantaloons that were patched and ragged and held in place by a mulberry coloured silk sash which was wrapped round and round his waist. In it was stuck a long dagger with a curving ivory hilt in a silver sheath. Above the waist, he wore a black shirt and a black waistcoat stiff with embroidered whorls and tight as a bull fighter's. He was bristling with other weapons too – several other knives, two pistols, a rifle slung over his shoulder and a bandolier of bullets. I came to know those pistols, knives, bandoliers and slung guns very well and saw them even on priests.

'I speak English. Little,' he said. 'Who you are?'

'Irish, 'said O'Brien quickly.

'English, me,' Cooper announced roughly. 'And this

here's Titheridge,' he added indicating the fellow with the bandage. 'English too.'

'New Zealand.' I added, last of all.

'How we know you not Germans? You must prove this.' demanded the new leader.

'How do *we* know you are not Germans yourselves?' retorted Cooper jutting out his chin and scowling.

'Look, old chap, we will give you name rank and number and no more,' said Titheridge with quiet authority, pulling out his identity disc. We did the same. 'That's the Geneva Convention, you know.'

The discs were duly inspected, and we were efficiently searched. The leader spoke rapidly to his men. He seemed to be giving orders. Then he addressed us: 'I am named Wolf. You stay here now. Like so.' He indicated our roped arms. 'Tonight, if safe, we will take you to beach. There, other English wait for your ships to take you to Africa.'

So saying he and his men left us alone once more, in the dark to await our deliverance.

***

2001

He arrived early, the young one, just after I returned from milking my goats on my land beyond the town wall and just as I started feeding the chickens. I saved a few more brown eggs to give to him. I called to him and offered him some fresh goat's milk to drink. It was still warm.

Ela na su po, I speak no English but he surprised me. He spoke some Greek – but not, of course, Cretan.

He had the key to the *spiti*. While he unlocked the door I returned to my kitchen to collect for him my gifts of eggs and raki. He was so tall he had to stoop to enter the house of Adoni's cousin. I opened the shutters to let in some light and I showed him the oil lamp I had brought for him. Adoni had forgotten to replace the light bulbs. I will telephone to him later. The *revma* was working – Adoni must have remembered to pay the bill, at least! So I turned on the fridge and placed the eggs and raki on the shelf. You must never pass eggs from one person's hand to another.

'*Efcharisto*,' he said with a sweet smile. Ah, such a one.

I ventured to tell him that I would cook him some breakfast and later clean the room. He came and sat at the table outside my house under the vine. I returned to my kitchen and cooked for him an omelette and fried a few *kalitsounias*. I know he will enjoy them. I walked over to him with a plate in each hand and smiled. He stood up and smiled too.

'*Efcharisto*,' he said and took the plates. We sat together as he ate. He seemed hungry and ate the omelette at once. He took a *kalitsounia* and looked at it.

'What is it?' he asked.

I told him that it was a pie filled with cheese and *horta*. '*Poly kala*.' I said.

He took a bite. They were just cool enough not to burn his tongue. He nodded,

'*Kala*,' he said with a broad smile.

I like his smile. Somewhere in the back of my mind his smile reminds me of someone. I will remember eventually. I am an old woman. It takes time.

'I am Kalliope,' I said pointing at myself. 'I am named for one of our Greek Muses. You know about them? There were nine. Kalliope was the Muse of epic poetry and the mother of Orpheus. The name means beautiful voice.' I laughed to myself for they always used to tell me that I never stopped talking, although they said nothing of the beautiful voice!

'Alexandros,' he replied in Greek. In Greek! 'Alex.'

Ela na sup o, he is fair. We Cretans are dark. He is tall; we Cretans are short and sturdy. He is thin. I like to see some muscle and flesh on a man. My Vassili was all muscle and sinew. A strong man, and brave. Such tight buttocks and hard thighs. And not only hard thighs. I remember his weight upon me and his passion. What a man he was! He feared nothing and no-one. He was bold and quick-witted. Yet he could be tender. He never beat me. Not once. And funny! How he made me laugh. And he brought me gifts of jewellery and this gold cross which is all I wear now that I am a widow.

How unlucky I am to be not just a widow, but a widow without handsome sons. I should have had sons. Are these tears I feel in my eyes? I love my daughters, of course. My daughters are pretty, clever like their father, but married and far away. Daughters are a mixed blessing. A mother needs sons. The son loves his mother. A daughter becomes a wife. A son is his mother's forever. Ah, *Panegyri*. I failed Vassili and I failed myself. I am alone. It is my Fate.

The young man with the fine blues eyes spoke – did not Alexander the Great have fine blue eyes? Here is another Alexander. I like the sound of his voice, low like a mountain wind, although I do not understand everything he says. When he speaks Greek to me – for I am Cretan – the sound of his accent grates and seems strange. Ah, he smiles and what a sweet smile. Such a sweet smile.

His words interrupted my melancholy thoughts. I had forgotten that he spoke my language.

'You speak the Greek!' I exclaimed. 'You speak the Greek very well!'

'I studied very hard,' he said.

'Holy Mother of God. It is a surprise.'

'I wanted to talk to you,' he said. 'You are my neighbour.'

A charming one, courteous also. I like the shape of his face: a strong jaw he has like a piece of carved olive wood, and no beard, I like that in a man, Vassili wore a beard all through the winter until Easter Day when he shaved it off to honour Our Lord, he said, and to prepare for the heat of the summer, with much soap and laughing, always laughing. He was laughing when he fell from the olive tree. He never laughed after that. Or breathed.

When my guest had finished eating, I fetched my broom and cloth and walked over with him to his room.

Adoni had left behind the iron bedstead, but no mattress or bedding. Just as well. I am sure that they would be full of fleas. But there remains one upright chair with a rush seat, and the built-in cooking facilities. Everything else he took away before two days and has not yet remembered to return them. *Ela na sup o,* the charming rogue will charge this young man many drachmas for the *spiti* even though it is bare and as God is my witness DIRTY!

Adoni's cousin, God rest her soul, kept the house spotless. Always she was scrubbing the table and sweeping the floor and in those days there were no tiles just bare concrete. No wonder she was peevish. Each day, she poured a bucket or two of chlorine and water on the path outside the front door to wash away the dust and the mess of the chickens – we all had chickens which roamed around freely in those days, and some of them were my chickens to be sure, but we did not fall out over this, *katholu*, no not at all.

Ela na sup o, Adoni's cousin would weep copious tears to think that this is the condition of her house today. Now, it is the home to spiders and, worse, scorpions and, even worse, rats. Yet, the young one does not seem surprised. Perhaps he thinks we all live like this. We are not peasants, *katholu*, no not at all. It offends my honour that Adoni has given this impression of us all. But what can I say? He is a man. I expect his mind is on the matters that concern men, not us women. What does he care for a house? It is women's work. I will come with my own broom, a cloth and my own bucket of chlorine and water and I will remove every cobweb and every speck of dust from every corner and every beam and shelf in the *spiti* until I am satisfied that Adoni's cousin will approve, although it would be hard to find anything to please her. Then I will make fresh *kalitsounias* with my soft white cheese and *horta* and give it to the young man for his lunch. He needs feeding!

I will telephone to Adoni and give him a piece of my mind and tell him to return some of the furniture to the spiti. Between us we will make this house fit to live in for the handsome young visitor. I wonder why he is here in Crete?

CHAPTER 5

1941

The fragrance of wild flowers and thyme was overpowering, and so was the stench of death.

When the Cretans had roused us after darkness I had wondered if they were going to take us out and shoot us. Instead, they untied us, but kept their rifles trained on us as they gestured to us to walk ahead of them out of the house. With two in front and two behind, they marched us out of the village and back onto the unforgiving terrain of the mountain and along the treacherous mule tracks which clung to the cliffs. On one side was sheer rock; on the other the precipice fell away sharply. The path was as narrow as any I had yet traversed and, in the dark, being pushed and shoved from behind and bumping into the man in front, it was as dangerous a journey as any so far.

And long.

On the afternoon of the following day, we halted finally at the edge of an olive grove. Wolf pointed. A few hundred feet below us I could see a huge red cross. It had been laid out over a field.

'English there.' said Wolf.

'It's a dressing station,' declared Cooper.

'Now we go,' said Wolf. We shook hands with him and the other guides and they melted away into the rough country and we were on our own.

During the march it soon became apparent that Cooper was as mentally and physically tough as the steel of his bayonet and that O'Brien was just the opposite. Cooper seemed to relish the challenges of the mountain which seemed to exhilarate him. He did not find it difficult to keep up with Wolf's pace and, in fact, it appeared that he wanted to go even faster. I suppose he was a natural soldier. Cooper could look after himself, but had no interest in the needs of the rest of us. He never offered to share the water in his bottle even though, by the following morning, the need for water had become an obsession, as we all had a raging thirst upon us until Wolf led us to a spring where we guzzled the water greedily. Cooper ate his biscuits and bread when we rested, but never shared them. After the unlimited generosity of the Cretan shepherds who had helped me, this selfishness was very apparent. But for all that, he was clear-headed and was not shy of taking a lead. He had corporal's stripes on what was left of his torn and dusty battle dress.

O'Brien, of the red hair and putty coloured face, had moaned continuously during our seventeen-hour march – about our situation, about his feet, his blisters, his aching muscles, his hunger, desire for a drink and, in the morning, the heat. The excess fat around his waist wobbled and spilled over his belt. He lumbered rather than marched and was so slow that he held us up by constantly stopping so that we were forced to wait for him to catch up and he soon became the butt of Cooper's colourful epithets. After a while, even our four Cretan guides lost all patience with O'Brien and his failings. After appearing to have a discussion about us, they maintained the pace, forcing us to keep up with them. It left O'Brien to flounder after us like a whale out of water.

I was surprised that he had ever passed his basic training and had been declared fit for duty.

'I gotta catch my breath, so I have, fellows. Give me a break.' he panted, mopping sweat from his waxy forehead.

His excuses infuriated Cooper who swore at him constantly. 'Break? I'd like to break your bloody neck,' he muttered and gave O'Brien a foul look. O'Brien looked aggrieved.

I had the greatest respect for Titheridge who was

wounded. A bloody and not very clean bandage was tied round a head wound which must have given him severe pain. He never uttered a word, but marched on doggedly with a set look and a clenched jaw. At one of the halts, I offered him my water bottle.

'You OK, mate? I asked.

'Oh, definitely, old chap,' he replied as he took a slug of water.

'Head wound?'

'Oh, just a scratch. Don't give it a thought. The Huns won't get me down.'

'You from England?'

'Just so. Family's from Surrey. Military, you know.'

'First action?

'No, actually, got a bit of a fright at a place called Dunkirk. Heard of it?'

Even in our backwater we had heard all about Dunkirk. 'Bad show', I said.

'Just a bit. Thought they'd forgotten all about us, actually, but I got away in the end. Almost the last to leave – in one of the little boats. Shot at all the way home. Leaking like a sieve. But we made it. Thanks for the water. Much appreciated,' he said, handing me the bottle and moving off like a man with a purpose.

After the Cretans had departed, Cooper took control.

'We wait here and then we advance under the cover of dusk,' he ordered. I agreed with his assessment of our position. It's what I would have done myself. Titheridge had slid to the ground looking very pale and close to fainting. I passed him some more water.

'Want some?'

'Yes,' he gasped.' Absolutely.'

'Why can't we make a dash for that dressing station?' O'Brien implored.

'You couldn't make a dash anywhere, you great lump of lard,' sneered Cooper. 'And you'd be a bloody fool if you did. You want to get shot?'

'There's a red cross for all to see, so there is. It's supposed to be safe! Why can't we?' He whined like a peevish child and it put us all on edge.

'I just told you,' snapped Cooper.' You stay put.'

O'Brien turned his head away looked sullen and sat down heavily. He took off his boots and inspected his bloody and blistered feet.

But I knew he had not been convinced and he kept up a stream of whinges and complaints for the rest of the afternoon, providing a counterpoint to the stuttering of gunfire and the explosions of bombs which continued without ceasing all around us.

'Shut up!' spat Cooper eventually' 'If you don't shut up I'll hit you over the head and that'll shut your bloody mouth, you fucking moaning Minnie!'

'I don't have to take that from you, you cockney bastard!' returned O'Brien showing a bit of spirit for once.

In reply, Cooper took the butt of his rifle and dug O'Brien hard in the ribs.

'If ... I'm a bastard, you can take that,' he spat. Titheridge opened his eyes and regarded the exchange through eyes dulled with pain. He looked like a rag doll. It seemed as if he wanted to intervene, but the effort was too much.

O'Brien curled up in pain hugging his side.

'I'll get you for that, so I will, you fucking arsehole,' he muttered, but very much under his breath.

O'Brien continued to moan occasionally, but his fear of Cooper gave us a period of peace from his irritating whinges. Around us the gunfire continued and the ground shuddered from explosions. The air beyond our position was filled with dust and smoke.

O'Brien had been quiet for quite a while, but I did not think he had given up on the idea of making for the safety of the dressing station. I looked at his pasty face, his slack mouth, disgruntled expression and rounded shoulders. Yes, I'd be glad to be rid of him and his constant complaining, I thought.

Titheridge seemed far from conscious and was giving me some cause for concern, while Cooper was lying flat on his back and snoring. I was dozing when O Brien suddenly leapt to his feet and made a blundering break for it, running headlong towards the tents of the dressing station.

'No! You fucking idiot!' yelled Cooper springing to his feet. Titheridge opened his eyes and struggled to sit up. I was on my feet too. There was a rattle of machine gun fire. O'Brien's body twisted and flapped and he fell.

'Bloody fool. Snipers.' remarked Cooper laconically. 'I warned him. No one else move,' he ordered. 'Stay exactly where you are or you'll get the same as O'Brien.'

He had a point. He and I flopped to the ground and slithered for protection into the undergrowth. Slowly and painfully Titheridge dragged himself across the ground to join us.

'We wait for dusk. That will give us cover.' stated Cooper.

'Absolutely' croaked Titheridge.

He said very little after that, although he was awake. Clearly his head wound was giving him trouble. Possibly he was drifting in and out of consciousness. Dusk approached and we edged along the goat track which took us to caves above the beach.

The stragglers of all nations were camped there: Jews and Egyptians, Syrians and Greeks, English, Scots, Welsh, Canadians, Australians and our own Kiwi boys. We were a tattered, forlorn, exhausted, hopeless lot, falling flat whenever a low-flying Stuka screamed overhead. Some never rose afterwards.

And, above all, we were thirsty.

There had been a rush for water in the caves. Helmets, pannikins, old tins, anything and everything had been put into service as containers. They littered the ground. Little did any of those parched men realise that the water was not pure like the springs to which we had become accustomed. Our own water bottles were sufficiently full from the springs Wolf had shown us along the way, so we did not refill them. We were lucky. We avoided the stomach cramps, vomiting and diarrhoea that soon afflicted a lot of the men sheltering in those caves and added to the general misery.

There was chaos on the beach below us. Slow-moving lines of men were formed up, but it was well past midnight when, from our sparse cover on the cliff, we made out the silhouette of the first destroyer as it slipped silently towards the crescent-shaped beach. The non-commissioned officers screamed commands as they tried to create order from chaos. Hour after hour, the lines of exhausted, gaunt men shuffled forward and stumbled on board the waiting ships.

'It's just like bloody Dunkirk all over again,' said a voice. There were murmurs of agreement. They hardly seemed to diminish before the last destroyer disappeared from view. A long, low groan swelled and spread along the lines of men, as the troops, realised that they had been abandoned, and sank to the ground like a chorus line of exhausted dancers.

Cooper swore as extensively and colourfully as I have ever heard a man swear. Although Titheridge was still standing beside us, he had drifted into sleep as he stood, or possibly into unconsciousness. I just felt numb. Frozen in time. So, it had all been a waste of effort: the marching, the pain, the exhaustion. To be abandoned by the navy at the very last. How could this happen and now what?

Dawn rose, and soon a blazing sun assailed us. About a mile away the Jerries were concentrating on some target with heavy bombing and cannon fire from their planes. I couldn't see over the rise to identify what it was they were targeting but I could see the black smoke swirling up into the sky and smell the acrid aroma of burning fuel and rubber.

We remained inert and in hiding all day, sitting ducks, hungry and thirsty, until the sun went down and until the planes gave up. At dusk we moved forward cautiously through olive trees some of which were still aflame or smoking, until we reached the road. It was littered with all the debris of a retreating army: ration tins, ammo boxes, masks, uniforms, even an officer's suitcase, but most important of all a couple of rifles.

'We'll have those,' stated Cooper. 'Check the boxes for ammo and get as much as you can,' he ordered. I began searching and took what we needed, filling the pockets of my battledress and trousers and the little square woven Cretan shoulder bag which I had been carrying since we left the village.

We came upon a burnt-out staff car. Little flames were still licking around the bonnet. Cooper grabbed my water bottle, produced an abandoned pannikin, splashed some of my precious water into it and set it to boil on the burning bonnet. Titheridge rummaged in his pocket and offered up a small block of chocolate and we melted it in the water. Then the three of us drank hot chocolate there and then amid the flames, the smoke and the destruction. Titheridge took little more than a sip but it seemed to do him good. I savoured my mouthful and Cooper guzzled more than his fair share.

Cooper nudged me and took me to one side.

'We can do better than this,' he whispered. 'You game?'

'What d'ya mean, mate?' I asked.

'Go back where we came from and wait. Just us two. We can escape from another beach. There's bound to be a boat we can get hold of.'

Titheridge was on the ground leaning his back against a boulder and slumped to one side, shaded by the branches of a small tree. His face looked grey and his cheeks were drawn tight across the bone structure and his jaw was clenched hard, his eyes dull and unfocused. He looked very ill.

'What about Titheridge? We can't abandon him like this.' I whispered. Cooper shrugged and moved away.

'How you feeling, Titheridge?' I asked.

At first, I thought he had not heard me. After a pause, he opened his eyes and said in a slightly slurred voice:

'Very thirsty and a bit muzzy, old chap, if you want the truth. Bit of a headache. Chocolate was a treat though.'

'Have some more,' I knelt down and handed him what was left in the pannikin. 'It'll do you good.'

He sipped slowly as if in a trance.

'Thanks. Think I'll just take a bit of shut eye' he gasped and keeled over.

Cooper returned to my side and took my elbow. 'C'mon mate,' he whispered in my ear, 'Titheridge is about as useful as a dish of cold custard.'

I looked again at Titheridge, lying limply prone among the rocks. His eyes were closed. He seemed to be unconscious. Cooper was already retreating into the grey and green undergrowth. He turned and beckoned me. I hesitated and he disappeared with a shrug of exasperation. He was right, Titheridge was a dead duck. Should I do the right thing and sacrifice my chances of escape and survival for a dying man.

For what advantage?

I hesitated. I liked and respected Titheridge. I thought he was a brave man. Cooper turned back and hissed at me to come. I hesitated and wrestled with my conscience. I thought about right and wrong. I asked myself again, should I sacrifice my own survival for a dying man?

Self, in the end, defeated selflessness.

I abandoned Titheridge with a pang of remorse. But in the end, I followed Cooper into the shadows.

CHAPTER 6

2001

I met Adoni, as planned, at his *kafeneion* in the town centre after breakfast with Kalliope. I ordered a Greek coffee and Adoni did likewise, but his came with a glass of raki. It wasn't yet eleven but I noticed that there were many old Cretan men clad in faded work shirts and denim jeans sitting in groups of three or four, each with a glass of raki and a coffee on the table in front of them. They appeared to be arguing vociferously with wild gestures or thumps on the table. Or so it seemed. But, in fact, when I became accustomed to it, I realised that this was just a normal discussion about the only subject of interest – the political situation.

Adoni registered my gaze.

'It is the custom,' said Adoni. 'We rise at dawn with the sun. We work at the olives. Then it is hot. We rest. *Tsigia.*' he called and he raised his glass in a toast. 'In my village, when I was a young boy, there were about 48 families, now we are very few. The young, they leave for Chania or Athens, America, as I did, or Australia. There they make more money in a week than we do in a month. Here we are poor. We are farmers. We must work the land each day. The earth is hard. We do not have enough water for the trees or the vegetables. It is hot. In winter it is cold. Then we must pick the olives for the oil. It is good oil. Very pure. Extra virgin you call it now. The work breaks our backs. But we make little money from it.' He leaned back in his chair and folded his arms across his chest.

'Adoni, I want to know if you can help me,' I said. Adoni nodded and fiddled with his worry beads. 'Let me explain. My Grandfather fought here in Crete in 1941. I have his diary from that time. He writes that he was helped by many Cretans. I know that they took many risks to help him and were very brave.'

'This is true,' agreed Adoni. 'It was a hard and dangerous time.'

'Do you remember it?' I asked.

'I was not born then but I know all the stories I have heard them many times. The bloody Germans were here in the town, at the Fortezza and living in the only hotel. They had motorbikes and trucks. There were many raids on the villages. They took from us everything they could find, our olives, our oil, our beans, our animals – sheep and goats and chickens, everything' he paused, as his mind reflected on the events he had witnessed. 'But we were a match for them, you know,' he growled, looking up at me with fierce eyes. 'We hid our food and our animals in secret places that they did not know about. But even so the times were very hard, you understand? There was starvation and danger.'

I nodded.

'Do you know, for example, the story of Kandanos?'

I had read about the destruction of the village in the guide book but I urged him to continue.

'Kandanos, you must know Kandanos. You passed through the village on your way here. A few days after the invasion of Crete, the Germans reached the village on their way to Paleohora. There was resistance; of course. They always resisted. The people did not know what was going on. They did not speak German. They were protecting what was theirs, as they always did – as they had against the Venetians and later the Turks. But these men, woman and children were civilians, not soldiers. They thought that the Geneva Convention protected them. But the German commander ignored these laws; they were not for him. He only saw that they refused to surrender so, in his anger and fury, he gave orders to kill all the men, women and children and to destroy the village, every last house, with dynamite and fire. So much blood. Entire families: mothers, fathers, grandparents, children all wiped out in one afternoon. So much pain. One house remains a ruin as a monument to the destruction. You may see it when you pass through.'

As my mind absorbed the horror of Adoni's words I watched the tourists ambling lazily past as tourists do, carefree, carrying their brightly coloured bags and bottles of water, making for the beach and bathed by the bright sunlight. The dark shadows of Crete's wartime past were far from their thoughts and why should it not be so? They were here to holiday and relax. My purpose was more complicated.

'So, Adoni, can you help me? I would like to find the village where my grandfather stayed. He was there for nearly a year and I would like to find the family who sheltered him. Would this be possible?'

'Maybe,' said Adoni, flinging his worry beads round and over his fingers. But his expression was fierce and not very encouraging.

'They, the family, were very courageous. Without them my Grandfather might not have survived – and I would not be here!' I joked.

Adoni grunted what for him was a laugh.

'My Grandfather writes of a village but he does not give its name, so I don't know where to start. But he does mention the names of some people who helped him.'

'What names?'

'The leader was called Wolf. There was someone called Rabbit.' Adoni guffawed loudly and took out a handkerchief to mop his face. 'And there were some women too. I would like to find them. Can you help me do this?'

He observed his raki, turning the glass around with his fingers.

There was a long pause as he considered. Then he said:

'Perhaps. I try.' he paused again and he jingled the coins

in his pocket.

I took the hint.

'Perhaps we can come to an agreement?' I suggested. I offered him a sum of money and although he demurred at first and shook his head vehemently, we finally agreed a fee and sealed the contract with a handshake.

'Tonight I call you. We can meet someone I know. Maybe he will help you.'

1941

We moved west using the sun as a guide. We knew from basic training that if we kept the sun on our left hand side, we would be staggering in the right direction away from danger, but also away from rescue.

My feet were now raw meat from burst blisters and every footstep stabbed me like hot knives. Frequently, Cooper was impatient and exasperated with me for holding him up, just as he had been with O'Brien.

'Get an effing move on for Christ's sake!' he yelled. 'Bastard, bloody clodhopper!'

It was clear to me by now that Cooper was a driven man, obsessive and short-tempered. He did not suffer fools gladly, and I was a fool. I could sense that he was fast regretting suggesting that I went along with him. He was reluctant to rest or to take into consideration that my feet were a pulpy mess and that every step was purgatory. I began to believe that I had been better off when I had marched alone and that I was paying a high price for Cooper's company. The more I was with him the less I liked him for his selfishness except where his own interests were concerned. He had no patience with weakness. I had found him callous in his attitude towards Titheridge and indeed O'Brien. He was self-absorbed and utterly single-minded where his own needs were concerned. He never offered to share his food or water. He wanted to control the situation completely and to travel at his own pace regardless of my needs. He was a thorough hard case.

The drone of the planes and the stutter of gunfire began again. Far below us, to our right, there was a road. We were hidden from their view but we could see a troop of German soldiers making a search of the surrounding area. A couple of stragglers were discovered in a gully and they emerged with their hands up. That could have been me I thought. The Jerries did not shoot them, as I half expected, but pushed them roughly to the ground at gun point. They tied them and left them trussed up, in full sun at the roadside, while the methodical search continued.

We slithered back into the shadows and inched on our stomachs until we reached the edge of the gorge and then slid and rolled down its side until we were out of view. Then we marched – or in my case stumbled and lurched – westward until after midday when there were few shadows to hide us.

'We'll stop now,' announced Cooper, without asking my opinion and he flopped down in the shelter of some rocks. As there was no alternative, I joined him.

'What do they call you?' he demanded.

'Lancaster. John Lancaster.'

'Where you from?' he said eventually. 'Norfolk?'

'No. Why do you say Norfolk.'

'Had a mate once, talked like you. He was from Norfolk.'

'I'm from New Zealand.'

'Where's that?'

'Thousands of miles away from here.'

'So how come you're effing here?'

'I volunteered.'

Cooper gave me a long withering look. 'You're an effing fool.'

I considered talking of King and Empire, duty, fighting for a free world, but decided that for Cooper these principles would have little meaning. So, I said nothing.

'Is it hot in New Zealand,' he asked eventually.

'Sometimes. Where I live it's very sunny.'

'Where's that?'

'On the north coast of South Island.'

'Is there a North Island, then?' Ignoring his ignorance, I explained that there were two islands, North and South.

'Well, I'll be buggered,' he said. 'Are they big, these islands?'

'Yes, big enough.'

'Do you have an effing job?'

I paused before I answered. I did not think it was any of his business that we had a big sheep farm and a couple of acres of apple orchards and I didn't feel like telling him, so I prevaricated a bit.

'Yeah, I looked after sheep.'

'Ah, an effing shepherd, like these effing peasants in this god-forsaken effing place,' he said, paring dirt from his fingernails with his bayonet.

'That sort of thing, yes.'

Cooper seemed to lose interest. I guess he didn't know much about sheep. After a pause I asked: 'And what about you? O'Brien called you a Cockney. What is that?'

'A Cockney is a Londoner who should be born within the sound of Bow Bells.'

'Bow Bells?'

'Some effing church in London. But I ain't. Hackney's my manor. Heard of it? It's in the East End of London.' Cooper started fiddling with the butt of his rifle as if he disliked the direction of our talk and it made me uneasy.

'No, not at all.' I lied. I had been going to ask him about his job, but I had read a book about the underworld in London, and Hackney had been mentioned. I rather suspected that robbery and violence were more in his line than any honest occupation, so I thought I'd keep off the subject.

'How did you get here?'

'Upset a few bad lads in Hackney. They said it'd be good for my health to see the world. So I joined the army. Didn't think there'd be an effing war.' Cooper's voice rose to a discontented whine and he seemed to be becoming agitated, his hands fiddling once more with his rifle and plucking at his uniform. 'And I've had just about enough of this shit!' he shouted.

He made me very uneasy. I decided to make myself scarce before matters got out of hand.

'I think I'll make a recce and see if I can find anything to eat. The food has run out.' I stated rather obviously. I had been thinking longingly for most of the morning of the shepherd's hut, the dry bread and the slices of fresh cheese. It seemed a good time to have a look beyond the trees.

Among the rocks, I came upon some small bulbs of wild garlic and green mountain dandelions. The whiskery leaves were bitter and nutty, but not unpleasant. Then I hit the jackpot. Standing alone among the shrubs, stood a single orange tree. I couldn't believe my luck: food and drink all in one go. I counted twenty oranges in its branches, so I picked the ones I could reach and filled my pockets

I returned to Cooper with my booty. He was slouched with his back against the rocks with a scowl on his face.

'Look!' I said, 'Oranges.' I offered one to him which he grabbed without thanks. He refused the garlic and dandelion leaves.

'I'm not eating that effing muck. You trying to poison me, you bastard?' he said with an angry sneer. I ate them anyway, making each mouthful count. I rolled his share of the oranges over to him and we started to suck the juice before we ate the flesh and then the pith and finally the peel, until only the pips remained.

The sweet juice was refreshing and gave me strength.

The food diverted Cooper from his bad humour, thankfully, and we set off again, if not with renewed vigour at least with a little more energy.

We glimpsed the sea on our left from time to time. The sun which had originally been behind us and then above us, now moved ahead of us and we followed its rays as they gleamed in the west between the clefts in the mountains.

We had agreed that it would be safer to approach a beach under the cover of darkness when we would be less likely to meet any German patrols.

'We got to look for a boat. Maybe a fisherman'll go out night fishing. I heard they do that,' said Cooper. 'Then we can grab him and make him take us out to sea. That way we can get to Africa.'

It sounded easy, but I had my doubts.

We scrambled down through the rocks, sending stones and small boulders scattering until we came to tamerisk trees lining the sand dunes. The beach and the ocean lay ahead of us. Cooper uttered a small cry of triumph as we spotted a small wooden fishing boat beached at the far end of the cove, close to the shore line. It was not large, but it looked seaworthy.

'Can you sail a boat?' I asked Cooper.

'Not much call for an effing boat in the East End. I'm better with a fast car. Can you?'

'Maybe. I had a boat in New Zealand.'

'Bloody hell.' For the first time in a long day Cooper smiled, revealing small rodent teeth. Then, without waiting for me he began to run.

'Hold on, Cooper!' I cried.

'I'm going down to the beach to check it out.' he said over his shoulder, adding, 'you hide over there in those rocks. Cover me in case there are any Jerries around.' And before I could reply he was zig-zagging through the trees towards the far end of the cove where I lost sight of him.

I waited a long time, lying flat on my stomach with my

rifle trained on the beach, straining my eyes to try to catch a glimpse of Cooper and the boat. There were no sounds of gunshots or of voices. There was no noise at all except the slapping of the waves on the sand and the moan of the rising wind. Darkness fell suddenly, as it does in the southern Mediterranean, and I could see nothing. I waited a long time until I was resigned to the fact that Cooper had gone without me.

I was cursing him in my mind, when I heard a scuffle and he flopped down beside me.

'You were a long time,' I said, as pleasantly as I could.

'Bastard fisherman took his time too,' he replied. 'I tried to do a deal. He didn't speak any English.'

Hardly surprising, I thought.

'Got through to him in the end. With sign language. Effing bastard said no. Wasn't fishing tonight.'

'We might as well leave now, look somewhere else' I suggested.

'No, not me, I need a rest,' said Cooper, rolling over on to his back, getting out his water bottle and some bread from his pocket which he did not, of course, offer to share. Then, he lit a cigarette and without any further word rolled over and fell asleep. I slept too.

I was a fool.

I woke at dawn. Cooper and the boat had gone.

CHAPTER 7

2001

'You want to go to Hora Sfakion. Why?' Adoni had demanded.

'I want to see the beach.'

'Beach? We have a good beach here. That place, it is nothing!'

'It's special. It's the beach the British Navy used to rescue the soldiers after the battle for Crete.'

'This I know. *Lipon.* You must take boat.'

'What boat?'

'Ferry boat. It leaves from the harbour each morning although today it has left already so you have missed it. It takes a few hours. Very nice trip. You can stop in the village drink a coffee, eat some lunch maybe, and return in the afternoon.'

'Is there a coast road? I have a car.'

'No. *Katholu*, not at all. No good! You must drive up to Chania on the north coast and after you must take another road down to the South.'

'That seems like snakes and ladders,' I joked. My feeble attempt at humour was lost in translation.

'What is snakes and ladders?' asked Adoni..

'Too complicated to explain. It's an English game.' I replied. 'Have you been to Hora Sfakion, Adoni?'

'Many years before,' he replied, with a vague wave of his hand which suggested no knowledge of Hora Sfakion at all.

As I drove the car across the mountains to the north coast, I wondered whether I would have abandoned Titheridge as he lay dying. I had had conflicting feelings when I read and reread my Grandfather's account of the debacle at the beach and his subsequent retreat.

It seemed to me from its length and its tone that he had written the account up long after the event. How far, I wondered, could I trust the account he had written? What had he omitted? What had he changed? How far had he exaggerated the situation in which he found himself…or indeed played it down?

Had I the right to judge? Had I the right to be shocked? What, I asked myself, would I have done in his situation. A life and death situation. How many of us have to face that in a lifetime? The phrase 'Judge not, that ye be not judged' fluttered through my mind, an echo from sermons in school chapel. In essence, when you boil it down, he found himself in a life or death situation. Exhaustion, fear and hunger all played a part in his decision. At such times, a man's judgement is distorted; right and wrong become blurred. Would I have remained with Titheridge at the risk of my own survival? Would I have stayed with him, helped him, ministered to his needs, held his hand for comfort, given him sips of water and watched over him till he died? Would he have died? Could I have helped him to survive?

How could I say?

How can anyone say who was not there, at that moment, under that pressure, under fire, at risk of being captured, hungry, thirsty and literally feeling the heat of battle?

And feeling the fear.

Not that my Grandfather ever admits to fear in his account, merely apprehension.

I tried to imagine my Grandfather as a young, untested, twenty-year-old, flung into a battle with terrible consequences and not as the tough, ruthless businessman that I had grown up with. Was that streak of steel always within him and was the war the crucible that annealed the metal or did the experience of war turn him into a man tough as steel?

At twenty how would I have coped? When I was twenty, I was a student, without a care, considering where the next beer and the next girl would come from. I was irresponsible, often rash, thoughtless and probably a bit arrogant. I was not fighting for my life. How can any of us predict what our actions will be *in extremis* when the chips are down and we are being tested as never before? So I will not play Solomon.

A road cut through the mountains. It was a new road. It was not the same road that the soldiers took in 1941. As I crossed the spine of the mountains which run parallel with the north coast, the sun disappeared and the temperature suddenly dropped. I shivered in my light clothes and turned on the heater,

I passed several white-painted villages, flanked by small pastureland, and drove on into a wilder, barren landscape. The road switched back and forth like a demented snake, dropped lower and lower, until all views were obliterated in a grey, sinister, swirling fog which curled and dipped like ripples of silk.

The Imbros valley which leads down to Hora Sfakion was swathed in cloud and the southern coast was invisible. I had read that the weather in late May 1941 was hot, and that many men had perished along the roadside from heat exhaustion and lack of water. Indeed, my grandfather's account corroborates this. The retreating troops had marched by a more direct route than mine across the narrowest part of Crete down through the Imbros valley to the sea. They were strafed all the way by German planes and chased by German motorised divisions. The slopes of scrub and small trees offered very little cover so that they were sitting targets every step of the way. In the cosy cocoon of my car, I had to work hard to empathise with their situation. At last, I emerged from the swirling mists and saw a glinting sea, and a bright beach, fringed with white buildings, illuminated by the sunshine.

'Is there a museum?' I asked testing out my Greek, when the waiter in the water's edge café delivered my espresso.

'No. there is nothing here,' he explained in perfect English. 'The museum is at Askyfou on the road to Chania.'

'I must have passed it.' I said smiling at him. 'There was a lot of mist in the hills. It was difficult to see much. This is Hora Sfakion, isn't it?'

'*Malista.*'

'So there is nothing here to commemorate the Battle for Crete?'

'*Malista,*' he repeated. 'Over there,' he added, waving to the far side of the crescent shaped harbour, 'is a monument.'

'I will look when I have finished my espresso. Thank you.'

'You are welcome,' he said, using the ubiquitous American phrase which has seeped into every language in every country you visit these days.

Hora Sfakion is a small village surrounding a crescent-shaped beach. White-painted apartments and hotels cling to steep slopes above the harbour. You are forced to pass through an arcade of eating places where you ran the gauntlet of desperate waiters who cling irritatingly to your arm as you passed by and implore you: 'Eat here. Fresh fish. Good price.'

The monument at the eastern end of the beach was erected jointly by the Australian and Greek governments. Where we lay wreaths of poppies at our war memorials to honour our dead, the Cretans lay palm fronds. Blue-and-white-striped Greek flags fluttered in a light wind on either side.

I shifted my gaze once more to the beach. I was astonished that it was so tiny. In my mind's eye I had imagined something far larger, like the sands of Dunkirk or one of the D-Day beaches. Its minute size explained the terrible, hotchpotch assembly of soldiers, the lack of organisation, and the mix of all nations desperately waiting for the evacuation, while the enemy Stukas and Junkers 52s bombed or strafed the unprotected men. The mountains, which fell almost to the shore, offered little protection. They were smooth and rounded, almost boulderless, quite unlike the rugged crags above Paleohora. There were few caves or clefts, very little sheltering shade and there were no groves of olive trees or oak as I had expected. The landscape reminded me of the bare back of an enormous hog. It offered little protection to the vulnerable troops. I shuddered at the thought of being trapped helplessly there.

Grandfather had never even reached the beach, but had been trapped on the hills above. He had assessed his chances and not rated them very highly. Urged on by Cooper, he had decided to slip away in the night under the cover of darkness. It would have given him a fighting chance at the very least. Who amongst us would have resisted the opportunity to retreat, set against the futility of staying with a dying man?

I sat on a bench behind the memorial and thought about those brave, ill-fated men choking the beach and those New Zealanders in the rearguard who selflessly maintained a defensive line, knowing that they were condemning themselves to captivity or worse, all for the greater good. I felt a choking in my throat and a pricking behind my eyelids.

I stayed there on the bench until a mini-bus disgorged a group of noisy tourists. They seemed to overwhelm that sanctified place. They talked raucously among themselves, laughed loudly, brought out cameras, pulled the tabs of coke tins and rustled packets of sandwiches, dispersing the ghosts.

I forwent the fresh fish, climbed back into the car and turned up the winding road for the Museum at Askyfou.

It was signposted well enough, but I suppose that I had missed seeing it in the mist and driven past. Rusting engines, plane parts, helmets and guns lined a steep path up to what seemed to be no more than a white painted cottage. But inside was a treasure trove. A dedicated collector of militaria would have paid thousands of dollars or pounds sterling for just a small part of it.

With great foresight and a sense of history, a Cretan guerrilla fighter or *andarte* had collected everything he could find lying around after the end of the war. It was not a hard task. The road to Sfakion had been littered with discarded weapons, ammunition, trucks, armoured vehicles and even, according to my Grandfather, an officer's suitcase. As the departing soldiers had boarded the destroyer that rescued them, they had been ordered to throw away their weapons and equipment. These had been quickly recycled by the Cretan *andartes*, but much remained abandoned. Propellers from Stukas, bombs (hopefully, not live ones), grenades and a whole arsenal of Bren guns, bayonets and bullets were crammed into one small room. While I was studying intently this amazing collection, a youngish Cretan woman silently appeared from somewhere behind the museum. I had noticed other houses and heard voices when I arrived and I had just caught a glimpse of a woman shelling peas or beans on a chair outside a door.

'*Kalimera*.' I greeted her.

'*Kalimera*,' she replied. ' Germani? Engliss?'

'New Zealand,' I replied.

She smiled: 'Welcome.'

She began to describe the collection very fast in broken English and a bad accent, as if she had learnt a script parrot-fashion, which she probably had.

'This Engliss gun, this Stuka German. This grenad Engliss, this cap Engliss, this passport Australian.' And so on. A stocky, muscular man entered. 'This father,' she said.

He introduced himself. 'I am Andreas Hatzidakis. My

father, he collect. Iss privet. Government no help.'

I took this as a hint for a donation and indeed gave willingly. The Greek government has been unable to take much interest in maintaining this collection, and indeed has very little money to do so. In England or America these artefacts would be on show in a major museum and not left where they were, partly rusting away on a remote Cretan hillside.

I had much to think about and digest as I retraced my steps along the same roads first to Chania and then to Paleohora and my rustic room in the Old Town.

Next morning a fierce, hot wind was blowing in angry blasts. It had rattled one of the shutters free and the banging woke me. I went to secure it and as I looked out I saw Kalliope battling with the unpredictable gusts in order to put her sheets on the washing line, which was strung along the path across her garden. The wet flapping cloth wrapped itself around her body encasing her like an Egyptian mummy as she tugged at the line, her mouth full of pegs.

I joined her and offered to help.

'*Oichi. Oichi.* It is not man's work,' she chuckled, as she unravelled herself and pegged the last sheet securely to the line. I rescued a towel which was soaring away towards the chicken coop and returned it to her. She smiles a lot when she talks – and she talks a lot, although I can only understand a word in three, as she talks so fast and with an accent. Her teeth are even and intact and white. She has sparkling, nut-brown eyes and there are merry laughter lines crinkling at the corner of her round face. A mass of iron grey curls spring around her head. She walks with grace, swinging her wide hips, as a woman does who has been a much admired beauty. Her legs are short, but her ankles are shapely. I expect she is as agile as a mountain goat. She seems very friendly and very helpful, full of Cretan hospitality and such a chatterbox. I think I am going to like her.

She picked up the empty laundry basket – '*Ela!* Come and drink coffee with me' and she sashayed into her house.

Coffee turned out to include a glass of raki, a slice of cheese and a spoonful of jam on a saucer

'What's this?' I asked.

'Spoon sweet,' she said, 'made from oranges and sugar. We boil it for many hours.' she added. 'Taste it. *Ine kala.*'

And it was. When she saw that I was enjoying it she piled another spoonful on the saucer and topped up my raki.

Kalliope's house stood opposite the cottage I had rented from Adoni. Hers was much more substantial: rectangular and standing two storeys high. The stone was whitewashed inside and out, and though simple was neat, clean and well cared for.

'How long have you lived here Kalliope?' I asked looking round at the sparse but immaculate kitchen

'I was sixteen.' she replied. 'My husband and his father built this house with their own hands,' she told me proudly. 'Our marriage was arranged between the families,' she said. 'It was the custom then, but Vassili and I knew each other, and,' she smiled and rolled her eyes, 'so we had already decided upon each other.'

'Was it love at first sight?'

'Perhaps. Vassili picked me out from the other girls. He only had eyes for me. I was very young and my Father did not wish to lose me. But Vassili was very persuasive. He and his father worked very hard for many months after a hard day's work on the land, or in the olive groves, to build this house, you understand. This was to prove to my family and the village that he meant to have me and that he was worthy of me. I moved in on my wedding day. I was very excited and so happy. My sisters and friends had spread rose petals on the bedspread. A new house is very special. But I was special to my man.' She let out a long sigh and an expression of sadness and regret passed over her usually happy face. I tried to picture her as she had been then – a young elated bride entering her new house for the first time.

'Children. Do you have children, Kalliope?' Her face clouded over and she suddenly became sad.

'All my children were born here. Three altogether. All girls. I was unlucky, just as my mother was unlucky

'Why?'

'A mother must have sons. I had girls. Girls leave. They go far away with their husbands. In the old days brides moved in with their husband's parents. Now they just leave to go away with their husbands for work, for jobs.' I later learned that this was a subject that Kalliope would return to again and again: her lack of sons was an obsession with her.

'And why must a mother have sons?'

'The son stays with his Mother. He always looks after her. God did not give me sons. My sisters have sons, but I was cursed! My Vassili is dead, so I am alone.' She fell silent, reflecting perhaps on her bad luck, and two large tears rolled down her cheek.

I wondered what to say. I did not wish to stir up any more of Kalliope's unhappy memories.

'But you must have family, Kalliope: brothers and sisters?'

'My Mother and Father are dead now, of course. God rest their souls.' Kalliope crossed herself furiously three times. 'No brothers. My Mother was cursed also.' More tears fell and dropped onto the table. I began to feel embarrassed and uneasy.

'Kalliope, *pou ise?*' called a voice from outside. Kalliope hurriedly brushed away her tears with her sleeve and stood up. I stood too, thinking of making my escape.

A woman, small as a sparrow and round as a barrel, breezed in like a barrage balloon in full flight. She was swathed in a brightly patterned, orange dress or rather in her case a tent. If it had been white I think helicopters would have tried to land on her! Her curly black hair kept escaping from her headscarf. She erupted through the bead curtain, beaming from ear to ear, kissed and hugged Kalliope energetically and handed over a basket of green leaves that looked like spinach.

'Iphigenia *mou!*' cried Kalliope, returning the kiss with gusto. She turned to me:

'Alexi *mou*, this is my sister, Iphigenia.'

The round figure twirled to face me, her brown eyes twinkling with friendliness, and seized my arms.

'*Kalas irthtete.* You are welcome!' she cried and planted a smacking kiss on my cheek.' How long you stay? You must eat with me at my house. You are a very good-looking young man, so blonde, so tall. Where you from?'

And thus she peppered questions at me like a machine gun while Kalliope made coffee and fetched biscuits. Under the onslaught of questions, I subsided into the chair while Iphigenia bounced around her sister's kitchen picking things up and putting them down, examining the bowl of oranges, picking up a bunch of oregano and sniffing it, opening the fridge and examining the contents, nibbling the biscuits Kalliope had placed on the table and all the while commenting and remarking, without any pause for breath. I felt as if a hurricane, a whirlwind or a tsunami had swept through the room. It reminded me of the old joke that when the mother-in-law comes knocking at the door the mice start throwing themselves on the traps.

When Kalliope placed the coffee on the table I attempted to make a move to leave, but Iphigenia prevented me.

'*Kathiste.* Stay, *pethia.* Where you from? Why you here? What is your name? Tell me.'

When you meet a force of nature it makes sense to throw in the towel and give in. Resistance is a waste of energy. A comedian once said that he had not spoken to his wife for eighteen months because he did not like to interrupt her. I felt very much the same. So I spent the next half hour answering Iphigenia's questions as best I could, aided by interjections from Kalliope, and soon she possessed pretty much the full story of my mission to Crete.

Iphigenia was such a bundle of positive energy that I was tempted to recruit her to be my guide. I was just about to form the words when she jumped up, kissed her sister, enveloped me in a huge crushing hug and bounded towards the door, bombarding Kalliope with instructions about their next meeting and aiming goodbyes at me.

She was a dear woman, but exhausting.

My Grandfather's diary does not give much detail about what happened after Cooper abandoned him on the beach and made his escape in the boat. There are just short, terse notes. I would guess that by this time he was suffering from the effects of extreme hunger and acute exhaustion. He must have been focused on survival and using every ounce of spare energy to keep walking. He must have had little energy or desire to write. He does note that he found a track that he thought he recognised and which he hoped would lead him back to the village where he had been captured by Wolf and the Cretan *andartes* and he struggled to follow where it led.

With Wolf leading the escapees, the journey had taken about seventeen hours. The return journey took my grandfather about a week. Towards the end, he records feeling light-headed, confused and hot and cold. He could only walk in short bursts and much of the time he was tottering with fatigue. In between, he had to rest for long periods. His wounds and cuts began to fester. This must have been the start of the fever which nearly killed him.

He saw the chapel first and that was when he knew he had made it to the outskirts of the village. Ironically, it was the dogs that saved him. They set up their usual cacophony of barking as he tottered towards the first house. It was the last sound he heard before he collapsed.

PART TWO

CHAPTER 8

1941

The door frame seemed to melt and sway as I clung to it. In fact, I was the one who was wavering. My legs seemed to liquefy and soften until they could hardly hold me. I felt close to collapse as the weakness from my illness swept through my body.

The sun blazed so bright when I stumbled outside that it dazzled me. It took some time to adjust my eyes to the intense light after the dim interior of my hideaway. The sudden rush of heat on my face was unexpected after the cool storeroom and so was the strong aroma of thyme. My head was thumping and I felt slightly sick and dizzy.

I did not know how long I had drifted in and out of consciousness, sick and hidden away in that small, dark space. I felt unsettled, confused and disorientated. Everything around me felt alien and strange, but awash with brilliant colour. I was so accustomed to the smell of goat and dung and dust that the fresh, hot air seemed, in contrast pure, clean and wholesome.

Two small, brown girls dressed in faded cotton smock dresses sat on a flight of steps teasing a ginger cat with a stick. Their legs were bare and tanned. I shifted myself until the door frame was between my shoulder blades and leaned back against its support to observe them. The steps of uneven stone led up to a terrace which was situated immediately above my hideaway. The cat hissed angrily and lashed out with a claw. The girls squealed and jumped onto their feet which were as bare as their legs. It took them a few seconds to see my drooping carcase, half in half out of the door. The sight of me must have startled them, for they dropped the stick and cried out a volley of words I did not understand in high-pitched voices and fled up the steps.

I had scared the children, of that I was sure, and I could hardly blame them for I guessed that the sight of a bearded, wild-haired man in dusty, blood-soaked clothes who appeared suddenly and without warning would alarm the stoutest heart.

I had no idea where I was and looked around me at the buildings. It was clear to me that this place was a small village. Most of the houses were box-shaped, single-storey and whitewashed. The building where I had been hidden was grander and larger. It was built of stone and lime-washed white to reflect the sun and repel insects. It was a long building, made up of two floors. There were rooms above where I could hear the excited chattering of the children I had disturbed, and stables and storerooms below for the animals, oil, wine, corn, olives and nuts and where I had been hidden. Small shuttered windows kept out the sun and double wooden doors opened on to the terrace.

A wide earth path meandered between the houses. It was scattered with clumps of yellow buttercups, scarlet poppies and wild mauve mallows nodding in the slight breeze. Beyond, there grew a tall brooding pine whose wide, spreading branches acted as a wind break. And further off, in the distance, lay the grey-green olive groves and a small vineyard. Through it all I could see the bright sparkle of the sea.

To my right the mountains rolled in graceful curves. They were richly carpeted in trees and shrubs which gave the look of green velvet, while to my left the cliffs soared sharply into high, bare crags of tawny and cream limestone. It was difficult to believe that not long ago I had crossed those very mountains on my own.

A large, well-tended kitchen garden flanked the house and was planted with neat regiments of vegetables. I recognised potatoes and tall, angular, spiky artichoke heads. Surrounding the rows of plants, was a hedge of prickly pear whose leather platelets and treacherous spikes provided a natural trellis for geraniums, supporting their great, round, tennis ball heads in startling fuchsia, pink and scarlet. Bushes of dark green, spiky rosemary and purple silvery sage completed the side nearest the house. Everywhere the air was filled with the sweet smell of herbs.

One of the small girls scampered back down the steps, chattering wildly, accompanied by a much older woman dressed in a faded blue frock and cream linen apron and with a black scarf wound around her head.

She shouted out, but I could not understand her and, fearing the worst, fell back into the shadows. She rushed to me and I waited for a knife between the ribs. Instead, she grasped my hands in hers, kissed my cheek and then crossed herself. One of the girls handed me a cup of milk and the other a piece of bread spread with creamy cheese. It reminded me of something, but my brain was too fuzzy to catch the thought.

In a high-pitched voice she uttered a torrent of words, but I understood nothing. Taking my arm she ushered me back into the room and led me back behind the tall urns where my straw-filled mattress had been spread on the earth floor. She seemed agitated and gestured that she wanted me to lie down in my hiding place and I obeyed. I felt weak enough after a few minutes on my feet in the hot sun and the store room was cool and inviting.

A shadow filled the door way. I saw the silhouette of a man and the outline of a rifle. I slid behind a tall pot until I was out of sight. The older woman rushed to the intruder, grasped his arm, and shouted a flood of Greek at him. He pushed her purposefully to one side and strode towards my hiding place. I shrank as much as I could into the farthest corner, into the dark and the dirt and the cobwebs. Dusty, white boots, baggy trousers and faded felt waistcoat loomed above me.

A Cretan costume – not a German uniform as I had feared.

I scrutinised his face.

Then recognition slowly dawned on me as he twirled the ends of his magnificent moustaches into points like the end of a spear.

'Wolf! Is it you?' I cried and struggled to my feet. Wolf grasped me firmly by the shoulders and slapped a kiss on each of my cheeks.

'My friend,' he cried, hugging me to him. 'Thank the Good Lord! You are feeling better?'

'I am.' I croaked weakly. 'Wolf, I am so pleased to see you. Where am I?'

'In my village.' He shooed away the woman and the two children who had accompanied her and we sat down on the straw.

'I tried to come back. It was the only place I could think of.'

'You collapsed at the chapel. Mavro led us to you.'

'That dog nearly crushed me once! But he saved my life!' I croaked. 'How long have I been here?'

'You have been very sick my friend. For many days. The woman of the house thought you would die. You had a fever. Also many wounds. Your feet were of blood. You cried out when she touched you here.' Wolf ran a hand over his ribs. 'The woman of the house cared for you. She is very skilful and has much good *farmaka*. Her daughters watched over you. We hid you here in the storeroom. For safety. You must stay inside,' ordered Wolf, grasping my shoulder again. 'You must not be seen, my friend. It is dangerous.'

'The Germans?'

'The Germans,' – he spat – 'you must know, are searching the whole countryside for British soldiers so you must not be seen outside. You must remain hidden within the house. We have the small boys on lookout. They will tell us if a German patrol will approach but you must have care. The Germans think they control Crete. The British have left for Egypt. But we, the *Palikaria*, we will fight to the death. We fought the Venetians; we fought the Turks; now we will fight the Germans. They have ordered us to hand over our weapons. They tell us that for each gun we hold back they will shoot ten men. *Lipon*, we have given them guns, oh yes! But we gave them the ones which were old and useless. The rest we have buried!' Wolf laughed merrily and then became serious again. 'We will never give up our land. We know the mountains, they do not. We will attack, attack and attack again.'

'And I must escape from the island. I must rejoin my regiment.'

'*Malista*. All in good time. First you must recover your strength and become well. Then we *andartes* will help you to escape. So, stay here for the present and rest.'

I felt profound relief. It's a cliché but I felt, like Atlas, as if the weight of the world had been lifted from my shoulders. I was safe for the time being and I was among people who would care for me and hide me until I could leave. I also felt a sagging tiredness and an overwhelming desire to sleep.

Wolf jumped to his feet in one swift movement

'Tonight we hold a *glendi* in the room above' he cried. 'It is the name day of my cousin. We will eat and drink and sing and tell tales. You will come!'

***

2001

Iphigenia was as good as her word. She announced herself by loud cries and an even louder battering at my door early that evening. I had just opened a beer and was deciding to re-read my notes on grandfather's diary and send a text to Hennery to update him on my detective work

'*Alexi mou. Iste etho? Alexi, pou iste?*'

The little round figure was standing in the lane beaming from ear to ear. 'You must come and eat with me,' she cried. 'Tonight! Now! Although we eat late here in Crete you will come now with me and Kalliope to meet my family and eat good Cretan *fagoto*.'

Refusal was impossible. Iphigenia was an irresistible force. I was swept away. Before too long, I found myself seated at a long table in a shady, cool courtyard which faced the sea and was filled with loquat trees, agave cactus and palms. Iphigenia bustled about as fast as her short legs would allow her bringing first raki and nuts and then dried fruit and curious spiral rings of pastry drenched in honey to the table.

'Drink! Eat!' she cried waving a hand towards the saucers and plates of nibbles laid before me on a plastic cloth.

Soon, various members of her family drifted in. I discovered that the apartment block behind the courtyard housed all the members of her extended family and that the young people were her grandchildren. Each one welcomed me with a handshake and the girls kissed me on both cheeks. I was surprised that most of Iphigenia's grandchildren were as tall as she was short – and slim. In fact, both granddaughters were extremely pretty with large brown eyes and rich, black curling hair which reminded me of the photographs I had seen of the famous Minoan women of Knossos. They moved gracefully, swinging their hips in the manner of their great aunt Kalliope and I could catch a glimpse in them of the young, lively and delightful women that Kalliope and Iphigenia had been when young.

The men clustered together round the barbecue grill which was roasting meat on the far side of the courtyard, smoking and drinking beer from cans as men do around barbecues all over the world. My grandfather's descriptions of the Cretan *andartes* always drew attention to their grand and luxuriant moustaches. Modern Cretan men still cultivate their moustaches and beards in the old traditional way, although these young men were mainly clean-shaven city boys. But when Iphigenia's husband finally arrived, any disappointment I may have had vanished at the sight of his ebullient shock of white hair, huge curling moustache and dark bushy beard streaked with grey and cut square to his chin like a spade in the old traditional style.

'This is my husband who is called Eftiki. He does not speak English,' said Iphigenia, introducing me. Eftiki took my hand and almost crushed it with his handshake and then filled my tumbler to the brim with red wine. He was a short and stout man with broad shoulders and a weather-beaten face, lined and tanned by the sun.

'He left school at thirteen to help with the family farm and before that he did not go to school much because of the war,' explained Iphigenia, 'but do not think that he is not a clever man. He understands figures very well and has now a big cement business to prove it. We do not starve!'

As Iphigenia and Kalliope, helped by the girls, loaded the table with dishes of lettuce dressed with lemon, salads of tomatoes, cucumber and onions topped with feta cheese, plates of wrinkled black olives and *kalitsounias*, cheeses and chips, I could well believe it. They piled my plate high with pork chops, chicken legs and spicy sausages and a pasta like macaroni cheese until there was no room left and I answered the usual questions, 'where was I from?' and 'did I like Crete?' and 'how long was I staying?' More people arrived, along with some children, and the room ebbed and flowed like the sea before us.

Two older men arrived who introduced themselves as Iphigenia's sons, Pavlo and Simon. By now the table was almost full and the volume of conversation and laughter had reached a peak .I could hardly follow a word. Although my basic Greek was good, it was difficult to follow a rapid conversation and I felt hindered too by the noise and the Cretan accent which was different from the standard Greek I had learned on my course in New Zealand.

I was bursting to join in and I attempted to explain to anyone who asked that I was retracing my grandfather's footsteps in 1941. I wanted to ask if anyone might have known him during the war when he was hidden in the area for a year, but I just couldn't keep up. Iphigenia plumped herself down beside me

'You like our Cretan food? Eat! Eat more! What I can give you?'

'No more thanks. It was delicious,' I said. 'Tell me, do you remember the war, Iphigenia? Does Kalliope? Does Eftiki?'

'I was a small child. Eftiki was just a bit older. He looked after his family's goats and sheep. Didn't you Eftiki?'

Iphigenia's husband leaned over and filled my tumbler. I noticed his well-cared-for hands and the long fingernails on his little fingers, which showed that he no longer worked the land.

'Until the Germans stole them, yes, I did. They killed our donkey too. Sometimes I was a look-out. We did what we could to make their life as difficult as possible,' he chuckled. 'Oh yes, we gave them a hard time, no doubt. We were completely united against them. But it was a long time ago.' He picked up the bottle of wine and, changing the subject, asked: 'You like this wine? I make it from my own grapes. It is called Syrah.'

'I make wine too,' I said. 'In New Zealand. We also have a grape called Syrah sometimes called Shiraz. This wine is very good.'

'It is a pity you will not be here in September. You could see our method.' He stood and moved away to replenish the other glasses.

I told Kalliope and Iphigenia about my trip to Hora Sfakion.

'I wanted to go there,' I said, 'to see the beach. My grandfather almost escaped but he was left behind as there were too many men and too few ships. That's when he wandered away and found a village near here where he was hidden. His name was John Lancaster. I am here to try and find members of the family who gave him shelter. I want to thank them for their bravery and kindness.'

Kalliope and Iphigenia sipped their wine delicately and listened intently but did not say anything.

'I don't know where the village is. That's the problem. It's around here somewhere. I have his diary but he is vague about names. I don't know much about the family either. There were six of them: father mother and four daughters. He also had a friend who was an *andarte* leader called Wolf. I am trying to track him down too, if he is still alive. Have you any ideas where I might start?' Kalliope and Iphigenia looked at each other and then at me and shook their heads.

'Sorry. It was a long time ago. It is hard to remember.' said Iphigenia

'And you and Kalliope were little girls?' I said. 'What was it like here in Paleohora?'

'We were children of the village,' said Iphigenia. 'The Germans were here in Paleohora so …..' a loud explosion stopped her short. One of the young men had let off a handgun into the air.

Two more loud volleys followed. There was a scrabbling in the vine overhead, a small thud and cheering from the young men. Some of the children rushed over to inspect the foliage on the far wall.

'Ah. He has killed a rat,' said Iphigenia blandly.

'Is it legal?' I asked.

'We have very strict gun laws here in Greece,' said one

of the young men, turning round at my question and showing me a solemn face. 'Everyone has a gun – or two or three! You must have a licence, of course, and you must not shoot birds at certain times of the year.'

'It is our culture. We are descended from warriors.' said Eftiki.

'We celebrate with guns.' added Pavlos. 'You must come to a wedding or a baptism. Everyone fires guns then.'

'Have you seen our road signs?' added Iphigenia. 'They are full of holes!'

'Target practice!' cried the young man who spoke before.

Soon, several more hand guns appeared and were passed round for admiration and inspection.

Suddenly, Iphigenia jumped up and waddled over to where two strangers appeared at the entrance to the courtyard. Kalliope rushed to her side. There was a flurry of activity and the guns disappeared under the table, up one of the girl's skirts and into the house hidden under a doll belonging to one of the children.

The new arrivals were ushered to the table with much fuss and hand waving and urged to sit. Raki was poured for them while Kalliope and Iphigenia piled food high on to clean plates. I soon saw the reason for all this hospitality. The two men were wearing uniforms.

The Police had arrived.

If they suspected what had been going on, the two officers said nothing. They uttered a toast of 'Yammas', drank the raki, refused the food and looked genially around the table. Most of the men were grinning and it seemed that the police officers shared the joke. They talked a while with Eftiki, drained their raki glasses, thanked the women and took their leave. No word was said about guns or gunshots.

Then Eftiki entered cradling a Kalashnikov.

***

1941

The upper room was thick and acrid with the smog of many cigarettes and it stank of sweat and feet. In the dim glow of the oil lamps and through the clouds of swirling smoke, I could just make out the pale, round shapes of many faces.

The upper room ran the whole length of the house above the stables and storerooms where I had been hidden. Broad beams supported a flat ceiling and wide planks boarded the floor. A raised platform ran the length of one wall. It was covered with brightly woven blankets of red, blue and yellow stripes. This was where the family slept at night and by day it acted as a seat. Before it was placed a long table of solid pine planks, supported on trestles and loaded with bottles and glasses.

There was not much space at the long table, but Wolf beckoned me to sit beside him and made room by nudging aside his neighbour.

'Come, my friend. Sit. You are welcome!' he cried. 'Meet my family,' He gestured to the many men seated around the table.

'That man, there, he is my grandfather.' He gestured to an old man at the head of the table. He was built like a tree trunk, compact and very solid. An impressive beak of a nose jutted from his face which was otherwise covered with a forest of hair, a beard cut like a spade and very long luxurious curling moustaches. He looked every inch the warrior. 'He is called Arkelos,' said Wolf.

At the sound of his name, the old man nodded almost imperiously to acknowledge me. I bowed my head to him. He slammed his glass on the table to get attention.

'*Kalas irthete*, my friend! 'He shouted in a rumbling and powerful voice. '*Tsigia!*' He swigged back the liquid in one go. Alerted by his voice, the others copied him and the table shook as they slammed their glasses down to make the toast. Arkelos reached out for one of the many bottles of clear liquor to replenish all the glasses around him as well as his own.

'My grandfather is leader of this group of *andartes*.' explained Wolf. He is a fierce fighter and greatly respected by everyone. We fight for the freedom of Crete.'

'Death to all Germans!' Wolf shouted and he slammed his glass of raki on the table; as before the others joined in. 'We will resist the Germans until our island is free. Look.' He continued. 'You see the white streak in my grandfather's hair? When he was young it appeared overnight. No one knows why. He looks like an animal of the country with white stripe on his head. You understand?'

'I think you mean a badger,' I suggested.

'*Lipon*. Badger. You are right. So, we call him by this name. Arkelos. The word fear is unknown to him. My grandfather is the father of fourteen sons, all very brave *Palikari*. These men here at the table,' continued Wolf, 'are the sons of his sons. *Lipon*, my brothers and cousins. My grandfather has twenty-seven grandsons. They are not all here, of course.' I thought that this was fortunate as I tried to commit to memory the blur of faces and the names Wolf listed as he introduced his multitude of relatives. But Wolf was talking again. 'I am named for him and so are many of my cousins.'

'Stavro, Nikos, Adoni, Yiorgos,Yanni,' he reeled off the names quickly, 'and another Wolf. We call him Little Wolf, although as you see he is not short.' continued Wolf. They each nodded in turn and raised a glass, but it was impossible to take it in. It was all a blur and, in any case, I did not understand a word of the language at that time and the names were alien to me.

'I won't remember most of these names,' I said. 'Too many are the same. Why do you all have the same names?' I asked.

'Because it is the custom to name each first-born son after his father's father and the second son after the mother's father and so on. This is why we all have other names.'

'Nicknames?' I suggested.

'*Ne*. Nicknames. I am Wolf, as you know. So we have here my brother Niko who is called Kouneli which means rabbit, See he has big ears. That is my cousin, called Zourida what is a small brown animal of the woods.

'Stavro sitting here beside me is my other brother. He is called *Okendra* which is a snake.' A small, ruddy young man with a bush of curly hair, a straggly moustache and wearing a dusty waistcoat decorated with many little buttons worn over a linen shirt with frayed cuffs, acknowledged me. He did not look at all snake-like and I wondered how he had acquired the nickname.

A man entered the room and I recognised him as another of the Cretans who had led us to the evacuation beach. This arrival was the cause for many more embraces and much back slapping. Hearty kisses were planted on cheeks in a manner I had rarely seen in New Zealand. And where it would not have been considered at all manly.

'Here is Lucky, my brother. Do you remember him?' I did indeed remember him because he had piercing blue eyes which I had not expected in a Cretan, an Errol Flynn moustache, and he was exceptionally handsome. He raised his glass. Wolf handed me one of my own and we drank a toast to each other.

Another tall Cretan came over to me.

'*Kalispera, Inglees,*' he said '*Kalas irthete.*' I had no idea what this meant but it seemed friendly.

'This is my cousin Andreas. We call him ...' Wolf said a name I did not catch and he poured us both a glass of raki and handed them over.

'You saw how we drink a toast,' said Wolf. 'You must do the same thing, Mr John.' I slammed down my glass on the table and cried '*Yammas!*' also. I had learned my first word of Cretan.

I wondered how many more toasts I must drink.

And how long the evening would last.

I was already beginning to feel muzzy and light-headed; not only from the alcohol but also from weakness and I realized that I was as yet far from well. I was already very confused. Everything was extraordinary and alien.

The women of the house started to load the table with food. Steaming bowls of snails swimming in a sauce of tomatoes, onions and olive oil arrived; plates of soft, white cheese, sharp and tangy which I remembered from the shepherds' hut where I sheltered at the start of my escape; boiled mutton, rice cooked in the salty, meaty gravy of the lamb and stewed green leaves which they collect wild and call by the name of *horta*. The pungent aroma of garlic swirled around me and acrid onions fought with the smell of roasting meat, wood smoke and the fruity fragrance of olive oil.

'Listen to that smell!' exclaimed Wolf. 'That's an old Cretan saying, you know.' At any other time I would have fallen on the food, but that night I had little appetite. My generous neighbours ladled a mound of food onto my plate, but I found it hard to eat more than a morsel. My shrunken stomach, after weeks of starvation, revolted and churned on the oil and raki.

The other men, hungry from a day of hard work, fell on the food with gusto, using knives and fingers which were soon running with oil and grease. They shouted toasts at each other, slammed their glasses on the table and reached for more food, piercing the meat with the ferocious-looking knives they usually wore tucked into in their sashes.

The evening mellowed. There was a golden glow from the oil lamps, swirls of cigarette smoke floated in spirals towards the roof, woodsmoke wafted from the log-burning stove and the effects of the wine took hold. Wolf bubbled with chatter and much of what he said must have been very funny as his companions rocked their bodies, held their sides and frequently slapped the table or clapped at his words. He twirled his moustachios, preened like a turkey cock and grinned with glee at the response to his word play. Jokes and stories tumbled from his tongue. Lucky or Okendra added their bit and, judging by the guffaws of laughter and the slamming of hands on the table, the tales were extremely funny and lewd.

Then Arkelos began to recite in a booming voice and the laughter died away.

'My grandfather is famous for his great memory. Now he will tell an old Cretan story in rhyme. He can do this for many hours,' whispered Wolf, winking at me. 'Soon we will start to sing and then he will stop! In this way we do not dishonour him.'

I saw Lucky and some of the men preparing to gather up their musical instruments and took my chance to speak.

'Wolf,' I said in a low urgent tone, 'I need to escape from Crete. I must rejoin my regiment and soon. Can you help me?'

'*Malista*,' replied Wolf, cheerily, twirling the ends of his extravagant, black moustache. He was a man of huge optimism, always cheerful and positive. His face was round and gentle, dominated by huge brown eyes which seemed to pop almost out of his head when he was excited or enthusiastic and a strong hawk-like nose, not unlike my own, which he appeared to have inherited from his grandfather. He seemed mild, but you misjudged him at your peril. He was the bravest man I ever met and a crack shot with a rifle. He laughed and joked a lot and his expressive face reflected every mood ... but underneath – as I learned – he was as hard and as true as steel.

'My Grandfather's band of *andartes* will help you. My uncles and cousins travel all over our mountains gathering information about the Germans. We have a network of contacts. We will find a way to get you to a boat and we will take you there when it is possible. You have my word. Trust me.' He clasped my hand and shook it vigorously to seal the deal.

'How soon?' I asked.

'Soon.' he promised.

In the days that followed, I soon learned that time is a very variable and inexact concept to a Cretan. It was pointless, I discovered, to ask the distance to any distant place. The answer was always 'one hour' or 'the time it takes to smoke a cigarette'. But often we would walk all day.

'Soon,' swore Wolf and slammed down his glass of raki. '*Yammas!* Soon. Next week. Maybe next month. This we will tell you. Now my friend, *siga, siga*. Enjoy yourself. Drink more raki. Smoke a cigarette.'

I took a cigarette but went easy on the raki. Already I felt weak from a creeping lethargy. My limbs felt heavy and difficult to control. There was a listlessness which I knew was partly due to alcohol but also largely the result of my ill health. Eventually, the faces in that smoky room began to float and merge like miasma on a lake in winter. I remember the harsh and strident tones of the voices, the clack of the worry beads as the warriors constantly flicked them back and forth over their knuckles and then Lucky picked up his lyra and the stirring notes of a melody cut through the rumble of Arkelos' poetry. Then bass and tenor voices entwined in harmony. Age-old, traditional songs of rebellion – against the Venetians, against the Turks, songs of love and desire, well-known and treasured by all the company, swelled and echoed to the rafters, punctuated by slamming glasses and the cry of: 'Death to all Germans!'

CHAPTER 9

2001

My Grandfather's diary does not identify Wolf and his family or Wolf's village, the village where he was hidden, by name. I suppose he thought that it was too obvious to mention, or maybe he feared that if the diary fell in to the wrong hands it could compromise the safety of the villagers. To him it was always *the village*. But there were clues to be found in his writings.

I settled down next morning, still bloated from feasting at Iphigenia's, with a pen and a pad of paper and the transcript of grandfather's diary to try to do some serious detective work. I drew several columns down the page and under each one I started to list the features of each village. It was a hiding to nothing. It did not take long to realise that I did not have enough information to work with.

I got up and made myself a cup of coffee while I pondered. There was a hammering on the door. I thought I recognised the insistent manner of it. I strode over to open it expecting to see the diminutive figure of Iphigenia standing there. I got the shock of my life. Resplendent in mirrored Ray Bans, a Nike baseball cap, a RELAX T-shirt, sawn-off camouflage trousers and Birkenstock sandals stood my old friend Hennery.

'Hennery! Explain yourself!' I demanded.

'I'm a nosy bugger, me.' declared Hennery, grinning at me. 'Couldn't resist the challenge, man! Got a last minute flight. No sweat.'

I poured him a beer and settled him into the chair.

The door opened and Kalliope entered, eyes ablaze with excitement and enquiry.

'This is Hennery,' I said, introducing her. 'He is my friend. He has come from New Zealand – to help me.'

Kalliope beamed. I could see that she was thinking 'Here is another young man to cook for'. She didn't seem to be put off by the earrings and long hair.

She kissed him warmly on the cheeks – and pinched them, which rather took him by surprise – and rattled away to him in Greek while I attempted to translate. Hennery meanwhile downed the beer and opened another can.

When she was satisfied that she had found out all she needed to know, she sashayed away with a little wiggle of her bottom at Hennery and we got down to facts.

'I'm trying to identify the village, Hennery, and I'm analysing the facts I've got,' I showed him my list. 'So you can give me a hand ... unless you want to crash out. Have you got jet lag?'

'No way, man.'

'OK. So what I've got so far is a village. It consists of several small hamlets, a mountain road, a few springs and a school.'

'Ain't much to go on.'

'No, but a start. Grandfather says he looked at the sea from the terrace of the family house and he says he watched some terrific sunsets over the western mountains.'

'What else?'

'Olive groves.'

'No sweat! From what I saw on my way here in the taxi there are olive groves all over the place, the country's thick with 'em, so that's not much help!'

'The old man mentions the German HQ in the town which was not too far away.'

'And you guess that the town is Paleohora, right?'

'Seems a good bet.'

'Evens I'd say! Burning question. You gotta a map?'

I spread out the map on the table and kept it in position with a couple of stones. It was not very detailed.

Hennery took out a biro and drew a rough arc round Paleohora. Much of the circle included the Libyan sea.

He looked at it for a moment.

'Not much help is it? Unless the village is under water.'

I adjusted the search area slightly and made a list of each village named within it in.

Hennery counted them out. 'Five main ones altogether. We better get going, man. You gotta a car?

'Sure you don't want to sleep off the jet lag?'

'I can sleep as long as I want when I am dead!' he retorted. 'Let's go!'

The first village we came to had a small church and a large olive press. I liked the little ribbon development of boxy houses with their bright pots of striking flowers lining the main road.

'The problem you have here,' said Hennery, 'is that this is the main road to Paleohora.'

'Too vulnerable to German patrols you mean?'

'You got it. No one would hide a man on the run here.'

'Anyway it is not high in the mountains, is it?'

'Give it a miss,' said Hennery, crossing it off the list.

A kilometre or so further away we located what seemed to me to be a really typical Cretan village. Water gushed extravagantly from a couple of pipes in the main square and filled the washing troughs with bubbles, keeping the surrounding air cool and providing a refreshing place to sit, observe and gossip. There was a white church with a bell and bell tower and a small churchyard. It was not a compact village, but quite large, with a tangle of little shady lanes and passages meandering between white stone cottages and leading outwards from the centre to small, heavily cultivated fields of vegetables and orchards of fruit trees, then away to the olive groves beyond.

'This is great, man!' cried Hennery, for a moment losing his cool image. 'This is real Crete – like in that movie *Zorba*.'

'But…' I hesitated, 'Grandfather suggests that his village was spread out and there's also no school.'

'Back to the car then.' said Hennery.

We travelled a few more kilometres from the town found only a straggle of houses intermittently located either side of the road and at the martyred village of Kandanos we turned round.

'That's a bugger,' said Hennery as we retraced our steps.' I could do with a beer.'

'At the next village, I promise,' I said.

It was farther than I had thought, along a road which ran east from the town and then twisted and turned up into the mountains.

'This is a bit modern,' said Hennery looking around him at rows of modern villas. 'Definitely NOT old Crete.'

'No,' I said. 'But here is a taverna. I'm buying.'

The friendly girl who served us cool beers and some olives told me that the taverna had formerly been a school.

'No sweat,' said Hennery downing half a litre at one swig and ordering another with a grin at the girl. 'This could just be it.'

From the terrace, under the shade of an ancient olive tree we could see all the way down a rugged gorge to the open sea.

'There's the sea,' I said, and ordered two more bottles. 'Grandfather could see the sea.'

'Yeah,' said Hennery swivelling his head from side to side,' but these houses look very new. Where's the old village? I can't see many village houses. My money's not on this one.'

We hesitated about staying and eating some lunch from a very tempting menu.

'Lunch at the next place,' decided Hennery. 'We're not finished yet.' And when I paid the bill and checked with my friendly waitress she told me that the village lost the sun early in the evening which pretty decisively ruled it out. We drove on.

1941

I have been ill again. The fever returned with a bitter vengeance. I have no memory of the days that followed. I don't know whether it was the amount of wine and raki I drank at the *glendi*, the oily food, the affect of the suffocating cigarette and wood smoke or whether my sickness returned because I tried to get up too soon. I don't think it was just a massive hangover as I have always been able to hold my drink, but the fever returned, and I recall nausea, sweats and a raging thirst.

I was fortunate that one of the older girls – I think it was the quiet one, Elenitsa – brought me a pitcher of water and bread soaked in milk each day, which was all I could swallow. Mama came from time to time and I remember that she forced me to swallow some foul-looking liquid which she called *farmaka* – which I now know means medicine. It was green, I recall, and tasted of pond life, but I think it was made with a herb rather like tea [here there is a note in the margin added in a coloured ink which says *dittany*].

All my joints ached and so did my kidneys. I could hardly lift my arms or legs they felt so heavy and leaden, and my head not only ached, but felt as if it were filled with cotton wool. My whole body was jelly. The weakness I felt then was appalling and time passed in a delirious haze. During this time I saw only the women. Mama checked on me from time to time and the little girls, who are called Poppy and Fifi, peeped curiously through the doorway to check on my progress but they never ventured inside.

I think it's now the month of July. It is certainly very hot. It means that I have been here in my dark hiding place behind the tall terracotta urns of oil for more than a month and I have remained hidden and ill almost constantly.

For about ten days now I have been doing exercises

several times a day – the routines that the army taught me. I was very weak at first and the effort was really hard; my limbs ached afterwards nearly as badly as when I had the sickness. I had to grit my teeth and force myself to make a start, but it was worth it. Now, some of my strength and muscle-power is returning to my legs and arms and stomach and I don't ache any more after the exercises. The big blisters on the soles of my feet have healed also, although bright red patches remain. I would like to go for a long run, but I am aware that I must not leave my hideaway for fear of being seen by strangers – and the Germans, of course. The villagers who live here know I am hidden and they are loyal to the family, I think. But I guess to any other people my presence must remain a secret.

As my fever and aches recede, I have become more aware of my surroundings and realised how isolated and lonely I feel. I have now been on my own for many weeks in an alien land among alien people fighting an arduous battle for survival. No comrades, no company, no fellow soldiers with whom to share a thought, a cigarette or a joke. Days have passed when all I have been capable of was lying prone and thinking. I have felt an outcast and abandoned. I can't speak the language at all and so I have no idea of what is going on and I have no way of understanding what the women and children are saying to me.

I dream a recurring dream that I am tightly encased in a spider's web and, however much I struggle, I cannot free my arms and legs from the threads which are wrapped tautly around me. I know that this is because I fear for my life. I cannot face the thought that my life might end at twenty.

How far can I trust these people? Even though they feed me and tend to my wounds I ask myself the question: Why? They seem kind, but why would they do this for me? In the end, will they hand me over to the Germans for a fat ransom to be shot or sent to a prison camp?

These thoughts are partly caused by weakness, I know, and my sickness, and also because circumstances have rendered me so powerless. I have lost any sense of direction. I am adrift. I am overwhelmed. I feel abandoned.

I, who am usually so positive and resilient, am as weak as a kitten and ready to shed tears like one of the little girls. Mama has been kind, if a little distant and brisk. The older daughters, also. They have tended me daily, but I cannot communicate with them, except in sign language.

Thank God that Wolf comes occasionally to see me. He can tell me very little of the progress of the war – or he chooses to tell me very little. I am not sure which. I have seen no other men except at the *glendi*. They must know that I am an escapee. How far can I trust any of them? Do they regard me as a lamb to slaughter? Are they waiting for an opportunity to betray me and hand me over to the Germans? Who will talk? Do the Germans now control Europe? Has all the fighting been in vain? Has England, the heart of the Empire, survived? So many unanswered questions....

And the most important question of all: will I ever see my family and friends again?

Who in the world knows where I am? No one will rescue me. How can they? My family must already have received the dreaded telegram that says I am 'missing in action' and, when they read of the calamity of Crete, it will leave them with little hope. I think of my Mother waiting anxiously for news of me. I am her only son. Mothers and sons: the cord is never broken. I think of my father clenching his jaw and sucking hard on his pipe in the way he has when he is fighting with emotion in the face of bad news.

I think of the farm: the green pastureland, the soft rolling hills of South Island, the bleating flocks of sheep in their curling coats ambling from hillock to hillock as they nibbled the grass. I think of my mother's roast mutton, mint sauce, plates of steaming home-grown potatoes, carrots and parsnips, and gravy and onion sauce, followed by apple pie made from apples picked in our own orchard. I think of my nosy, effervescent sisters giggling and gossiping as they milked the cows, churned the butter and made cheese in the dairy. I picture the inlet at Mapua where my blue-painted boat was moored and I recall the feel of the cool water on my flesh as I swam naked in the creek and the gentle lapping of the waves against the jetty as I fished.

I picture my bedroom under the eaves of the sloping roof of the house that my father built, for himself and his fiancée, in the summer he took over the parcel of land he had used all his savings to buy – built with a little help from his friends, the skill of his own hands and copious amounts of beer. I think longingly and a little wistfully of my soft bed, with its comfortable spring base and feather mattress, as I lie on the lumpy mattress of straw and shrubs on the earth floor of my hideaway. My dormer window at home frames a view of the smoky hills and beyond them the jutting mountains. The gay red gingham curtains were made by my Mother on an old black and gold sewing machine which she operated with a foot treadle. She was a keen seamstress and loved making things to adorn the house. Each room is packed with the curtains, tablecloths, and chair covers she sewed each evening while we listened to the radio. She spent hours embroidering counterpanes and table runners and all the quilts were assembled by her from tiny lozenges she cut out of old skirts and dresses. She often said, 'John, it should be practical, but beautiful. Why make something ugly when you have to look at it every day?'

The interior of our home was a testimony to her care and skill and sense of what was pretty and proper.

My Pa supported her and was proud that she was so capable and practical. When time allowed from the farm work and animal husbandry, he never failed to make a repair, to construct shelves and benches, oil hinges and ease a sticking door, all for her comfort,

This hot dry land where I now find myself, with its majestic cliffs, wild mountain pastures and deep gorges, is stark, outlandish and barbarous to me. Everything is alien and unfamiliar: the food, the customs, the dress and most of all the language which divides me from people as effectively as barbed wire around a prison camp.

What future is there for me?

2001

'Acogiras,' said Hennery, reading from the guide book, 'has long had a reputation as a very holy place.'

It certainly had a wonderful atmosphere. In the yellow painted *kafe* where we stopped, a group of men were playing backgammon. The click of the tiles and their occasional cries of triumph punctuated our sips of beer. We ordered Sofia's special omelette, and it arrived fat and golden and bursting with goodness. The young man who served us said his name was Lucky and looked a true Cretan warrior for he had magnificent curling moustaches that reminded me of my grandfather's descriptions of Wolf. I wondered if they were related.

He told me that there were many churches in the village. We spent an hour or two after lunch visiting them. We found caves which had been homes for hermits and visited them too. We saw an impressive whitewashed monastery, dedicated to ninety-nine saints and built into the side of the cliffs. The caves where the monks had lived were still darkly visible. Lucky also urged us not to miss a delectable waterfall and mossy green bathing pool.

I am sure I saw a nymph appear in its cool clear waters who beckoned me in to join her.

'You're pissed, mate,' said Hennery.

But the shadows were lengthening into deep purple as the sun disappeared behind the cliffs so I may have been mistaken. My grandfather had mentioned none of these (he could not have ignored the nymph!) and so I crossed Acogiras very reluctantly off the list.

At every place we checked and rechecked the time of the sunset and searched for the remains of school houses. It was all worthwhile, as it gave us an excuse to make regular stops at *kafeneions* for cool beers and freshly squeezed orange juices, and offerings – they call them mezes – of olives and nuts, chunks of cold cucumber, slices of those big, succulent beef tomatoes which seem to be flavoured with sugar and sunshine, and little lumps of feta cheese, which always accompanied the drinks.

We eliminated any small clusters of houses we spotted along the way.

'I've been here less than twenty-four hours, mate, and I guess I've seen more real Crete in that trip than many tourists do in a fortnight,' said Hennery, looking very pleased with himself.

'True. But do any of these places fit the formula?' I retorted.

'Not yet,' said Hennery. 'I can keep going if you can. No sweat.'

CHAPTER 10

1941

Fifi and Poppy, the little girls, are not twins. I thought they were. They look very alike. They have the same round faces and big brown eyes, pointed chins and wiry, curly hair which they tie back with coloured ribbons. They are both small and agile and dart about like kittens on short sturdy legs. I guess that they might be aged five or six. They are cheerful and bubbly little characters and very open and friendly.

I have learnt this fact because they have decided to teach me to speak Greek – or rather Cretan. They have taught me simply, as children do. They speak to me slowly and in plain, uncomplicated language and with many gestures, giggles and much miming. We started first with names. They pointed at themselves and said their names, Fifi and Poppy which were easy for me to understand and remember, as the names reminded me of characters from a French farce I had seen in Wellington before I left for this endless war.

They showed me the chickens, the dogs, the cats, the goats and sheep and even pointed out a rat and a lizard or two and named them. They pointed to the bread and cheese and eggs on my plate and told me what they were called. I soon learnt the words for water and milk and wine.

The word 'raki' I knew from the start!

They led me by the hand into the garden to look at the plants and they named the potatoes, tomatoes and beans. I learned the words for a tree and wind and sun, hot and cold. They pointed to my clothes and possessions: my very grubby and stained shirt, my combat trousers, my precious boots, my belt, rifle, knife and named each one for me.

I wrote down the words on a piece of paper in my notebook as I heard them – I will never be able to write Greek – and learned them by heart every day. It was like being back at school, but much better fun. I began to look forward to the time each day when they would appear in the doorway of my hideaway and start a new lesson.

Go! Come! To have and to be. I soon picked up the verbs from their gestures and constant use.

The terrible two, as I started to call them, were utterly unselfconscious. They laughed and giggled and rolled their eyes as they acted out the words they wanted me to understand and learn. It was rather like the game of charades we used to play at home at Christmas. They clapped their hands with merriment when I understood. Fifi raised a finger and said its name, Poppy giggled and pointed to her nose, her eyes and her lips. Fifi pulled Poppy's hair and after a scream and a tussle I knew what they meant and added that word to my vocabulary list. Face, arms, legs, hands and feet soon followed.

Poppy mimed walking and I noted the word down. Fifi put her fists to her eyes and wailed. I wrote 'to cry'. When I laughed at their antics they told me the word for laugh. Fifi curled up in a ball on the straw and squeezed her eyes shut. Poppy shouted the word for sleep. Each day I leaned a little more and what's more I looked forward to my lessons. I wanted to please them, and I felt that I was doing something positive – and it kept boredom and a longing for home and family at bay.

Soon we moved onto feelings: How are you? I am well. I am ill. I am hot. I am cold. I am happy. But never I am sad. The terrible two did not think it necessary to teach me this word. Yet there were days when I did feel sad, I have to admit it, with an overwhelming longing to see my Mother, my Pop and the farm.

'What is your name? My name is John.'

'*Oichi*. Yanni.'

'OK. Yanni, then. I will be Yanni, as I am in Crete.'

The terrible two made good teachers. Only small children would have had the time and energy to spend teaching me. But I was surprised at their patience and determination. They giggled at my accent and I think they were endlessly amused by my mistakes but were so involved in and proud of their roles as teachers that they did not get bored or consider giving it up. It became a matter of pride between all three of us that I would master the complicated language and even Mama remarked eventually that I would soon pass as a Cretan.

2001

'Wolf. They called him Wolf,' I said, addressing a much-lined old man, seated at the rear of a wide terrace facing the mountains. He looked as if a sudden gust of Cretan wind would blow him away he was so thin. A shepherd's crook rested on the chair beside him. Adoni walked over to him and took his hand, kissed him on the cheek and asked him how he was.

'*Kala. Kala. Panda kala*.' The old man nodded slowly. 'I am the head man of this village,' he said to me, raising a skeleton like hand slowly in a sketched greeting.

'*Kathiste*. Sit, sit.'

We did as he told us. He called out an order, in an unexpectedly powerful and deep voice for someone so frail, to a person inside the house. An exceptionally pretty young woman appeared from within with glasses and a small carafe of raki and a saucer of rusks on a tray.

'*Oriste*, Grandfather,' she said, dropping a kiss on his white hair and smiling at us.

I had met Adoni that evening at the bar he favoured in town. Hennery had finally succumbed to jet lag and had crashed out on my bed where I left him. Adoni and I took a coffee and the inevitable raki and observed the evening volta. Now that I understood Adoni's reserved nature a little more fully, I knew that any confidences could not be rushed that I must allow him to take his time to frame the words in his rusty English, decide what to tell and what not to tell and above all to weigh the consequences of what he would tell me.

Adoni flipped his worry beads from finger to finger. At length he said:

'There is a man I can take you to meet up in the mountain. I spoke to him today and he will meet you. He is a very old man. He remembers the war. He may be able to help you.' I felt a rush of excitement and agreed immediately. I almost said 'No sweat.'

Adoni drove his pick-up at harebrained speed up the switch back road to a remote village high in mountains. He jerked the gears up and down and pumped the brakes as we swerved and squealed around deep corners on what felt like two wheels. A smooth drive it was not; the pickup eventually bunny-hopped to a halt on a patch of bare land which flanked a long, low house of yellow-washed walls and metal-framed windows. Blue and white painted gourds were festooned along a rope which was slung like bunting across the frontage. Small boulders, also painted blue and white, marked out the garden in which old oil cans were planted with roses and geraniums. On the other side of the road a chain rattled and a dog barked.

We entered an enclosed vine-draped terrace through a long front room – the winter bar. Whitewashed walls were hung with a picture gallery of photos in black and white, or sepia, of Cretan warriors, tough mountain men with curling moustaches, posed stiffly in their waistcoats, pale linen shirts, baggy pants and white boots. Curved daggers were slotted through their sashes and bandoliers slung crosswise over their chests. My grandfather had described just such men in his diary. They looked like dangerous bandits and they glared at the camera with a challenge in their eyes. Ancient guns of different sizes and ferocious-looking knives hung on the wall. It was a reminder that this ancient land was a thread away from a warlike past.

'This is a museum.' I remarked, looking around and thinking back to the astounding collection at Askifou.

'No. No museum. Just a private collection of the family,' replied Adoni as we walked through to the terrace. 'Very brave men.'

I had with me a list of the names which my Grandfather had mentioned in the diary the names of the men of the village and of the cousins and other relatives who had helped him. I hoped that the old man could identify some

'Wolf was the leader of a group of *andartes* here,' I said.

The old man exhaled noisily like a horse.

'Everyone was an *andarte* here, Wolf was a common name.'

'My grandfather was a soldier. John was his name. Maybe you knew him as Yanni,' I said,

'English? '

'From New Zealand. He was hidden in a village here during the war. 1941–2.'

'There were many English hidden here.'

The old man took a long drag of his cigarette and let his gaze sweep over the distant mountains which were fading to a deep purple.

I felt that he was weighing up the pros and cons of giving up some nugget of knowledge that he possessed. Slowly, he exhaled once more.

'There were many men called Wolf.' he repeated finally. 'And every village hid a soldier.'

'But you could have met my grandfather? I persisted.

'How can I know that thing?'

'He looked a bit like me? Did you ever meet someone

who looked like me? Tall, blond?'

His head turned towards me and he stared at me intently, while he twirled the ends of his moustaches. I felt sure that something I had said had struck a response. Dusk was falling; the mountains were purple silhouettes. A pause hung in the air.

'Maybe. Maybe not. There were many English on the island for many months.'

'My grandfather writes of a man called Wolf.' I repeated.

'As I said, it was a common nickname. It was given to brave men.'

'The Wolf's brother was called *Kouneli*. That means rabbit doesn't it?'

The old man's laughter erupted like a train emerging from a tunnel, and he relaxed a bit and finished his raki.

'Yes.'

'Another *andarte*, a brother I believe, was a musician. He played the lyra, I think. It's like a violin isn't it? Can you remember him?'

'I remember him,' said Adoni flashing a gold tooth. 'He was called Lucky. Now he is very famous. He plays *rembetika*. This is our folk music of Crete. He has recorded CDs. He does not live here, of course, but he comes back sometimes.'

At last, a clue I could pursue. 'Where does he live? Perhaps I can contact him and speak with him.'

'I don't know. Athens, maybe,' said Adoni vaguely.

'Some men,' interjected the old man, 'the fathers of many children – are called *misotragos*.'

'And what does that mean?'

'Billy goat!' He cackled with laughter and revealed a mouth missing a few teeth. Adoni laughed too.

'There was no TV then,' he added, 'and no electricity. They had nothing else to do!'

I laughed rather falsely as you do when you are trying to

ingratiate yourself. I wanted him to talk. I wanted to get him on my side to allay his suspicions of me and get him to give up what he knew. But what did he know? Adoni had said this man would help me, but I was getting nowhere.

'My grandfather mentions another man in the village, a man who was a crack shot with a rifle just like Wolf. He was called Simadis.'

'Many men are called Simadis.' He answered sharply

'But a man who was a crack shot?'

'We are Cretans! We are born with a gun in our hands. Every man is expert with a rifle in these mountains. We hunt all the time. Have you seen the signposts riddled with holes? They are used for target practice.' I had seen them and remembered what Iphigenia had said.

'There is many a cuckold who can shoot a hole through a ten drachma piece at 500 metres.' said the old man. I wondered if this was really true.

'So you don't remember a Simadis who was a crack shot?'

'I may know of the man you speak about ... or not.' He tossed the raki into his mouth and slammed down the empty glass. 'I can't remember.' He regarded me for a long time with dark, watery eyes and twisted the ends of his moustaches which, I was beginning to realise, was a characteristic gesture. I felt sure that he was on the brink of saying something revealing and I waited tensely. In the end something made him shy away from any revelation.

Once again I felt I was meeting a brick wall.

'It was a long time ago. I am tired. I don't remember nothing. *Katholu.*' He rose stiffly and picked up the wooden crook which had been propped beside him and he walked, slowly and laboriously like an actor playing a sick man, into the house. Disappointment overwhelmed me. I felt weighed down with fatigue as my excitement evaporated and my hopes disappeared. I realised that I had been banking on this meeting to reveal everything I needed to know about my grandfather's life in Crete, his village and the family who saved him. And I realised sharply that I had been naïve in my expectation. Nothing comes easily. Adoni poured me a glass of raki and shrugged.

'He is old. He does not trust you. Maybe another day.'

'I don't have long, Adoni, that's the problem. I can't wait. I can't give him time to trust me. I guess I'm stuffed!'

On the way home I tried one more time. 'Tell me, Adoni, my grandfather writes a lot about the girls of the family. There were four daughters.'

'Many fathers had many daughters – and many sons … we did not have TV to keep us busy then, remember!' Adoni repeated the old man's joke, cracked a laugh and the pickup lurched madly towards the grass verge.

'But there were only four daughters and no sons. Does that throw any light on what I want to know?'

'Throw any light,' repeated Adoni, 'what means this?'

This is a tactic to divert me. I thought to myself: to put me off. I felt a brick wall looming closer.

I ignored him and persisted.

'There were four girls. He calls the two youngest the terrible two as a joke but their real names seem to be Fifi and Poppy or at least that's what he calls them. Have you any idea who they were?'

'A man with no sons is to be pitied,' mused Adoni. 'It is a *katastroph*.' He braked hard as we turned into a tight bend. 'You must ask Kalliope. She will remember the names of the women of the villages better than I can.'

'There were two older girls as well as Fifi and Poppy. 'They were called Tonia and Elenitsa. Did you know them? 'I persisted.

Again Adoni paused a long time before answering. 'You should ask Kalliope, he repeated.

***

106

1941

Poppy and Fifi are very excited. They have been given a puppy as a present and they have been playing with him outside the house. He's a mongrel really, tan-coloured, half terrier, half mountain dog. He has an intelligent eye, a slate grey head and a long nose for sniffing out game. The Cretans do not train their dogs to work to a whistle or commands as we do in New Zealand. They are rarely used to herd flocks of sheep either, though sometimes the men take them out hunting. They keep their dogs chained or tied to a rope. Their job is to guard the house and to bark at the approach of anyone – as I know only too well. After a while the dogs become melancholy and listless, and bark or whine at the slightest disturbance like a gust of wind or a passing rat. I had skirted many villages to avoid dogs: one barks, they all bark and alert the entire neighbourhood.

'The new dog is called Spitha!' cried Poppy excitedly as the puppy struggled from her arms. He wriggled to the ground only to be scooped up by Fifi who started kissing him.

'"*Spitha*" means spark,' continued Poppy. 'Isn't that a good name for him?'

'Where did you get him?' I asked.

'From me,' replied a rasping voice. I looked round and saw a short, dark muscular man with a rifle flung over his shoulder descending the steps from the house. He regarded me thoughtfully, as if he were weighing me up.

'*Yassou*,' he said and stuck out his hand. I shook it.

'*Yassou*,' I replied briefly. I was still struggling with Cretan or Greek and, anyway, I decided to be circumspect. I did not yet know if the stranger were friend or foe, so I held my tongue further in case I gave myself away.

'It's my cousin, Simadis!' shouted Poppy 'He found Spitha for us.'

There were so many cousins that I had no idea who this Simadis was, but I wondered if I recalled his face from the *glendi*. Simadis offered me a cigarette and struck me a light. For the first time he smiled revealing very large, white teeth like a horse.

I nodded took the cigarette and decided not to say anything except my name.

'Yanni.' I said drawing on the cigarette while I thought of my next response.

'Simadis! Simadis!' called out Fifi and he turned away towards them. Spitha rushed up and started jumping up enthusiastically onto his thighs. Simadis shouted something harsh at the dog. It started to bark so he kicked it away with his boot. Poppy cried out and Fifi scooped him up and ran into the storeroom. Simadis shifted his gun onto his shoulder and strode away.

'Who is Simadis?' I asked Wolf when I saw him next.

'My cousin,' answered Wolf.

'You have many cousins,' I remarked. 'It's confusing.'

'Simadis and I share the same grandfather, Arkelos. Simadis is the son of my uncle.'

'I have not seen him before. Was he at the *glendi*?'

'Simadis has been in Rethymno until now. He has been with a group of *andartes* who are resisting the Germans in the hills above the city.'

'So he is an *andarte* also?'

'*Malista*. And a very brave man. He is an expert with the gun. He can hit a target with his rifle at 300 metres. When we hunt together he never misses and he always he kills the most birds and animals.'

'A useful man to have around.' I said. 'Is this his village? Does he live here?'

'Yes. Here in the village, but much lower down, by the school. He looks after his mother who is a widow. My Uncle, his father, died in the battle for Crete in May. He was shot by the Germans near Kandanos. You know what happened at Kandanos? It happened just last month.'

We fell silent and, after Wolf had told me the harrowing story of how the village had been razed to the ground, concentrated on our cigarettes.

'Has Simadis returned to the village for good?' I asked eventually.

'Only God knows,' replied Wolf. 'He has been away for some time. His mother needs him to help her. They have a big *kipo* and flocks of sheep and goats.'

'Is he the only son?'

'Of course not,' laughed Wolf. 'We are strong men here in Crete; we breed sons. Simadis has brothers, but they are also away from here, up in the mountains. Some also are in the Greek army and we do not know what has happened to them. But he is the youngest. It is his responsibility to care for his Mother's needs.''

'And any sisters?'

'No. no sisters.'

'Is he married?'

'Who would have him? He has teeth like a horse!' cried Wolf slapping his thigh. 'I am joking. Now is not a good time to be thinking of marriage,Yanni *mou*. Life is dangerous and life is short. We must wait until this war is over, before we take wives and make sons. When we have conquered the Germans we can think of marrying.'

I saw Simadis at the house quite often after this, always alone, and always with his rifle slung nonchalantly over his shoulder. He would sit with Nektarios, the children's father, without speaking; endlessly smoking cigarettes he rolled himself, his eyes raking the landscape as if waiting for something to move so that he could take a pot shot at it. He was courteous and charming to the women and seemed to tease them in a light hearted way for they giggled a little and swished their skirts as they ran inside the house. Mama was always kind to him and I often saw her pat his arm or touch his shoulder as she passed him. He never left without her giving him a parcel for his mother. But I never saw his mother. She never left her house to accompany him on a visit. Locked away in grief, perhaps.

The terrible two had spent a lot of time playing with Spitha. She turned out to be a bitch with a gentle, amenable nature and I showed them how we trained our dogs in New Zealand. Soon, they taught her to sit down or lie down at their command, to come at their call and to beg for scraps of bread, despite Mama tut-tutting at the waste. With beaming pleasure they paraded Spitha in front of Simadis and showed off his tricks. Simadis smiled his horse smile and gave each of them a small coin and told them to go away. They ran off squealing with delight.

***

2001

Hennery slept like the dead for twelve hours while I saw Adoni and met the old man in the mountains, but after two cups of coffee next morning he was full of plans.

'We missed a couple of villages yesterday, so we must get going, man. How was your detective trip?' I told him that I thought the whole visit had been fruitless.

'No sweat! It's down to us, then. Let's get going.' Hennery has boundless energy once he's awake and it's a factor in his success. We headed out of town once more and up into the wild mountains.

The road snaked back and forth in huge loops. Hennery pointed out several clusters of houses in small groups of three or four situated alongside the road. We paused, examined them and drove on. I am sure we completely missed some houses altogether, so completely hidden were they in olive groves or folds in the mountain.

Presently, we came upon a group of five or six cottages

of whitewashed stone sitting above the road, I wondered again if I had found the right place, but the lay-out did not seem to reflect my grandfather's descriptions very much: the cottages looked east to the mountains and did not face the sea. The dogs started to bark, so once more so I nosed the car up the hill until the road stopped winding and arrowed straight along the top of a plateau with a view towards the mountains of Sarakina and the valley of Kandanos. It was scrubland or *garigue*, high goat country of rough shrubs and prickly oak. I spotted groups of goats grazing and heard the bleat of a sheep.

'Hey, look!' shouted Hennery. 'What's that, man?'

He had spotted a cluster of red tiled roofs nestling below the road. I slowed the car and we took a good look. A rough track seemed to lead there. I nudged the car forward gently and round the bend we came upon a sizeable hamlet.

'Is this it?' asked Hennery who leapt out of the car before it stopped and ran down the steep slope towards a large, domed bread oven. The path narrowed as it passed a long tall building and ended in a blue metal gate. I followed it and saw that the path turned right.

The house, when we found it, had changed a little. It was not quite derelict. Some of the plaster had fallen from the outside walls, revealing the stone core. One shutter hung drunkenly from rusted hinges. Others were missing. Green paint peeled. Wood showed through, grey and pitted with age. Weeds grew out of crevices in the stone walls. The outside flight of steps was crumbling; a wild tangle of vine branches tumbled down into a dense thicket. But the steps led to a wide terrace which ran the whole length of the façade.

'We've found it! No sweat. Who would have believed it?' cried Hennery foraging for his camera. 'Gotta get some photos, man!'

At ground level a pair of double doors was loosely wired together. I pushed them apart and entered. Something flew at my head and I recoiled. I guess it was a bat. As my eyes adjusted to the gloom I could just make out tall terracotta urns ranged against the wall. Everything was covered in a layer of dust, and strings of cobwebs hung like stalactites from the rafters. The familiarity of these objects gave me a strange feeling. I was convinced I was seeing for the first time the place my grandfather had lived in for more than a year.

I was in touch with the past at last.

'Hennery, come look! I've flown thousands of miles to find this place. I think this is the very house and the very room where my grandfather was hidden.'

'Hidden in Crete.' said Hennery, looking around. 'Awesome!'

Using the torch on my mobile phone I flashed the beam around.

'Look, there's a wooden ladder. It looks a bit rustic. I hope it's safe.'

'See if there is a trap door to the upstairs,' suggested Hennery. And sure enough it was there. And it was open. The first rung creaked when I put my weight on it, but it was solid enough so I decided to take a chance and climb up the dozen or so rungs.

With my shoulders through the gap I peered into the upper room, almost expecting to see Tonia, Elenitsa, Mama and the children sitting at their work. I had read about it so often that it seemed very familiar to me. The floor was covered in dust, rat droppings and the detritus of years. But it was without doubt the upper room that my Grandfather had described. I ducked as another bat swooped at me before veering away up into the rafters. But in a second I was through the trap and into the room.

Light filtered through the shutters and I crossed to open one. As golden light flooded into the room I was able to see clearly. I could pick out the ledge around the wall where Father, Mama and the girls had slept. A long scroll-backed wooden sofa was pushed against another wall. The horsehair padding was spilling from splits in the fabric of the cushions on the seat. A table faced the doorway, the straight-backed, rush-seated chairs pushed back from it as if someone had just stood up. A set of corner shelves held clay and pottery bowls and earthenware plates. Cooking pots hung from hook above a trough-like sink. The single tap was rusted and encrusted with limescale.

'You know, except for the layers of dust,' I said to Hennery who was poking about in corners, 'I feel as if the family has just left the room and is about to return.'

'Spooky, man!'

I went outside on to the terrace and into blinding sunshine and sat on a low wall and looked around.

'What have we got?' said Hennery when he joined me. 'We can see the sea. Look there.' And sure enough the sea was visible through the dip in the mountains, deep blue and sparkling in the sunlight.

'And the mountains all around.' I added.

'There's a garden of some sort over there, although it looks quite overgrown to me and what's that great big cactus plant holding up the geraniums? It looks like something out of a Wild West movie!'

'The old man mentions those. I remember. It's a prickly pear, I think. They could be the same ones.'

'What else did he say?

'He said there were olive trees.'

'Plenty of those.'

'And a vineyard.'

'I can't see one. Perhaps it's overgrown too. We should walk around and have a look.'

'And a tall pine tree.'

'So what's that over there?' asked Hennery waving his hand towards a lofty tree.' Is that big enough for you?'

We ran down the steps and walked along the path which meandered between several empty and decaying houses and back towards the car.

'What does he say about the layout of the village? Does he mention this bread oven?' Hennery pointed to a square, domed and whitewashed lean-to. 'That opening's wide enough to slide in and roast a whole lamb!'

'They probably did. Loaves too and fed the entire village. He does mention a bread oven but it was downstairs in the storeroom.'

'So let's go back and have another look.'

We retraced our steps and Hennery followed me into the store room again. My eyes squinted to adjust to the shadows and then I saw it through the rear doorway in the far room

'What's this?'

'A bread oven! No sweat.'

CHAPTER 11

1941

'*Ela!Ela!* Come! Come!'

A scuffle and a pair of tanned feet scrambled down the ladder as one of the terrible two appeared.

I jumped up and ran towards the door.

'*Oichi! Oichi! Epano!*' No! No! This way upstairs!' Fifi cried and grasped my arm and pulled me towards the ladder. As my head appeared through the trap door into the upper room I could see Mama and the older girls bustling about in great haste gathering together clothes and bags and sacks.

Before I knew what was happening to me, a giggling Tonia had grabbed me and slipped a voluminous black cotton skirt over my head and Elenitsa wriggled me into a baggy black linen blouse over my shirt. I removed my voluminous Cretan trousers. They wrapped a sash around my waist and Mama completed the outfit by winding a light woollen scarf around my head and face like a nun's coif.

Grabbing their shoulder bags and sacks, Mama and the girls made their way towards the ladder. I followed. Suddenly Elenitsa shrieked out:

'His boots!'

They froze in horror as they regarded the army issue boots on my feet. Tonia and Elenitsa darted about the room looking in wooden chests, under benches, on shelves for some suitable footwear while I sat on the floor and removed my boots.

'Give me!' yelled Mama from the base of the ladder and I threw my boots down to her. Grabbing them, she plunged them deep into the cold bread oven. Tonia found a pair of slip-on *papoutsia* and while I crammed them on to my feet, the girls slid down the ladder with an ease of long practice and I followed more gingerly in my unaccustomed and uncomfortable footwear.

In the storeroom, where I had my den, Mama had torn apart my straw mattress and flung the pieces away around the room. She took my boots and pushed them deep into an urn of pistachios nuts which stood beside the window, swept up my few belongings and threw them into the back of the bread oven. I grabbed my diary and pencil from the heap. She flung herself through the window. We followed. Then she closed the shutters, and we ran from the rear of the house and melted into the cover and shade of the olive trees. With Mama leading the way, Tonia, Elenitsa and the terrible two followed along the barely perceptible tracks which led away from the hamlet. I brought up the rear flapping in my unaccustomed costume and ill-fitting shoes.

We ascended rapidly through the olive trees, keeping to the shadows until we reached the scrubby outcrops of mountain boulders. Here we paused to take a breath for it had been hard and lung-pounding work climbing uphill and scrambling up the terrace walls and over boulders, untangling the branches that caught at our clothes. I found it difficult enough coping with my skirt and blouse not to mention the slip-slopping shoes.

Mama carried a shoulder bag slung diagonally across her chest and held a sack-like container in one hand. She was a thin, slight woman and yet her wiry strength gave her the stamina to move quickly and with the agility of a goat and to maintain a fast pace. Tonia and Elenitsa also had shoulder bags. Tonia wore a cloak and Elenitsa had wrapped a homespun blanket around her shoulders like a shawl. Even the little girls carried a little bag each. From the direction of the hamlet we heard the stutter of machine gun fire. We stood frozen like statues for a moment. But it was too far away to harm us.

'*Germania*,' uttered Mama and spat. I saw her clasp her hand round the carved handle of a large and glittering knife which was tucked into her waistband.

'I kill the girls and myself before the Germans take us,' she spat. 'But first I will slit the throat of a German.'

'They look for English,' explained Elenitsa. 'They look for you. They reach to the house of Felix but he sent Young Felix to tell us of this. Now we must hide.'

We set off again, always climbing steeply, until we came to a tumble of rectangular boulders, half the size of the sarsen stones at Stonehenge, limestone grey, and patched with mossy green lichen. A clump of grey-leaved bushes straddled one side of it and a twisted olive tree rose in front like a sentry. Behind it, and barely perceptible to the naked eye unless you were almost upon it, there was a narrow cleft in the rock. Mama slid through and we followed.

The opening led into a sharply sloping passage which soon widened out into a large chamber with a domed roof. A shaft of light filtered down from a cleft high up and illuminated softly the jagged spurs of rock which made up the walls. The cave was roughly round and was about some twelve foot in diameter at the widest point. Towards the rear it narrowed again and fell away into murky gloom but I could detect the tinkle of water and guessed that there was a spring located somewhere there in the darkness.

Mama struck a match and in its short glow found an oil lamp which she lit and I saw that this hideaway had been used before. Bracken was piled against one wall ready to sleep on. Boxes of ammunition were stacked farthest from the entrance. Woven bags hung heavily from jagged pieces of rock. These contained roundels of hard cheese, some of which we ate later with hard lumps of bread, called *pakimarkia*, also stored in woven bags, dipped in olive oil and softened. There were flagons of oil and wine, and raki too, which the women never drank but which was offered to me before we slept. Even small logs of wood were stacked in neat piles. My impression was that this cave had been prepared for a siege. I was told later that it was mainly the work of the women who had started to prepare this secret hideaway as soon as they heard of the German invasion.

When Mama had dropped her bag, I heard the chink of coins. She had rescued the family's fortune. The rest of the gold she and the girls wore as bangles on their wrists, as earrings and necklaces. Tonia's sack contained bread, Elenitsa had carried olives and the little girls had carried cucumbers and tomatoes.

We collected some of the wood and Mama built a small fire, making sure that the wisps of smoke which spiralled toward the opening in the dome were too insignificant to give our sanctuary away and soon the chill of the cave was lifted by the crackling fire and illuminated by the warm glow of the fire and of the lamp. Then Tonia and Elenitsa wrapped the cloak and the blankets around the bracken and made cushions for us all to sit on. I was astonished at the military precision with which Mama had regimented her troops. Mama removed the deadly looking knife with a razor-edged blade from a sheath stuck in her sash and began to carve bread and cheese into portions for each of us. She waved it at me her eyes glittering in the firelight.

'If the Germania comes, with this I kill them. If I cannot kill them, then I kill the girls and then myself.' she said again. It was a shocking statement, but Mama was a realist. She knew what to expect after the news of the massacres at Kandanos and other places. She knew that she would receive no quarter from the Germans if she and the girls were caught with me. It was a sacrifice I thought I could not allow and that I would rather fend for myself than put this wonderful family in such danger.

'I go,' I said.

'Now, no.' ordered Mama.

'Tonight, we stay here,' Tonia assured me. 'Here we are safe.'

The terrible two nestled into the bracken cushion and soon they were asleep, head to head, snoring gently like a couple of hedgehogs. I watched the glow of the lamp which highlighted Elenitsa's cheek and painted a golden wash down one side of her body. She looked like a Madonna in a renaissance painting. Her long eyelashes curled and stroked her cheek as she gazed pensively at the flames of the fire as they flickered red and gold. I wondered whether she was thinking of her mother's fierce declaration. Her glossy black hair was drawn back from her forehead into a dark cotton headscarf, the way she wore it when she was working in the *kipo*. Her eyebrows were thick smudges of charcoal. She clasped her arms round her slim body as she sat before the fire. Perhaps she sensed that I was regarding her because she raised her face to mine and smiled an almost apprehensive smile. To me it was enchanting.

So, finally, we ate, rested and waited.

Later next day, Young Felix slid silently into the cave to give us the all clear.

'They have looted to the last doormat,' he informed us.

Slowly, and by a different and easier route we returned to the hamlet.

The Germans had searched the house thoroughly; tipped up tables and chairs, turned out the wooden chests. Out of spite they had smashed some of the urns in the storeroom. There was a mess of oil and walnuts but the urn of pistachios had escaped their scrutiny and my boots had remained hidden from their prying eyes. They had taken what food they could carry: olives, cheese, corn, vegetables and fruit from the garden. Most, but not all, of the chickens and rabbits were missing, but fortunately the bread oven had not interested them and so I retrieved my belongings later, smelling of ash, but useable.

We were clearing up the mess and putting the house to

rights when Wolf appeared.

'*Yassou!*' he cried. '*Ise* …..'And then he paused as he saw me in my woman's clothes. He did a double take, his eyes popped and he fell into howls laughter which shook his whole body until he was bent double, clutching his arms around his stomach.

'Yanni,' he spluttered and advanced on me, clasped me in his arms and still gurgling with laughter planted two huge kisses on my face.

'Yanni *mou*. I love you. You are so beautiful. Marry me!'

Soon everyone in the room was crying with laughter. The shock, the horror, the anxiety, the tension of the day before was released and forgotten.

Suddenly, there were screams from the children outside in the wrecked *kipo*.

The Germans had shot some of the dogs.

The girls had found the corpses, but not those of Mavro or Spitha who had escaped the cull. It explained the machine gun fire we had heard as we ran through the olive groves. It could have been so easily all of us. Better dogs than humans, I thought sombrely. As Mama, Tonia and Elenitsa comforted the little girls; I took a shovel and buried the dogs. The earth was like iron and it was long, hard and sweaty work, but it was a small way to compensate the family who had saved my life at such an enormous risk to themselves.

2001

Hennery and I drove back to the town and lunch in high spirits. I collected my transcript of Grandfather's diary from the cottage and over a beer and a plate of small fish in a taverna facing the sea. I read out to Hennery the extracts from the diary about the village as grandfather had written them.

When I had finished, Hennery rocked back in his chair gazed at the view while his computer mind sifted and analysed the information. Finally he said:

'The facts fit, man, but we should make a list of all the details, go back to the village and check them out. Just to be sure. So what are we looking for?'

'A big house in a small hamlet.'

'Spot on.'

'A house with two floors with a terrace above and storerooms below.

'That fits.'

'The sun sets behind the mountains in the west.'

'We should check that.'

''A vegetable garden and a small vineyard.'

'We should check that too. Anything else?'

'The bread oven.'

'Definitely saw that! There were two! Eat up and then we'll go.'

Which is exactly what we did.

Each point on the list matched what we found in the village.

Then we entered the house once again through the storeroom and it fitted exactly the description my grandfather had given of his hideaway.

We climbed the ladder to the upper room. There we identified the ledge where the family had slept and where my grandfather had sat on the night of the *glendi*. I even found a dusty and moth-holed blanket of faded red, blue and yellow stripes when I lifted the lid of one of the wooden chests. Dust and worse had settled over everything. I saw rat droppings which looked like black peppercorns over the floor and the table and bird droppings spattered on the surfaces. Each time we disturbed something, motes of dust sailed into the air and were picked out in shafts of sunlight. The room smelt stale, musty and mildewed.

I stood for sometime taking it all in. Yes, this was definitely the place, but why had it been abandoned? Hennery was ferreting away in corners.

'Look!' said Hennery. 'Photos.'

They had spilled onto the floor from an album of dark fake leather. They had evidently fallen from a book shelf that hung drunkenly from the furthest wall. He shook the dust from them and shuffled them into a neat pile and handed them to me.

'Do you think there's a picture of your grandfather in here?'

'Yes! No, Hennery. I don't think the family would have owned a camera in the nineteen forties and during the war? In any case, I guess that all cameras would have been banned and seized by the Germans, wouldn't they?'

Hennery nodded.

'You have a point there, Alex.'

He handed me the pile of photos. I blew off the dust and wiped them against my shorts to clean them. When we examined them closely we saw that these were photos of people from a later era. The poses were stiff and formal.

'I think that these are wedding photos.' I said. 'Look, these girls in their lace veils and stiff-skirted gowns must be brides.' They threw shy glances at the camera from under their eyelashes.

'Look at these guys in fancy dress!' laughed Hennery.

'No, Hennery, not fancy dress. I think that they are wearing the full traditional Cretan costume. My grandfather describes it in the diary and they are wearing the white boots of a Cretan *Palikari*.' The grooms gazed rigidly at the camera, chins raised, jaws stiff with a challenge in their eyes.

'No sweat. Is that how they dressed then? Imagine wearing all that palaver in the heat.'

'Well, the old man mentions these clothes several times

in the diary.'

'You know what? You should take these photos with you and show them to Kalliope or Adoni or even the old man in the mountains if you want to. One of the faces might jog a memory.'

I nodded.

The photos were not absolute evidence of my Grandfather's presence in the house but they were a start.

***

1941

'You come with me!' ordered Wolf one morning a few days later 'But first you must wear this.'

He threw a bundle of clothes at me. I picked out a pair of dark baggy cotton trousers which looked as if they had come straight from a Turkish harem, the type they call 'crapcatchers'. I climbed into them and then picked up a dark blue felt waistcoat. I pulled it on over my shirt. It had a crossover front and an exasperating million buttons. After I had struggled to do them all up, Wolf said:

'I think I loved you better as a woman but now you look like a real Cretan – except for the boots!' Any boots were rare as hen's teeth at that time and so precious that when the soles wore out the men repaired them by using the treads of rubber tyres.

'I'll wear my army boots,' I said.

'*Po, po, po,*' said Wolf, making a face and screwing his forehead into furrows. 'Let me think about that. No, it is too dangerous. If you are captured your boots will give you away as an English soldier and if they take you they will torture you. Now we have word that the Germans will begin a search of the mountains. No, you must wear your sandals for now – like a woman!' And Wolf burst into peals of laughter slapped his thigh and then twirled his moustaches, then added:

'Come, my friend, we have work to do. Let us see if this disguise works.'

I followed Wolf out of my hideaway and into the open. We walked up through the hamlet passing no one until we reached the water source. Some of the women waved at Wolf and stared at me with open curiosity as Cretan women always do when they see a stranger.

'We tricked them!' cried Wolf when we were out of earshot. 'No one recognised you! *Kala, kala.* Now we go to Simadis's house.'

'I must try to escape,' I reminded Wolf as we walked. 'You said you would help me. I am a danger to the family.'

'Naturally, you wish to escape, my friend,' replied Wolf, frowning hard. 'And I will help you as I have promised, but first we must find someone we trust, a man with a boat or you must swim like a fish and Africa is a long way.'

'I can sail a small boat,' I said. 'There was a little inlet not far from where I lived in New Zealand and I had a small sailing boat for fishing, so I know a bit about it. Can we borrow one?'

'Or steal one!' added Wolf with a laugh. 'The Germans have taken most of the fishing boats. Many of the beaches are well guarded. Some are mined and very dangerous. Only recently a young boy stepped on a mine and was blown into a thousand pieces on a beach near here. Remember that the Fortezza contains a regiment of Germans. *Lipon*, I will find out what I can. I will also try to contact a British agent. We have no one here in our area, but maybe in Chania…. I will try.'

I was frustrated and impatient, but also resigned. Alone I was powerless. Nothing could be achieved without help.

'You must remain here, my friend, with us!' cried Wolf as he slapped me on my back and grinned broadly.

When we arrived at Simadis's house a group of the

andartes were already gathered there. No one recognised me. Wolf introduced me as Yanni. I nodded and said nothing as I did not yet fully trust my skill with the Cretan language. I fielded a few searching looks but not a word was said in challenge. The men had too much respect for Wolf to question who accompanied him. I still did not have a clue as to what we were going to do until I saw a group of pack animals loaded with wooden boxes, barrels and bundles of sacking which looked as if it was wrapped round rifles,

'These many things we must take to the *andarte* group at Temenia, but first we will take a raki together.' announced Wolf.

Simadis passed round a bottle and we all took a swig and thus made bold we set off in a single file of men and beasts.

It was a long, demanding trek over terrain with which I was very familiar after my own long march, but it proved uneventful. We stopped at a stone hut and broke for food, water and raki around two in the afternoon, leading the animals off the trail into an olive grove and tethering them to the trees in the shade. Stavro started playing a game of throwing stones. He challenged us to throw against him.

'The one who throws shortest pays for dinner!' He shouted. Stavro would lay a bet on anything. When he didn't have money he staked his knife, his dog and even once a cat! He was an addicted gambler but in his company it passed the time and naturally it was not Stavro who paid for dinner that night or ever. He was unbeatable.

We felt safe from attack by the Germans and so fell asleep on a carpet of leaves under the gnarled, old trees.

Simadis got up first and led us on until dusk when we reached a small village of whitewashed houses facing each across a steep, narrow, cobbled path.

'This is the house of the headman,' said Wolf as we halted. 'He is also the doctor. He is the leader of the *andartes* around here and he is in contact with the English. These rifles, ammunition and supplies are for the resistance here.'

The doctor welcomed us into the house while some of the men led the pack animals into the stables and other stowed away the equipment.

'Say nothing,' whispered Wolf to me. 'I want to know if they think you are a Cretan.'

As I could understand Cretan by now, but was still not entirely fluent, I was happy to obey him.

We feasted on food served to us by the doctor's nervous, plump wife, drank uncountable rakis and smoked home-grown tobacco while the headman conferred with Wolf, Lucky, Bunny and Simadis while I remained silent.

We slept that night on straw and brushwood in an outhouse and were up at dawn for the return journey. And no one had made any comment about me.

It was a bright clear day. The sky was very blue. Buzzards circled on the distant thermals, but as they came closer we realised that they were not buzzards at all but German search planes methodically criss-crossing the mountains and valleys.

Instinctively, we separated and slithered for cover beneath the dry prickly shrubs of the undergrowth and waited.

It was some time before the planes withdrew and the sky became clear once more.

'*Ela*. Let's go!' ordered Simadis. Wolf threw him a glance which said 'Who is in charge here?'

We reached the donkey trail once more but soon found ourselves in wide open country at the top of the plateau.

A lone spotter plane appeared from behind the cliffs as if it had been lingering like a cobra waiting to rear up and ambush us. The guns sputtered viciously as the plane's engine whined in an ear-piercing dive towards us. Once more we scattered into the safety of the shrubs and rocks as the bullets spat around us angrily.

Simadis returned fire with his rifle and so did Wolf but the range was too long. Some of the others gave us covering fire as we delved deeper among the rocks and trees looking for cover.

'Spread out,' ordered Wolf. 'Pick your target. Don't all fire at once!' The plane circled around and swooped again, engine screaming as it dived and we felt the rush of racing bullets.

Then there was a grunt of pain from Lucky who was a moment too slow running from a boulder into the protection of an oak tree. His body contorted and twisted amid spurts of blood as he fell in the open, unprotected ground.

'*Malaka!*' swore Wolf. 'Lucky, he is hit!'

Lucky writhed and twitched in the dust and then slumped unconscious as blood spread on to the earth from his leg in a large puddle. The plane swooped once more and turned for another attack

I was on my feet and moving before I knew what I was doing. All the old training kicked in. It was a reflex action, I suppose. I certainly wasn't trying to be a hero. Keeping low and. snaking across the dusty ground I zig-zagged to where the inert body of Lucky was lying. I felt the breeze of a bullet whiz past my back and heard another ricochet off a rock nearby, sending chips of stone in a shower into the air. One of the pack animals screamed and reared before collapsing in a mess of grey matter.

I reached Lucky and grabbed his shoulders. 'My leg,' he groaned.

'This will hurt Lucky,' I warned him, as I pulled him across the open ground. 'Hold on.'

The plane roared above my head and bullets spattered around like hailstones. The *andartes* continued a volley of rifle fire and I could hear the sound of metal striking metal.

A lucky shot tore into the fuselage and an engine spluttered and croaked above my head.

I heard Wolf and Simadis yelling encouragement as they reloaded their rifles and then Wolf was by my side and together we pulled Lucky into the safety of the trees.

'My leg,' groaned Lucky again.

'Better your leg, Lucky, than your arm if you want to be the best lyra player in Crete!' yelled Wolf robustly.

Lucky was bleeding like a pig. At first I feared that a vein had been severed, but as Simadis tore his shirt into a bandage and when we wiped the gore from his thigh we saw that the wound was long, but not deep.

'Lucky, you are lucky,' said Wolf gruffly. 'You will not die!'

The damaged aircraft limped away from sight. The other *andartes* gathered round. I was slapped on the back, my hand was shaken.

'Well done, English!' they cried. So, they had never been fooled about me, I thought.

'Let's get him back home,' said Simadis.

'Mr John. You saved my brother's life. You are an *andarte* now.'

'The debt is mine, I hope I have repaid you for looking after me and hiding me for all this time.'

We made a makeshift stretcher, unloaded the goods from the dead donkey and reloaded them onto another animal.

We slung the stretcher between Wolf and myself and set off one more.

After the attack, we sent Bunny ahead as a scout. It was hard going and we were all exhausted.

It was late afternoon when he ran up to us with the news that a small German patrol was approaching. We took Lucky's stretcher and hauled it up away from the track among some craggy boulders and laid him down gently in the thick foliage of some carob trees. The others led the pack animals further away from the path of the Germans and tethered them among a stand of scrubby trees.

We spread ourselves out scrambling as fast as we could into the cover of a small gully where we could see but not be seen. We cocked our rifles and lay on our stomachs to await the approach of the enemy.

'Wait until I tell you to shoot,' Wolf had ordered before we dispersed. Simadis had glanced at him and I did not like his expression. The look seemed to question Wolf's right to take command.

It is possible that the Germans might have passed us by in total ignorance of our presence, but at the last moment they were alerted by the clinking of the harness of one of the pack animals and they stopped to listen.

'A goat,' said their sergeant and they may yet have passed on, but Simadis was already shooting. It was contrary to Wolf's orders and it may well have been a disaster for us all if Simadis had not been a crack shot. Fortunately, every bullet met its mark. The others joined in. The German troopers fell where they stood. Simadis sprinted down the track swiftly followed by Wolf who shouted at him:

'I told you not to shoot until my order!'

'And when would that come?' sneered Simadis. 'They are the enemy. I killed them. I killed them good!'

'You fool! There will be reprisals for this.'

Simadis shrugged and was inspecting bodies.

'Four dead, two wounded.' he announced and spat. 'Cuckolds and donkeys!'

'And what do we do with them now?' demanded Wolf.

'Slit their throats,' retorted Simadis.

'Is that what you Communists do? Then you do it because I won't!' Wolf shouted back.

'Cuckold!' cried Simadis and withdrew his knife from his sash. I thought at first that he was going to attack Wolf but then without remorse and ignoring the pleas of two wounded troopers he did the deed.

And seemed to relish it.

'Now we must hide or bury them,' sighed Wolf.

It took an hour of backbreaking work. We lugged the bodies to a small cave dragged them inside and covered them lightly with earth and blocked the entrance with brushwood.

'Let the wild animals do the rest,' commented Simadis.

'If he had waited,' muttered Wolf, 'they might have passed us by without seeing us. Now there will be a big problem. Remember Kandanos?'

Wolf and Simadis argued much of the way back to the village. They spoke too fast and with too much anger and passion for me to catch what was being said, but I know that Wolf, who was usually so even-tempered, was incandescent with rage at Simadis's folly.

Simadis left us before we reached our hamlet. When Nektarios heard from Wolf what had happened he gave orders that messages be sent to the other houses on the mountain and told the women and children to prepare to leave for the family caves.

Wolf, Bunny and I once more heaved up Lucky's stretcher. It felt heavier with every step and we followed Mama and the girls to the cave. A discreet message was sent to the doctor and meanwhile Mama did what she could to make Lucky comfortable. The *andartes* headed to the hills above the hamlet and slept under the stars. The village lay silent and deserted. From first light we waited for the Germans to come and take their revenge.

'Now they will take their revenge, I am sure,' Wolf muttered in a serious voice.

We were not disappointed. The patrol arrived later that morning at the foot of our mountain. The buildings were by now deserted and silent. The Germans began to set fire methodically to each one. Because the mountain was dotted about with small hamlets this made it complicated for the Germans to burn down everything in one fell swoop.

It was one of those scorchingly hot days which make

you gasp for breath as if you were in front of an open oven door. There was a powerful and unpredictable wind which tore at the vegetation and gusted like a noisy child having a temper tantrum. The flames spread quickly: I watched the golden tongues of light flicker and catch, and curl round and devour the dry grass. The flames moved quickly and easily across the *kipos* and among the olive trees which began to catch and smoulder. Soon we could pick up the smell of acrid smoke even up in the high pasture. Wolf began to look worried, the furrows in his brow deepening.

'They'll set the whole mountain on fire,' said Wolf as we lay on watch together. It was an anxious wait and time passed very slowly. I might even have dozed off from exhaustion.

It must have been a few hours after midday when two things happened.

The wind dropped unexpectedly.

In the sudden silence we could hear the crackle of the flames. But without a wind to fan them they finally dwindled to nothing and all that remained was the scorched earth and the pungent smell of the smoke.

And then Young Felix found us.

'They've gone,' he announced breathlessly as he scrambled up to where we lay. 'The Germans have gone. I watched. I climbed high into a pine tree. And I hid there. No one could see me. I watched it all. The Germans were afraid that the fire would burn their vehicles. They jumped into their jeeps and drove away!'

'And the fire? Has it spread far?' asked Wolf.

'I was not alone, me. The other boys were with me like birds on the branches. The leaves hid us and we stayed very still. The Germans did not know we were there; they could not see us. We climbed down from the trees when the Germans were far away and it was safe for us. We made a chain with buckets of water from the cistern and we poured it onto the flames. Then, there was no wind; it dropped suddenly and so we stopped the fire spreading.'

'Brave one. You all risked much,' Wolf said patting him on the shoulder. 'How many houses are burnt down?'

'The homes of Dimitri and Stelios are completely destroyed. This I know. Old Anna's has no roof. Some of Dimitri's olives are gone, but I think the rest are saved. The Germans loaded animals onto their jeeps – if they could catch them! They smashed everything else! But no one is hurt. Nektarios's warning reached everyone in time and all the women, children and old people are safe in the caves.'

'*Panegyri*. God be thanked,' breathed Wolf, crossing himself. 'Felix, you did well, pethia mou. You are a hero and the other lads. '

'Am I an *andarte* now?' asked Felix.

'You are still too young, *pethia mou*. But you will be my first choice when you are older, no doubt. Wolf handed Felix his water bottle. 'Drink, *pethia mou*. But now … I want you to be my runner.' Felix let out a sound between a sigh and a grunt of pleasure.

'Here take this.' Wolf took out the dagger from his sash and handed it to Felix. 'This is your reward.' Felix ran his hand over the carved ivory hilt, grabbed Wolf's hand and shook it and then ran off.

'The Germans will return,' said Wolf. He looked resigned and exhausted suddenly, his ruddy face grey with fatigue.

'Why so sure?' I asked.

'Let me tell you this, my friend. News reaches us all the time of the revenge and punishments they exact on the villages. In one village the Germans herded everyone – the priest, the doctor, the teacher who was the cantor, the women, the children and the old people into the square. The cantor who had a mellow baritone voice which was renowned for many miles around began to sing the memorial songs to give the people heart. Then he began the Cretan National anthem and they started to join in, one by one. Then the Germans opened fire … and you can guess the rest.'

'Why do they behave like this? It is so brutal. And it breaks the Geneva Convention.' I said.

'Because they can. Because they are afraid of us. We do not behave like a conquered people and we never will!' Wolf uttered vehemently. 'They think they can terrify us into surrender. Let me tell you another story I heard: three brothers were captured. Imagine the feelings of their mother. The Germans lined them up in the square and shot them.'

'Why?'

'Only God knows I do not. One was married and he did not die from the bullet. He rose up; his wife screamed. The German officer went over to him took out his pistol and shot him in the head. His Mother fainted and his wife screamed again in anguish. She fell to the ground and beat the earth with her hands in her pain and grief. The German walked over to her and kicked her in the stomach – in case she was pregnant, you understand. Then he hit her with the butt of his gun and crushed her skull.'

The thought disgusted and appalled me: 'These are war crimes.'

'No doubt, but they will never be punished, my friend.'

'Why not?'

'If the Germans win the war nothing will happen because, of course, they are the victors.'

'And if they lose?'

'Politicians will decide who is punished. Can you trust politicians, the cuckolds? No, my friend only the ordinary people suffer. But I hold to this truth, and that is that the Cretan people have never surrendered and will never surrender: not to the Venetians, not to the Turks and definitely not to the Germans!'

CHAPTER 12

2001

I didn't want to frighten Kalliope or put her off helping me, so I left Hennery exploring the bars and picked a moment when I could talk to her alone without giving her a shock. Late that afternoon, I offered to accompany her to watch her milking the nanny goats.

They were tethered together with the kids in a small field between the fortress and the beach. Kalliope strode ahead swinging her hips in the characteristic way that she had, her big plastic yogurt pots which she used as buckets swinging lightly from either hand. In the golden warmth of the early evening dappled light spilled through the olive trees and a slight breeze rustled the branches and made them shiver in a shower of silver and gold.

'Once there were many,' she explained, indicating the animals, 'but now there are only two of each. I have need of no more. I have no man now that my Vassili is gone to the good Lord above. No, I have need of no more. I make yoghurt and cheese. Some yoghurt I will sell to a hotel and the rest is for me – and for you.' She flashed her brown eyes sideways at me and grinned flirtatiously.

I watched her as she collected a small log from under an olive tree and placed it next to one of the tethered female goats. I had often noticed small logs or stones lying around, seemingly at random, alongside the road or at the edge of a field. I now knew that each one had a particular purpose and was placed there awaiting the moment when it would be used to sit on as Kalliope was doing or to secure a plastic pipe or an olive net.

Clucking her tongue and softly crooning endearments to the nervous animal, Kalliope coaxed the nanny goat to come to her. Hitching up her skirt above her knees and sitting with her legs wide apart she placed the bucket between her knees and began to pull at the teats. The milk squirted into the bucket in a warm creamy waterfall. When she had done she slapped the animal on its rump and it skittered away with a bleat like the cry of a child, as far as the length of its chain would allow. She stood and offered the bucket to me.

'Try.' she ordered. I dipped a cautious index finger into the liquid. Thoughts of salmonella or TB passed through my mind, but as I did not wish to insult her I licked it anyway. It was warm and sweet, rich and creamy and slightly tangy with the taste of cheese.

'*Kala*,' I said, and Kalliope grinned.

'*Poly kala.*' she said.

Pulling the next goat to her, Kalliope began the milking process again and soon a second bucket was filled. Then she reached in the pocket of her apron took out a handful of feed and scattered it broadcast across the carpet of dead leaves and grass. She stretched and smiled with satisfaction of a job done.

'Thanks be to God,' she said crossing herself. 'The milk is good.'

I took the log and replaced it under the olive tree where it belonged and then reached out to carry the pails for her.

'*Oichi. Oichi.* This is not man's work,' she said, but she did not resist when I took the pails anyway.

'Now we return to my *spiti* and you will eat with me. Where is your friend?'

'He's discovering the town,' I lied. 'He'll be back later.'

At the house, when Kalliope had placed her pails in the cool room behind her kitchen, she poured me a beer and placed a saucer of olives and thin wedges of graviera cheese in front of me. Then she lit the gas burner and poured oil into a frying pan.

My vivacious neighbour owns a clutch of chickens

which lay eggs with yolks of startling yellow. She has goats who give her rich creamy milk. In less than five minutes she placed on the table before me an omelette of these eggs and this goat's milk, filled with onions and boiled potatoes.

I was almost dazzled by the plate of gold. I waited for her to turn down the TV and settle down at the table with me

'Kalliope,' I said after a mouthful of egg and potato, 'this is delicious.' She nodded and smiled.

'*Malista.*'

I took a deep draft of what Hennery would call the amber nectar.

'I have something to tell you, Kalliope. Today, I visited a village and I think I found the house.'

'What house?' Kalliope asked raising her head and looking steadily at me.

'The house where my grandfather was hidden!'

She said nothing. The air of light-hearted gaiety of a few minutes before had evaporated and she suddenly seemed tense, apprehensive, waiting.

'It's high in the mountains about twenty minutes in the car away from here. There's a small group of houses there now but no one lives in them. Do you know where I mean?' I waited for her to respond but, unusually for her, she still had nothing to say. Was this was the right moment to ask Kalliope about the photos?

'I found some photographs in one of the houses. Wait while I fetch them.'

I left her sitting quite still, gazing at the TV with the sound turned down and returned to the cottage for the sheaf of photos Hennery and I had retrieved from the abandoned house.

'Here they are,' I announced when I put them down on the table in front of her.

She picked up the group and shuffled slowly through them. Then her eyes filled with tears and they spilled down her cheeks and onto her blouse.

'Kalliope, help me if you can,' I urged softly, taking her other hand. 'I am sure that my grandfather was hidden in that house. Hennery and I found these photos there today. Did the woman in the photo live there also? Is she one of the girls my grandfather mentions? Please tell me.'

Kalliope mopped up her tears and studied the photos intently then she said in a wavering voice:

'*Ai! Panegyri!* 'She uttered with a sob. 'Adonia.'

'Adonia – who is she?'

'This is my sister Adonia.'

'Your sister!' I shouted and she jumped.

'*Ela na su po.* Adonia is my sister. This is the photograph of her wedding day. See this handsome *Palikari*. It is her husband.'

She clutched the photos to her chest and then put them down gently on the table and mopped her eyes on her arm.

'But my grandfather never mentions an Adonia in his diary. Did she live in that house?'

'Yes.'

'And did you?'

'Yes, of course.'

'But I still don't understand my grandfather never mentioned you or Adonia in his diary. Never.'

I felt puzzled and deflated. Hugely disappointed. I'd not found the right family after all.

'It's the wrong house.'

'It is the house of my parents.'

'Who are dead?'

Kalliope crossed herself: 'Yes, God rest their souls.'

'And that is why it is abandoned?'

'Yes.' she whispered.

'Then I am wrong. It is not the house I am searching for.' I felt like a deflated balloon. I had been so sure that when Hennery and I found the village and the house that they both fitted the descriptions in my grandfather's diary so accurately that we were both certain that we had found the right, the only, place.

Kalliope remained unusually silent, then asked finally:

'The girls you are looking for? How many were they?' .

'There were four. Four sisters.'

'Four sisters? How were they called?'

'My grandfather called them Tonia, Elenitsa, Fifi and Poppy.'

'*Panegyri!*' exclaimed Kalliope. 'Say again the names.'

'Tonia, Elenitsa, Fifi and Poppy – four sisters. Do you know them?' I cried eagerly.

'Oh, yes, I know them. How can I not know them? See, this one, this is Tonia here in the photo. Tonia is what we call Adonia for short. And Elenitsa was my eldest sister. It means little Eleni.'

'Who is Fifi?'

'You met her yesterday,'

'You don't mean Iphigenia.'

'Yes, Iphigenia is my sister Fifi.'

'So, Kalliope, who are you?'

'Me? I am Poppy!'

'Poppy! I don't believe it!'

'It is short for Kalliope.'

'And was your father called Nektarios?'

'Yes, he was, God bless his soul.'

'So you did live in the house in the village where I found these photographs.'

'*Malista.*'

'Kalliope?'

'Yes.'

'Can I call you Poppy?'

'Of course.'

'You are the key to all this.'

But I wondered how much she would reveal.

***

1941

'What will you do after the war, Wolf?' I asked, tossing my cigarette butt into the embers of the fire. Our group of Wolf, Lucky and their brothers and cousins sprawled and lounged or sat cross-legged or even lay asleep in the shelter of a wide deep cavern where the smoke of a fire could not be seen outside. It was late afternoon and the light coated the mouth of the cave in gold.

We had rested all day after a particularly difficult evening the previous night.

Wolf and his group had left the village at dusk in twos and threes. The cave was the rendezvous. News had reached them via a runner that allied planes intended to make a drop of arms and ammunition, supplies and stores around midnight. Their instructions were to lie in wait and listen for the drone of the plane. Lighted flares were to signal the location to the aircraft and the group were then to collect the arms and boxes of equipment as they parachuted down to earth.

High winds had aborted the plan twice and high winds had sabotaged the drop the previous night. This was their last chance. The plane circled, Wolf's men lighted the flares and signalled. The parachutes were released. But fierce gusts of the famous Cretan high wind had blown the precious cargo hither and thither onto the mountain.

So the long night began. It was treacherous and exhausting work to locate and collect from inaccessible ledges, the branches of oak or olive trees, and rough terrain the many boxes, even with the light of a lantern. By dawn it was clear that much of the consignment was still missing. Wolf called a briefing of the men at the cave and then sent them out again. The search continued for another couple of hours. It was increasingly dangerous as the German lookouts, also undoubtedly alerted by the sound of the plane, would have sent off patrols at first light to search the area. Wolf called a halt by about mid morning and we congregated in the cave and stored what had been gathered. Then we slept until late afternoon.

'What will I do after the war?' repeated Wolf twirling his long curly moustache. 'Why, steal sheep!' He grinned mischievously, slapped his thigh and rumbled into laughter which echoed around the cave and caused a stir among the sleepers who grunted and rolled over on their cloaks. It is almost a mime show when he talks.

'I will go to America and make my fortune, like my father. My father was a middle son. There were fourteen brothers and sisters. He had nothing to inherit. So he ran away from the village when he was very young and he took a boat to America. There he worked for many years, maybe ten, and saved his money. Then he returned to find a Cretan wife. He looked around, but he did not like what he saw. One day he was visiting our cousins in another village across the mountains and he saw in the house a small girl maybe two years or three. She was very pretty and very lively. She tried to seize the knife from his sash. He thought that this was a sign that she was fearless as well as pretty.

'I will marry your daughter,' he said to her parents at once and he slapped down a bag of money.

'I return now to America,' he said,' but when she is of the age to marry, I will come for her.

'When the girl was about 14 she was still very lively and also very beautiful. In fact, she was regarded as the most beautiful girl in the village. Our cousin, her father, had offers from three or four men who wished to take her for a wife, but my cousin had given his word to my father and felt bound by honour – and the gold – to keep his daughter for my father, although they had received no news of him.

'But my father had not forgotten and later that year he arrived back from America. He immediately went to see our cousin and made his daughter his wife. That is how my father married my mother!'

'So your father learnt to speak English in America.'

'*Malista!* And that is how I can speak English. I asked him to teach me. '

'Have you always lived in the village?'

'You have forgotten the Turks, God rot them!' he spat.

'The Turks?'

'Remember that the Turks ruled Crete for many generations. My village was a Turkish village. When Crete became independent, the Turks left for Turkey. They left the land and abandoned their homes and farms. My Grandfather, Arkelos, was born in Sfakia, but he too was a middle son. He decided to find land of his own. He came to our village. The olive groves were burning and the Turks were running away. The price of land was low and it was not difficult to find an empty house, an olive grove and some land for little money.'

'Or no money at all?' I said.

'As you say, nothing at all. *Katholu*. My Grandfather was a fierce warrior, the bravest of the brave. He took what he wanted and soon he had olives and goats and sheep.'

'Which he stole?'

Wolf grinned: 'Sheep stealing was natural to us. It impressed the women as well as the men. I ask you, what woman wants a man who is afraid to steal sheep?'

'And then what happened?'

'My grandfather took a wife and had fourteen sons, as you know. We are a big family of *Palikari*. Some remain here, some have died of illnesses or in fights and others have land in other villages and my father went to America to seek his fortune.'

'If you get to America, will you return to Crete when you have made money?'

'I am Cretan. My heart is always in my village and in Crete. I will make money and then I will open a taverna. I will return.'

'And your brothers?'

'Lucky wishes to be a musician, if God wills. Bunny wants the farm and Stavro will gamble and steal sheep, I am sure!'

As dusk fell again, Wolf ordered us to restart the search. It was hard, exhausting and treacherous work as we slid on unstable earth and tripped over rocks, struggled along terraces either in pairs or alone, aware only of the grunts and mutterings of our companions. By dawn we had located and collected much more of the drop which we ferried back to the cave. We made one last foray. I spotted a wooden ammunition case suspended by its parachute strings high in a pine tree. The white silk hung and flapped in the wind like a flag of surrender and a signal to any German patrol. I scrambled up the trunk using each branch to haul myself aloft like a seaman up the rigging. After a few minutes I reached the parachute and began to haul it in.

Voices floated up from below. I was about to call out thinking it was one of our group of searchers when I detected an accent which I knew with deadly certainty was not Cretan.

'Was it here you saw the parachute,' said the voice in German.

'Ja. I believe this is so.'

I froze against the branch along which I was lying, hugging the parachute silk under my chest and hoping it was no longer visible, but keenly aware that the ammo box was still suspended below me.

The two German troopers continued to talk and by the rustling I heard seemed to be searching the base of the pine tree. I hoped that they would not decide to climb as I had done.

I heard the click of a lighter as they lit cigarettes and felt the tree tremble as they relaxed against it. If they looked up and examined the tree really closely or had binoculars I knew I was done for. They smoked their cigarettes and chatted together and the time passing by seemed endless. I dared not move, but my position was extremely uncomfortable and before long I developed pins and needles in one of my legs. I gritted my teeth against the discomfort and tried not to shift my weight. In the end it was unbearable and very slowly and with as little movement as possible I realigned my body .The Germans seemed to hear nothing and continued to chat.

Suddenly, with a rapid flapping of wings and an agitated cawing two buzzards swooped down from their eyrie in the crags above me. The distant sound of gunfire must have disturbed them from their nest. The shock of the noise, the sudden onrush of air and the swiftness of the birds' dive brought the soldiers to their feet and scared them so much that they ran for cover into the rocks. I heard them shout and draw their pistols and start shooting into the air. The next few minutes were a chaos of gunfire, shouts and cawing, then all became silent. A century seemed to pass while I waited for the Germans to return. But they had been terrified by the unexpected power of the predators just above their heads, whose wing span was over four feet and whose talons could tear the heart out of a sheep. So they had run away. At length, I pulled myself up into a sitting position and blood flowed again into my leg. I waited even longer before I pulled up the ammo case and then I sat in the cover of the branches clutching the booty to my chest.

I stayed there for the rest of the day while I heard intermittent semi-automatic and rifle fire echo off the walls of the cliffs. At dusk, I took the decision to make a move on the basis that all the Germans would have withdrawn to the safety of their base. I was hungry and thirsty and drained from tension. I hoped that I would find that Wolf and the group would all be safely returned to the cavern and so I hauled down the box and set off to rejoin them.

***

'No sweat.' exclaimed Hennery when I recounted my meeting with Kalliope. 'No sweat. No sweat.'

'I was bowled over.' I said.

'So Kalliope is Poppy and Iphigenia is Fifi. No sweat.'

'Not what we expected though, was it?'

'A real breakthrough. Now what?'

'Questions. Questions. Questions.'

'And another drink,' grinned Hennery. We drank, we ate and we discussed. Darkness fell, the lights in the harbour twinkled, but our thoughts were back in 1941.

'I want to know everything she can remember,' I said decidedly, forking a calamari in batter.

'Will she tell you though?'

'I want her to flesh out the characters for me.'

'Have you thought that some of them may still be alive apart from Poppy and Fifi? How old are they now? About sixty-six? And what about Elenitsa and Tonia, Wolf, Lucky and Bunny. Wouldn't they be in their seventies and eighties?'

'It's a long shot, I agree. I think Wolf was about twenty when he rescued my Grandfather.'

'Hey! And what about Simadis?'

'I got the impression that he was older.'

'He's probably dead, then.'

'Even if they are dead, surely Poppy can tell us more about them and my Grandfather. '

'Before he became a cussed bugger, you mean?'

Hennery and my grandfather had never hit it off. One look at Hennery, his tattoos, his earrings and long hair and my grandfather had dismissed him as a layabout and good for nothing and had disapproved loudly of our friendship whenever he got the chance.'

'You knew him, Hennery, so I won't argue with you. He

was difficult.'

'Bloody understatement!'

'Maybe they saw another side to him. They helped him after all. They liked him. He was Wolf's friend. He was brave. And he was very young. Just twenty. Younger than you and me. How would we have been affected by all he went through?'

'Fair point.'

We drank the beer and we both thought about the twenty-year-old Lancaster and the effects of war

'Did you say he never came back here?'

'It appears so.'

'Why wouldn't he? It's a great place. Great food, man!' Hennery had demolished a large portion of moussaka and chips and was now eating his way through a sugar-dusted portion of sponge cake which the waitress had brought with a small carafe of raki and which she said was on the house.

'He had the money, he had the opportunity, and he writes so admiringly of them – they had been so generous and kind to him too.'

'I agree that it's a mystery, but he didn't. And he never talked about Crete. Never a word. If I hadn't found the diary stashed away in the attic we would never have known any of this.''

I speared a slice of cake. 'You know there are pages torn out of the diary?'

'No sweat.'

'I wonder why. I wonder if they would have explained anything.'

'Well, mate, no doubt about it, we have to do some more detective work.'

'I've just remembered about the old fellow in the mountains that Adoni took me to see. I am sure he was holding something back. And another thing: he mentioned Lucky. Lucky is famous. He's a musician in Athens and still gives concerts apparently.'

'Yeah, man, you could fly to Athens and back in a day and try to meet up with him, I suppose. It's an option but it's easier to get to work on Poppy and Fifi and see what they will tell us. '

'First thing tomorrow.'

'And you don't have much time. Just gotta do it, man. Just gotta do it.'

I sat up until the hour was very late and I was getting chilled. I knew that I should get some sleep. But Hennery was right. The fortnight was disappearing fast, and I didn't have much time. My head was spinning with questions but not finding any answers. At dawn all sleep was irrevocably lost, so I got up and fetched a coke as quietly as I could so as not to waken Hennery, then returned to my sleeping bag with a notebook and pen just as the first slivers of grey light began seeping into the sky.

I thought of all those dawns that my grandfather had experienced when he was alone and on the run. In the grey light it was hard to believe that, within a few hours, the sky would be an intense aquamarine, clear of clouds, and that the sun's heat might be fierce enough to fry an egg. It was a day the tourists would relish, a day for lazing on the beach, taking a swim or messing about in boats. Not for me, though.

Questions swept through my mind in a mad race. I jotted them down as fast as they arrived. Who were the family? Who was still alive? Lucky I knew about, but what of Wolf, Bunny, Stavro and Simadis? Where were they? What could I learn of them? Poppy was definitely the key to everything. And in a few hours I would see her.

PART THREE

CHAPTER 13

1941

The cauldron heat of August wrapped itself over the mountains like a blanket and smothered our energy. Work on the land slowed down. The vegetation turned burnt umber, brittle and dry. Water became a slow trickle in the spring as the land became parched and arid.

'Yanni you must be ready at sunrise.' Mama had warned me at supper the previous night. 'We make an early start. We will walk together.'

I asked where we were going and why.

'We are going to a small church dedicated to the Holy Virgin. It is her special day, *Panegyria*. There is a festival dedicated to her at another village. We will walk there through the olive groves along the donkey trails. It is a very important holy day to us,' she continued. 'Everyone will come from all the villages around to this special church. You must wear your Cretan costume. You speak Cretan quite well now, but say as little as possible. There will be many people there. You will be unknown, but say nothing. There may be people who come to spy for the Germans.'

Despite the danger of the last few months, everyone was determined to turn out for the Feast of the Assumption on the fifteenth of August as it is the most important festival, after Easter, of the Greek Orthodox Church Calendar.

'I will take care. I will keep my mouth shut.' I promised.

Elenitsa handed me a white linen shirt.

'It is new,' she said, 'I made it. Wear it under your waistcoat.'

I also wore the crapcatcher pants and wrapped a sash around my waist and a headband around my head. When I finally pulled on a pair of old boots I think I looked the part of a Cretan shepherd dressed in his best.

The little church was no more than a tiny, whitewashed stone chapel surrounded by a courtyard. Mama and the girls went inside. I followed and watched them as they lighted thin taper-like candles, placed them into the brass container of sand which acted as a holder, crossed themselves before the altar and kissed the icon of the Virgin, which was surrounded by small bunches of flowers. I then joined Nektarios and the other village men outside in the courtyard. They stood in small groups, chatting to each other. It was an opportunity to make deals and smoke cigarettes. Only the old widow women, dressed in black, remained inside the stuffy chapel where the priest intoned the liturgy and where the cantor sang the responses in a clear strong baritone which carried out into the open.

I too smoked a cigarette and observed. People continued to arrive, until about one hundred men, women and children of all ages had gathered in the open area in front of the chapel. I recognised the faces of families from our village. Towards the end Wolf, Lucky and their brothers arrived and finally Simadis, escorting his mother who was not old and infirm, as I had always imagined, but upright, stout and fierce-looking with black eyebrows running in a thick line across her forehead. I was surprised that he had come. We had not seen him since his argument with Wolf the previous week. But here he was, bold as brass and acting unconcerned as he greeted the men he knew with a handshake or an embrace.

The priest emerged from the gloomy interior to stand in front of the chapel. He carried a large book which looked like a Bible in his arms. It was bound in embossed silver. The cantor swung a censer and the smoke wafted through the air leaving an aroma of frankincense and pine. A rope was pulled and a bell rang. The priest set off, his robe flapping in the wind, accompanied by his acolytes, to walk around the perimeter of the church, followed by the more devout members of the congregation. Then he finished off with a long prayer in front of a table piled high with the special round, sweet bread baked for the occasion. He blessed it and one of the helpers withdrew a large knife from his belt and cut it into pieces. I expect he had used that self same knife to slaughter a goat or dig in the earth. The worshippers lined up and priest took the chunks of bread, blessed them and gave them to each person as they passed in front of him. The women often kissed his hand as he spoke and blessed their foreheads.

By now it was about mid morning and the heat was growing despite a gusty wind. The crowd drifted into the dappled shade of the olive groves where it was cool. They sat on the beds of olive leaves in groups. The children, free spirits, released now that the church service was over to let off steam, played and chased exuberantly among the trees. On one side of the clearing a rank of trestle tables had been erected covered with white linen cloths. A group of women, Mama included, bustled about setting out baskets containing bread and *kalitsounias*, cheese and olives. Behind them Young Felix, sweat pouring down his face, was cheerfully turning a huge spit which was roasting a couple of sheep and on another open fire sat a huge cauldron containing stewed goat and pilaffi rice. Smells of olive oil and roasted meat and woodsmoke filled the air. The German occupation was forgotten for a short while.

'Come!' ordered Wolf, twirling his moustaches and licking his lips. 'Now we eat!'

'Simadis is here,' I said, 'I saw him in the crowd. Have you made up your quarrel?'

'Ah, Simadis, Simadis.' sighed Wolf. 'What a man! He believes no one and nothing can touch him. He thinks he lives a charmed life. He escaped from the Germans on the mainland after fighting for many months in a long and bloody battle with our army – what was left of it. He did not receive a cut, not one. He sailed to Crete on a small wooden fishing boat, a caique, although the risk was huge so early in the spring for the seas are treacherous and unpredictable and very dangerous. Storms and wind blow up in an instant. He was lucky he was not shipwrecked and drowned. I don't suppose he even got wet! *Lipon*, once again God was on his side. He has been fighting since the start of the invasion of our island with the *andartes* around Rethymnon. They have been attacking the German troops and convoys and stealing arms and ammunition. Very dangerous. The Germans shoot first and ask questions afterwards.' As he talked, Wolf piled a plate with meat and pilaff and passed it to me. 'You know your one-eyed English man, Pendleton?'

'No. I'm from New Zealand, remember.'

'Your Pendleton, very famous archaeologist at Knossos. Much loved, honoured and respected by our people. He knew everyone; he knew every mountain, had climbed them all. The Germans shot him dead in the first days of the invasion. The cuckolds! On sight, even though he was wounded and could not defend himself. *Malaka*. But Simadis, he fights like a tiger and nothing touches him. *Lipon*, he has the right to be arrogant.' Wolf loaded his own plate, tucked a bottle of wine under his arm and gestured to me to pick up some tumblers and follow him into the grove.

'But what he did last month endangered us all.' I said. 'And there must be one leader who gives the orders and one alone. That stands to reason.'

'*Vevea*. You are right, of course, but Simadis is a law unto himself, as my Mother tells me they say in the Bible.' Wolf shrugged his shoulders, dismissing my point. 'And no, he does not apologise either, but Simadis is Simadis. I must accept him as he is for we need every man we can get and we must work all together if we are to free Crete from the Germans, so I forgive him. And now we must eat. We stole the goat from our enemy Mavroyannis so it will taste extra good as it was free!!'

Flagons of tawny country wine and honey-coloured retsina appeared. Nektarios and several of his companions began moving from group to group filling cups or glasses.

By midday the sun was very hot, but the wind was still blowing in fierce unpredictable gusts which cooled the air. The olive trees cast a gentle shade over the feasting groups. The men sat together drinking and smoking apart from the women who did neither but who moved serenely from group to group serving the food to their menfolk and children before eating themselves, just as they did at home.

Simadis ambled over to join Wolf and his brothers a flagon of wine in his hand. Perhaps it was a peace offering, and before long Lucky, now recovered enough from his wound to play, tuned up his lyra and began to pick out the old familiar melodies. First one voice took up the tune, then another, until there was an energetic choir. As the drink took hold, the tune became discordant and rowdy as the words were slurred and the notes were missed. The girls nudged each other and giggled at some of the bawdier verses, but did not join in.

No Cretan male can hear music and song without jumping to his feet and dancing. It demonstrates his power, his agility, and his strength. It is a sign of his masculinity. He can't resist the sound of the lyra and the bazouki. In Minoan times bull leaping entertained the court of King Minos. It required great skill and gymnastic ability.

Cretan dancing still does.

Lucky stroked the strings of his lyra as if they were the skin of a woman. The opening notes of the melody caused a loud shout of recognition and Wolf was on his feet in an instant. His brothers joined him and then Simadis. It seemed that music had the power to settle all quarrels. The young men linked up with each other, arms flung over each other's shoulder and began the intricate steps. At first, the movement was slow and the footwork simple: a few steps to the side, a few rocking movements forward and back as the weight changed from foot to foot and then they moved the circle on. The speed increased and the footwork became more complex. Wolf sprang lightly into the circle and clicking his heels together began a sinuous snake-like swivelling of his hips while he wrapped and unwrapped his feet around his calves. He raised his arms above his head and clicked his fingers in time with the beat of the music. I thought he was very good and watched him in admiration.

Until, that is, Simadis replaced him. Then I saw what real skill was.

Every one of Simadis's muscles was controlled like a coiled spring. He moved stealthily like a panther, at first, then sprang high into the air and clicked his heels together as he rose on the spring. He landed lightly in a crouch and placed one hand on the floor. Next, he circled his whole body around it, swinging his feet over and around a tumbler full of wine which Wolf had placed on the floor. By now everyone was clapping in time with the music. Stretching out, with his hands on the floor Simadis supported his whole body and raised the wine tumbler with his mouth. The crowd roared and clapped. Next, he jumped to his feet, shimmied over to a small table and lifted it up it with his teeth high above his head before Wolf relieved him of it!

Simadis executed a back spring, landed on his feet, folded his arms across his chest and then crouched low kicking out his legs like a Russian Cossack. Wolf placed a wooden chair in the centre of the space and held out his hand to Simadis who vaulted onto the chair and did a handstand onto the back just as, with perfect and precise timing, Wolf sat on the seat. The audience gasped in admiration, then roared their approval. Simadis looked majestic, drawing the collective eyes and sighs of the women. You could see how a man could attract a girl just through his lithe movements, agility and athleticism. The eroticism was palpable.

With one fluid movement he let go and landed on his

feet to cheers and claps and returned to the circle of men a self-satisfied grin on his face. No other man was prepared to dance solo after that and the circle disintegrated and made way for the women.

The girls danced slowly and gracefully with stylish footwork.

Elenitsa is refined and poised, slender and upright as a cypress, elegant and willowy, almost sorrowful and intense. She is lovely to look at, although she is not beautiful. There is something in the dreamy expression of her large eyes which is sorrowful and enigmatic. It is a faraway look of otherworldliness as if she is detached from the rest of us and lost in the movement of the dance. She is solemn and does not smile often intent on what she is thinking, excluding us all.

By contrast, Tonia is a star performer: flirtatious and vivacious, spirited, flamboyant and effervescent, all flashing eyes, curling lips, sinuous hips and good-humoured jollity. She drew all eyes to her with her panache, all eyes except those of Simadis. He watched only Elenitsa with a concentrated burning intensity. He moved to the front of the audience and never took his eyes off her as if he were magnetised by her. Was she aware of it? I don't know, but she did not dance for long after he appeared. He made to move towards her when she stopped as if to meet her and speak to her but she avoided him and soon slipped back to her place among the women.

Eventually, the heat and the wine and full stomachs took over and people reclined and slept on the cushion of olive leaves among the vines. Peace descended and tension melted away.

We were woken by distant machine gun fire. Fear and apprehension surged and there was a flurry as the women hurriedly cleared away and packed up and as the men checked their knives and guns and held urgent discussions. Everyone was rattled and disturbed. It was a false alarm but it was a reminder that trouble is never far away.

I suppose it's fair to say that I had not really taken much notice of Elenitsa before she danced, except on the night we had hidden in the cave. I knew her of course. I had known her all along, she had cared for me all the time I was ill with gentleness and efficiency. She had brought my food, offered me drinks of water but I had not really noticed her. She was part of the furniture, you might say, along with Mama and Nektarios, shadowy figures on the fringes of my insecure hold on life, always there, always present but in the background. Fifi and Poppy were prominent in my life, teaching me and playing in my presence, including me in their thoughts and plans. Tonia, with her wit and bubbling humour no one could overlook. Her huge personality, laughter and jokes, made her unmissable and unforgettable, but Elenitsa was always a pale shadow of her other more boisterous sisters. She was more formal, more restrained, more conscientious; the right hand of her Mother whose orders she obeyed dutifully. Tonia would often question her Mother's requests and, even more often, fulfil them reluctantly. Elenitsa was quietly obedient. Fifi and Poppy were too young and treated too indulgently to have to take much responsibility. I suppose because Elenitsa was the eldest of the four she took on responsibility more readily as a matter of course.

Each day she went quietly about the chores of the house and garden: feeding the chickens, watering the vegetables, collecting water in pitchers from the spring, fetching and carrying for Mama. She helped to make cheese, after she milked the goats; she cooked the endless stews and helped to bake the bread. She always seemed busy. In the quiet afternoons when the family rested in the cool of the house, Elenitsa set to at the loom to weave the brightly coloured wool into lengths of cloth while Tonia pretended to do the mending , chatted and complained of the heat, of fatigue, but in a manner that always made you laugh and never gave offence .

Elenitsa was not beautiful. Not even immediately attractive. She did not draw the eye as many girls did. I was used to the loud, strapping, blonde farm lasses of New Zealand, not a quiet, composed Cretan village girl. Her skin was sallow and her body sinewy and thin. She had large and mournful brown eyes and abundant dark, curly hair which she usually restrained modestly under a headscarf.

That day of the Assumption Elenitsa was dressed in her best clothes – a colourful heavily embroidered Cretan costume. The tight waistcoat and full skirt gave her curves; her curls were tied with a ribbon. Instead of heavy shoes suitable for the farm, she wore light slippers. The heat and the excitement gave her cheeks a glow and, lost though she was in the dance, her eyes sparkled. Above all she smiled which was a rare thing.

Suddenly, she was beautiful.

***

2001

'I was a child. No one notices children – or thinks that they hear and understand.'

'Tell me everything.' said Alexi to me.

'When Lancaster – or Yanni as we called him – came to us he was ill, very ill. His skin was black and blue from bruises where he had fallen. He had a big wound here.' I fluttered my hand across my rib, 'and another here,' and I ran my hand down my arm from the elbow to the wrist. To show him 'He was covered with sores. And his feet. Oh, they were not good. They were ... how do you say? I do not know the word.'

'Festering,' Alexi suggested. 'Going bad.'

'Yes, you are right. And he had a fever. Water poured

off him. He was shaking like the leaves of the tree in a wind.'

'Shivering.'

'*Ne*. He staggered to our village and fell down. This is so. He fell at the feet of my cousin, Wolf. *Ela na po*, your grandfather was very thin. He looked like a skeleton. He was covered with marks from stones and trees. His uniform was very torn.'

'In tatters.'

'He wore over his back the skin of a sheep. It held many biting things.'

'They sound like fleas.'

'He had many bites on his arms and legs.'

Alexi was waiting by my door before breakfast time. He gave me such a fright that my heart – which is not so strong as it was – beat harder when I saw a man there, for I did not know it was him at first. I could tell that he was impatient to talk. He followed me into my garden when I went to feed the chickens. And he followed me as I threw the corn and then took the hosepipe to water my vegetables – asking questions, questions, so many questions.

'The men carried him into the room below where we keep the stores and laid him on the floor on a bed of straw. Then my mother and Elenitsa, my oldest sister, came to him. They cleaned him of his blood. Then my Mother sent Elenitsa away. She was a young girl. It was not proper that she should see the naked body of a strange man. Then my Mother took off his clothes for they were filthy and smelling bad and put good *farmaka*, which my mother made from herbs and oil, on his wounds. She gave him a tea to drink of dittany, which is a cure for many terrible things like snakebite but he was soon unconscious again. Then Elenitsa returned and sat with him many hours and watched over him, tried to make him take water and bathed his face. We wanted to see him also but Elenitsa always sent us away. My Mother called us to her knee and put her arms around us. She told us that we must not say a word to anyone. This was our family secret. "What goes on in the house must stay in the house," she said. "No one must know." Then she made us kneel before the icon of the Holy Mary and make a solemn promise that we would never say anything of this secret to anyone. *Katholu*. Not at all. Of course, we did not want to make the Virgin angry, or to upset my Mother, whom we loved very much, and so we crossed ourselves three times and promised never to speak a word. And we never did.'

'How long was my grandfather ill?'

'He stayed like this for many days. He did not wake up. The fever was very bad. My Mother did not think that he would live because he was so thin and weak. He muttered words but we did not understand what he was saying, because, of course, he was speaking the English. When he called out in your language, Elenitsa had to quieten him because we feared that others in the village would hear him.

Later, he sometimes woke up and Elenitsa made him drink the dittany tea and she gave him some bread softened in goat's milk as well. He could not swallow easily and could not eat solid food. He was very thin, of course, for he had starved. You could see the bones of his body sticking through the flesh. Elenitsa cleaned the cuts each day and put on new *farmaka* which my mother had made.

Ela na su po, my Mother knew many things about herbs. She collected the wild things from the mountains. Some she dried, and stored in cotton bags, some she mixed with oil or animal fat to make a *crema* for cuts on the skin. The men often cut themselves with knives or on trees and thorns when they worked in the fields and, sometimes, when they were caring for the flocks of goats and sheep, they were kicked or bitten by the animals, snakes even, and sometimes she even looked after bullet wounds or stab wounds. When the men drink too much raki sometimes they fight. It is their way. But my mother cured them all.

Some herbs she boiled to make a drink which sends you to sleep. I told you that dittany cures the bite of a snake. It also stops the baby, and sometimes a girl had need of this. My mother helped with everything and made many medicines for them. All the village came to her for *farmaka* and she had a reputation for success. Today, I think that she would have been a great success as a doctor or a nurse. My cousin in Athens is a doctor. My Mother would have been a good doctor.'

'So, my Grandfather came to know Elenitsa because she nursed him.'

'No. When he became conscious once more, my Mother sent Elenitsa away. She could not leave a young woman and a young man alone together. It was not our custom. When your grandfather woke up, my Mother nursed him herself and Elenitsa did my Mother's work.'

'It gave them a lot of trouble as well as being dangerous,' Alexi said.

'This is true but,' I replied, 'we Cretans would share our last crust of bread with a stranger. It is a matter of honour. It is our custom to help strangers. At first, your grandfather was very weak from the fever and from his injuries. For many days he could not sit up at all and then he could not stand and he had much pain from the rib. But slowly, slowly he became strong. He could not walk. His body would not let him. But he was young and he was a soldier. He had been very fit.'

'He had worked on the family farm until he joined the army and he rode horses so, yes, he would have been fit.' Alexi agreed.

'Yanni was strong. He had a strong heart.' Stronger than mine, I thought. It is beating so fast at this moment I have to catch my breath. I gathered up the eggs from my chickens.

'We used to creep to the door of the storeroom to watch him. Through a gap. Like spies. We were – what do you say? – fascinated, as young girls are, and I think very naughty.' Alexi laughed and took my arm as we returned to the house.

'My Mother had forbidden us to go into the room so we peeped in from outside. We saw him make exercises with his arms and legs. One day I remember he got up and staggered to the door. This was the first time, you understand. We ran away upstairs in fear when he came out of the door. We ran away to call my Mother. That was the first day he got up. I remember that it was just before the name day of my cousin Pavlo so that must have been the end of June.'

'So, Poppy, my grandfather must have been ill for about a month. I guess it would take about a month or six weeks for a cracked or broken rib to heal.'

'This is true. You say right. But later, when he was strong again and he could walk, he would join the men and sometimes my Mother, Elenitsa and Tonia. He would offer help. Ah yes. He was kind and helpful that one. We liked him and came to trust him as a big brother.'

'I want to know about the men. Who was Wolf? He was the leader was he not?'

'Ah Wolf. *Ela na su po*, he was the bravest of the brave: a real *Palikari*. A leader of men, like his Grandfather, Arkelos, who was famous for his great courage against the Turks. Wolf was bolder even – dare I say it. And funny. I loved him and Fifi loved him. He was our hero. Everyone loved him. He and Yanni – as we called your grandfather – were very good friends. They did many daring things together.'

'Where is Wolf now? I came to see him.' Alexi said to me urgently. 'What is his real name? Is he alive? Where can I find him?'

Suddenly, I felt a shiver come over me like a cold finger running down my back even though the sun was warm. I said to myself, 'This man is asking too many questions' and asked myself, 'Do I want to answer? What does he really want of us? How far can I trust him?' The past is the past and the past does not always bring happy memories. *Katholu*, no, not at all. So, I did not invite him inside to drink a coffee with me as I should have done.

He seemed impatient: 'Who was Wolf?' he demanded.

'Wolf was my cousin.' I answered.

'And what was his real name?'

'He was always called Wolf.'

'Is Wolf alive? Does he live here? I want to meet him. He can tell me so much.'

I crossed myself rapidly and touched the little gold cross at my neck: 'No, he cannot help you, for he is dead, God rest his soul.' Alexi's face fell. I could tell that he had pinned many hopes on finding the heroic Wolf and hearing his version of events. He tried once more.

'What about Lucky, Bunny and Stavro?

'Lucky is in Athens. He is famous. He plays the lyra.'

Everyone knows this, I told myself, and you can buy his CDs here in the town in a tourist shop. I am giving away no secrets.

'Stavro too is dead. He was killed later in the war. But who is this Bunny?'

'My grandfather calls the other brother Bunny.'

'Bunny? Bunny? I don't know this name.' I could say this with truth.

He looked so very disappointed that I felt sorry for him and thought about saying more, but these secrets are not my secrets. I must talk to Fifi and ask her for her advice.

'At this time,' I said, 'there were many men, how you say, on the run. We were not the only family in the village who were hiding English or a man from *Afstralia* or *Neo Zealandia*. Because the Germans were in charge we were united against them. We wanted to do anything to help the enemies of Germany.'

'How safe was it?'

'Not safe – no, not at all. The German patrols came to the village sometimes. But Young Felix and the other young boys kept watch and warned us. The Germans took everything they could carry away – sacks of rice and corn, or nuts or olives, eggs, chickens. *Ola.* They came on foot or on motorbike, so they could not steal everything. We would collect our things take them with us and hide in the caves above the village until they had gone.'

'Yes, my Grandfather says this in the diary.'

'The young boys took the flocks of sheep and goats high into the hills also. I remember that Young Felix's family had a donkey.' I will tell him this tale because it will make him laugh, I thought.

'Felix's family did not want to lose the donkey, of course. Felix was on look-out and when he saw the German patrol marching to the village. He ran to hide the donkey. The donkey was stubborn and would not move and Felix had to push and tug and hit the obstinate animal with a cane until it finally moved, and then with much difficulty. He dragged it to the river bed where there was some water for it to drink and he hid it among some oleander bushes. He thought everything was *endaxi,* but he forgot to hide the wooden saddle we put on donkeys when they carry stones or sacks. This the Germans found when they searched the house. As Felix ran back for this saddle, a German trooper caught him and hit him with the butt of his gun. Young Felix was not more than eight years. He was frightened, of course, but he said nothing.'

'But also very brave.'

'Yes, also very brave. But the German had a gun and he was a very fierce man. He forced Felix to lead him down the gorge to the river bed to where the donkey was hidden. The German took the donkey.'

'I hope the donkey gave the German a lot of trouble.'

'Well it was a stubborn donkey. It had a bad temper. It kicked out with its hind legs and tried to bite, so the

German shot it dead.'

'What use was that?'

'No use at all, but it made the German feel good, powerful, a man. But he was a cuckold!' I should not have used that word, but it is true, the German was a cuckold. A bad man! While the German was taking the donkey, Young Felix ran away and so you could say that the donkey saved Felix's life.'

'Were there any reprisals?'

'Yes, but what could they do then? There was no one to shoot except the donkey because everyone from the village was hiding in caves that the Germans did not know about. So the Germans went to our houses and made a mess, took what they could carry away, smashed the rest and left. We ate roasted donkey. It is not as good as goat!'

I stood up then and took off my apron. I tried to look determined. '*Signome*, Alexi. Forgive me, but I have to go.'

I must see Fifi and ask her advice. Can we trust this young man? How much should we tell?

CHAPTER 14

1941

'This man. Very bad man. Mavroyannis. Black John,' whispered Wolf behind his fist, coughing to disguise his words

Short, but muscular, built like the trunk of an olive, dressed in dusty and faded Cretan costume, pot belly forcing the lower buttons of his waistcoat open, he stood legs apart, square head topped with thinning curls, wild wire-wool beard, very black. His broad hands were lighting a cigarette, while his eyes swept through the crowd like a searchlight. They alighted on Wolf, raked him up and down, then stared at him challengingly. I could detect, even at the distance of some yards, that this man exuded power and aggression. I felt the might, the vigour and the vitality of his personality crackling like electricity, even though it was not directed at me.

The market bustled and buzzed around us, smelling of earth and sweat, garlic and Turkish tobacco. Above the noise of the rumbling carts, the braying of discontented donkeys and the chatter of the shoppers, the stallholders' cries of '*Favas! Marula!*' swelled up as they tried to drum up trade, even though they had very little to sell except beans and greens. That was the reason we were here, Wolf and I, to sell or barter some sacks of beans for flour and cigarettes.

We had set off from the village in a chilly mist before five. This was the first time I had ventured into the town.

'I can get you a *taftotita*,' Nektarios had told me one day.

'What's that?'

'A paper: a Cretan identification card. All it needs is

your thumbprint. The Mayor, who is my cousin, will see to it for me. You must have a Cretan name. Papayiannakis Yanni seems fine to me. You can easily pass as a Cretan. You always wear Cretan costume now?'

'I guess so. I am pretty tanned now and my skin is sallow anyway. But wait a minute what about my blue eyes?'

'Do not concern yourself. Many men here in Crete, especially those from Sfakia have blue eyes. Lucky has blue eyes. Some even have red hair!'

Nektarios, as he promised, had acquired my card. Wolf had long before provided me with my Cretan outfit and the children had taught me to be fluent in Cretan. I was well equipped for a trip to Chania.

It was now nearly midday and oppressively hot. The crowd was thinning as the heat increased and the stalls emptied. The quantity of produce was small enough anyway, after the Germans had impounded or stolen the best of it. For a moment, a space had opened among the black-clad widows and wide-hipped mothers who comprised most of the shoppers and, standing by the corner of a bullet-riddled wall, Wolf had spotted him: the bad man.

And he had spotted us.

'*Ela*. Come, we will walk' directed Wolf, taking my elbow and guiding forcefully me to the edge of the crowd.

Wolf took out his tobacco tin, rolled a cigarette and lit it, inhaling deeply. He offered me one as an afterthought. That he had forgotten his usual good manners was a clear indication of the turmoil he was feeling inside.

'Who is he?' I asked.

Wolf tugged his moustaches. 'Holy Mother of God!'

'Is that all you are going to tell me? Which is it? Holy or the Mother of God?' I asked. Wolf hesitated for some moments and I could tell that he was wrestling with himself while he thought about what he was going to say to me. Eventually he made up his mind:

'You know what is vendetta?'

'I think I do. It is a blood feud between families, isn't it? Families fall out and no one is ever forgiven.'

'Sometime we forgive. Maybe ... after many years. The families can marry to end a feud or we become godparents to the son of our enemy. But this man, he will never do this, not even if the world is coming to an end. He is like his father and his grandfather before him. They like blood. They like to kill, to torture even.'

'How did this happen.'

'Many years ago, in my grandfather's time, this man's grandfather – a man called Manoli – stole a flock of sheep belonging to my Grandfather, Arkelos. Manoli and his sons took the flock from our sheepfold and drove them away to his own land on the other side of the mountain. They had captured my grandfather's youngest son, the shepherd boy who looked after the sheep. They burned his feet with the hot blade of a knife and then they tied him up with a rope. He was only ten years. Eventually, he escaped and crawled back to the village after many days to warn us. He was very brave. My grandfather cried an oath to the saints to get revenge and he set off with his sons. They were armed to the teeth with guns and knives. They had also their hunting dogs and they rode on horseback. But old Manoli was waiting for them. He was as cunning as a hungry wolf. He set a trap and as my Grandfather and my uncles and their cousins rode through a small pass in the mountain they were attacked.

It was a bloody battle.

My grandfather has the heart of a lion, as you know, and his sons took after him in courage. They fought a bitter battle. They vowed to recover the sheep or die in the attempt. The sheep, you know, were very valuable. With our sheep we were rich. Without our sheep we were poor. Our families would starve in the winter cold without a sheep to roast. So, they fought for many hours until Manoli was shot with a rifle and badly wounded by my grandfather who, as you know, can kill a rabbit at a hundred yards, and several of old Manoli's sons were injured. This forced them to retreat to their village for safety. This was a great shame to their honour. In this way, my grandfather was able to recover most of his flock of sheep.'

'Except the ones they had already eaten.'

'*Vevea.* You speak true.'

'And for this you have a vendetta?'

'Old Manoli died a few days later of his wounds and for this reason the family vowed on the icon of their church never to forgive. They will do us a bad turn every chance they get and always have. They tell the story from father to son and pour the poison into the ear to each child which is born so they never forget. They will kill us if they can.'

'What even now? Even with a war going on?'

'*Especially* with the war. It gives many bad men the best chance to take revenge. Our enemies can burn our village, steal from us, rape our women, shoot us dead and they can blame the Germans for everything. Already this year my uncle lost some good sheep he was hiding in a high pasture known only to us. We suspect Manoli was behind it.'

'But you said Manoli was dead.'

'*Malista,* but that bad man there, he is also called Manoli. He is the grandson of old Manoli.'

While Wolf told me his tale we had moved slowly towards the edge of the crowd and turned to our left towards a small side alley which led to the sea front, but as we turned into it we were confronted by Manoli himself who had skirted around to cut us off. He was standing there four-square before us, his jaw jutting forward menacingly and his hand at his waist on the hilt of his dagger.

'Cuckold!' he rasped and spat at Wolf's feet. I wondered if Wolf, that bravest of men would respond likewise. 'Your father was a goat shaker!'

'Manoli! Son of a Turk!' replied Wolf in a voice hard as

granite. 'Your mother made love to a donkey!' The ancient enemies stared at each other, neither wishing to look away first, or to give ground. I would have intervened but I was unsure of my disguise and knew that if I spoke I would be betrayed by my accent so I coughed to break the deadlock.

Manoli gave me a look ominous with malice and I felt a shiver run down the back of my neck.

'Who is this, donkey?' he demanded, jabbing a grime encrusted finger towards my chest

'A friend,' said Wolf briefly.

'A friend.' mimicked Manoli. 'You have no friends, cuckold!' Manoli spat again and took a step closer.

I could feel Wolf tensing by my side, balancing his body ready for an attack and I knew that he was itching to fight for his honour. Equally, I knew that if I spoke and tried to diffuse the situation my cover would be blown and I would put Wolf in even more danger.

'Manoli, we are two. You are one. Do you think you have a chance against me and my friend here, alone in this alley?'

'I can fight a hundred men and win!' bragged Manoli. 'You son of a whore!' As he discharged this insult he reached for his dagger and withdrew it from his belt.

Wolf, quick as a flash whipped out his own dagger and slashed it towards Manoli's face. Manoli was quick on his feet for a stout man, but not quick enough and the blade of Wolf's dagger drew a line of blood from Manoli's cheek. I too reached for my dagger and at the same moment realised that also tucked in my belt was my revolver which I pulled out and pointed at Manoli as he staggered back, wiping the blood from his face with his free hand.

I don't know whether I intended to shoot him at point blank range there in the back streets of Chania, but before I made that decision a group of women turned from the sea front into the far end of the alley, chattering and laughing together.

Taking the opportunity, Wolf grabbed my arm.

'*Ela*, come!'

We abandoned Manoli who was trapped between us and the women and we turned and ran back the way we had come into the enveloping cover of the crowd.

'I wanted to kill him,' gasped Wolf as we gulped for breath. 'I could have killed him. I should have killed him!'

'I don't forget! 'Manoli had shouted after us, his words echoing off the walls of the alley as we ran. 'I don't forget your friend!'

'He will remember your face,' said Wolf. 'He will look out for you. Also he saw the revolver. It is yours. It is British army.'

'Don't worry, Wolf,' I reassured him. 'There are British weapons everywhere here on Crete. They were scattered all over the north coast after the battle and down the Imbros valley. It is not so unusual.'

'He will remember it. He will think about it and finally he will know,' said Wolf.

'Know what?'

'That you, my friend, are British and in hiding. He will find a way to denounce you – and me – and all of us.' Wolf fumbled for his cigarette tin which revealed his agitation at the thought.

'Then I must leave the island,' I replied. 'You know that this is what I want.'

'Forget it, my friend. I did not mean this. You are safe with us. Let us collect our bags and return to the village.'

Wolf was uncharacteristically silent on the return journey. Everyone noticed it. We had, I suppose, come to rely on Wolf's good humour to enliven our trips with jokes and tall stories so that we were too full of laughter to notice the passing miles. The others in our group eyed each other, each aware that something was wrong with Wolf. There were a few feeble attempts at conversation but after a few miles this dwindled and all that was heard were the hooves of the trotting horses.

'You are glum, mate,' I said eventually. Wolf let his horse fall behind the others and I did likewise.

'I should have killed him when I had the chance,' said Wolf bitterly, tugging at his moustaches in an agitated manner with his free hand.

'Manoli, you mean?

'Who else? The cuckold!'

'That would have been very foolish, mate,' I replied. 'Maybe you can kill a man here in the mountains in a fair fight but in the centre of Chania? That would be madness!'

'Still I should have killed him. He will not rest now until he kills me.'

'Or me!' I said as merrily as I could in an attempt to cheer him up. 'If the Germans don't get me first, he will!'

Wolf lapsed into silence as he continued to dwell on the encounter with Manoli.

And the horses ambled slowly onwards.

'That young shepherd was a brave kid,' I said eventually in an attempt to divert Wolf's thoughts. 'The one who was tortured. What happened to him?'

'He was my father,' said Wolf shortly and fell into silence. Then he added: 'My father would have killed Manoli if he had had the chance.'

'Not in the centre of Chania he wouldn't unless he was a fool. I'm sure he was no fool. Look, Wolf, you are a very brave *capitan*. No one doubts that, especially not your family. You did the right thing today. If you were arrested and locked up in Galatas Jail, it would help no one. Forget today happened, at least for now, and concentrate on helping me to escape. If Manoli denounces me, I don't want the Germans coming to the village to arrest you or your family.'

Wolf's head came up from his chest were it had been resting in gloom.

'You are right, my friend. Manoli won't come near the

village. It would place him in danger from all of my family. In Chania he is safe as he is in his own village. He will try to injure me another way but we will be on our guard. I will speak of this to my men.'

'Say that he attacked you but that I prevented the fight,' I suggested as a way to protect Wolf's sense of honour. 'I will say if I am asked that you saved my life.'

At last, Wolf grinned, twirled the ends of his moustaches and sat up straight in his saddle at last.

'You have the solution my friend. This I will do!'

Wolf was still subdued for the rest of our ride but, as his mood changed, so did that of the group and though there were no tall tales or songs or jokes, we arrived at the village in a lighter mood.

***

2001

He is haunting me, this Alexi. He was standing with his back against the wall of his cottage when I returned. The friend who looks like a hippie was with him.

I remember when the hippies first came to this town. They camped on the beach; they tied their hammocks to the tamerisk trees and slept in them each night under the stars. They washed in the sea – if they washed at all.

This was a small town then – little more than a village for the fishermen and their families. It was not like it is today with many bars and tavernas. Oh no, *katholu*, not at all. There was an *ouzeria* for the men to meet and drink together at the crossroads, although no respectable woman would be seen there. My cousin owned a taverna where his mother cooked good Cretan *stifado* and there was, I remember, another near the beach. The hippies came and they ate and drank; how they drank and – God forbid that I should remember – they sunbathed without clothes, yes, naked on the beach, just like the day they were born. The women of the town would never go there to be shocked by the sight of so much naked flesh. No, *katholu.* They swam from the beach of pebbles in the east and left the beach of sand to the strangers.

Panegyri! What can I do now? These two will not leave me alone. I like Alexi, although I am not so sure about his friend who has disfigured himself with studs and who wears earrings like a girl!

They invited me to go with them and to drink a coffee. I agreed as long as it was at Adoni's bar where everyone knows me and will not raise an eyebrow at me, a widow, alone together with two young men.

'You told me that Wolf is dead,' Alexi said to me. 'So is Stavro, you say. Lucky is in Athens and you don't know who Bunny is. Yes?'

I nodded an agreement. Better not to say anything. Fifi, when I consulted her, agreed that this was the best thing to do.

The one who looks like a hippie said something to Alexi who translated for me:

'Hennery just said to ask you about Simadis.'

'Ah,' I said and paused while I thought about my answer. Luckily, the girl brought the coffee which gave me some time for reflection. I think I prefer to talk of Simadis. Then I can avoid talking of my parents and sisters.

'Simadis! Simadis was what we call an enigma. You understand what I mean?' Alexi nodded and translated for the hippie. '*Ela na su po,* he was a man who was difficult to know and understand. He was a man of many moods. One day, sunshine; another, black clouds. You were never certain how he was going to react to you.

'Fifi and I we were small children, you understand. We saw things simply then, in black and white. We liked Simadis because he gave us a dog as a present, and other things too. We did not receive many presents. Presents were special. Later he carved for us a wooden doll from the wood of the mulberry tree which is soft and easy to work. But we feared him too because he could change his mood as quickly as a gust of wind changes direction. Lancaster we loved always. He was steady. He was special to us. We taught him to speak Cretan, you know. He showed us how to train our dog Spitha and he taught her tricks. His mood was always balanced like the scales. But when a dark mood came over Simadis he scared us. Then he was gruff and scowled at us and kicked the dog.

'Mama and many of the older women seemed to like him. With them he took the trouble to show a special face, to be charming and amiable. With us he did not bother to hide his moods. He could make them laugh with jokes and he knew how to wrap them around his little finger with flattering words and a soft voice like a cooing dove. They were sorry for him and kind to him because he cared for his mother who was poor and whose husband had been murdered by the Germans. I must say true: he was to her a good son.

'And yet....'

I tried to put into words the feeling that Simadis gave when he was in a bad mood. It was unsettling, frightening. 'We felt that a dark mood could break out at any moment and so we always felt that we must take care in his presence. We were on our guard'

'We say walking on eggshells'

'*Malista*. Children sense these things like animals do. The adults had their mind on many other things: their work, their children, money, business, the war....but we children had less to occupy us so we would observe and we knew to keep far away from when he was in a black mood.'

I felt I was getting into deep water, so I decided the change the subject.

'You know he was a wonderful dancer. So athletic, so manly. When Lucky played the lyra the women waited for

Simadis to get up on his legs and dance and they were so pleased if he picked on of them to be his partner.'

'I remember that my Grandfather describes how well he danced at the Feast of the Assumption,' Alexi said.

I paused for breath and Alexi began to talk rapidly in English to translate what I said for the hippie – what is his name? Hennery – I suppose I must remember to call him that.

'Wasn't Simadis a crack shot?'

'What means crack shot?'

'An expert with a gun.'

'Ah, yes. That's why they called him Simadis. This is what his name means. The other *andartes* admired him enormously because he could kill anything from a long distance and he knew no fear. They would follow him and obey his command. He was recklessly brave, I think. He challenged Wolf's right to command and this made Wolf angry as Wolf was the chosen leader, but the men preferred Wolf in any case as he was very brave, funny and popular. Simadis they admired and respected, but feared.

'Simadis had spent some years away from the village before the war. He was older than Wolf by four or five years, I think. No one knew what Simadis had done on the mainland of Greece. There were many rumours, which he never denied or confirmed, of ambushes and throat slitting. "Didn't he strangle a man with his bare hands?" they asked. "How many men did he kill single handed?" We never knew what was true and what was a lie or an exaggeration, but because he had this dark and secretive side to his character every story seemed possible.

'You could not be sure of what he was thinking. Always he wore a mask. He smiled often enough, but not with the eyes. His eyes were cold and dead. Perhaps once you have killed a man this is what happens to your eyes, no? But he was very brave, we all knew that and we forgave the rest.'

'My   grandfather   thought   that   Simadis   was   a

Communist.'

'*Malista*. Certainly. After the war Simadis disappeared again to the mainland. The Communists were very strong at that time. There was fierce fighting. It was war between brother and brother, cousin and cousin.'

'A civil war.'

'Yes that is so. A terrible time. Most people believed that Simadis had joined the Communist side. That life, the fighting life, suited him.'

Alexi leaned forward and fixed me with his beautiful blue eyes.

'I got the impression that he was interested in your sister, Elenitsa.'

Ah. I was waiting for this. I hoped that my chatter about Simadis would divert his mind but no, not at all. He is a determined young man, I will say that, like a dog with a bone.

'*Ela na sup o*. You could say that he was obsessed with Elenitsa. Of course, we children did not realise this at once but we observed that his eyes always rested on her for a long time when she was present and after a while we began to remark his attention. Little children notice these things; then Fifi and I would nudge each other and giggle – quietly of course, so that he would not notice and become angry with us. But always he looked at her. His eyes burned into her and while she was in the room he would always be telling jokes and laughing and charming the other women to get her to take notice of him.'

'He showed off,'

'*Alithea*. Yes. He worked hard to get her attention. He was like an actor before the audience. It was all calculated. But he was not allowed to give her presents. It was not the custom.'

'Perhaps that's why he gave them to you and Fifi!'

'Ah! Don't say that and break my heart!' This made me laugh and perhaps Alexi was right. 'He gave gifts to Mama instead: like birds that he had shot, bunches of fresh herbs or dittany he had picked in the high mountain or maybe a hard cheese he had from a shepherd. Mama did not like to accept these presents because she felt that his poor widowed mother needed them more than she did.

'And how did Elenitsa react to this?'

'Elenitsa was a very modest girl, you understand, very reserved, almost shy and I do not think that she was aware of his interest at first, but he did not try very hard to disguise his feelings and when she became aware of them she was, I think, uncomfortable.

'He made excuses to visit our house every day, and, if Elenitsa was not indoors, he would go to find her in the *kipo* where she was weeding or watering the vegetables. He would even help her carry pitchers of water from the spring! This was not man's work, no, not at all, and no other man did this except for your grandfather. At first, Elenitsa ignored Simadis without being impolite, but later she tried to avoid being in his company. Once or twice she hid below in the storeroom.'

'With my Grandfather.'

'Well, I expect he was there.'

Oh. *Panegyri!* Now we are on dangerous ground!

'So she did not avoid my grandfather?'

'She was comfortable with him because she had nursed him. She was accustomed to him like a brother. And then, he was handsome like you, Alexi' – that made the hippie snigger – 'the same pleasant manner, the same blue eyes and identical nose and his temper was neither hot or cold.'

'*Yassou!*'

'But here is Adoni so I must leave you now,'

God be praised, Adoni has saved me in the nick of time from this interrogation. I feel that I have said enough, perhaps more than I should. Am I singing like a canary?

***

1941

'We make the best wine in the world!' declared Wolf, who was never downhearted for long, as he took the steps to the terrace of the *spiti* two at a time at the crack of dawn one morning in September. 'It tastes of apricots and figs, raisins and almonds, strawberries, geraniums and more. It is ruby red or rich tawny. It is nectar. It is ambrosia!!!'

'You never exaggerate, Wolf, do you?' I challenged him with a grin.

'Look at those grapes,' he demanded pointing above his head the where fat bunches of round, black grapes dangled heavily from from the criss cross poles which supported them. 'Are they not perfect?'

I had to agree. One long, thin, gnarled stem reached up many feet from the ground to the canopy of meandering branches and leaves above our heads, which bowed and twisted under the weight of the substantial bunches of fruit. It seemed hardly possible that one slender stem could provide enough nourishment for the bounty above us. The sun had ripened the grapes until they smelt of honey and shone with stickiness.

'Crete has been famous for its wines since ancient times.'

'I expect you will tell me that King Minos drugged the Minotaur with his best vintage!'

'Only God knows, but I can tell you that we grow many different kinds of grapes in our villages here in Crete – Mavro, Aspro, Retsina. Look around you – every house has its own grapevine as well as vines in the fields and they are all wonderful!'

'Wolf, mate, you could sell ice to the Eskimos!'

'Forget Eskimos whoever they are. We have every kind of grape here: grapes for wine, grapes for eating, which, as you know, are green and sweet as honey. We also have small, dark grapes which we dry in wicker baskets in the heat of the sun. They become brown and chewy and very sweet like *carameles* and we eat them in winter.'

'They sound like raisins to me. My Ma puts them in cakes.'

'But the best grapes are for making wine. And wine is for drinking. It makes you happy and ready to sing and dance. It helps you forget your worries. That's what it's meant for. And to get drunk! Oh, yes! It's no use for anything else! And,' added Wolf, 'I hope to press at least 400 litres this year unless the bloody Germans steal the lot from me!'

The papery leaves of the grapevine above us gave dappled shade to the terrace all summer and now the fruit would give us wine to drink all through the winter. Today, the grapes were at their absolute best, ready to be picked and pressed.

'We must pick now at this moment without delay before it is too hot, otherwise the grapes will spoil.' Wolf instructed.

It was a family affair, like most things in the village Everyone took part and had a job to do, even little children like Poppy and Fifi.

We men spent the morning perched precariously on rickety wooden ladders cutting the stems of the fruit with sharp knives and letting the bunches fall down with a gentle plop into the wicker baskets below. I could just spy men and women hard at work on the other terraces too and small figures in the vineyards below us working along the rows like ants, cutting bunches to pile their baskets with fruit. The *kipo*, which measured more than two *stremata*, was planted with straight lines of vine bushes, heavy with dark wine grapes.

A donkey waiting to be loaded with baskets was tethered in the shade of an olive tree and nibbled idly at the dried grass. Old Arkelos sat beside him leaning his back against the tree trunk observing the younger and spryer members of his family as they toiled with bent backs to harvest the crop that he owned, and from time to time issuing a volley of insructions to them in a deep, gruff voice which could have carried across two valleys. The families moved through the vines like a swarm of locusts and the buckets grew heavier with their purple cargo until the sun had passed the meridian and it was time to load the baskets of fruit and for the donkey to haul them away.

Up on the terraces of the *spitia* the glare in our eyes blinded us and droplets of sweat from the heat rolled saltily into our eyes and soaked our shirts until they were wringing wet. Dust and twigs attached themselves to our sweaty arms and branches tore at our skin till the blood ran and mingled with the sweet juice and salty sweat.

Our girls placed the full baskets of grapes on their heads and transported them into the cool cellar where the round vat constructed of stone awaited them.The children swept away the refuse into piles which they put into buckets and threw away onto the rubbish heap.

We had picked our grapes by midday and, with relief, removed ourselves into the blessed coolness of the wine cellar.

We spread thick layers of thyme branches onto the bottom of the vat and then the girls tumbled the rich, black and green grapes on top of them.

'Now off with your boots and your pants!' cried Wolf and we stripped to our underpants to a chorus of giggles from the unmarried girls and spicy comments from the married women .

'*Panegyri*, what muscles! What thighs!'

'*Oichi*. He is bandy!'

'He is hung like a donkey! What pleasure for his wife!'

'He has no wife. Do you want him for yourself?'

Buckets of water had been lined up along the wall and

we plunged our feet and legs into them and splashed the water over our arms and faces. It was cool and refreshing after the blistering heat.

'Bah! Dirt improves the taste!' muttered one of the old men who had come to observe and offer his opinion, but not to help.

Wolf, quickly followed by Lucky, Bunny and Stavro launched himself over the side of the vat and into the mountain of juicy grapes. I hesitated for a moment, took a deep breath and I too vaulted onto the juicy mass. The grapes were soft as a pillow and slippery as mud. Skins exploded under the soles of my feet as I slithered into the fruit. The skins popped and juice squirted between my toes and covered the bottom of my legs. The twiggy stems scratched and tickled my feet. Then the juice began to trickle and then run, rich, blood-like, purple, and finally flood down the stone lip of the spout and into the waiting tub.

The sweet heady scent of grape juice and sugar was overpowering. While we trampled the grapes, Poppy, Fifi and the other children ran backwards and forwards, carrying pitchers of the purple juice from the press to the cool back room where the tall earthenware urns were waiting for the wine.

Treading grapes is hard physical work. The constant knees up, knees down movement, like marching on the spot on the parade ground, with an energetic grinding of the feet on the down step, quickly makes the muscles of your thighs start to ache and your feet sore.

Mushing the grapes to pulp was easy at first, but after that it got more difficult as the pulp became dryer and the juice dwindled to a trickle.

'What we must do now,' stated Wolf, 'is to push the remaining pulp against the wall here and press it hard. This will allow the juice to run freely into the centre of the floor and towards the lip of the press.'

It's not surprising that we slid and slipped against each other and fell into the precious liquid in a tangle of limbs with yells from us and shrieks of merriment from the women. At last, we clambered out matted with pips and skin and twigs and purple and sticky with liquid and, as I licked the gooey liquor off myself, I felt that I was tasting all the goodness and bounty of summer.

'We have made more than 400 litres!' shouted Wolf later. 'It's a record! And it is going to be good wine! In two months, God willing, we will sit together on the terrace of the *spiti*, look at the moon and drink the first glasses of our new wine!'

A month or so later on a spectacularly wet evening our whole village, men, women and children, set off, despite the driving rain and the gusty wind to trek to the raki still or *rakokazano* . The raki still was illegal, because raki could only be made under licence which had to be bought – 'And who was going to pay for that?' said Wolf – and anyway no one cared about the law! A spiralling wisp of smoke signalled to us where to go. The secret raki still was hidden – or not so hidden – in a stone hut on one of the high terraces above the village. The villagers were very merry already with anticipation and excitement, joking and chattering like birds about the *glendi* to come, despite the whipping they received from the wind and rain as they forced themselves upwards through the gusts and mud.

The hut was partly hidden from view, partly derelict and built of large stone slabs. It belonged to Nektarios. There were no windows, just wooden shutters which were barred against the wind and rain, but the rain still penetrated through gaps in the bamboo lining of the roof. This did nothing to dampen the exhilaration and exuberance of the group crammed into the hut. The floor was roughly stamped earth. A few old car tyres were stacked against the wall and I noticed more than one *andarte* eyeing them speculatively, for tyres made good soles for repairing damaged boots. Along the wall, old timber planks were stacked, along with scythes and spades and hoes encrusted with soil and in various stages of rust and decrepitude as well as coils of rope and wire: all the paraphernalia of a farm store.

And in the centre of the room stood the object of our veneration: the large copper boiler.

Nektarios and a group of companions had been hard at work for some time before our arrival, and the boiler was already hot from the bonfire beneath and steam hissed from the funnels which projected from it and warmed the night air.

The planks were soon disposed on trestles and tables set up. The women, who had not accompanied us empty-handed, began to set out clay pots and wicker baskets of food.

Making raki is an excuse for a party and while the steam condensed and the warm raki began to fall drop by drop into glass containers, the village settled itself on benches and stools around the table and prepared for a feast.

The room was warm and moist and smoky from the bonfire and cigarettes and soon I forgot the chill of the stormy evening outside. The air smelt rich, spicy and aromatic with alcohol fumes.

Nektarios and his group of expert distillers sampled the liquid regularly as they analysed it for strength and purity. There was no shortage of eager helpers. Comments flew among them about the level of the alcohol content and the density of taste. And there was much loud debate about it.

I could soon see that this was a ritual deeply rooted in the ancient traditions of Crete – as old as the land itself. Perhaps the exact same process took place in Minoan times in the vast labyrinths of Knossos.

'Did you know that the word 'raki' comes from the Ancient Greek, *rakos*?' cried Wolf. 'My teacher at school told me that. It means rubbish! Ha! Ha!'

'So what about *tsikoudia,* know all?' I challenged him.

'I know that too! It comes from the word *tsikoudi* meaning the shavings of the fruit and the pips.'

'I bow to your superior knowledge, my friend. There is nothing more to be said.'

By now, half an oil drum had been erected on its side, supported by metal legs. Its bowl had been filled with charcoal. A side of goat was roasting on a spit above it and on the wire below large pork steaks were grilling, oozing fat, and skewers of lamb rolled in oregano. Tiny glasses of the new raki were passed around for our opinion and bottles of tawny red country wine appeared on the table. The merrymaking had begun.

'I thought we had pressed all the grapes,' I said. 'Were these put to one side especially for this?'

'*Katholu.* Not at all,' said Nektarios who sat down beside me and wiped the drops of sweat from his forehead with a grimy rag and shared with me a flask of his new wine. 'This is what is left over after the grapes have been pressed in the *patitiria.* Do you remember?'

I nodded as I recalled the sloppy heaps of brown mush; leaves and pips and stalks which remained after we had extracted the grape juice just a month before.

'*Lipon,* we put it in barrels and there we let it lie until now. This is the *strafila.* In that time it ferments. Then it is ready for us to use to make the raki. Here in this *kazani.* As you can see, we are boiling it over a fire of thyme and other shrubs to give a good flavour.

'So, when it is in those glass containers and has cooled down, we can drink it. Is that what the party is for?'

'No. No. *Katholu.* We must throw away some of the first liquid. It is no good. Then we must wait for the alcohol to get stronger.'

'How do you know when it is ready?' I asked.

'We know from its taste,' replied Wolf.

'And experience.' continued Nektarios. 'Then we put

the rest back in the *kazano* and heat it again. We call the first 10% heads, next 30% is hearts and the last 20% is tails! Hearts is about 70 degrees. It is far too strong and dangerous for the head, as I can tell you, from drinking it when I was young and foolish! That is why we put the water with it so that we reduce the strength and potency to about 40 degrees.'

'How do you know when it is 40 degrees?'

'We know. We can tell by taste.'

'So you have to keep testing.'

'*Malista.* Yes. That is why you must have a hard head!'

'Or maybe you will fall down asleep before the evening is ended!' added Wolf.

'I have woken up on the floor in front of the boiler more than once before now! *Tsigia!*' admitted Nektarios.

Elenitsa and Tonia approached the table with plates of pork steaks and *souvlaki*. Fifi and Poppy followed with country sausages and pots of warm beans. The women carved the bread into slices for us to use as makeshift plates and to absorb the oil and the juices from the meat. Elenitsa smiled at me warmly as she passed. I noticed how soft the planes of her face looked in the glow of the oil lamps as she served the food. She looked happy and relaxed and serene.

Then Lucky put his lyra under his chin and began to play a haunting melody. The stones seemed to listen and then dance and the intoxication began.

CHAPTER 15

2001

'Well, you have about 8 days left!' announced Hennery, as he came up to our loungers on the wide sandy beach and shook himself, like the shaggy dog he resembled, all over my blockbuster novel. When I complained, he just laughed and flopped down on the lounger beside me. 'And a lot of loose ends to tie up, man.'

'Very loose ends. So what do we have so far?'

'We have found the house.'

'Which is abandoned and empty and really no help. I don't get the impression that anyone has lived there for years.'

'We have found the village,' said Hennery opening a tinnie and swatting of a fly in one fluid movement 'Want a slug of the amber nectar' he asked. I shook my head.

'But there's no one living there, either.' I continued, 'It's abandoned too; everyone has moved away.'

'I suppose there's no work – or excitement. Believe me, this place is beautiful and great for a holiday and everyone we have met has been kindness itself, but I wouldn't want to live up there with no jobs, no money, and no internet! No way!'

'Just olives, sheep and goats which are really hard work and don't pay that much. But at least we have an idea of the place where Grandfather was hidden. That's important to me.'

'So how does that help you?' said Hennery with a belch. 'Heck this stuff is fizzy, man!' he said belching for a second time.

'Because at least I can visualise it now. I can picture his very hiding place. I've seen the earthenware urns. And the bread oven, don't forget that!'

'Yeah, where he hid his boots!'

'It's just helpful Hennery to picture the layout of the house and the hamlet and you have to admit that it's very picturesque. I like the rough stone and the terracotta tiles,'

'And the not so whitewashed walls! I took lots of photos, man.'

'Good. I like the atmosphere too – kind of peaceful. Good for the soul.'

'Don't you get all philosophical on me, man. Soul indeed. I suppose it's because you had a uni education?'

'As if you didn't! Any way, at least I've got a soul – somewhere.'

'I never got the impression that the old man had much soul – hewn out of granite, I thought. He made no secret of the fact that he didn't like me.' declared Hennery without acrimony.

'Didn't understand your lifestyle, mate. Up late, looking unwashed and hairy, that's what he thought. Not to mention the earrings which nearly gave him an apoplexy! Thought you were a right layabout. You two were chalk and cheese.'

'Instead of which I'm a genius, man, and on my way to my first million!' Hennery made it a joke but I more than half believed him. 'He liked you though, didn't he?'

'In his own fashion, perhaps.'

Hennery rolled over on the lounger with all the grace of a large Labrador and toppled over into the sand. 'Shit' he said jumping up and shaking sand off all over me. 'Hey, I've had enough of this. Let's go up to the village one more time and have another snoop round in case we missed anything. How about it?' I had no objections so we cleaned up, put on our togs and took to the car.

'He left you the Double L vineyard in his will, didn't he?' said Hennery as we drove up the winding switchback road. 'Lancaster and Lukos. You know that's a strange spelling of Lucas. I wonder why he did that.'

'Just to be different, I guess. To stand out from the crowd. 'I said, paying close attention to the road and not to Hennery.

'Did your Ma mind? That you got the vineyard, I mean.' he continued.

'Not really. She wasn't interested; or wasn't allowed to be interested. She said he always ignored any suggestions she made.'

'As a mere woman. I'm being deliberately sexist here, Alex!'

'She had a good brain, my Ma. Went to college and all that. But because she was his daughter he took the view that she had to obey him, I would think.'

'No sweat!'

'Anyway she is a director of the company and has been for years, so she doesn't lose out financially. It's curious to think that he changed from farming to cultivating a vineyard because he got the idea all about vines from living here.'

'This is really olive country, though. There must be thousands on this mountain alone and some of them look really old and gnarled; some of the trunks must be two metres around.'

'Planted by the Turks, I expect and they were here 400 years, so they must be ancient. The guidebook refers to several one–thousand-year-old olive trees. We can see one on the way back, if you want. It's outside Kandanos.'

'Do you think he considered farming olives before he decided on a vineyard?'

'He made wine here. He made raki. He picked olives, but I suspect he chose grapes because there was a better market for wine. The olive was not much known in NZ in those days and everyone likes a tipple, a glass of wine. Yeah, I think he saw more potential and profit in it. And he was lucky that our land at home has the right soil, aspect and climate to produce a bustin' red.'

'I'll drink to that! And look there's the village vineyard itself, over there, although it's mightily overgrown.'

'Let's take a closer look.'

'And photos,' stated Hennery lifting the small state of the art digital camera from his rucksack.

So we did. The vines were in poor shape and hardly pruned at all. I could not identify a variety, but the soil when I ran a small clod through my fingers was reddish clay, quite friable and seemed rich. The gnarled vine stem which climbed up onto the terrace of the family home looked strong but very old. I think its roots tapped into an underground spring because there was no one to water it and yet it thrived. Wolf had said it gave good wine and I regretted that I would not be around in September to watch the grape harvest, if there was one any more, in this village.

We sat on the low terrace wall and looked down the valley to the sea through an ocean of waving silver grey olives.

'Poppy says you look like the Lancaster she knew. Do you think she's right?' said Hennery.

'Possibly. I'm tall, I'm blond. I have blue eyes.'

'And the Lancaster nose. Definitely the same nose. Dead ugly, man. Perhaps he saw himself in you?'

'My nose is aquiline I'll have you know Hennery, you philistine. It's ... er ... refined, slightly long, I'll agree, but not ugly at all!'

'Sounds like you're describing a wine, man!'

'Did the old man see himself in me? Could be. He trained me to take over the vineyard. He was insistent about that. If I hadn't, maybe I would have ended up a bum like you Hennery, mate!' I made a false punch at him Hennery dodged and pretended to fall off the ledge.

'Thanks a bunch. But, you know, it put him in the driving seat because you were very young, weren't you? '

'When I started learning the business you mean?'

'Exactly.'

'I don't know that I had much choice. I was expected to work in the vineyard in the holidays or in the press or the bottling plant. I got paid, actually. I got to know the business inside out in a practical way. I got to know the lads in the fields and the girls on the conveyer belt. And everyone knew me. I had to follow him around from about the age of twelve.'

'I think it gave him power over you. He wanted complete control.'

'If so, it was probably a reaction to the fact that he had no control over his future when he was hidden here.'

'No. Agreed. It must have been frightening, man. I don't think I'd have liked it. In fact, I don't think I'd have coped at all well.'

'No one knows, really, what they are capable of until they are faced with it, do they, Hennery?'

'He was completely lost really, no way of contacting home, no way of knowing if he'd ever get home again.' said Hennery, thoughtfully.

'The diary is quite upbeat most of the time, but, yeah, I agree with you, Hennery, his life was dangerous and uncertain every day. He never knew if he would be discovered or run into a German patrol. He could have been killed or arrested and imprisoned at any time and he had the well-being and safety of the family to think about too. Always living with the thought that his very presence condemned the family, the village even, to terrifying reprisals. I think he was very aware of that and he was very lonely at times. He had no one.'

'He had the girls in the family. Mama was kind to him.'

'At a distance.'

'Wolf was his friend and the other brothers too.'

'Yeah, he really admired Wolf. They got on really well.'

'But then again Simadis was always lurking in the background. Very unpredictable. A malevolent force, like a scorpion lurking in the shadows ready to sting and poison. I saw one yesterday, you know, in the bathroom, so I bashed it. It wasn't going to get me, the bastard!'

'Simadis must be late eighties now so he's probably dead. Young Felix could tell us a lot; he was around all the time. But who is he and how do we find him? I'd like to know if Tonia and Elenitsa are alive. I'd like to find out what happened to them. Especially Elenitsa. And all the others: the list is endless.'

'I'll have to talk to Poppy again. Squeeze what I can out of her.'

'You could always go to Athens and try to make contact with Lucky. He's famous. Should be easy to track him down.'

'Back to Poppy again.'

'All roads lead to Poppy.'

***

1941

Mama roused us all as the first light streaked across the smoky sky. She gave each of us a cup of warm water and a handful of rusks accompanied by voluble instructions about our tasks for the day. Chattering like birds, the females bustled about as preparations began for the first day of the olive harvest.

It was the custom that the families of the village joined together to help each other each day of the harvest. Nektarios, Mama and the four girls were joined by Wolf, Lucky, Bunny and Stavro. Even their aged Grandfather, leader of the *andartes*, Old Arkelos, came to watch over the work and offer endless advice and instruction. Young Felix, and his mother and father, his father's brother along with his hatchet-faced wife, arrived laden with tools and sacks, baskets, food and drink. They chattered at the tops of their voices as they trotted along, swapping gossip and old familiar jokes and their laughter bounced around the valley, the noise echoing off the cliffs.

The men marched into the olive groves, led by Old Arkelos and Nektarios. They carried special cudgels curved at one end with which to beat the olive drupes from the branches of the trees and home-made triangular wooden ladders tucked over their shoulders and under their armpits, with which to climb into the tree in order to shake the branches.

The women and children followed with the nets, baskets and sacks. They spread the nets under each tree. Nektarios propped the ladder against the first old gnarled twisted tree trunk and climbed it. He started to batter the branches with his cudgel to loosen the drupes which tumbled to the ground and onto the nets. The women and girls collected the fruit into wicker baskets. When each basket was full the children held open the sacks while the women poured in the olives from each full basket. The work was back-breaking and hard but the women were cheerful and sang old traditional songs as they worked.

Slowly, the weak wintery sun peeped from behind the mountain peaks and little by little rose into the grey sky. By the mid-morning break, the sky was blue and the air was warm.

The men stopped work and gathered together to share a bottle of raki between them. Old Arkelos began reciting one of the epic poems he loved, while Wolf and his brothers winked shamelessly at each other behind his back and mimicked him: they had heard it all before. But before long they joined in and added a true Greek chorus to the old man's words. Nektarios and some of the other men seemed to be arguing, shouting loudly and waving around their arms about. Their antics caught my eye but they were just talking politics which they always do with great passion and much hot air. Mama passed round pitchers of water and the girls lay on the ground groaning with relief as they stretched their aching backs.

Eventually, Tonia and Elenitsa hoisted themselves onto their elbows and whispered together. Tonia animated as always and Elenitsa serene and dreamy. Suddenly, I felt an overwhelming desire to join them. I picked up a pitcher of water and wandered casually over to where they were reclining.

'More water?' I asked. They sat up and offered me their tin mugs to refill and gestured to me to sit with them.

'This is hard work,' I commented. It was a lame thing to say but it was all I could think of at that moment.

'Yes, it is,' replied Tonia.

'But necessary,' added Elenitsa seriously. 'Without the oil we cannot live.'

'Some of these trees are very old,' explained Tonia waving her arm to indicate the gnarled and twisted trees. 'They were planted before the Turks,' she made a face, 'and maybe even before the Venetians. Papa says they are perhaps a thousand years old. Look how round are the trunks. Elenitsa and I cannot join our hands around them they are too wide.'

'Are these good olives?' I asked.

'*Vevea*. The best, of course. Here we make the best, the purest olive oil in all Crete. You have tasted it. You know this.' I didn't think I could tell the difference, but I didn't say so.

'I don't think I ever tasted olive oil before I came here.' I replied with what tact I could.

'You mean you don't cook with it in your country. You don't put it with *horta*!' cried Tonia, opening her eyes wide in astonishment.

'No. Not In my country.' I shook my head and made a face of apology. The girls exchanged glances mixed of amazement and horror and then giggled.

'Then what do you use?'

'My Mother uses lard usually. Or sometimes butter.' I

explained what butter and lard were only to receive grimaces of disgust and wrinkled noses.

'*Po, po, po. Kako.*'exclaimed Tonia.

'I do not like,' remarked Elenitsa more gently. 'The oil we use for many things – for cooking and for our lamps. It is very important. We eat the olives as you know.'

I picked a fallen olive from the net and tried it. It was bitter.

'This is very nasty,' I said.

'Ah! That is because you cannot eat it raw. First you must prepare the olive.'

'How do you do that?'

'We wait until the olives have turned from green, as they are now, until they are the black. Then we put them in salt and water in a barrel. We change the water for many days and after some weeks we put a heavy stone on top to keep the olives under the brine. We add more salt when we must. In the spring the olives will be sweet, not bitter and ready to eat.

'How can you live without the olive in your country?' asked Elenitsa. 'We use it for everything. When we and our sisters were born our mother washed us in water and salt and then rubbed our skin all over with oil before she wrapped us in cloth.'

'What you don't have you don't miss!' I joked.

'What means this?' asked Elenitsa looking at me sideways through long lashes which curved and brushed her cheeks like the fronds of a fern.

'Well. We don't have olives in New Zealand, as far as I know. We don't know that they are good so we don't want them ....' I faltered as I watched those wonderful lashes brush Elenitsa's olive skin. A tendril of black hair had freed itself from Elenitsa's headscarf and it curled onto the silky skin of her neck where I saw a light sheen of sweat. I inhaled slowly and deeply and I could detect a mixed aroma of cedarwood and lemon which had collected in her white apron, her dusty black skirt and dingy patterned blouse and on her skin. I felt the scent envelop me and overwhelm me like a wave.

My head began to pound. A rush like a stream in flood set my temples tingling. Beads of sweat to broke out onto my forehead. I suddenly felt light-headed and dizzy. The trees seemed to dance before my eyes and the daylight flickered on and off like a torch sending Morse code. A sensation welled up from within my body setting my heart beating faster and faster until I felt hot and drunk. All this lasted only no more than ten seconds but it was an intensely powerful sensation. I had a sudden overpowering desire to take Elenitsa in my arms and kiss her lips, run my fingers over her skin, remove her headscarf and let her curls coil around my fingers. Instead, I pulled myself together with a huge effort of will took out my tobacco tin rolled a cigarette and lit it, taking a long draught and allowing the smoke to calm my body.

'Why is your olive oil so good?' I asked weakly.

'You must ask my father.'

I took the opportunity to stand up although my legs felt weak as jelly. 'I will. I'll go and find him now,' I said – and I escaped.

'We are high here on the mountain.' said Nektarios. 'Mountain olives give better oil than the ones on the plain or near the sea where they absorb the salt from the air. Our trees like the rocky soil. They like the moisture from the morning dew and the dry heat in the afternoons. Look at Old Arkelos, aged eighty-two and strong as a bull. Why? Because each day he takes a rusk or two and soaks them in olive oil, sprinkles them with rigani or perhaps thyme, some sea salt and eats them. Sometimes, he drinks a raki glass of olive oil also. My great grandfather was the priest in my village and he lived to be more than one hundred years. He rubbed himself every day in oil, he ate olives, and he drank good oil.'

'How long have the olives been in your family, Nektarios?'

'I got the trees from my father and he from his father and his father before him. My grandfather told me that our family had lived on this land and looked after the olive trees before the Turks drove out the Venetians and that was many hundreds of years ago.'

'How many trees do you have?'

'Maybe 500. Each tree is part of my family. Each tree has been around for 1000 years. He is an old man, like my ancestor. He has seen many things, many generations. You cut him down. The wind tears off his branches, the sun or frost or snow scorches his leaves. They will not kill him. He will not die. There is always a rebirth.' Nektarios, usually a reserved man, much like Elenitsa in character, spoke passionately as he talked of his olives and looked at the trees fondly. 'Anyway the trees need us and we need them. The old people, they like to rest under an olive tree. They always choose the olive tree, not the fig or the mulberry or chestnut, always the olive'

'Why?'

'Because it has just the right amount of light and air. The rustle of the wind in the leaves keeps you cool. The shade stops you burning in the sun. You can fall asleep under it and dream good dreams. Another tree, like the fig will give you the headache.'

'Why do you store the oil in those big urns?' Those earthenware urns, tall enough to hide one of Ali Baba's forty thieves, had been my close companions as long as I had been hidden in the store room

'It is better for the oil to be stored in the dark and the clay takes all the acid from the olives. You can put oil in the same urn each year for more than a man's lifetime and nothing will happen to it. It will not turn bad.' said Nektarios in his gentle, quiet manner and smiling at the thought, like a fond parent of a treasured child. 'I am proud of my oil. It is the best round here. Everyone agrees this.'

I could not tell whether this was true or not as my palate was not well enough developed to identify the nuances like a connoisseur although I liked the fruity and spicy taste. Cod liver oil, which my Ma used to force down me to keep me regular, as she put it, is all we have in New Zealand and this oil was definitely not it.

'You must roll the liquid round on your tongue,' explained Nektarios, 'and relish the flavour when you dip the bread into it.'

'I can tell the difference in colour: bright green, shimmering gold or dull yellow. Maybe one day in the future – if there is a future – I will learn to appreciate it properly.' I said.

Nektarios continued. 'The oil varies from year to year, you know. It depends on how much rain comes, how hot is the summer, or how strong is the wind which, as you know, can be very fierce here, or if we get disease. There are good years and bad years, as God wills.'

Yes, I thought. You cannot control the elements.

For the rest of the morning I had to will myself not to stare at Elenitsa all the time. I felt as if we had met for the first time and each time I caught the perfume of cedarwood and lemon I felt breathless and something stirred within.

Concentrate hard, divert your mind, I lectured myself, and I hit out at the olive tree above me with such tremendous force that it sent down a shower of drupes and branch broke off – which earned me a disapproving glance from those around me. Once, I hit Wolf by mistake.

'*Malaka!*' yelled Wolf. 'What you do, you cuckold!'

After that I focused as hard as I could on hitting the branches with accuracy and just the right amount of force while missing Wolf aloft on his ladder.

Still, I could not prevent my eyes from searching out Elenitsa, drawn like an iron filing towards a magnet or, better said, like a bee towards the flower. I could not prevent myself from dwelling on the sinuous curve of her rump and the apple-like swelling of her breast as she bent and stretched over the baskets of fruit.

After the sun had passed the midway stage on its journey from east to west, Mama judged it the time to call the girls to help her unpack a large wicker basket of bread and hard white cheese, hard boiled eggs and bowls of olives. She laid a large shallow dish of potato cooked with onions and cheese on the nets and distributed spoons amongst the family. The other families had come similarly prepared with cheese and *spanakopita* pies. The wife of Old Arkelos contributed a large round baking tin of bean stew with herbs. The scent of oregano and onions and garlic floated among the trees as each family ate and shared their food. A flagon of pink country wine appeared and was sloshed into mugs among the men while the women drank the warm water.

Later, we rested, cushioned by the fallen olive leaves and our backs supported by the olive trunks. The terrible two curled up like kittens against their mother. Old Arkelos resumed reciting his epic poem, continuing from where he had left off earlier in the day.

'How many more verses?' I asked Wolf.

'Five more hours, at least!' he replied with a wink and a twirl of his moustachios.

I lay back and observed Elenitsa. I saw her with new eyes. I saw Elenitsa for the first time as women in her own right. Before this, with Mama and her sisters she had merely formed part of the women of the house. I had not seen her as an individual.

Now, at this moment, every feature and characteristic took on a new brightness as if a dirty painting had been cleaned to reveal fresh, sparkling, brilliant colours.

If, previously, I had considered her at all it was not as a woman with any claim to beauty but just as a collection of features: eyes, mouth, chin cheeks. Now I was captivated by her full curling lips and her dark expressive eyes which promised passion. Yet her eyes and her proud, thick eyebrows and firm pointed chin also held a warning. They said: I am a Cretan woman: courageous, strong, honourable, pious and proud.

The gods do not smile on those who pursue such a woman with ignoble intentions. I was confronted with a dangerous path. I could choose it or reject it; follow my senses or contain them. This family had saved my life and put their lives at risk for me. I decided that I would uproot the burgeoning seedling of my desire and crush it under my heel before it had a chance to grow any more.

After a rest, the hard work began once more and we worked until the light began to fade. A willing family can harvest a lot of olives in a day, but it is back-breaking work. The old folk shuffled home bent double and fell into bed too tired even to eat or undress, while the young girls spent hours complaining and groaning in the lamplight as they attempted to pick the splinters out of their fingers which had come from scooping up the fruit from among the fallen leaves.

I had started the day feeling battle-fit, but by dusk even the muscles in my arms, neck and shoulders ached and so did my back.

But, despite my recent good intentions, I could not resist offering to carry Elenitsa's basket as dusk fell as we returned to the hamlet. She refused.

'It is not necessary,' she said. 'It is not man's work. Take a ladder.' she ordered gruffly, not meeting my eyes.

The olive picking took four days of back-breaking work. But jokes and songs, good humour and laughter, food, wine and a sense of camaraderie helped the time pass quickly. I tried not to look at Elenitsa too often. She kept away from me and always seemed to be in the company of her mother or sisters, as if she too sensed that something had changed between us and she needed their protection.

When all was finished, some of the sacks of olives were loaded onto the donkeys that the Germans had not stolen. The rest were loaded onto carts. I joined Wolf and his brothers and some of the other young men and together we yoked ourselves to these carts. Then we all set off for the press.

***

2001

'Everyone said I was the prettiest girl in the village!' Poppy giggled, rolled her eyes and lifted her chin. 'It used to make my sister, Fifi, so mad because she wanted to be the prettiest girl in the village but no, it was me. Later, after the war when we were growing into young women there was no shortage of young men who wanted to visit our house, take us for walks in the olive groves and even marry us. Oh yes!'

Poppy did not need much persuading to talk about herself after a little gentle persuasion in the form of a gift of a large box of sticky cakes from the bakery and I encouraged her. This was a way into the past, I thought and I hoped that I would then be able to persuade her to talk more about my grandfather's relationship with the family. Hennery had decided to take himself off to explore Chania, so I was left alone to tackle Poppy once again.

'*Ela na sup o*, Tonia was the practical joker. She had a great sense of humour. You would find peas in your pillow. She had put them there. Or seeds inside your blouse which made you itch. She once put a frog in my bed. It jumped out at me and I believe that I jumped even higher from shock. Certainly my scream was heard all over the village! That was how she was. She was a great flirt too. But really she loved only one man and did it to make him jealous because he hid his real feelings. Mama often scolded her, but not too much. We all loved her.'

'What sort of girl was Elenitsa? Tell me about her.'

'My oldest sister? She was soft, like a dove, and gentle. She was not a chatterbox like Tonia. She sat quietly either sewing or making lace. She preferred to listen.

Elenitsa was a serious girl like my mother. We were the naughty ones. My Mother sometimes said that we were the children of the Devil, but she did not mean it, of course. Your Grandfather called us the terrible two. We were always playing jokes and laughing and running and dancing. No, not good girls at all. But Elenitsa was grave and sensible and thoughtful and obedient too. She never gave my mother any trouble, not like Fifi and me. And although she liked your grandfather very much she always behaved with dignity. But you could see she liked him and he liked her.

And we watched them. They would glance at each other sideways when they thought no one was watching, but we were watching. Sometimes their hands would touch, as if by accident, and we would nudge each other and try hard not to giggle when we saw them. Many times, he carried Elenitsa's pitcher of water from the spring to the house. He helped her spread the washing on the bushes. He helped her weed the *kipo* and collect the vegetables into sacks. We laughed and giggled because this was not men's work, you understand, but he did these things because he liked her and because he was grateful that she had cared for him when he was ill. He watched her in the afternoon when she was making the lace or when she was weaving at the loom.'

'Was she pretty?'

'Pretty? Not like me! She had a beautiful smile. I remember her smile; and her teeth were white. But when she sat quietly her expression looked a little fierce, like the hawk. Her eyes slanted like almonds and they were brown. The eyebrows above were straight, not bushy like mine. Her chin was pointed, her hair was dark, of course, like mine, thick and curly and in those days we grew our hair long. Elenitsa's hair fell to her waist like a waterfall. Now we can go to the hairdressers and have it cut, as I do. ' At this Poppy tossed her curly and coiffed head. 'This is how my Vassili liked it.' Her eyes filled quickly with tears. 'Ah Vassili ...'

I knew that if her thought continued in this direction there would be more tears and expressions of regret at the lack of sons. To divert her, I said quickly;

'It was when you were picking the olives that my Grandfather first became interested in Elenitsa wasn't it?'

'*Vevea*, and my Father and Mother noticed something also.'

'What happened?'

'I think it was because he always helped her more than the others. He always seemed to be by her side. One morning she overbalanced and fell from a ladder and he caught her in his arms. I think he held her too long. My mother noticed this and she told my father, I think. Elenitsa was frightened that they would be angry with him and send him away, but even then she said nothing about her feelings. Then they spoke with him.'

'And were they angry?'

'No. My father loved him. "You are the son I will never have," he told him. It was my mother's great shame and disappointment that she had no sons, only daughters. Just like me.'

I held my breath as we approached dangerous ground once more and waited for Poppy's tears to fall. But Poppy was in the grip of the past. 'And four daughters too! One after the other, and each time she hoped and prayed for a son. She was very upset about it. It was a great grief and disappointment to her. My father accepted Fate, for he was that sort of man. So he took your grandfather for a private talk while they walked in the olive groves. I followed them. They did not see me for I was clever and hid in the trees so that they could not see me, but I could hear their talk. My Father said: "Tell me, with truth, if you have feelings for my daughter Elenitsa".'

'*Ela na su po*, you know when we are young, we are passionate, we are obsessed and we want the world. Lancaster told my father that Elenitsa was the moon and stars to him. My mother asked Elenitsa about her feelings for your grandfather and she said that he was the moon and stars to her!!'

CHAPTER 16

1941

Vivid green drops dribbled slowly into Nektarios's cask. The air hung heavy with the fruity, rich fragrance of blackcurrant as the last of the olive oil was pressed. Clothes and hair, skin and nostril absorbed the aromatic and spicy scent as it saturated the air. The discarded mash of crushed skin and pips lay in a pile. The monumental round grindstones grumbled to a halt, the Hessian sacks lay folded against the wall, and the donkey that provided the power had been untethered and stood quietly outside nibbling at his feed. The final pressing of the family's olive oil was complete.

Nektarios clasped the hand of Dimitri, the owner of the press, and slapped his shoulder in appreciation.

'It is good-quality oil, the best grade,' pronounced Dimitri. 'You should be pleased.'

Nektarios nodded his agreement. Mama and the girls smiled.

'The oil will provide for all our needs, for cooking and lighting for the whole year ahead. And there will also be a surplus which will sell for a high price as the quality is undeniably good – if the Germans do not seize it first.' said Nektarios. He patted the cask fondly. 'Relax, my friends, rest and take satisfaction at a hard and long job well done.'

Nektarios offered cigarettes to the workman and soon the smell of tobacco overpowered the scent of the oil.

Dimitri fetched a bottle of raki and poured liquid into glasses which he handed round to the men.

'*Tsigia!*' they cried.

At that moment Young Felix hurtled through the door of the press.

'*Ti egine!*' demanded Dimitri irritably, aiming a swipe at Young Felix's head, for he was tired; it had been a long day.

'*Germania*. They come. They are on the road below the church,' panted Felix gasping for breath before he disappeared through the back door and out onto the path behind the press.

'Guns,' shouted Nektarios. 'Quick! Hide them!' The men with pistols flung them into a barrel of oil.

'And knives,' ordered Nektarios.

Mama and the girls scurried round collecting knives, pulled up their petticoats and hid the weapons in their underclothes.

The roar of a truck engine left us in no doubt that Young Felix had not been lying.

A tall, upright young German lieutenant, in an immaculate uniform, accompanied by a hefty Sergeant, strode into the yard and looked round menacingly. Behind them the truck containing four private soldiers was parked.

'*Achtung!*' commanded the Lieutenant. 'I see you have oil.'

'*Malista*,' said Dimitri, without any expression. 'This is an olive press.'

The Lieutenant studied him sternly trying to make up his mind whether Dimitri was merely stating a fact or being insolent. Then he barked a series of orders at the troopers, who marched into the room and began to load the casks and urns of newly pressed oil onto the truck, while the Cretan men looked on with resigned expressions on their faces.

Nektarios said moderately: 'Lieutenant, you are taking all the oil of our family. It must feed us and give us light for a whole year. Is it necessary for you take it all? We must live.'

The officer regarded him with a mixture of contempt for his pleading and satisfaction that he had the power to do exactly as he wanted.

'The German Reich also requires oil.' And he nodded to the troopers to continue loading the barrels onto the lorry. 'Now I require your identity cards. At once!'

Nektarios and Dimitri fumbled into their pockets and produced their grubby *taftotita*. Mama glanced anxiously as I produced mine. It looked alarmingly new and unused. The officer scrutinised it for a moment while I held my breath. If I were unmasked now it would be the final blow to the family who would all be shot for harbouring an escapee.

'*Namen?*,' he demanded.

'Papayiannakis Yannis,' I said. He glanced at my card and I sensed then that he could not read Greek. My work clothes were grimy from dust, stained with oil and mucky with bits of olive seed, twigs and skin. I know I looked the part of a Cretan farmer. Would the German question me further? I guessed that he did not know much Greek and possibly no Cretan at all. After a second glance at my card he passed it back without further comment.

He then checked the other identity papers while rapping out orders to his troopers.

Mavro, the large dog, who had been standing still beside Elenitsa who was holding his rope, began to bark, unsettled by the tone of the officer's voice.

'Keep still, Mavro,' she ordered, as he tried to wriggle himself free from her grasp. Instead the dog began to bark rapidly. Spitha, the puppy that belonged to Poppy and Fifi began to jump up and down, yelping and yapping as he added his voice to Mavro's.

The sergeant regarded both dogs with a malicious scowl. He took out his pistol and shot Mavro without a word. The huge dog collapsed to the floor. A trickle of blood oozed from under his head onto the floor. Its stench mingled with the sweet smell of the olive and the acrid smell of tobacco and cordite. The children fell on to their knees beside Mavro, whimpering in shock and despair and this irritated the sergeant even more and so he shot the puppy as well.

The little girls burst into noisy sobs, but Mama hushed them:

'Silence! Be brave, my children. You are Cretan women, the daughters of *Palikari*. Remain silent before these *Malaka*.' The shock of Mama using a swear word silenced them at once.

The officer said something sharp to the Sergeant and both men turned on the heels of their shiny boots and marched out of the press and back to the truck. It roared into life and sped away leaving us all stunned and numb with shock.

The troopers meanwhile, had untethered the donkey and the horses which had transported the sacks of olives to the press and led them away.

The little girls sobbed pitifully over the corpse of their puppy until Tonia gently pulled them away, hugged them in her arms and then began to mop up their tears. Elenitsa knelt down beside the big dog, blinking away her own tears but not uttering a sound. She kissed the top of his old head and gently stroked his black coat.

At first, we didn't notice it, but Mavro trembled very slightly.

'Look at Mavro,' said Elenitsa with a shaking voice. 'He moved.' She bent down again to inspect Mavro's body. 'The sergeant has missed him. Look! The bullet has only grazed his head and it has stunned him. He lives, thanks be to God.' She stroked his shoulder gently and I recalled the time when I had first seen her with Mavro. It was the day when I had been hiding exhausted in the little chapel after my long walk from Hora Sfakion after we lost the battle for Crete. The dog had nearly betrayed me then, but later it had saved my life. I felt that we were connected and I did not want him to die.

'He will live, and with Mama's care he will recover,' she said. 'Dry your tears, little ones.'

This calmed the children a little.

'*Malaka!*' spat out Dimitri. 'Turks! Sons of cuckolds! May they choke on the oil! I wish I had had time to piss in it before they stole it!'

This made Tonia laugh and soon we were all swearing and laughing together, more as a relief from the shock of the German attack than from any real amusement. But it did us good.

'At least they left the raki.' remarked Dimitri wryly, as he filled glasses and passed them round. Even to the women

'Drink it,' he said. 'For the shock. And then to the caves.'

Young Felix had run with the speed of Pheidippides, the heroic messenger who ran from Marathon to Athens with the news of the great defeat of the Persians, hurtling and scurrying down the donkey tracks until he reached the dry river bed where he knew that Wolf was at a meeting with other *andartes* at a house by the bridge where the road passed to the town.

Wolf came to us later at the family cave and told us what had happened:

'Young Felix showed great courage. No one could have run the distance any faster. He reached us covered in dust and bloody from scratches and scrapes. He was completely exhausted and he could barely speak. He told us what had happened at the press. His quick thinking gave us enough time to plan an ambush.

'As you know the bridge is narrow and made of wooden planks. We knew that the truck would have to slow down to cross it. We fixed a rope across the road just after the bridge. We ourselves we hid underneath the bridge.

Lucky and Stavro held one end of the rope and we tied the other around a big boulder.

Young Felix volunteered to act as lookout and to warn us when the truck was coming, even though he was utterly exhausted, which he did.

When the truck crossed the bridge, Stavro, Bunny and

Lucky and also some others tugged the rope hard. It stopped the truck, which fell on its side. We shot out the tyres and before the officer and sergeant could recover we had them caught. The sergeant who was driving had hit his head on the screen and was knocked unconscious. The officer was thrown clear and he too lay unconscious on the side of the road. We tied up his arms and legs.

'Then we waited for the soldiers to arrive with the horses and donkeys. When they saw the crash they ran to help the injured men and then we rushed them and overpowered them.'

'Did you shoot them?'

'Never. For that they would take many of our men and shoot them.'

'The reprisals.'

'Yes. One German, ten Cretans. We took their weapons and uniforms tied them up in their underwear and left them at the roadside. Ha. Ha.'

'We saved what oil we could. Lucky, Bunny and Stavro loaded it on to the animals. We will return it to Nektarios. Also we took the tyres from the truck. You can guess why, my friend!'

'The petrol we siphoned off. We have taken everything up along the river bed to a cave where it will be hidden until the Germans stop searching for it.'

'You have thought of everything, Wolf.' said Nektarios. 'Bravo. Will they search?'

'*Malista*. Our spies tell us that we caused a real uproar,' Wolf laughed showing a wide expanse of teeth and slapped his thighs merrily.

'The Germans are furious, but no one was really hurt and they do not know who to blame.'

'Will Nektarios and the family be safe?' I asked him.

'They will stay here in the family cave until this all blows over. The Germans will not find them here. And furthermore they only saw you all at the press. They cannot identify you easily.'

'Are you certain?'

'They would have to search many mountain villages to find you. They have not the time.' he added reassuringly.

We stayed in the cave for more than two weeks, coming down to the village at night to collect what we needed and check the house and the remaining dogs.

Mavro remained at the press where Dimitri looked after him until he returned to good health. Animals have a remarkable ability to recover from injuries and Mavro was a strong and healthy dog who was fighting fit after a month. Spitha did not recover.

The little children remained tearful and sorrowful for a long time. Mama was not sympathetic.

'Be grateful and give thanks to God, *pethia*. No one was hurt. God protected us. Young Felix, Wolf and his brothers are heroes. Do they wish to see tears and hear cries and sobs? No. They saved our oil and now we have most of our supply for the year. We can cook with it, eat with it, and preserve with it, light our lamps with it. What is the death of a puppy compared with that?' The children nodded silently and sadly. But I did not hear them speak of Spitha again.

'Now you are a proper Cretan,' Elenitsa said to me with a smile.

'How is that?'

'The German saw your *taftotita* and he did not suspect a thing. You passed for a Cretan and your papers also. Now you are one of us'.

'It is as God wills,' I said.

I hid my relief that I had passed a severe test. I had been unprepared for what happened. We had all been unprepared for what happened. Felix's quick thinking had saved us from disaster. Mama was right. He was a hero.

***

2001

Ela na su po. I was young of course. I myself do not remember exactly but I have heard the story so many times that I cannot now tell what I remember and what I have been told many times by others.

We had just woken from the afternoon sleep. It had been raining and it was misty outside. Mama made us all cups of coffee to warm us up and passed a cup to Papa. My sisters unfolded their embroidery and Mama drew up her chair to the loom. We could not have been more relaxed or cheerful. The war might have been far away at that moment.

The clatter of boots shattered the peace and then we heard voices shouting. Your grandfather's immediate reaction was to dive for the ladder and shin down into the cellar and hide himself behind the bread oven. We had had no warning that the Germans were searching the mountain.

Young Felix had not been on look-out that day, he told us later with much insistence.

'I would never have let you down,' he said indignantly, jutting out his chin and standing a little more upright. And we knew this was true. Felix was brave and honest and true. Another boy from another family had been on look-out that afternoon and because he was tired, or because of his own laziness, he had fallen asleep. We relied heavily on this system of early warning. This mistake left our village unprotected for we had no idea in advance of the German patrol.

The shouting was interrupted by woeful cries from the women in the other cottages as the German boots crashed into their homes. They told me later that the sergeant raised his gun and threatened them with it. Next thing, the Germans flung open the door and marched into our house shouting for our father. We were very frightened, of course, Tonia and Elenitsa pushed their chairs over the hatch to the cellar and sat together with a big blanket they had seized and which covered their knees and also the floor, and they pretended to be mending it. We ran to our Mother and she flung her arms around us to protect us. One of the soldiers pushed over the table and smashed all the glasses and cups and another swung the butt of his rifle at our pitchers of water so that they fell and shattered and spilled water all over the floor. The soldiers were very aggressive and shouting all the time loudly and we thought that they would kill us. My father stood up and asked what they wanted.

They wanted him.

The troopers seized and bound him with rope, all the time bellowing at us like the donkeys they were and waving their guns around. They marched our father out of the door.

'But he has done nothing! Leave him!' cried Mama.

I only saw my mother panic once and it was at that moment.

'Please let him go,' she pleaded. We began to cry until my mother pulled herself together and told us to shush. Even the dogs started a cacophony of barking. We were terrified that the Germans would start a search and that they would find your Grandfather. We knew that if he was discovered we would all die. The sounds of shouting and cries and wails mixed together into a wild chorus like the birds at dawn, but far noisier.

It was incredible, but it seemed that the arrest of my father was the sole purpose of the German's visit and once they had captured him and, of course, smashed up everyone's houses, they left as suddenly as they had come.

'But why?' sobbed Mama later. We never saw her weep and we were very frightened by this. 'What reason? We have done nothing.'

Tonia and Elenitsa sat either side of her stroking her hands in between mopping up their own tears. We sat silently on the floor at her feet. We stayed like that for many hours and grew cold. I suppose we were too shocked to move or to drink or eat.

Eventually, your grandfather rejoined us. I remember him cautiously poking his head through the trap door and then climbing from the ladder into the room. He lit the oil lamp, for we were sitting there in the dark.

'I will go for news,' he said. 'I will find Young Felix and his father. They will know more. It is dark now and I will not be seen.'

The news from Young Felix's father was very bad. Without any warning that afternoon the Germans had started to go from village to village and house to house, to round up any men they could find.

'How did Old Felix avoid being arrested?' Mama asked.

'I believe he had seen the Germans enter the village and at the last minute he had escaped into the sheep hut he has in the high mountain until the coast was clear.'

'They say we are helping the Allies,' Old Felix explained to Lancaster. 'They accuse us of being traitors and spies and that we must pay: ten men for one German killed.'

'It was against the Geneva Convention, of course.' said Poppy. 'We knew that. It was a war crime. Wrong or right it was German law because they ruled the island. They could do what they wanted and the German General at that time was very cruel and sadistic.'

'Where did they take Nektarios?'

'The Germans took Nektarios and also men from nearby villages. They tied them up and they put them in the olive factory in Paleohora which they were using as a jail. They announced that each day they would execute a number of them as a punishment and as a warning to others. They said that our men were traitors and that they were helping the enemy. There was talk at that time of a big parachute drop of supplies from the Allies in the White Mountains. The

Germans claimed that all the Cretan men all over the *eparchi* were involved.'

The next few days our nerves were taut as a bow string. The little shepherd boys set up a chain of lookouts and no one dared to sleep in the afternoon. In fact, most of the women of the village and the old men left their houses and retreated to the family caves. They only returned the village in ones and twos and very cautiously to feed any remaining chickens. In the gloom of the cave, the women moved silently like wraiths, merging often into the shadows. The rest of the day they sat in tense silence, sewing or making lace. Wolf and his brothers and other groups of *andartes* also disappeared and met with the agents of the English where they planned reprisals and attacks.

'What did my grandfather do?'

Your grandfather was very frustrated because he felt useless and unable to help. Eventually he took himself off into the higher crags where he sat carefully hidden but able to watch the mule tracks which led from Paleohora to the north. For three days he told us that he observed soldiers on the move. He heard the roar of lorry engines bringing troops to the end of the road where the mule tracks led into the village. He heard the screech of motorbikes as they roared up the safer tracks. He heard the clatter of marching boots as the foot patrols marched from hamlet to hamlet. The peculiar acoustics of the mountain meant that the noise carried clearly and he said he could hear the Germans shouting orders or talking amongst themselves. He heard the rattle of machine gun fire as the Germans systematically went from hamlet to hamlet, house to house, to arrest any men they could surprise. But by this time the men had melted away and in frustration the Germans destroyed anything which they could not take away with them. He saw the smoke rise from hamlets where they had burned what they could not take away.

We were fortunate in this because our house was not

damaged for the Germans did not visit it again. They already had Nektarios in the prison. But elsewhere ruined urns, smashed furniture, rivers of oil and wine were testimony to the fury, rage and spite of the thwarted German patrols.

A week of intense anxiety passed. Our disquiet increased. The news which filtered back from Paleohora was terrifying. Executions took place each day. There were no trials.

Each day Mama grew whiter, the skin stretched across her cheekbones tight like a bandage and her fingers clenched into tight fists. Like a faded flower she drifted through the daily routine or sat in the cave with sightless eyes, her mind elsewhere.

She ate little and nor did my sisters. Fifi and I did our best to stay silent and not blurt out our opinions as we usually did.

By now, the news of the purges in Paleohora had reached all parts of the mountain. I thought that Mama would collapse from the strain and I think that only our need for her held her together.

'You are Cretan women, *pethia*,' she said. 'You will be brave.' I think she was convincing herself too.

On the tenth day Mama returned alone to the house as she had each day to feed the chickens: miraculously one or two had survived the destruction.

She was stooping down to fill the water bowl inside the old store room which housed the chickens when she was aware of a shadow in the doorway behind her. Thinking the worse she rose up, crossed herself and turned to meet the barrel of a gun.

This is what she had expected in her heart each day when she returned to our house. She had prepared herself for this moment and at this moment, after so many days of fear and anxiety she no longer dreaded this thing.

She stood with the courage of a Cretan woman

determined to face her Fate. Instead she fainted. There was no barrel of a gun in the doorway.

The gaunt, dirt-encrusted and ragged figure of a man stood there.

My father!

The Germans had released him suddenly without warning. They did not give a reason. They came to his cell, they shouted his name. He crossed himself, uttered a prayer and called goodbye to his comrades. They marched him into the yard; they led him to the wall. He was blinded by the sudden light and was expecting to see the firing squad. They pushed him forward and he found himself in the street. He stood very still waiting for a bullet in the back but the door shut behind him and he was all alone. He stood for a moment longer, bewildered and then he realised that he was free.

He ran.

***

1941

Young Felix is a reliable, intelligent, and sturdy lad who is well able to take care of himself so no one worries much about him when he remains alone in the high pasture guarding the goats for weeks on end.

Goats will eat anything. They are voracious; they can strip bare a *stremata* of pasture land in the wink of an eye. It is the job of the shepherd boy to move the goats from pasture to pasture before they graze the tender shoots into oblivion, for it is necessary to protect the land and allow the growth to recover in order for it to be eaten again. So the herd must be moved every few days, and the shepherd boy must do this.

Young Felix looked after two herds of over 100 animals

both Nektarios's and Wolf's. It was a big responsibility for a young boy, but he was well trusted and trustworthy. He slept in one of several small stone huts built for the purpose up in the high mountains. Each time he left the village he took with him a *sakoula* of dry bread or *pakimadia* and some hard cheese such as *graviera*. Water he could find from a nearby spring and milk he could squeeze freshly for himself from one of the nanny goats in the herd. When the cheesemaker passed by, he left Felix some soft white cheese and from time to time Felix's mother trekked up to find him, bringing with her a clay pot of stew or beans.

It was a hard and lonely life for a young boy but Felix was independent, resilient and tough and seemed to thrive on it; he amused himself through the lonely days by playing the flute. In time, he was to play with Lucky. In recent months he had proved a reliable lookout and sometimes runner for the *andartes*. His ambition was to join them as soon as possible because he wanted to fight for Crete against the Germans.

When Young Felix turned up with cuts to his face and arms, and a bleeding wound on the forehead and his body black blue with bruises, there was much anger at the tale he told. The women clucked and fussed around him with potions and lotions, then Nektarios and Wolf immediately summoned the men of the village together to hear his tale. A less well respected and trusted boy might have been suspected of losing the goats through negligence – perhaps by sleeping on the job – but Young Felix was too well liked and conscientious to be suspected of these faults.

'Two nights ago,' he explained, 'men with guns and sticks came among the goats. With shouts and whistles they began to drive them towards the north. Of course, I ran after them, shouting at them to leave the goats alone and calling them cuckolds and worse but they just laughed at me. I ran back to the hut for my rifle and I fired at them, although I have to admit that I missed.' Felix said this in such a tone of sorrow, mingled with disgust, that some of the men laughed although when he glared fiercely at them they cut off the sound quickly.

The *banditi* turned and came for me with knives and sticks but I could run faster and climb like a goat too. Only one man reached me and tried to hit me but me I struggled from his grasp. I bit his hand and then ran like Hermes and he did not catch me again. Then he shot at me with his rifle and it grazed me here on my forehead. I felt the wind from it whistle through my hair, but I did not stop, no, not at all, until I was far away from them.

'You did well, *pethia*.' said Nektarios.

'No, not at all. I am free but the goats, I fear, are captured.' replied Felix woefully.

'We must know who did this thing!' cried Wolf. 'And find our goats.'

'Felix,' said Nektarios. 'Who were these *banditi*? What can you tell us about them?'

'I think they were men from Sfakia.'

'Of course!' shouted Wolf vehemently, slapping his thigh.

'Why do you think this?' asked Nektarios quietly. The effort to speak seemed too much.

'I think I have seen before the man who chased me.'

'Well?'

'It was some time ago when I was younger, before the Germans came. I saw him in a *kafeneion* in the town. There was an argument and he was shouting. That is why I remember him. He was short and built like the trunk of an olive. I was surprised that he could run so fast after me and catch me for I am as fleet as Pheidippides. He had a great big fat belly too like a woman who is with child – like this.' Felix made a big balloon with his hands and for the first time he grinned.

'What else?' demanded Wolf.

'Well, he had a very black beard, thick and woolly like

the fleece of a sheep.'

'You describe many men of Crete, *pethia.*'

'His hair was thin, yes, thin but with curls. I could see the skin shining through his curls in the moonlight.'

'This is no help Felix, my boy,' said Nektarios. 'Think again.'

Felix remained silent looking at the ground. He appeared to be concentrating hard. Eventually he said:

'When he came after me, I told you that I bit his hand and now, I remember, I bit something hard and metallic. Then he tried to shoot me and I ran. After that,' said Felix slowly as he tried to recall the event in his mind's eye, 'he had to climb up the rock after me as I was above him. I saw that I had bitten a ring on his finger. A ring of gold.'

'Yes. Yes,' said Wolf, impatiently. 'I wear a ring to sometimes, so does Nektarios here. It means nothing.'

'*Vevea.* But I saw the ring shining in the moonlight. The ring was most unusual. It was carved in the shape of the head of a ram, with curling horns of gold and stripes of green enamel. '

'I knew it!' cried Wolf triumphantly and casting a glance at me. I nodded for we both recognised that ring.

'Manoli!' cried Wolf.

'If Manoli it is, then we must take all care.' Nektarios sighed. His face was drawn and he appeared too tired as if the effort to care was too great a burden.

'Oh, he is a bad man,' uttered Wolf.

'If you go after him for our goats,' Nektarios warned him, 'you put yourself in great danger, Wolf, so do nothing hastily.'

The village men murmured in agreement for Manoli was not unknown to them. I guessed that Wolf would use all his powers of persuasion, his charm and his good humour to win them round to his way of thinking.

'*Pes mou.* How many men accompanied him, Felix,' demanded Wolf.

'I am not certain, but I think that there was Manoli himself and two others, maybe three. It was dark, you understand, but, yes, I think I chased away three *banditi* and then Manoli came after me, so he makes four.'

Nektarios patted Felix on his head.

'Leave us, Felix *mou*, and take some rest at your mother's house while we consider what we must do.'

'Revenge!' cried Wolf when Felix had left the room. We laughed but it was no laughing matter.

I did not sense a great welling of enthusiasm for this undertaking. Some of the elders hesitated to support Wolf and voiced their reluctance accordingly, for he appeared unusually vehement, hot headed and angry as he put forward the points in favour of his scheme. I thought he was still smarting from the shame of his withdrawal in Chania and that he wanted revenge for that more than the recovery of the goats. Nektarios was measured in his arguments. Nektarios wanted the return of his herd, no doubt, but he was wary of starting a vendetta with a man of Manoli's reputation – a man from Sfakia in particular, where vendettas lasted as far back as time itself. He did not exactly argue against Wolf's plans but he examined each suggestion in a serious and thoughtful manner and let the others debate the futility or possibility of each plan of action. Wolf pulled his moustaches irritably, shifted in his seat, huffed and puffed and grimaced when the argument went against him and drank a lot of raki from the bottle at his elbow.

'We have a bigger enemy,' said one. 'We should reserve our guns and ammunition for fighting the Germans.' There were nods and murmurs of agreement.

'Without my herd, I suffer a great loss!' cried Wolf, becoming testy.

'So does Nektarios but he does not shout loudly like you, Wolf!' said another.

Wolf looked at Nektarios for support.

'I cannot afford the loss either,' said Nektarios quietly, and then he paused while the room finally fell silent and the men waited for him to continue. He took his time as if the effort of putting forward an argument was too great.

'I fear that we may start a vendetta with Manoli and this is not the right time. Our fight is with the Germans. We must concentrate our energy and arms on that.'

'We must go, and we must go now!' Wolf shouted. He was now slightly drunk and becoming agitated in his frustration His greatest strength was always his charm and his sense of humour. They always won men to his side. I could see no signs of them now and I felt that the support he took for granted was melting away.

'In the dark,' sneered one.

'Well, at dawn,' conceded Wolf. 'First light.'

I watched the faces in the lamplight. Wary, reluctant, undecided, wavering, perhaps even tired of the endless debate. It was not my battle, I thought, so I left Wolf to it and went to bed.

Next day, I found myself accompanying Wolf, his brothers and other *andartes* on a search for the stolen goats. Somehow he had won the argument: he was elated, full of jokes and tall tales. His enthusiasm raised the men's spirits. He showed no sign of the crashing hangover that he ought to have been suffering.

We marched north into a cold, biting wind that froze our cheeks, until we came eventually to the goat pasture and Felix's hut. The mud was churned up from where the goats had rushed around in panic but it did not take long to find clues and then follow the tracks made by their hooves. Surprisingly, the tracks led north, although Sfakia is to the east.

'I think Manoli has taken the herd and hidden it' cried Wolf. 'He hasn't made for Sfakia at all! We must follow the tracks.' he continued. 'My guess is that they will lead us to a cheese hut or sheep fold and he is planning to keep them out of sight until all the fuss dies down!'

We broke for a rest inside Felix's hut out of the wind, ate some bread and cheese and drank raki to warm ourselves and, about two in the afternoon, set off again still marching north into the teeth of the bitter wind.

The terrain of gullies and outcrops of rock was as wild and unforgiving as it always is when walking in the high mountains of Crete. Fortunately, we were just below the snow line, but it was icily cold.

Ahead of us reared a huge jetty of white limestone. We were dropping down below it, sliding on the scree when we disturbed some wild buzzards that flew suddenly out from their eyrie over our heads with a rush of air and flapping of wings. We rounded the corner in single file and suddenly there was Manoli who had his back to us and was in the process of relieving himself. He turned in alarm. We fled for cover and so did he.

'If I had been at the front I could have shot him,' fumed Wolf.

No one had the advantage of surprise. But we had the advantage of the high ground above the rustlers and waited, guns loaded and trained on a small gap in the rock, where we guessed Manoli and the gang were hidden. I don't know what made him decide, but Manoli kept out of sight. We waited.

Suddenly we heard horses' hooves. The gang must have had their horses tethered nearby. They were making a fast tactical withdrawal. Wolf, Stavro and Lucky fired in unison and Manoli slumped over his horse's neck.

'He's wounded,' cried Wolf triumphantly. 'We got him.'

'Not entirely,' said Stavro. 'They've all got away and we can't follow as we are on foot! And so Manoli lives to fight another day!'

***

CHAPTER 17

2001

'*Ela na su po*,' said Poppy, 'My father returned from the prison and he was much changed. My father was a gentle man, you understand. His temper was mild as a spring day. He was slow to anger, thoughtful and quiet like Elenitsa. But, my father's moods became black as night. He was no longer himself.

'When Mama spoke to him it was not that my father ignored her, it was as if he did not even register that she was speaking to him. Her words fell on deaf ears.

'If he heard her, perhaps his poor, tortured brain could not make any sense of what she was saying to him and so he appeared not to understand her words.' Poppy sighed. I felt tears were imminent.

What is the imperceptible line which divides sanity and insanity? I wondered. Do we all tremble on the edge of that abyss? In times of great stress does the brain simply shut down to protect itself? Does it lower a drawbridge and surround itself with unseen curtain walls to keep out any invasive thoughts that can harm and damage the already wounded mind?

'Mama would massage Papa's forehead,' continued Poppy, 'and draw the hair gently away from his head while he drooped in the chair, limp and motionless like a puppet. It was as if he felt nothing at all. How do you say it? Numb?' I nodded. 'If Mama took his hand, it rested limply, like a wilted plant, in hers; if she pulled him to his feet from his chair and led him to the door and outside onto the terrace he would follow as meekly as a small child. Then, if she let him go, he would stand where she left him still as a sightless statue. He would gaze at the misty, grey mountains without seeing them. He was disconnected from us all and from his surroundings too.

'At first Fifi and I would creep up to him and wrap our small arms around his legs. When he was fit and well and we did this he would cry out in mock horror and struggle to be released. It was a game we always played – to capture our father in this way and he would always pretend to be angry and roar at us like the dogs at a stranger and then we would giggle and release him and start all over again. We tried this game but he did not move or shrug us off. We waited for his roar but he made no sound at all.

'We would cry *"Baba!"* to attract his attention. Sometimes he would slowly turn his head. *"Baba, ela!"* We would then take his hand and he would look at us without seeing us and then we would cry and run away for he was a stranger to us.

'*Ela na su po*. Before his arrest my father had been a happy and contented man. He was not a man who became angry quickly. He was mild, but not weak. No, not at all. He did not argue with our neighbours except about politics, of course, when he would condemn the government and call all politicians cuckolds and thieves! He was a respected in the village – no house was closed to him. Many came to him to seek his advice, for his opinion was well regarded.

'He loved our family; he did not beat his wife as many husbands did and he was kind to all of his children even though we were merely girls and he and Mama had longed for sons. He was a satisfied man, fulfilled by his life. He planned and organised the work of our farm with method and energy. He worked from the first light of day until the setting of the sun. He was prosperous from the profits of the olives, the sheep and the goats. He sold our wheat and was known for making good red wine and the surplus he sold also. *Lipon*, he appeared easy-going, but he was astute and shrewd. He didn't miss much. He was regarded as far away as Chania as a successful man and few dealers or farmers in the district dared to cheat him or give him short measure.

'But in his present state, our father cared little about dealing, buying or selling. After his return from prison he became silent, nervous, morose and miserable. He began to shake. Then he found that he could not walk without tottering. And eventually he became too ill to get out of bed.

'"I have pain everywhere," he complained, "In my back, my head, and my legs. All over my body. I hurt. God help me."

'Mama boiled up her herbs and dosed him with *farmaka* but it did no good at all and after a while he pushed the mug away.

'My father's face became grey, dark smudges developed under his eyes, his cheeks sank and his grey skin sagged under his chin. He could hardly bear the light. It hurt his eyes, he said. He could eat nothing. "The food tastes like straw," he complained. He pushed away the food Mama prepared. He became wasted and thin: a man existing behind a glass barrier, trapped in a vacuum, one step removed from the world's activity.

'"I cannot think. My head is full of sheep's wool'" he said. "What is happening to me?"

'Later, he described to us his daily battles to capture his thoughts which, he said, evaporated like wisps of mist when he tried to grasp them. He felt that his mind was suspended in ice, or like amber in stone. He felt powerless. He tried, he said later, very hard to regain control of his mind, but he failed.

'"I believed I was mad." he told Mama. It made us cry.

'"I fought a hard battle," he said, "but the more I tried, the more the pain and the shaking in my body and the confusion of my mind increased. I became bitter and angry at my impotence. I know that I lashed out and uttered harsh and threatening words to those around me: cruel words, bitter words, designed to hurt those who when I was in a sane mind I loved better than the entire world."

'Mama hid her despair. If she wept many tears – and I am sure she did – she did so secretly so that we never saw her grief. She did not want us to be frightened. She was strong as the rocks and mountains that encircled us.

'"Papa is not well," she explained to us. "Look after him."

'So, we sat with him and tried to amuse him and hold his attention in the simple way that children do. We told him our childish stories; we brought him small gifts of flowers or nuts or fruit, even a mushroom once, I remember.

'He would try to lift his head from the mattress but the effort was usually too much for him. Sometimes he would struggle to hold out a hand, which trembled like the wing of a moth hovering over a candle flame, and pat one of us on our arm or head. Often, like a man caught in a dream, he would stare at us vacantly without really seeing us at all.

'I loved my father very much,' said Poppy. 'We all loved him; he was a kind of god to us all and we obeyed him because we loved him and because we believed he was right in all things. He was a man. That is how we thought at that time.

'Then he became a stranger to us, a demon, a foul fiend, as some would say, possessed by the devil. Everything we did was wrong and angered him. Nothing could please him. At first we were puzzled and then frightened. That was when we began to avoid his company. We hid from the bitter, cruel assault of his words.

'My father's arrest and imprisonment changed everything; it transformed him and made him a stranger in our eyes.

'All our young lives, so far, our family had been happy and secure even when the Germans came and stole from our village and wrecked our houses. After my father became ill, we felt that our world was shattered like a broken clay pot.

In desperation Mama went to your grandfather.

"'Yanni," she said. "What can I do? You must help me find a way to restore Nektarios to the man he was."

"'It is impossible – for the moment." Your grandfather took her hand and kissed it, a thing he had never done before, and replied. "We must let time heal him. His mind is wounded, just as if he had a wound from a bullet or a slash from a knife. This takes time to repair itself, you know that. He has endured much and the shock has been great."

"'We have no sons. What can I do?" said Mama, in a voice trembling with an emotion which she failed to disguise. "There is no other man in our family who can help us now. Our cousins and uncles are fighting far away for the freedom of Crete. Some are dead, others are injured or in prison. I have no one. Will you help us now? We need you!"

'Your grandfather did not hesitate to reassure her. "I will help you as much as I can. We must protect him from anxiety and from worry. I can take over the business of the farm – the olives, the wood, the animals. Are you are certain that there is no other man who can help you?"

"'No one, Yanni. There is no one. I need you. We all need you." she pleaded. I had never heard my Mother plead in this way before and her voice trembled with the emotion of it and the depth of her feeling. "You know, Yanni, how we do things here," she said looking intently into his face. He could see how close this usually strong and capable woman had come to crumbling.

"'Sheep, certainly, I know," he said. "My father farms sheep in New Zealand. I have helped him all my life since I was a young boy. Our methods are not Cretan methods but, at the end of the day, sheep are sheep. I will get Young Felix to help me with the goats. He's a good lad. The olives are already pressed, thank God, and we have the oil safely stored unless the Germans come again to steal it. The olive groves I can clear of weeds. Wood, I can chop. I can put my back into it and the exercise will do me good and make me fitter. As for the rest we'll cross that bridge when we come to it."

'"May God bless you," breathed Mama, as she crossed herself.

'"I owe you my life," replied Yanni. "I will do anything I can to repay you."

'He did not let us down.

'Nektarios, meanwhile, lay prone on his mattress, wrestling with suffering as the pain gripped his limbs, his eyes gazing into shadows and fighting his demons.'

***

1941

Dusk. Time to leave the cave. The sky was streaks of pink and amber; I could just glimpse the last of the sun in the west, fading, sinking slowly between the mountain peaks and throwing them into silhouette. I stayed in the family cave most afternoons after the morning's work was done. It was cool and it was safe: safe for me and safe for all; my absence from the village put no one in danger. The Germans liked to raid the villages in the late afternoon when everyone was sleepy and had relaxed their guard. Women, children at home alone were sitting targets for reprisals. The Germans would drive up from town, surround the village with a cordon and then start indiscriminately rounding up any people they could find. I finished my roll-up cigarette and stubbed it out carefully by habit, in the dust by my side. The smallest spark could set off a forest fire when the undergrowth was dry as tinder. As I raised my head, a shadow in the mouth of the cave obliterated the light of the setting sun. The silhouette of a tall man filled the entrance. He moved slightly and a finger of golden light caught the side of his face.

'Simadis,' I said with some relief, relaxing tense muscles.

'Yes, it is me'. He stood over me, his rifle hanging easily from his arm, the blade of a sharp knife glittering in his sash. 'I have come for you,' he said sharply.

I rose to me feet. My first thought was anxiety for the family, for Elenitsa. Was he a messenger of bad news?

'What is it? What has happened? What do you want?' I demanded urgently.

'Want,' he repeated in a queer, choked voice. 'Want? I want you. *Ela*. Come.' He beckoned me.

'Has something happened?'

I jumped up and moved towards him. He ushered me through the mouth of the cave. I half turned to ask another question and saw stars. A fierce bang on the back of my head sent me falling through the cover of trees and I rolled onto the flat ground below the cave. Shafts of pain pierced my skull like hot needles. I felt groggy. Thought was confused.

The last rays of the sun glinted on the metal barrel of the gun which was pointing straight at me. Words died in my mouth. Simadis scowled above me. Before I recovered my senses and before I could stagger to my feet, he was bending over me with a rope and had me trussed, like a goat, around the waist.

He pulled me up, recovered his rifle, and pointed it at me again.

'Move.' he ordered. I stumbled forward. He followed and I could feel the prod of the gun's barrel in my back.

Through waves of nausea and a thudding pain in my skull, I tried to determine exactly what he was planning to do. Was he going to hand me over to the Germans? Or worse, kill me? Surely, Simadis, the fiercest of the *andartes*, was not a man to betray even me.

'Simadis,' I tried to gasp. 'What's this about?'

'Don't speak.' he ordered. 'Move!' and he prodded me in the back with his rifle once more.

I stumbled and staggered through the dead undergrowth and the groves of trees until presently we reached a small round hut built of rough stone backing onto the rock. There was a rudimentary roof of corrugated iron panels, bamboo and small branches. I recognised it as one of the temporary huts they used for penning up sheep and goats. He pushed me inside. It smelt strongly of the sour reek of goat pee. Plenty of droppings on the dirt floor under my feet confirmed the identity of the last inhabitants.

It was almost totally dark inside for by now for the sun had set and the hut had no windows.

'Take off your clothes!' Simadis ordered.

'What?'

'Your clothes. Off. Now!'

'Mate, you cannot be serious.'

He was.

He drew his knife and waved it in my direction dangerously.

I obeyed.

Although my arms were pinioned to my waist, I had enough freedom of movement to remove my baggy Cretan trousers. I kicked off my sandals and he knelt to bind my ankles. Nakedness in such circumstances is a weird feeling. In the changing room after Rugby, in the ocean, in bed with a girl, it seemed normal, but wearing no keks, and facing a man with a grudge, is alarming. It removes yourself respect, it strips away literally all your self-worth and leaves you feeling fragile and vulnerable. It reduces you to nothing.

He whipped the rope away from my arms. I lunged at him with my fists but inevitably he jumped out of reach and I overbalanced and fell heavily on my left arm.

'Hurry!' he shouted hitting me round the head with the

butt of his rifle hard enough to make the world spin. Sitting up clumsily, I slowly and reluctantly unbuttoned my waistcoat. I shrugged it off and eased my shirt gently over my head. He pulled me to my feet and then tied my hands behind my back. I tried to struggle, although I felt weak and dizzy, but he hit me again on the side of my face and I fell to the floor once more, my cheek in the dust and goat pellets. Soon, I was trussed like a sheep or goat before slaughter which, at that moment, I felt was my likely fate.

'Look, m-, m- mate,' I managed to stutter. 'What's this all about?'

'You don't know?' Simadis spat at me, looking furious and dangerous at the same time.

'Haven't an idea?' I tried to grin as I said it, but it was more of a grimace.

'Elenitsa.'

'Elenitsa. What?'

'She is mine.'

'Don't know what you mean, mate.'

'I watch. I see how you look at her. You help her at the spring. She likes you for this. You hold her hand. This she also likes. But she is mine. Before you came it was understood that she was to be my woman. Now she looks only at you, and she is cold to me. But she is mine. I will kill you and she will forget you.

'Simadis, you're wrong!' I lied, despising myself for the betrayal, perjuring myself to save my skin.

'Take her, Simadis. Elenitsa is yours, mate.' I hated myself for denying her. Did St Peter feel the same way when he denied Jesus? But my life was at stake.

Simadis gave me a long cold stare.

'*Malaka!*' he swore and spat. 'You will die here. No one will find you until you are a heap of bones. They will think you were shot by Germans or *andartes*.' He kicked me violently in the stomach and, for good measure, a second time in my kidneys and I passed out.

How much time passed I cannot say. The sheep fold was pitch black when I regained consciousness. I could have lain there for ten minutes or for ten hours. I lay with the flat of my cheek and my side in the dirt and let pain wash over me. It was too much effort to move. My head throbbed, my kidneys ached and I had a monumental stomach ache. I raised my head slightly and felt immediately sick. I lowered my head again and waited for the nausea and trembling to pass. I heard a weak voice, but it was my voice, groaning with the pain. My mouth felt bone dry. I desperately wanted a drink. And I was cold. Very cold. For this, I had survived the Battle for Crete, fever and illness only to die in a hovel on a filthy floor, stinking of goat shit: dirty, naked and in the dust.

I think I drifted off into unconsciousness again for the next thing I remember is wakening and seeing a chink of light under the rough wooden door of the hut.

Daylight or moonlight, but which: day or night?

I lay hog-tied and helpless, filthy and in pain. Thought floated elusively across my mind but I could not catch it or make sense of it. And I drifted off again. Later, still shivering and trembling, my brain seemed to engage and I remembered the words of some officer from my training course.

Self-belief.

Always believe. Believe that you will survive. Believe. The difference between survival and death, men, is all in the mind. Robust and positive thought. Clear logical thought will get you through.

Rule Number One: make a plan. Plan your survival. Never give in. I thought of all the hardships I had already endured, the battle, the marches, the injuries sustained. I thought of Elenitsa. I thought with anger and loathing of Simadis. I felt hot with hatred. Channel it, I thought. Use it. Clear your mind and assess the situation.

I moved my trussed wrists experimentally and I

discovered that in his haste Simadis had tied the rope rather loosely. Fighting pain and nausea, I twisted and wriggled until the rope which pinioned my arms slipped upwards. The effort left me weak and sweating and the nausea returned. I almost gave up and lay down on the floor once more. Even the goat shit and dust seemed inviting. I steadied myself and took some deep breaths to relieve the pain. Then, performing like a contortionist at a travelling fair, I managed after a long struggle and with many breaks to slide the rope up to my neck and over my head. With the rope now slack I could now sit upright although my hands and feet were still tied. Leaning forward, I was able to loosen the rope binding my ankles and soon my legs were free. Paralysing pins and needles shot up my limbs as the blood pounded into starved muscles but enduring it was worthwhile: I was able to sit up.

By now my eyes had become accustomed to the dark inside the hut and I had got my night vision. The moon must have risen and moonlight and starlight filtered through the slats of bamboo into the room. I could just discern the stone of the walls nearest me. The hut looked bare: merely an animal pen, not a storeroom. I edged on my bottom to the wall nearest to me and then cautiously shuffled to my feet. With my front and hands against the wall I walked crabwise along it searching methodically for any tool, any stone, anything at all which would help to release the ropes on my wrist.

Do not give up, I urged myself. Slowly, I made a circuit of the hut, feeling the wall with my fingers, but by the time I had reached the doorway I had found nothing and my arms and wrists were grazed and bleeding.

The door was a simple timber construction of long rough planks with short braces nailed across them near the top and bottom. The shepherd who built it had used long nails to pinion the planks together and had bent the ends of the nails down at right angles to stop them protruding. I examined each nail by carefully stroking my fingers along them. The top bar was too high and offered no help, nor did the centre. But when I sat down and investigated the bottom brace I found a nail which protruded a couple of inches.

I desperately needed a drink. My mouth was parched and my tongues felt twice its normal size and too big for my mouth. My head pounded and so did my side. I was sure that Simadis had cracked another rib when he gave me a good pounding with his boots and my kidneys ached.

Survival depends on positive action, I told myself. Keep going don't give in.

I knelt facing the door and held my wrists against the nail. I held the knotted rope to the nail and began to work it backward and forwards in an attempt to loosen the rope or cause it to fray. It was hard work on my knees, in the dust and I soon got pins and needles again while all the time I was fighting the pain in my ribs.

Keep going. Don't give in to that bastard, I told myself.

How many hours passed I have no idea. Pain and exhaustion blotted out any sense of time passing: each second was a struggle. Eventually, I became aware that the moon was high in the night sky and a dim beam of light penetrated the hut. I felt some slight shift in the knot. This gave me some hope. I felt another slight shift. I continued working in this way for a long time. It was painful, the effort was huge and I found that I had to take longer and longer rests between my efforts. My thirst continued to rage. I thought I would go mad with it.

I must have fallen asleep from exhaustion again, or become unconscious from the agony, because I was woken by a sharp crack and crackle of lightening overhead, followed closely by the boom of thunder. Torrential rain thudded on the corrugated iron roof and drips began to slop onto the floor and dribble down the walls. I stuck out my parched tongue and lapped the liquid from off the wall. Like the spring months before, it saved my life and gave me the energy to attack the rope again.

I decided to use my teeth to attack the fibres of the knot. After spitting out gouts of dust and fibre I decided that the nail was a better option. Doggedly I continued as the light became stronger. I kept having to stop to relieve the pain in my rib and the circulation in my legs.

Survival is a state of mind. Keep going, I told myself. Keep positive.

I kept at it.

The knot released with a jolt and I fell sideways into the dirt. I banged my temple on the floor but the pain no longer mattered. What mattered was that I was finally free.

I felt an electric surge of adrenalin rush through my body. Relief made me laugh hysterically for a moment. I took a grip mentally. I was free.

But naked.

It was hardly the best state in which to walk across the mountains, after a violent storm, find a village, walk in stark naked and terrify the widows and the children.

The morning light filtered through the gaps in the bamboo ceiling and around the frame of the door. I checked around the hut again and spotted something high up stuffed into a gap between the wall and the roof supports. It was a rough hessian sack of the type they used to collect the olives in. I reached up and pulled it down. Dust and cobwebs encrusted its folds and fell out when I unfolded it. I was filthy with dust and goat droppings which stuck to me like burrs after you have walked through a field, so I was hardly in a position to be particular. I shook it well to get rid of any insects and inspected it for scorpions. This was not the moment to receive a scorpion bite. Returning to my trusty nail, I used it to tear some holes in the base and then I pulled it up over my legs like a pair of baggy Cretan trousers. Decency restored.

But I still needed protection for my feet. Although I knew that Young Felix and his friends ran through the undergrowth without shoes, the soles of my feet were not hard enough to withstand the thorns and twigs and tough grass of neither the scrub nor the biting rock.

I scanned the hut again but it was bare.

Simadis had latched the door but not locked it. I went outside into the weak watery sunlight and looked around me. Simadis had taken away my clothes with him. Perhaps he had buried them or stowed them in a cleft in the rock. I searched, but I found nothing.

Gingerly, I walked around the perimeter of the hut, taking great care where I put my bare feet. At the rear, I found a spring trickling into a small pool. I fell to the ground and raised my lips to the trickle and let the cool fresh water drip into my parched mouth.

I lay like that for some time letting the water wash my face and sipping the liquid slowly. Then I washed my filthy, stinking body as best I could and also the sack which I laid on some rocks to dry in the weak sun. I sat with my feet in the muddy pool and relaxed my aching frame. I drank some more water and slowly some strength returned to my pulverised body. I stayed a long time in the sunny spot allowing some vigour to slowly return and I thought about my next move.

I spotted a small piece of sheepskin trapped in a bush. It was sufficient to wrap round one foot and provide some protection. I bound it securely with long pieces of tough grass. When the sack was dry I dressed. It took a long time to find a covering for my other foot. It was a fig sapling which came to my rescue. Feeling a bit like Adam discovering original sin in the Garden of Eden, I pulled off the leaves carefully avoiding the sap which causes a bad rash. Young and supple and wide as a tea plate, the leaves made a thick sole when pressed in a pile. I tied them over my remaining bare foot with more strands of grass. Thus elegantly attired, very weak physically but mentally determined to overcome any challenges I encountered. I started walking ... and thinking of how to deal with Simadis if I saw him.

Before long I came upon one of those small, white painted, stone chapels that stand hidden among the groves of trees: chapels that are built by a family often in gratitude for the birth of a longed-for son or as thanks for surviving a life-threatening illness.

Testing the door, I found, as I had expected, that it was unlocked. I entered. It was shadowy and chilly but it contained what I needed and what I had been looking for. On one of the stone ledges that acted as seats lay draped, as I had hoped, some brightly woven covers. I took off the sack and wrapped the scratchy wool around my body and over my shoulders. Now I could tear up the sack into strips for my feet. There was an embroidered linen cloth edged with lace on the altar, but somehow I could not bring myself to take it. What I had was adequate for my needs. Then, I sat by the altar behind the wooden screen and rested as I had done many days before when I had first arrived in the village and Mavro had found me.

When I stirred, every part of me was stiff and aching. The pain in my rib was like a dagger thrust and my head was sore and throbbed. I longed to remain there and rest. To stay meant to die of exhaustion and hunger. I forced myself to move outside. I guessed from the position of the sun and its weak warmth that it was now after noon. I calculated that I had no more than four hours to find food and shelter before the light went and the cold returned. I would be lucky to survive another night exposed to the elements. I could also calculate where the south lay and I knew I needed to travel south. I was in poor physical shape and hungry. But I had come this far.

Survival is in the mind

I drank some more water. I forced myself to move. Slowly, inch by careful inch, I moved among the rocks and scrub where I found a stout stick like the shepherds used, to help with my balance and support me.

I set off with the sun as my guide on a southward path.

***

2001

We were surprised when Lancaster did not appear and join us at dusk for supper but not concerned. By the time we had cleared away the food and washed the plates, cutlery and glasses a mood of apprehension began to take hold of us. Mama looked more serious than usual and snapped at us as we prepared our beds ready to sleep. Elenitsa looked drawn and her cheeks became hollow as if she were sucking in her cheeks. I did not recognise the look then, but later after he had gone from the island I became very familiar with that look. No one spoke their fears but what we thought was that he had been captured by the Germans.

'Yanni will return soon,' said Mama briskly whisking and shaking the blankets as she prepared the bed for us. 'Perhaps in the morning a message will come. Or your father will have news from the *kafeneion*.'

My father was now much stronger in his mind and his energy had returned also. He renewed his interest in the world around him and in our affairs. He visited the *kafeneion* once more and met the men of the village. But when he returned that day he had no news to reassure us and was surprised that Yanni had not reappeared.

I slept well that night and so did Fifi because we were young and energetic and a full day of activity tired us out, but I do not think Elenitsa or Mama slept much, for in the morning they looked washed out. Even Tonia seemed subdued. My father left us at first light to see if he could find Yanni or at least hear news of him. So, we waited all day, tense and anxious and jumping at every shadow and every sound of a footstep. By now we all loved Yanni very much.

'What news?' demanded Mama when my father returned from searching the cave.

'Nothing, *yineka mou*. Yanni has been in the cave as we expected. There was a small pile of cigarette butts on the floor by the place where Yanni usually sits. But no Yanni.'

'Did you ask the other men? Did you go to the *kafeneion*?' insisted my mother.

My father explained that he could not ask outright in the *kafeneion* if anyone had seen Yanni because of the presence of strangers and because Yanni's own presence was supposed to be a secret, but over coffee and raki there was no talk among the men of the villages of any German raids and arrests taking place.

'If Yanni has not been captured, has he left us?' I asked tactlessly.

'No! *Katholu*, not at all!' cried Elenitsa fiercely. 'He would never do that! Not without telling us!' Then she ran from the room in tears.

And, you know, this was the first time, I think, that she revealed the depth of her feeling for Yanni in front of us all.

So, the next day passed. Fifi and I finished our chores and went off together to search all the hideaways and small caves that we knew of and planning between us what we would do if we found Yanni lying injured at the bottom of a gully or unconscious under a tree and how we would rescue him and bind up his wounds. Children plan such things. They are always the heroes of their own adventures. We found nothing, of course; no sign of him at all.

That night, just after we had snuffed the lamps and snuggled down in bed there was a fierce storm. Tremendous claps of thunder echoed almost ceaselessly around the valley. The lightening crackled and spat. Great flashes illuminated the mountain, forking into the valley and then the rain came lashing down in huge torrents. It battered the tiles on the roof and built up into a great river which overflowed from the roof splashed like a waterfall onto the terrace and streamed in under the shutters and through the doors. We were fully occupied with finding pans to put under the drips. It was a wicked and fearsome night and we did not get very much sleep until the storm had passed away to the south after many hours. I am sure that we all thought of Yanni and where he was in that terrible storm.

CHAPTER 18

1941

Once again I survived through the kindness of strangers – and the guard dogs.

During the day the weather had deteriorated: the sun was obscured by dark purple clouds, a vicious wind whipped up and the temperature plummeted to freezing. By late afternoon the sky was a sullen yellow ochre behind swirling black clouds.

I faltered through the rough undergrowth, rocks and trees and the sound of my stumbling footsteps or my scent set off a chorus of dogs barking. A cottage appeared. It had been hidden from my view by a small stand of stubby oak trees, the kind that the goats eat. It was too late to turn back and I was too shattered even to bother to contemplate it. I stood motionless trying to think what to do through a brain clouded with exhaustion.

One of the guard dogs raced up to me and stood at my feet slobbering at the mouth and barking furiously. I told him to shut up in a feeble voice. I must have spoken in Cretan for a male voice called out roughly asking me who I was.

I couldn't see him but I knew he had already seen me so I knew it was useless to make a run for it even if I could have found the strength which I knew I could not. I decided that pretence was useless so I told him I was a stranger to these parts and that I was lost.

A squat man appeared through the trees, enveloped in a heavy cloak and with a red scarf wrapped around his head and chin. He levelled the barrel of a rifle at me while the dogs bared their teeth and jumped up at me. I feebly raised my hands.

I presumed him to be the owner of the dogs. He looked me up and down and assessed my strange attire with some astonishment. I looked such a sight and so little a threat that he laughed a loud barking laugh. He called off the dogs and beckoned me to follow him to the house.

He took me inside into the warmth and told me to sit. He was still holding the rifle. But he called out to the woman of the house for a blanket and some raki.

The cottage was a long low building of stone with thick walls and small windows. There was a stone floor covered with rag rugs, and a double bed in a recess over which was thrown a brightly coloured woven blanket. Guns, knives and tools hung on the wall. The *zomba* roared merrily. On it sat a large stew pot. The smell of wood smoke mixed with the aroma of goat and garlic was intoxicating. An oil lamp threw a yellow glow over the centre of the room; a small candle flickered on the corner shelf in front of the icon. A typical Cretan house, in fact. A small hope flickered in me that this might be a haven and a sanctuary for me, perhaps.

The woman of the house was, I noted with surprise, very much younger than her weatherbeaten husband, very small and very pretty. She entered from another room with a blanket and a sturdy Cretan cloak which she handed to me. I wrapped my freezing body in it and drew as close as I could to the flaming stove. The woman disappeared and returned quickly with a glass and a raki bottle and then fetched a bowl and poured me some *stifado* from the pot on the top of the *zomba*. The man put down the rifle where his hand could reach it and poured out the raki and cut a slice of hard cheese.

'So, stranger, why do you wander the countryside so oddly dressed?' he demanded, as I crammed the bread and cheese into my mouth.

I paused before I replied. I could hardly reveal the truth of what had happened to me: it was too incredible. I had not yet had time to decide how I was going to deal with

Simadis if I ever got the my hands on him and so I answered that I had been attacked and robbed of everything I possessed by some bandits and nearly lost my life also.

I don't know whether the answer really satisfied him, but he seemed prepared to accept what I said with a nod.

'How many men were there?'

I decided to embroider a bit in the Cretan fashion.

'Four, maybe six, all heavily armed with rifles, pistols and knives,' I said. 'They took my mule and my gold and then all my clothes. They gave me a good beating and tied me up and left me to die in the mountains. But the rope was loose and I escaped. God be thanked,' I added piously, crossing myself for good measure.

'This I can see,' he replied. 'We have not heard tell of bandits or sheep rustlers here. In Sfakia, perhaps. They are lawless brigands there, but our mountain here is peaceful.'

I said nothing.

'And so, stranger, where is your village?' he asked. I thought that I had better not name my village in case it caused complications later, so I made my answer deliberately vague.

'In the south, close to the coast,' I replied.' You know of Paleohora?'

He nodded, so I was warned to take care with my story.

'I was travelling to Chania to make a trade when I was attacked. I was totally lost when your dog found me.'

'He is a good hunting dog.' he told me. '*Lipon*, you are from Paleohora? It is a day's walk from here. My name is Pavlo and this is my woman, Sofia. We are mountain people. I can see that you are injured for you are black and blue and are covered with much blood. The bandits certainly gave you a pasting, the cuckolds. My woman will care for you. You may rest here for the night and tomorrow we will help you return to your village.'

I put my hand on my heart in thanks and told them I was called Yanni.

'Thank you,' I said.

And thank you for believing my feeble tale, I thought. Soon after the woman cleaned my wounds and covered them with ointment. She then fixed me a bed in the other chamber. I staggered through barely aware of what I was doing as pain and fatigue overtook me. I wrapped myself in the cloak and blankets and fell into an exhausted sleep.

Next day, after a night of fitful sleep and lurid dreams in which blood and blows featured heavily, I woke in great pain from every inch of my body. I have a fuzzy memory of Sofia forcing me to drink a hot liquid from a mug at times but the following many hours or so were a blur.

Snow had fallen while I slept. The wind had blown it into drifts against the outside walls of the house. We were wrapped in a cocoon of snow. I knew none of this. I woke, finally, painfully stiff and sore. A luminous silvery light infiltrated the shutters. The house was silent and my room was cold. I struggled to rise from the tangle of cloak and blankets. I rolled from the bed and hobbled to the next room.

Sofia sat close to the *zomba* working with her spindle. A can of water was steaming on the stove as well as a large pan of stew. Sofia rose and smiled and fluttered her eyelashes when she saw me while on the far side of the room Pavlo was struggling into a heavy sheepskin coat.

'You had a lucky escape, my friend,' said Pavlo. 'It snowed in the night. Look, you can see.' He gestured to the window. The landscape outside was pure shimmering white where the snow had fallen. It festooned the branches of the olive trees which drooped and curled under its weight.

'You can go nowhere today until the snow melts so you must stay here and eat and drink with us. '

'*Malista!*' added Sofia enthusiastically.

'If I had not found you, you would have died from the cold. Now I must go out again and find out what has happened to my sheep and goats. '

Sofia gave me a tin mug of warm milk to drink and a plate of bread and cheese to eat and a hug around the waist. I flinched which was not the reaction she expected and she made a face.

'I have much pain,' I said. 'And thank you for your care.'

'*Kala*,' she said. 'You live.' She busied herself making me a coffee and I staggered to the chair opposite hers and lowered myself very delicately onto the seat.

'It snows,' she said. '*Para poly*. There is much. We are high here. We are trapped for today. My man has been in and out since first light clearing a path to his animals. When it stops freezing the snow will melt. Here drink this.'

I thanked her and sipped the thick black liquid and gnawed at some bread and cheese.

Then she placed a bundle of clothes on my knee and let her hand drift over my thigh.

'You can wear these,' she said.' I will help you dress later, if you are in pain.' she added.

'Thank you, but there is no need.' I replied. 'I will manage.'

I considered how close I had come to a second death, exposed and in the snow. Simadis's desire to kill me by means of exposure would have certainly been realised if I had not found shelter with these Cretans strangers ... although Sofia was almost too kind.

The Cretan code is almost contradictory: on the one hand the vicious vendetta and on the other kindness to strangers. The poorest villager will give all that he has to a passing stranger: it is a matter of honour. A traveller is always welcomed into the household. Food and drink is pressed on him. He is given a bed for the night and a cloak to wrap himself in. Bed bugs come free. Many times Wolf travelled to and from Chania sure always that he would find somewhere to stay overnight if he was delayed on his journey. Many times he sat in the fields or rested in the shade of the olive trees to share in some olives, bread and oil given him by a stranger in the certain knowledge that he and his family would offer the same welcome and hospitality to any similar stranger who passed by their door.

The kindness of strangers.

The bitterness of enemies.

My thoughts turned to Simadis. Simadis, who had tried to kill me in the most violent and sadistic way. Simadis, who was not kind to strangers. Simadis who was eaten alive with the bitter gall of jealousy. An evil maggot had burrowed into his brain and it was consuming him. A red mist blinded him to reality. I now realised that he must have been spying on me for weeks, and watching my movements while he plotted and planned to kidnap me and remove me from the scene. He must have stalked me just like he hunted in the mountains for animals and game for the pot. It was common knowledge that I went to the cave nearly every afternoon and he must have waited for an opportunity to follow me.

They don't call jealousy the green-eyed monster for nothing. It camps in your head. It festers like a wound. It is not an emotion which is in any sense rational. It is warped and twisted. It is a grotesque perversion. It becomes a monstrous, evil obsession. It dominates every waking thought. You cannot think of anything else.

Simadis coveted Elenitsa and bitterly resented me. Each time Elenitsa looked at me or spoke to me or laughed with me or walked with me, each time I helped her with the pitcher at the spring or carried her sack or helped her weed the *kipo*, a dangerous sword must have twisted in Simadis's distorted mind. It must have – had indeed – driven him crazy, ballooned out of all proportion and blinded him to any consequences.

Since the olive harvest, Elenitsa's growing warmth towards me, must have increasingly driven Simadis crazy with jealousy and made him more and more suspicious of me as a rival. His feelings of hatred towards me must have escalated to such a height that he was jealous of the very air that I breathed and obsessed madly with the idea of getting rid of me.

The red mist of jealousy was irrational of course, because in the end Simadis could not control Elenitsa's emotions. He could not force her to love him. Simadis needed to feel in control of the situation. And his plan made him feel in control. What he did not realise was that his life and soul were actually controlling him. His violent and threatening behaviour just demonstrated the blind obsession which gobbled him up. He could not control Elenitsa, but he could control me. In his warped mind he must have thought that if he got rid of me, removed me as a rival, Elenitsa would fall into his arms. Consumed by this delusion, Simadis thought that he had hit upon the solution: he would kidnap me and leave me to die on the mountain. This would absolve him of any responsibility for my death. The elements the wind and cold would do his job for him. Then Elenitsa would be his.

I knew that there was no cure for jealousy and obsession. When – if – I returned to the village I would have to accept that Simadis would always be watching me, spying on me, waiting like a wild cat preparing to pounce on me.

I considered how I was to deal with him. At that moment I wanted to kill him – an eye for an eye. I recalled the words of my officer who had told us that revenge was a dish best eaten cold. I should plan my revenge with cool logic.

Options: Kill him – and be killed in return. Set off an enduring vendetta. Not something I was keen to do.

Proclaim his wickedness to the whole village; describe in every gory detail what he had done to me. But, I was the outsider. Why would they support me against Simadis who was one of their own? How could I be sure that they would not abandon me, reject me, stop helping me, and betray me to the Germans?

Simadis was admired for his courage. He was a crack shot; he was admired for that too. But he was also capable of a ruthless attempt at murder. I wondered if I was his first victim. What had he experienced during the fighting in the North where atrocities were not punished and more likely encouraged? The first killing is the hardest, so they say, the second is easier. After that killing becomes a routine activity. There is a blurring of right and wrong. War contaminates; it dehumanises.

I could stay away from the village, never return, and abandon all that I loved. Would that be the best decision for everyone? Not for Elenitsa, perhaps. But for me?

Stay away, I told myself, look for help elsewhere. Try to make for the coast and look for a way to escape from the island. I now knew that boats rarely sailed in the treacherous seas of the winter months. Already the snow was a reminder of the harshness of the elements and how quickly the weather could bedevil any plan. Where could I remain safe and undiscovered until the gentler winds and seas of spring?

I could now speak Cretan well. I could pass as a Greek who knew the Cretan language, although I would never be taken for an islander. I could answer any enquiries by saying that I was from Northern Greece where my fair hair and blue eyes would not be out of place.

Could I place my trust in the kindness of strangers while I wandered from village to village looking for a way to escape from the island? It was a risky strategy. Could I chance it? It briefly crossed my mind that here in the isolated farmstead of Pavlo and Sofia I could make a temporary home. But then I discarded that idea. I needed to live with a family where I could be passed off as a visiting distant cousin. Pavlo and Sofia and I might make uneasy bedfellows. Already Sofia had flirted with me; she was a very desirable young woman and knew it. There was a big difference in age between Sofia and her man and I suspected that Pavlo had his hands full satisfying her needs. For me, that way danger lay.

The alternative was that when the snow cleared and my body had healed a bit I should return to the village. At that moment the pain from my bruised body was so intense that I was glad the snow was forcing me to stay put and rest.

If I returned to the village what would I say or do? How would I explain my disappearance to Elenitsa, to Wolf, to the family? How would the family, especially Elenitsa, react? Furthermore, I did not know what story Simadis might have concocted about me. What lies had he told? Had he spoken of me at all? Had he kept silent about our encounter? Had he denied all knowledge of me? If so, and I kept quiet about his behaviour, would that help me? Would that keep me safe?

While I pondered my options, Sofia had been busy mixing liquid in a small glass.

'Drink this,' she ordered, handing it to me. 'It is for the pain. I see you have much pain. You suffer.' She stood behind me and gently massaged my shoulders. She stood close enough for me to feel her clothes against my sore back and to smell the musky aroma of her skin. She moved closer still and slipped her hands over my shoulders and on to my chest. I turned to look up at her forcing her to move slightly away.

'What is it?' I asked, indicating the thick brown liquid in the mug I held.

'It is good *farmaka*.' She said moving closer again. 'It is the juice from the poppy. It will make you feel sleepy.' She bent her head, nuzzled my ear and kissed the hollow in my neck. She moved to face me, placed her hands on my shoulders and leaned towards me.

'Let me help you to the bed.' She said lowering her face to mine. Her lips were soft and curving and very tempting.

'It will help get rid of the pain and I can help too.' she said softly. I placed the mug and not her lips to my mouth and looked at her over the rim.

'Thank you, Sofia. Your man will return soon and then I will go to bed.' She shrugged and moved away and we passed the time in silence until Pavlo returned. Then I made my way unsteadily to bed.

Sometimes the best decisions come in that dreamy time between sleeping and waking. My mind drifted as I warmed myself under the blankets and as the power of the potion began to take effect.

For Elenitsa's sake, I decided, I would return to the village. I would become a full member of the family and I hoped that this would throw a cloak of protection around me. I would say nothing about Simadis's treatment of me. And I would wait in silence to see what he would do next. I would be prepared and I would be always on my guard. We would hold the secret of what had happened between us, but no one else would know unless Simadis told ....

[At this point pages appear to have been torn out of the diary]

***

2001

I overheard it all. *Ela na su po.* I did not intend, how you say, to eavesdrop. I was curled up on the sleeping ledge in the corner. No one noticed that I was there. I had been asleep, I think, when their talking roused me and I was interested, of course, in what my father had to say to Lancaster.

Your grandfather returned, in the end, after many days.

He told us he had been beaten by bandits. We did not question this because Yanni had always been honest with us. Elenitsa could not hide her joy.

The sun had already set that evening so my father and Yanni sat in gloom, the only light came from a small oil lamp on the table. After many weeks of pain and suffering my father seemed to have become restored, if not to his former self, at least to a man who was able to function nearly as well as he had before his arrest and imprisonment.

'Yanni,' he said pouring your grandfather a raki, 'I have not been blessed. I am not young. I may die tomorrow in this uncertain world. I may be arrested again. I may be shot; only God knows and it is as God wills. If I had a son he would defend and care for my family. He would work for them.'

'You have Wolf. He is like a son to you.' Your grandfather replied.

'Wolf is his father's son. There lies his loyalty. He is accountable to his own father and his own family. My family needs the protection of a man. These are terrible times.'

I heard the clink of glass as the men drank a toast to each other. There was silence while my father considered his next words. Then he said: 'Yanni, I have not been blessed with a son. It is the great sadness of my life and of my woman. In my eyes, you are to me the son I never had. You could be to me a son for all the days of my life.'

I tried to understand what my father was saying. Yanni could be to him a son. What did this mean? Was he going to adopt him? I had heard of such things taking place. Was it possible?

My father continued: 'Elenitsa's mother has spoken to me. She has told me of how much you have helped us on the farm and in the fields and groves while I was ill. I can see this anyway with my own eyes. You cared for the sheep most skilfully. The goats too.' He paused. 'She has also observed you and Elenitsa together. Tell me now with truth if you care for Elenitsa. Tell me what you plan to do. My daughter is a precious rose. I will not allow you to bring sadness to her life. If you care for her,' he paused, 'you … could take her as your own … and be the son of my old age.'

All this my father spoke slowly, hesitating over some of the phrases as if uncertain whether to speak the thoughts in his mind, as if they were too precious and too vital to be voiced out loud.

I listened very intently to what my father was saying for now I was very interested. I stayed very still for I did not wish to be discovered and sent away.

'Tell me with truth in your heart, Yanni.'

'Nektarios, I will not lie. I too may die tomorrow,' said your grandfather. 'We may all die tomorrow. We do not know what the future will hold. The war may never end. The Germans may be the victors. I may be captured and executed. I could stay here in this remote village and, with luck, outlast the war. I can pass for a Cretan. I could give you what you want, the son of your old age, I could give you grandchildren too. In my heart I care deeply for Elenitsa, but on the other hand … I am a soldier. It is my duty to return to my regiment.'

'If it is your desire to leave us, we will not hinder you. If you choose to remain with us Elenitsa will come to you willingly. She will respect, honour and obey you in all things. You will become my son. You will have Elenitsa's dowry and a room in which to lay your heads and live your lives together. If you are unwilling, I salute your sense of honour to your army and your country.'

I heard my father pour out another raki. I heard the clink as the glasses touched each other. He said, 'A toast to Crete and death to all Germans.'

'*Yammas*,' replied Yanni.

'But,' continued my father, 'if you are unwilling to

choose Elenitsa you must be moved to another place of safety far from Elenitsa's eyes.'

'Unwilling!' Yanni cried. 'No never. A dowry does not matter to me. We don't have dowries in New Zealand. I would like a wife like Elenitsa and I do care for her. I am a lonely man, far from home, far from my mother and father. You offer me a home, a family and above all a place of safety.'

'Safety.' said my father. 'What safety do we have?' and when he said this I was very frightened and did not wish to hear more. 'Safety? It is as fragile as a leaf in the wind. The Germans are still increasing their patrols. They want to tighten their grip on the island. You know that their aim is to round up escapees like you. They are scouring the countryside on foot. The raids on the villages happen every day. They round up innocent men like me for no reason except that we are Cretan and they want to crush us.' My father's voice became loud with anger. 'And they are searching from the air. The planes fly low down the valley to the coast. We see and hear them. We have watched them as they circle overhead round and round like huge malignant buzzards. And other planes are dropping supplies to their troops in the mountains and valleys. Do you remember that only last week Wolf returned in a mood of great triumph after recovering a box of German supplies which lay smashed in one of the high reaches where he hides his sheep? The German grip on this island tightens every day.'

'Nektarios, you are right, as always.' replied your grandfather. 'Nektarios, I do not need time to make up my mind. Nektarios, if you wish it and if you will give me your blessing I will take my place in your family as a son should. In Cretan costume and with a Cretan name and papers I can go anywhere and with much more safety.'

My father stood up: I heard the scrape of his chair. I heard him move toward Lancaster. I opened my eyes just a little, you understand, so that I could peep and I could see through my eyelashes that he grasped Yanni's shoulders, hugged him and kissed him on both cheeks. Then he called for my Mother and my sisters and in the commotion and excitement I slipped over to join them.

'*Ela na sup o*. They say that love, a cough and money cannot be hidden!'

It was not a traditional wedding. Oh no. How could it be? It was a time of war and hardship.

Lancaster was not a Cretan man. He was not of the Orthodox Church. Many things were different.

Tonia, Fifi and I rose early and helped to get Elenitsa ready. We bathed her and then smoothed rose water over her body. We washed her hair with fresh water from the spring and rinsed it with water perfumed with lavender. We sat in the morning sun and combed Elemi's hair in ripples over her shoulders while it dried. We took it in turns to recite the traditional *mantinades*. They are little rhyming verses of two lines, you know.

Today the sky is shining, today the day is shining,
Today the eagle is marrying the dove.

We took her wedding clothes from the cedar chest – clothes which Elenitsa had woven and embroidered, ever since she was a small child, in preparation for this special day. That was our custom then. First a white linen shift, then long pantaloons and white stockings. We wound a long red sash around her waist and helped her shrug herself into a dark blue, long sleeved jacket which she had embroidered in red and gold thread. There were many little buttons but Fifi and I had little nimble fingers to pop them through the tight loops. Finally, on top, we tied an embroidered, fringed apron. She slipped her feet into new black shoes. Under her new shoes Tonia and some of our girl cousins had written their names because they believed and hoped that name that was wiped off first was the name of the girl who would be married next! I know that Tonia secretly hoped that it would be her name. I had seen her look at Wolf and I recognised the signs. Inside the shoe it was the custom to put a tiny pair of scissors in order to protect her from witches, swearing and curses.

'Witches?' Alex enquired.

'*Malista*. We all believed then in ghosts and spirits and the power of curses. Maybe swearing did not bother us!'

Your grandfather had bought for Elenitsa a golden cross on a chain for her wedding gift. I don't know where he got it. I expect Wolf bought and paid for it for him. She wore it around her neck. My mother came to Elenitsa and placed a lace veil over her head. Our Mother had worn this veil on her own wedding day. It had been crocheted by our Mother's mother. It was very precious and the design was very beautiful. It showed love-birds and roses. My Mother kissed Elenitsa gently and tenderly as she placed the veil over her hair.

'Blessed be the hour,' she said.

Mama led her onto the terrace to show Elenitsa to our Father.

'Wife,' he said. 'Our daughter is like a rose in a basket.'

Elenitsa kissed the hands of our father and our mother. In turn they kissed her forehead. This was our tradition.

'I bless you, my daughter,' said Father.

'I bless you, my daughter,' said Mother with tears in her eyes.

Lancaster had spent the night with Wolf at his house. And there the men prepared him for his wedding day also. He dressed in his Cretan outfit. Wolf's present to Lancaster was a pair of new white leather boots. Where Wolf found boots from I don't know. Boots of any kind, as you know, were very difficult to find in the war and very expensive to buy. It was a symbol of how much Wolf loved and respected your grandfather that he did this thing for him.

Do you know that we had to cut the soles not from leather but from rubber car tyres?'

I nodded for my grandfather had noted this in his diary.

'But Wolf found some white boots. He was very good at that sort of thing – and they fitted – and Wolf gave them to Lancaster for a wedding present. How fine he looked. Lancaster left those boots behind when he escaped. Elenitsa took then and put them in her cedar chest and I saw her hold them and look at them while she wept.

When Lancaster was ready the shooting began. The men fired their rifles and pistols in the air to celebrate, to get rid of demons and to make God hear!' Poppy crossed herself as she always did when she mentioned the name of God.

Then Wolf, Lucky, Bunny and Stavro and the other *andartes* led Lancaster to our house. He came before my father and my father blessed him also.

'My daughter is the cypress of our garden,' said my Father, 'the rose of the grove of heaven.' He was not a poet, as you know, but these are the words that they said in those days. 'Now we give her to you. Take care of her as a husband should.'

Mama took both their hands: 'May pain and worry be a stranger to you both,' and raising her eyes to look your grandfather straight in the face, she said. 'Be kind to her.'

By now Mama, Tonia, Fifi and I were all weeping, but they were tears of happiness for we loved Elenitsa very much and we also loved Lancaster. We also knew that we were not losing Elenitsa so we were happy not sad.'

In our custom, a bride leaves her home to live in the house of her husband's parents and there she helps his mother in all the household tasks. But Lancaster had no parents. My mother and father already regarded him as the son of the house: the son that they had never had. He had no other home in Crete so we knew that our lovely Elenitsa would remain with us.

After they were married, my Father welcomed the whole

village and all our cousins and friends back to our house. We served a great feast which lasted the whole day and into the night. Before midnight, I curled up on the corner of the raised platform and fell asleep despite the noise of the singing and dancing. Perhaps you have seen our dancing?

'Yes, my grandfather describes the feasts and the dancing in his diary. You really know how to celebrate!'

'Ah! The men, they dance like warriors, springing higher and higher. One man, I remember, I expect it was Simadis for he was a very good dancer, jumped onto the table while Wolf placed a tumbler on top of a bottle. Then he sprang onto the glass and balanced on one leg while he drank a toast to the bride and bridegroom!

The others clapped in time with music from Lucky's lyra and the bouzouki and roared him to the rafters. Another man, I don't remember who, leapt onto a chair did a double flip just like an acrobat and landed on two feet in front of the bride. In one house in another village they danced so hard that the floor collapsed into the room below!

Before Elenitsa and Lancaster entered the room which had been prepared for them, the men threw down onto the floor their leather belts. The idea was that Elenitsa and Lancaster would have to walk on them and this would make them strong like the belts and never get sick.

Then Elenitsa threw a pomegranate with all her might hard onto the ground so that it smashed into many pieces and the seeds scattered left and right all over the floor. Many seeds meant many children and happiness forever.

Elenitsa clapped her hands and exclaimed in a voice trembling with emotion: 'Many children and much happiness for us, Yanni, my love!' And our lovely, serious, serene Elenitsa burst into tears of joy. The rest cheered as they shut the door.

The next day Simadis left the village.

***

2001

'Did you know they got married?' demanded Hennery after Poppy's bombshell. 'You never told me, man!'

We had left Poppy and taken the short walk to the sea front, found a bar and ordered two large beers while we digested this most unexpected news.

'No, I didn't. He never wrote a word about it. I feel blown away.'

'It's awesome.'

We sat in silence. The sun, the rocks, the pounding waves receded as my spinning mind tried to make sense of it all. I took a swig of cold beer and idly pushed a handful of olives into my mouth.

'There's a gap in the diary after the kidnap, Hennery, where pages have been torn out. You can check. Honest.'

'Didn't that give you a clue?'

'No, not really. It never crossed my mind that the gap was important. It was just a gap. Could have been for any reason.'

'You wouldn't make much of a detective then would you, man?' commented Hennery tartly but with a grin that meant that he didn't mean it.

'I suppose I assumed that the pages had been used for some other purpose – for lighting a fire, anything at all and that the fact that they were missing did not mean anything significant. Everyone tears pages out of a notebook don't they? There doesn't have to be a sinister reason does there? I never gave it a thought. What Poppy told us – it's a real shock. Not what I was expecting at all.'

'Surprise is an understatement, man!'

'You could say that.'

'So the old man was very economical with the actualité – isn't that the phrase, man?'

'Devious would be more accurate.' We lapsed into silence again. Dusk fell. The moon rose shedding a shaft of light over the sea in front of us. We ordered more beer.

'If he married Elenitsa,' said Hennery eventually, 'why didn't he return to Crete after the war?'

'The simple answer is, Hennery, I don't know.'

'He doesn't mention a wedding at all?'

'No. Nothing at all, *katholu*, as Poppy would say. He writes about being kidnapped and he writes a lot about Simadis's jealousy and Simadis's behaviour in the village but then nothing at all until he makes plans to get away from the island. That's where the torn-out pages should be.'

'So he could have written about the wedding but later decided to censor the whole thing. X-rated!'

'Could be,'

'So why didn't he just chuck out the whole diary?'

'Who knows? But he didn't.'

'He stashed it away in the loft and there you found it after his death. I wonder why he did that, man.'

'Sentiment.'

'Sentimental? Your grandfather? He had all the sensitivity of a brick.'

'Perhaps he just simply stuffed it up there and forgot all about it.'

'Mmm.' Hennery considered this possibility, but his expression did not suggest that he was convinced. After a pause he said, 'So he fell for Elenitsa. But does he say anything else about her?'

'Yeah, a bit. He mentions that he fancied her and that he kisses her, but that's all. He writes far more about Poppy and Fifi – the terrible two. And Wolf. I could more easily believe that he was in love with Wolf!'

'Sounds like he definitely decided to cover his tracks, man'

'But not until later, Hennery, after he returned to New Zealand. I am convinced now that the missing pages mean that he wrote about her, about them both, at the time.'

'And deleted the evidence!'

We ordered more drinks and idly watched the evening *volta*. Thoughts, questions, ideas flooded through my brain. Hennery's voice broke into my thoughts.

'How could he abandon her and the family after all they had done for him?'

'Men abandon women and children all the time, Hennery. Fact of life.' Disappointment with my grandfather made me speak harshly.

'And he never returned to Crete, the bastard!' exclaimed Hennery.

'No and never spoke about it. I asked my Ma before I came to Crete and she said he had never mentioned that he was even in Crete during the war.'

'So he kept one of the most important years of his life a complete secret? Never said a word?'

'Not to me or Ma.'

'Like I said: devious.'

'Yeah, but he doesn't come across like that in the diary. His personality then was essentially a young, fresh, honest, upright young man who enlisted to fight for empire and country with strong ideas on right and wrong.'

'Well, man, he certainly changed later!' retorted Hennery as he stood up. 'Gotta point python at pan, man.' he explained. When he returned he said, 'He married your grandmother and they had just the one child who is your Mother, is that right?'

'That's about it.'

'And you know, Alex, what it means?

'Go on,'

'The old man could have been a bigamist.'

'Yep, I had thought of that.'

'No fucking sweat!'

Around us tourists were laughing and joking, relaxed and in holiday mood. The tavernas were filling. People were drinking and eating. Music floated from the bars. Lights twinkled. A holiday atmosphere surrounded us, while I was confronting the complete destruction of the foundations of my whole family history. Everything I had accepted as the truth of my life and family was collapsing in ruins around me. Had Poppy felt this too? Had certainty crumbled for her when I crashed into her life? What was the truth? My grandfather a bigamist; my mother illegitimate? What did that make me?

'Alex, your Mother's name is Helen, right?'

'Sure.'

'So, man, work it out. Helen is Elenitsa in Greek.'

'Bloody hell. I never made that connection either.'

'I always said you were thick! The old man named your Ma after Elenitsa.'

'Doesn't that make him sentimental?' Hennery just made a face and took a gulp of beer.

'The next question is – and now we have to know – what happened to Elenitsa? Where is she? Is she alive?'

'Ask Poppy.' said Hennery. 'You know, man, we should tread gently; we may have opened up a can of worms here. Poppy must have worked out pretty soon that Lancaster married again in New Zealand when you turned up saying you were his grandson. Talk about shock! I'm surprised she didn't have a heart attack. No wonder she was reluctant to talk about it. I am amazed she talked to you at all. In fact, I'm surprised she didn't curse you!!

'Perhaps she was curious. Perhaps she wanted to know what happened to Lancaster in the end.'

'Poppy is your rellie, you know, Alex. So is Fifi. Cheer up, man! You have a crowd of Cretan cousins!'

I said, 'No sweat.'

PART FOUR

CHAPTER 19

1942

'*Ela*, Yanni, come with us today,' said Lucky. 'You are family now. You saved my life. I owe you a debt. We are blood brothers!'

The *kafeneion* was a large vaulted room behind a wide terrace hung with gourds and set back from one of the main tracks that the shepherds used. I could tell that Wolf and Lucky were well known there and welcome visitors, as the raki appeared as soon as we set foot inside.

'You are one of us,' added Lucky.

I could easily pass for a Cretan now. My skin was tanned to a walnut brown and my blue eyes simply proclaimed that I was a man of Sfakia and if I was a shade too tall for a Cretan it could be explained away easily because many men of Sfakia were as lofty as the mountains which surrounded their strongholds and gave birth to them. My Cretan was almost fluent and my accent was good and hardly gave me away. If I was challenged I knew that as each area had a separate accent I could say that I was from the east of the island. I had my *taftotita* and my name was Yanni Papayiannakis.

No one could resist the hospitality of this *kafeneion* with its small cups of muddy coffee which arrived at the table remarkably hot, strong and sweet

'Like a woman!' commented Wolf with a grin.

The raki came in small copper pans and the mezes, even in a time of great hardship, were conjured up out of the kitchen by the woman of the house. On this day they had produced small quarters of hard boiled eggs and cold cooked giant beans in oil and oregano. Tasty and filling.

It was after midday and the *kafeneion* was full of dusty, working men who had come in from the fields and the groves and stringy old men escaping their wives. This time of year was devoted to the clearing-up of the weeds and undergrowth below the olive trees, pollarding the mulberries and pruning the olive trees and fruit trees.

And bonfires.

There is a prehistoric pull towards a bonfire: the challenge of getting the twigs to catch light from a tiny spark, the sudden rush of flames, the brilliant colours of red and orange, the heat and the roar. Each day, curls of smoke could be observed spiralling up from among the trees.

There was a pungent smell of woodsmoke, must, sweat and damp percolating through the room. The raki and the coffee relaxed us and the noise level was the usual high-pitched cacophony of shouts and arguments about the war and politics and the clack of backgammon counters that always occurred when a group of Cretan men were gathered together.

Nevertheless, our group was cautious in our conversation. Walls have ears, as they say. We did not believe that we had collaborators among us as we knew or recognised most of the crowd there that day, but you never knew who might be listening. We were very well aware that the Germans employed bribes and spies to collect intelligence for them. And you could never be too careful

We had been sitting in the corner of the *kafe* for about an hour and were drinking our third raki when Wolf who was sitting opposite me and facing the door which was on his far left suddenly stiffened and stopped talking in the middle of one of his jokes. He threw a sideways glance from his eyes without moving his head to Lucky at his left hand

'Do not move any of you,' he muttered in a low voice. 'Do not turn round, Yanni.' Of course, I immediately wanted to do exactly that.

'What's up?' I asked.

Wolf leaned forward. 'Manoli,' he whispered.

Lucky gave a low whistle, leaned back in his chair and checked the knife in his sash.

'So what?'

'*Tipota*. Nothing. This man, very bad man,' said Wolf.

'We know,' I added. 'We've met him before,'

'*Malaka!*' he said through gritted teeth.

'*Siga, siga*. He has not seen us,' said Lucky looking out of the corner of his eye. I was burning to look round and it took all my will power to resist and stay as I was.

'Is he alone?' I asked.

'He came inside with one other.' said Wolf. 'He may have men outside.'

'Relax,' said Stavro. 'He did not come here for you. It's just a coincidence.'

'He will not cause trouble here,' said Lucky with probably unjustified confidence.

'Only God knows,' returned Wolf looking down into his raki glass. 'He is our sworn enemy.'

'We can just walk out?' I suggested.

'We are not cowards! We are *Palikari*!' retorted Wolf, thoroughly roused and twirling the points of his moustaches and tossing his head. 'We do not give way to such a cuckold!'

I smothered any reply. What we did next was Wolf's decision, not mine, but if I was discovered all three of us knew that there would be trouble for everyone in the room.

'He has walked to the other side of the room.' reported Lucky. 'He is sitting. His companion also. He has ordered drinks. He has joined some men – of Sfakion, I think.'

I could feel that Wolf was very tense. I was tense myself. Manoli was the last person on the island that we wished to meet. But Lucky was, as ever, calm and relaxed

'We do not move,' he said. 'We continue to talk as if

nothing has happened.' So we hunched over our drinks and waited.

'He has seen me, I am sure,' said Wolf after a few minutes of intense uneasiness. 'He is looking this way. *Malaka!* He is getting up!' All the muscles in my stomach tensed with apprehension.

'He comes,' said Wolf.

'Son of a Turk, who have we here?' Manoli demanded, with a threatening sneer on his face and a malicious look in his eye like an angry bull when it catches sight of some red cloth. He planted his legs apart, thrusting out his bulky stomach in a challenge.

'Cuckold! You know us!' cried Wolf jumping to his feet.

Lucky put out a restraining arm. 'Brother, take care,' he warned. 'More bread is eaten with honey than with vinegar.'

Wolf and Manoli stood eyeball to eyeball. The noise of the room died away to nothing and there was silence. Men put down their drinks and turned their eyes our way.

'You whoreson goat fucker!' Manoli shouted and spat on the table.

'*Episis!* The same to you.' retorted Wolf.

'If you were my dog, I would give you poison!' shouted Manoli and roared with laughter. There were some stifled sniggers elsewhere.

'If I were your dog I would eat it!' riposted Wolf and there was laughter around the room. Manoli went red in the face.

His hand shot to his sash and the handle of his knife.

Bunny stood and punched Manoli in the stomach before he expected it. Manoli doubled up with pain and before he had time to recover, Wolf seized the dagger and held it to his throat.

While Eftiki pinioned his arms, I drew my pistol.

As Manoli struggled, his companion had crossed the

room. He didn't help him but he stared hard at me.

It was Cooper.

At that moment the *kafe* owner fired a shot in the air from his own gun.

'Enough boys. You are all banned. Get out!'

Manoli was scarlet with rage and I was white with shock.

Cooper, of all people, here?

The brothers released the struggling lump of gristle and fat that was Manoli. Wolf took the dagger and tossed it out of the window but I kept the gun trained on the poisonous wretch until he strode in fury to the door flung it open and left. I hoped he did not have a gang of men outside ready to attack us, or that the men of Sfakion would not take his side and jump on us. The entertainment over, the customers turned back to their drinks and their conversations and the noise level rose again.

Cooper continued to stare at me intently.

'Quick!' said Wolf,' let's go out through the kitchen. Manoli may have men out front who will come after us.'

'So will those men from Sfakion, make no mistake,' said Stavro. 'Want a bet, boys?' Wolf threw some money on the table and sauntered nonchalantly towards the rear of the Kafe. We followed and I left Cooper staring at my back. Then we ran through the kitchen and into the safety of the trees.

'I have been recognised,' I said as soon as we were safe back in the village. 'We're in for trouble! Cooper recognised me!'

'Who is this Cooper?' asked Lucky.

'An English soldier. He was with the group you led to Hora Sfakion. What's worse is that he may have recognised you or Wolf or all of you. We were together for seventeen hours on the trek to Hora Sfakion, remember. Later, he and I escaped together but he abandoned me on a beach. I thought he had sailed for Egypt. I don't trust him.'

'*Malaka*,' said Wolf. 'Are you certain?'

'I am sure of it.'

'*Malaka*,' repeated Wolf.

'I have to leave, as soon as possible. I can't stay here and put you all at risk. It's too dangerous.'

'*Malaka*,' said Wolf for a third time. 'You must go to the cave immediately and stay there.'

'What can I say to Elenitsa?'

'Say nothing. I will tell her that there is a strong rumour of another German search for escapees and that you have hidden. She will understand and anyway she can visit you at the cave. You will have fun!' Wolf's eyes twinkled and he slapped me on the back. 'Much fun!' Wolf can always find the funny side of every situation and turn it into a joke. That's why we all love him.

Meeting Cooper gave me food for thought. I knew he was a self-serving bastard. I knew I couldn't trust him; he had done me a bad turn. I knew he was ruthless and cruel and had a very murky, if not criminal, past. I had long ago forgotten all about him. So much had happened to me since. I had never expected to meet him again and I was convinced that he had left the island when he had abandoned me on the beach. Yet here he was in the company of Wolf's greatest enemy, Manoli, a man as aggressive as him, a sadistic, violent and brutal gang leader. Birds of a feather. It made me very uneasy.

I tried to reassure myself that our meeting was just a very unfortunate coincidence. Perhaps he had forgotten all about me. It was possible that I had misread his stare and that he had not recognised me at all. After all I dressed as an *andarte* and I had only spoken Cretan. Manoli knew Wolf and the others and maybe remembered me from our previous encounters. Cooper might have been interested in any one of us. But anyway, I would be gone from the island before he could do me another bad turn. I decided to put him out of my mind.

I remained in the cave.

I had not seen Wolf for over three days but, as he frequently disappeared into the mountains for days on end on secret business, passing on messages, acting as a runner and gathering intelligence, this was not cause for concern. Then, he reappeared looking his usual merry self, twirling the ends of his moustaches and looking relaxed.

'*Ela*, come,' he said. 'Come to the village. Now we eat together.'

At the house the women fussed around the men and produced what food they could. But food was still scarce. The seeds had been sown but the seedlings were no more than a few stalks high in the *kipo* and supplies of grain and nuts and olives from the previous year had dwindled until we were literally scraping to the bottom of the urns. But somehow they always found a goat to slaughter when the men returned and there was always plenty of raki to drink.

We sat together on benches and chairs in the golden glow of the oil lamps in the upper room. This might be the last time I do this, I thought, as I looked at the familiar faces of my companions. The women were dim figures on the fringes of the room or just voices down below in the kitchen.

The raki bottles littered the table. Wolf began to tell a long rambling story about a man and a goat and the room filled with laughter. It could have been any ordinary gathering, but it would be my last. Smoke from the lamps and from the cigarettes eddied in curling wisps. The men slammed their glasses on the table and shouted toasts: '*Tsigia! Yammas!*' It was all so familiar and, yes, this might be the last time I would experience the warmth and the hospitality of the Cretans.

Wolf passed me a chunk of goat meat on the end of his knife and leaned towards me.

'You must be ready tomorrow night,' he whispered. 'It is all arranged. Say nothing to anyone, especially the women. They must know nothing.'

'You mean, I am going, leaving the island?'

'Yes, my friend, you and others, other English. Lucky has spoken with a man of Elafonissi. He has a big fishing boat. He is leaving tomorrow night from a small beach near there. The weather is good, the tide is right. There is no moon. But no one must know. If the women find out they will weep and then they will make a fuss. People will then suspect that something is going on. We must slip away silently. Bring nothing you cannot pack in a bag. You have your gun still?'

I nodded.

'Kala, Bring it. Do not say a word of this to Elenitsa unless you wish to stay.'

A surge of excitement and a lurch of regret. Yes, I wanted to get back to the army. I had joined the army to fight a war to destroy Nazi Germany. I had seen first-hand what the Germans were prepared to do to women and children. The Germans now controlled the island and were crushing it with an iron grip, hammer on anvil, destroying any man, woman and child who stood in their way, flagrantly ignoring the Geneva Convention with bloody reprisals and burning villages. I had seen for myself the smoking ruins of a village, inhaled the sickening stink of burning flesh, witnessed the planes dropping death from the sky. The terror, the starvation, the violence; I had experienced it all. And for this reason alone I would take my chance to try to escape so that I could fight once more to set these people free.

And then I remembered Elenitsa and the family and a huge wave of despondency and regret poured over me like a cold bath of water. 'Am I soldier or am I a coward?' I asked myself.

That evening I put on the remains of my army uniform but wrapped the knotted Cretan headband around my forehead as a souvenir. Lucky had come to me with a deadly sharp knife with an intricately carved ivory handle.

'This is a present from me,' he said, hugging me in a tight embrace. 'You saved my life. May it save yours.'

I wound the dark red sash around my waist. I slipped Lucky's gift carefully among its folds.

I took my gun and began to check it.

'Yanni *mou*, what are you doing?' Elenitsa stood in the doorway. I had not heard her approach. I did not know how long she had been observing me as she always moves so quietly like a cat.

'I am cleaning my gun as you can see, Elenitsa *mou*.' I replied evenly. 'I am going with Wolf and the *andartes* tonight. Do not worry I will be back soon.' I lied.

Something in my manner must have given Elenitsa a warning or a premonition for she stared at me intently, her large solemn dark eyes filling with tears.

She came and stood beside me, and put her arm around my neck and kissed my cheek and then nuzzled her nose into the hollow of my neck.

'I love you,' she said simply. 'May God go with you.'

The tender way she looked at me, with her eyes filled so trustingly with love and tears, made me swallow hard. This was not easy. I wanted to say goodbye but knew that I must keep my plans a secret in case it jeopardized the whole mission.

'Bless you, Elenitsa *mou*.' It was all I dared to say. I said it very gently and kissed her in return to prevent any more questions.

I looked down at dear little Elenitsa tucked in the curve of my arm. Her smooth skin, her curving eyelashes, the gentle serenity of the expression on her face; it made it hard to leave.

Mama and Tonia had prepared food for the mission. It was impossible for me to say any goodbyes. So I kissed them all on the forehead as I left.

'God go with you,' said Mama gently, and she made the

sign of the cross over my chest. I wondered if she suspected anything. I followed Wolf and Lucky in the direction of the setting sun.

We took the track from the village down to the valley floor and followed the dry, rocky river bed to the foot of the next mountain peak, which I knew we had to climb. But I was fitter now than at any time since the Battle for Crete and I was exhilarated at the thought of escape. And at first the going was easy. We marched silently as we had done so many times before together.

It was a long trek down into the valley floor and along the river bed then up the opposite slope until we picked up one of the ancient donkey tracks which led us even further west. We stopped after about two hours at a tiny, white-painted chapel tucked into the side of the cliff where a small cluster of Cretans was waiting.

'Why have we stopped?' I asked Wolf.

'We wait. Others will join us,' he explained.

The Cretans were quite agitated and smoked incessantly, fiddled with their guns, took their knives out of their sashes and tested the blades against their thumbs. Minutes passed uneasily.

'They are late,' muttered Lucky.

'Then we will wait no longer,' decided Wolf. 'If they do not come in the next minute we will go.'

We were just on the point of breaking nerves, when noises behind us put the group on alert and shadows emerged which turned into men. The new group consisted of British soldiers in uniform and Cretan *andartes*. The Cretans embraced each other with hugs and greetings. With breaking horror I realised that the leader of the new group was Simadis. I looked at him with mixed and confused feelings. He caught my eye and scowled before looking away. This was a man I had not laid eyes on for nearly three months and then he had shown himself to be my implacable enemy and almost murdered me. What would he do to me now if he had the chance?

Wolf and Lucky embraced him in the Cretan manner and seemed to be on friendly terms with him. Then Wolf and Simadis, Lucky and the others set off again. As we marched on I could hear the soft tones of their whispered conversation. The new group and I followed.

I felt more on edge than ever. Simadis had tried to harm me once, would he attempt do so again? A small nudge from him and I could slide silently into oblivion off the track and into the void below. I decided to keep as far away from him as possible.

We trekked on, always travelling west, slipping and tripping, dislodging a cascade of stones from time to time, always in danger of tumbling off the path. It was pitch black and we only had the light of the stars and the form of the man in front to guide the way.

We halted later on at a spring and drank some cold water. It was refreshing and welcome. Another group joined us there.

'Well, mate,' said a voice in my ear, 'who would have thought it!'

I spun round. 'Cooper!' I exclaimed.

'The very one,' he said with a smirk.

'You bastard. You bloody bastard; you abandoned me! Fuck off.' Attack is the best form of defence I thought. Cooper did not look put out at all.

'Yeah, well you know how it is: every man for himself, ain't it. Gotta look after Number One.'

'You certainly did that!' I glared at him.

'What are you doing here?' He asked with not much curiosity and apparently unmoved by my frosty attitude.

'Same as you, I suppose.'

'Escaping from this God-forsaken island.' he spat a gobbet of saliva onto the ground.

'I thought you had got away.'

'Almost. Bloody boat sank. Full of holes. Had to swim

for it. Luckily no bloody Germans around where I landed so I kept on the march until I came to a village.'

'Where was it?'

'Bloody miles away from here. Big village called Kako something. Kaky poo if you ask me! Been with Cretans ever since. All goat pongs and interfering old witches in black, nosing about and gossiping. Stopping you talking to the girls. Effing men always cleaning guns and sharpening knives, shouting, and singing their bloody mournful songs or going off for days on end to God knows where. Then coming back and drinking raki till they fall over. Raki's choice though. Got plenty of that and lots of sitting on my arse, doing fat all.'

I nodded. What could I say? His views of this island and this people were so different from mine. I decided to ask him about Simadis:

'Your leader, the man you came with tonight. Did he live there?'

'Yeah, turned up a while back. Seems to be a cousin or something. They are always cousins, aren't they? He went off with the leaders into the mountains all the time. Bloody good shot though. His name's Simadis. Always sounds as if he's shouting or arguing the toss to me. I call him Bad-Tempered Bastard. He never liked me, always eyed me like he doesn't trust me and wants to slit my throat.'

For once, I felt that Simadis and I were in agreement. Cooper deserved to have his throat slit. I had to admit that Simadis had good reason not to trust Cooper, when I recalled wryly Cooper's behaviour the last time I was with him. I offered no comment.

Then I recalled my last meeting with Simadis who had tried to kill me, who was insane with jealousy about Elenitsa and me, not rational, and driven by a desire for revenge.

And here? Was Simadis friend or foe?

'There are five of us in our group. How many are you?'

'Just me, so far. We may pick up more, I think.' I said cautiously.

'Who are your leaders?' demanded Cooper. 'Where you from?'

I was about to answer, when I hesitated. Something about his sly manner and the blunt way Cooper questioned me made me decide that I should be cautious. If anyone of us was captured in this escape attempt and interrogated by the Germans I did not want to betray Wolf, Lucky and the others by revealing their names or the name of our village to Cooper.

'Never met them before,' I lied. 'I … I was told to meet them at a cave and we came on together from there.'

'Yeah, right. But you must have been sheltering somewhere all this time. Where was it?' persisted Cooper.

I paused and got out my cigarette tin and rolled one which I offered to Cooper and then made one for myself while I considered my answer. I thought of Elenitsa, Tonia, the children, Nektarios and Mama. My friends. My saviours. Nothing, I resolved, that I would say would put them in any danger. I would not reveal anything about them. Why would I trust Cooper? He had abandoned me without a thought for me and the last time I had seen him he had been in Manoli's company. That bold, bad man.

'I've been moving around from village to village, Cooper. Living in caves at night, being fed by villagers during the day. That sort of thing. No special place. Just moving around.'

I don't know if Cooper believed me for I could not see his expression in the dark but he seemed to lose interest and did not try to question me further.

Sometime after midnight, the wind changed and I could feel it blowing on my face. The land began to dip downwards and I sensed that we were heading for the sea. Then suddenly, I could hear the whisper of the waves and I knew from the salt tang on my lips that the beach was ahead of us.

Cooper had melted away into the body of the men. Probably aiming to be first in the queue, I thought sourly. We tramped downhill, following a steep track which switched backwards and forwards on itself towards the sand dunes.

I felt the power of a body thrust hard against mine. I lost my balance and tumbled awkwardly over the edge of the track. Luckily, my downward fall was halted by a stunted tamarisk tree which stopped me from plunging further down. It entangled me in its branches which cut and scratched me but it probably saved my life. I'm pretty sure that whoever pushed me did it deliberately, but it was done in such a way as to seem accidental. Simadis, I thought.

As I scrambled up to a ledge there was the sudden stutter of machine gun fire and a voice yelled: '*Halt! Raus!*'

The Cretans melted into the sand dunes and the cover of the tamarisk trees and prepared themselves for a battle.

An *andarte* slithered down to join me in my place on the ledge below the path. It was Wolf.

'*Malaka!* We have been betrayed,' he said ramming his rifle into his shoulder and taking aim.

'Are you ready, my friend?' he continued in a terse voice. 'The caique waits in the shallow water off the beach. You must escape if you can. God speed you. Go well. *Kalo taxidi!*'

The Germans shouted at us to surrender and followed the order with a round of machine gun fire.

Two of our party ran forward in panic across the dunes holding their hands high above their heads in the familiar gesture of surrender. They twisted and fell as they were shot in cold blood by the merciless German machine gun.

'Lucky and the others will try to attack the Germans from the rear.' Wolf told me. 'They will kill them, one by one, with rifle shots. And then they will slit their throats. Not one will remain.'

In the dark I could not see any chance of that working but I did indeed hear several shots and cries break the night.

The fishing vessel had retreated farther out to sea. I decided that it was now or never. To come this far and to be captured and sent to a prison camp after so long on the run; I knew I could not face it, so I decided to take my chance. Do or die. I crawled and slithered as rapidly as possible through the sand dunes towards the shore line, the waves and the hovering boat. Wolf remained where he was. Someone fired to cover me. It could have been Wolf. It was the last I saw of him.

I dived into the shallows, lunged through the breaking surf and icy waves, fought my way through the current and swam for my life towards the boat until I reached its side. Willing hands grasped me and pulled me aboard. As I gasped for air and choked up sea water on the deck I glimpsed Cooper struggling across the sand and I saw with disgust that he was waving a white cloth of surrender in his hand.

'Don't shoot! I heard him cry. 'Don't shoot. I surrender.'

I didn't give him much of a chance with the Germans after what I had already witnessed. I expected them to shoot him down without mercy after what had happened to the last two but, as he staggered towards them, the gunfire ceased.

In the silence he shouted: 'Don't shoot! You can't shoot me. You promised. You promised I'd be safe! Don't shoot me! I told you everything!' He had nearly reached the machine gun nest when a voice cried out:

'He betrayed us. He betrayed us all!'

I recognised the voice immediately. It was Simadis's. There and then without hesitation he shot Cooper in the back. Cooper twitched like a demented puppet for a moment and then fell onto the sand.

'He betrayed us!'

These were the last words I heard as the caique's engine roared into life and the boat sped away from the beach towards Africa.

Six of us escaped that night.

I sailed for freedom and left my friends Wolf, Lucky, Bunny and Stavro and the other *andartes* in Crete to fight for their lives and the freedom of Crete ....

[*At this point the diary ends*]

***

2001

'He was betrayed,' Poppy whispered. 'Wolf returned alone. Blood. There was much blood over his clothes. My God,' she crossed herself rapidly many times. 'I cannot bear to think of it even now. We did not know about the others.'

'Elenitsa rushed from the house. Her face it was white. "Yanni!" she cried out in a piercing voice. "Where is Yanni?"

'Betrayed,' uttered Wolf. 'We were betrayed and we were ambushed. The *Germania* knew. They knew we were coming.'

'Did Yanni escape,' screamed Elenitsa. 'Tell me.' She began to tear at her clothes and her wails echoed right round the valley. Wolf took hold of her arms and pulled her to him.

'Elenitsa *mou*, this I cannot tell you for certain,' said Wolf gently.

'Why not! Why not,' cried Elenitsa, shaking him off. We were so shocked to see her lose control in such a dramatic way as she was usually so reserved and quiet. We had never before seen Elenitsa like this. To tell the truth the intensity of her reaction frightened us.

'He was beside me on the beach, Elenitsa *mou*,' Wolf croaked and reached out for a pitcher of water which Tonia had brought for him. He was encrusted in dirt and blood and his face was white and haggard.

'I told him to run for the boat. I gave him covering fire. I did all that I could but, with truth, my cousin, I did not see him reach the boat. It was not yet daylight and the waves hid him from my sight.'

'But if he reached the boat, he must have escaped. He must!'

'This I did not see, Elenitsa *mou*. A bullet scraped my forehead. See the scar. I was knocked unconscious. I blacked out and for a short time I saw nothing. *Katholu.*'

Elenitsa flung herself to the floor and beat the earth with her hands. She tore out clumps of hair and wailed. I still hear that sound today and it breaks my heart.' Poppy's eyes filled with tears and they rolled down her round cheeks in a torrent.

'I am sorry if this is upsetting you, Poppy,' I said. 'I did not intend to distress you. Can you go on?' Poppy mopped her eyes with her sleeve. Hennery fished into the pocket of his shorts and drew out a remarkably clean handkerchief which he offered it to her. Poppy smiled wanly at us both and continued in a trembling voice:

'We waited for news. Each hour passed like a day.' I tried to picture the blanket of despair that must have settled over the house.

'News came that the escapees had been rounded up and taken away to prison at Galatas, It was a place of horror.'

I had read of Galatas Prison where there was no water and where prisoners were forced to sleep in the open, where torture and intimidation were practised as routine, and summary executions took place. Indeed a place of horror.

'Did you know that Simadis and an Englishman called

Cooper were also there on the beach that day?'

'Of this Cooper I know nothing.'

'Simadis shot Cooper.' There was a silence as Poppy took this in.

'Why,' she paused, 'why did Simadis shoot this man Cooper? What was Cooper to him?'

'Simadis accused Cooper of betraying everyone.'

'*Simadis* accused this man Cooper?'

'Yes. That's right.'

'And then he shot him?'

'Yes. Simadis shot Cooper,' I reiterated. Poppy thought for a moment.

'But we always believed that Simadis had betrayed them. Bunny told us. It was Simadis's revenge on your grandfather. No one talked of an Englishman called Cooper.'

'In the heat of battle, Poppy, they may not even have been aware of Cooper. He was not known to them. No, Poppy, my grandfather definitely writes in the diary that Cooper pretended to surrender to the Germans. He ran onto the beach with his arms up in surrender. Then he cried out that they should not shoot because he had told them everything and because they had promised to protect him. That made him the traitor, the betrayer, and that is why Simadis called out that Cooper had betrayed them all and that's why he shot him.'

'But Wolf said nothing of this.'

'Wolf was knocked out for a short time. Wolf did not know what happened.'

'And you say that Simadis betrayed no one.'

'Not according to my grandfather. He didn't like Simadis so he had no reason to defend him, did he?'

'Yet for all these years we have believed Simadis was a traitor. *Panegyri!*'

'It's true. Simadis was guilty of many things but he was not a traitor.'

'We blamed him. It was unjust.'

'Did Simadis return unharmed?'

'Almost without a scratch. That seemed strange to us. Simadis returned just after Wolf who was hurt. Simadis went at once to Elenitsa and told her that Lancaster was dead; that he had been shot and died in the waves and the sea took him. Again her screams pieced the air like the cries of a wounded animal in a trap. It made us shudder.'

Despite Elenitsa's torment, Simadis came calling every day. He was not sensitive to her pain. He was obsessed with Elenitsa. He begged her to marry him each time and always she refused. Elenitsa was like a stone: a cold, hard, granite stone. He ignored this and persisted. The pressure was great on her. A widow's life is a hard one as I know only too well.' Poppy sniffed and sighed. Hennery patted her hand. 'Many thought that she should take Simadis as a husband. He would provide for her. She had been married only a short time and to a foreigner. She was lucky, some said, in a time of war, to find a good Cretan man who wanted her for his wife.

But Alexi *mou*, understand this, how could she think of anyone but Lancaster? And even had she not been utterly devoted to Lancaster's memory she could not find it in her heart to forgive Simadis for kidnapping him. For Lancaster had told her of this. Simadis was condemned by his own actions.

Elenitsa shunned him. We all shunned him. We hid from him. She turned from him and would not speak words to him. Finally, she cursed him.

Slowly, slowly, the men returned. Lucky was wounded by a bullet which scraped across his shoulder and the doctor had to come.

How long Simadis would have continued to put pressure on Elenitsa to marry him I do not know, but Bunny returned with shattering news. Bunny had hidden for many weeks alone in the mountains and when he thought it was safe he returned also. But without Stavro. We waited for a long time and then men brought back news that our dear, brave cousin, Stavro, was dead. We could not bury his body. We wept.

'And Bunny told us that Simadis had betrayed them.'

From then on Simadis was treated like a wild dog. No one spoke to him; no one would have anything to do with him. They spat on him as he passed. They cursed him. I curse him still. He had betrayed us all.' Poppy looked directly at me and Hennery with hatred for Simadis in her eyes.

'No, he hadn't, Poppy.' I said. 'Everyone had jumped to the wrong conclusion. It was Cooper. Cooper was a German spy, a collaborator. Cooper was utterly ruthless and was ready to aid and abet anyone if it was in his own interest. I expect the Germans paid him to betray the escapees and offered him his freedom in return. We know he was part of Manoli's gang of sheep rustlers and we can only guess that they were all spies and collaborators working for and paid by the Germans. We know that Manoli and Wolf were deadly enemies. Manoli saw his chance to get even with Wolf and was paid his thirty pieces of silver into the bargain.

'Simadis was much wronged. He did not betray my grandfather. That is certain. There is no reason to believe that what my grandfather wrote in the diary about what happened and what was said on the beach was not true.'

'*Panegyri!* What have we done?'

'Nothing. You have done nothing, Poppy.'

'But we were unjust.'

'You didn't know, that's all.' I reassured her. 'What happened to Simadis?'

'He left one day without warning. We heard from him no more. '

'He did not come back after the war?'

'He never returned. His reputation was destroyed. No

one respects a traitor.'

'Which he wasn't,' Hennery interjected.

'We heard that he fought in the civil war on the side of the Communists. He may have been killed. But we heard no word of him after that.'

'Simadis was just another casualty of war.'

'Ay me.' gulped Poppy mopping her eyes, 'God forgive us.'

CHAPTER 20

2001

The old man was sitting in the same spot in the same position on the terrace as he had been when we had left him the previous time. He might never have moved since last I saw him. He greeted us with a flick of his fingers and a slow nod of the head and stuck out a bony hand. It looked fragile but his handshake was crushing. He did not rise from his chair.

'You have returned,' he said.

'We have returned, as you requested,' I said and thanked him for seeing us again.

Hennery and I had been summoned by Adoni to his bar.

'I have news for you, my friends,' he announced as he drew his chair close. He clicked his fingers and nodded to someone unseen inside the bar. Three coffees arrived immediately.

'The old man we visited before telephoned to me. He wants to talk to you again. We can go now if you want.'

'I hope I can come too,' said Hennery eagerly. 'I am enjoying this detective work.' Adoni clicked his worry beads between his thick fingers and his gold rings flashed in the sunlight, but he remained silent.

'Why does he want to see me?' I asked.

'He will tell you himself. The choice is yours.'

Hennery was already standing up and gulping down the last of his coffee. 'Let's go, man,' he demanded.

We went.

But this time I drove my car with Hennery in the back and Adoni sitting beside me to guide me. Hennery was thrilled by the sight of the *kafeneion*.

'Old Crete.' he uttered. 'Awesome!'

We greeted the old man and went through the usual ritual of raki and toasts. Then he leaned back stiffly in his chair.

'Costa is my name,' he said.

'Costa,' I repeated and paused while I digested this information. Another dead end. 'There is no one in my grandfather's diary called Costa. I am afraid we have wasted your time.'

I looked at Hennery and he grimaced and shrugged his shoulders. I could tell that he was as disappointed as I was. We had placed too much value on this meeting.

Costa regarded us and twirled the end of his magnificent silver moustaches. He sat up straight and squared his shoulders.

'You may know me better by another name.'

'Yes?'

'As Wolf.'

I jumped to my feet.

'No sweat!' exclaimed Hennery, slapping the table with his palm.

I shook Costa's bony hand.

'Wolf! Wolf. You are the hero of my grandfather's diary!' I exclaimed. 'He writes so much about you.'

Wolf inclined his head.

Hennery and I embraced him, Greek style, and grabbed the raki to toast him.

When we had calmed down a bit and digested this golden nugget of information I asked: 'Why did you not tell me when I visited you before?'

'Forgive me, my friend, for saying this, but you were a stranger to me and Adoni here. We did not know you. *Lipon*, we did not trust you.'

I could see that he had a point. 'But I told you I had come to find the family who saved my grandfather and to thank them.'

'A worthy reason,' said Adoni clicking his worry beads over his fingers. 'If true.'

'What do you mean?' demanded Hennery.

'Consider this, my friend.' said Costa looking at me with faded chocolate eyes. 'How are you called?'

'Alexander Dunbar, Alex. '

'And you are the son of?

'Helen and Nick Dunbar,'

'Your mother is called Helen?'

'Right.'

'She is the daughter of Lancaster or Yanni as we called him.'

'Right again.'

'*Lipon.* You present yourself to us as his grandson. And we say to ourselves: how can this be possible. We thought Lancaster was dead. He died on the beach as he tried to escape. He was betrayed. We say this must be the son of another. We say this cannot be true. We say that Lancaster was married to my cousin Elenitsa. Again, we say how this can be!' Costa paused and twirled his moustaches between his fingers.

'We ask: is Lancaster alive? Why he did not return to Crete? If this stranger is his grandson, is it possible that he has another family? If this is so, he betrayed our Elenitsa.'

'Costa,' I said, 'We knew nothing of this. Truthfully. My grandfather died a few months ago. I found his diary when I was clearing out his house. I read it. It was amazing.'

'Awesome!' added Hennery.

'You were a brave – what's the word – *Palikari*. Courageous, kind and generous to him. I wanted to visit Crete, follow my grandfather's footsteps, find you and meet you and the family in order to thank you. I knew nothing of a marriage. There is nothing in the diary about my grandfather marrying Elenitsa. Sure he mentions that he liked her, but there is nothing more.'

'And it was a shock, man, I can tell you, when Poppy told us yesterday.' added Hennery. 'No sweat.'

'Tell me, are there not laws in your country about a man marrying two wives together?'

'Bigamy? Of course.'

'Then you will understand our distrust of you.'

'Agreed.'

'It shocked us too. I can tell you, man' added Hennery.

'I can't defend what my grandfather did or explain it.'

Costa looked at Adoni and then at us. Finally, he said:

'And another thing. Have you come to find out who betrayed your grandfather? Do you come for revenge? The point is, we do not trust you or why you are here.'

'Fair comment,' said Hennery.

'I hope I can persuade you to trust me now.' I said. 'I don't mean you any harm. I have learnt this week many things which I did not know or expect and which have shocked me. I am still trying to piece the story together and to try and make sense of it.' I took a sip of raki. Costa and Adoni regarded us with stony expressions.

'I am glad you survived the war, Wolf,' I said, changing the subject. 'Did you go to America as you planned?'

'*Malista*. After the war I took a boat to the USA and I worked there for many years. '

'Did you buy a bar like you said you would?' asked Hennery.

'*Malista*. I bought a bar and then another. Then one more. Five altogether. I bought and sold and made money. I worked hard. America is the land of opportunity. I sent for Tonia and she joined me.'

'Tonia! Do you mean Elenitsa and Poppy's sister?' exclaimed Hennery. 'No sweat.'

'Yes. I married Tonia and we had fine sons and daughters. We returned here with our money and I opened my taverna in the town as I said I would. And bought this bar here for my retirement.'

'This is the bar where you and my grandfather met the bad man, Manolis, isn't it? – just before he escaped.' I said.

'How did you know that?' asked Adoni.

'I recognised the painted gourds hanging outside. My grandfather mentions them. They are very distinctive.'

'Many more than before. Yes . It is the same. I stay here and I have a very capable manager at my bar in town. He is sitting right here.' He gestured to Adoni.

'Adoni and Tonia I might have guessed. It's a family naming thing isn't it?' said Hennery.

'*Malista*. Family first,' nodded Costa. 'And my granddaughter looks so like Tonia when she was young, I am reminded of her every day.'

'Reminded.' I repeated.

'Tonia has gone to God.' announced Costa, crossing himself. We murmured regrets.

'It was some years ago. I am eighty. And if you think my poor granddaughter is stuck here living a peasant life I will tell you that she is studying for a degree in economics at the university at Rethymno, she speaks four languages and is staying here merely to write her thesis in peace and quiet and because she likes to help me and give me company.' Costa paused and twirled his moustaches once again in just the way my grandfather described. I felt the atmosphere lifting.

'So...' he said slowly, 'I am a hero. '

'My grandfather writes about you all the time. You were his hero. He admired you enormously. I think he would have followed you anywhere.'

'What stories does he tell?'

'The missions, the wine and raki making, rustling sheep, the encounters with Manoli; it's all there.'

'So long ago. I have forgotten it.'

'I will get copies made for you all, and translated, if you like.'

'He was a good friend.' stated Costa. 'Why did he

betray Elenitsa?'

'I can't answer that question. Hennery and I have been discussing it and trying to find a solution. The young Lancaster you knew was not the grandfather I knew. He was a changed man and something changed him.'

'We may never know,' said Hennery, 'but I can definitely confirm that when I knew him he was what you Cretans call a *Malaka*!'

Everyone laughed and it broke the tension.

'Wolf. I'll always think of you as Wolf. It has been a privilege to meet you and to put a face to a hero.'

Wolf inclined his head and twirled his moustache ends.

'They are magnificent moustaches,' I said. 'They are just as my grandfather describes them. I should have recognised them as a clue to who you are.'

'Awesome,' agreed Hennery.

'Adoni tells me that your grandfather owned a vineyard.'

'Yes. It's called The Double L Vineyard – Lancaster and Lukos – although we don't know why he chose the word Lukos as we usually spell it Lucas.'

'Well, my friend, in Greek the word for Wolf is Lukos.'

At first we were struck dumb and then Hennery choked out: 'No sweat.'

'Lukos means Wolf.' I repeated.

Costa nodded: '*Malista*.'

'So he named the vineyard in honour of you. You taught him to make wine after all. He never forgot you.'

'And by the way,' added Hennery, 'it produces some of the best red wine in New Zealand. He was a very successful business man.'

Costa nodded his head and laughed: 'He had a good teacher! Yes, Yanni was like a brother to me. When he did not return after the war we all thought that he was dead. We mourned him as a brother. Now the story you tell brings pain and sadness to my heart. He broke his promise to

Elenitsa and thought no more of us. This I do not understand. *Katholu,* not at all.'

'It's a mystery to us too,' said Hennery. 'But he didn't forget you. He named the vineyard after you, and Alex's mother after Elenitsa.' Then we were silent while we took stock of this paradox.

Hennery eventually broke the silence:

'Just one more thing, as we are tying up loose ends,' he added. 'What happened to young Felix? He was a great lad. Definitely, good as.'

'Young Felix, as you may expect, is old Felix now,' said Adoni dryly, tossing his worry beads through his fingers.

'Is he alive? Does he live here?'

'He is indeed alive and he lives in the town,' said Adoni.

'Great! Can we meet him.' Demanded Hennery.

'You have already met him,' smiled Adoni, flashing his gold teeth.

'Already? Who?'

'The husband of Fifi.'

'No sweat!' said Hennery.

***

2001

She wept. She wept always. Every day. She wept as she went to the well, she wept as she fed the chickens, she wept as she weeded the *horta,* she wept as she wove at the loom. At night she sobbed in her bed. She soaked her pillow with unceasing tears. This I know for I shared my bed with her. She shunned the bed she had shared with your grandfather. I knew I could not comfort her although I tried. I put my arms around her waist and I felt her body shaking with sobs but always in silence.

When she heard a step she looked up immediately,

expectantly. If she was seated inside the house she placed herself so that she could always face the door. If she glimpsed a tall shadow she thought looked familiar, she jumped up with hope in her eyes. Always, she was looking for him, waiting for him, yearning for him. She seemed to weep for a year or more.

She wept when she fed the baby. Silently she wept. Big tears fell from her eyes and rolled down her cheek and dripped onto the baby, on to her dress, any place.

'Stop, my child,' said my Mother. 'Stop. It is bad for the milk. It is bad for the baby,' but still she wept.

Even the baby could not shake her out of her misery. The baby was beautiful and very good-tempered. It had big blue eyes after the father and long eyelashes after the mother. It gurgled and laughed and beamed on us like a bright angel. We played with it like a doll. We loved it with all our hearts and so did she. And then when it started to talk, Elenitsa's tears stopped and she spoke to the child instead of weeping. She spoke to her child of her wonderful one, her brave soldier, her handsome hero. Over and over again she told the child Yanni's story: of how he had been a hero in a great battle, how he had walked across Crete all alone, how he had been left behind by the ships and how he had found our village, found her. How sick and ill he had been and how she, Elenitsa, had nursed him back to health, how they came to know each other, how they fell in love, how her father and mother were pleased for they had no son of their own and how Yanni was a son sent to them to look after them in their old age. How they were married and so, so very happy, and how Yanni had to go and leave her because it as his duty to return to fight for his country in Africa or maybe Germany and how she was waiting for his return because one day, yes, one day he would return to her and his child.

The months passed and then the years followed. The child grew. It was healthy and strong, but hope slowly dwindled away and was lost to Elenitsa.

One day Elenitsa was working on the *kipo*. She was cutting *horta* with her sharp knife and she slashed her finger. It happens. There was much blood, but she washed the wound and Tonia spread cobwebs which are good for healing and some purple ointment over the wound and she bound it with a fresh linen cloth.

Later that day Elenitsa began to shiver and feel very cold. She decided to lie down. It was the afternoon and we all slept. Later when we rose again, Elenitsa said that she felt faint and sick. She asked for the baby, kissed it and wept. She never rose from that bed. By nightfall she was unconscious and by day break her body was cold and still as a marble tomb.

We were silent with shock at the speed with which God had taken our lovely Elenitsa from us. It is our custom to bury the body at once. By night fall she lay with Mama in the family tomb. We returned from the church yard in a silent file. Now we all wept.

***

2001

'It's a bombshell.' said Hennery.

It was a lot to take in. I could not say anything for some time. I remained in silent thought. Poppy mopped up her inevitable tears, while I tried to make sense of all that she had revealed to me.

I am a pretty tough cookie. Previous girlfriends have called me insensitive among many other things, usually just after we have just broken up, but I could not help being very moved by Poppy's description of Elenitsa's deep pain, suffering, anguish and distress. Her death shocked me. It was so sudden and so unexpected. Perhaps she had not wished to continue to live a life of such grief and misery, despite the child. For her, the future was as full of desolation and sorrow and as bleak as the harsh Cretan mountains in winter.

And the birth of the child itself to Elenitsa and my grandfather left me reeling.

When I told Hennery his reaction was predictable enough

'No sweat!'

He frowned while he considered what I had told him, his acute brain sifting and analysing the new information.

'So Elenitsa is dead?'

'Yes.'

'So we'll never be able to meet her and get her to tell her side of the story. That's a bummer, man.'

'Yes. I had so many questions I wanted to ask her.' I felt a great sense of disappointment and loss and Hennery looked glum and gazed at his full glass of beer but did not seem inclined to drink. In front of us on the beach the children squealed shrilly in the bright glare of the sun, splashed in the shallows or made castles in the sand. The world of war was decades away and at the same time seemed to sit on my shoulder. Under the shadow of the palm-frond umbrella in front of the beach bar it suddenly felt chilly.

'Lancaster and Elenitsa had a child? That's a bombshell, man. I didn't think about that!' Hennery exclaimed at last. 'Was it a boy or a girl?'

'I was so shocked I didn't ask.'

'It means your Ma has a half brother or sister.'

'They might be dead.'

'This gets crazier and crazier,' cried Hennery. 'Elenitsa is abandoned by her man, has a baby and then she dies. The child becomes an orphan. It's like something out of Charles Dickens. It's bizarre.' He threw a peanut at a marauding cat.

'He never knew he had a child.'

'Serves him right, man.' retorted Hennery who was becoming increasingly waspish and moralistic about my grandfather's behaviour. 'If he'd come back here he'd have found out wouldn't he?'

'Which raises another point. Was he a bigamist or not a bigamist?'

'It depends on when Elenitsa died.'

'That means we must find out the exact dates and knock that mystery on the head.'

'You may not be the son of a bastard after all, man.'

'It's no joking matter, Hennery, and we can't ever – repeat *ever* – breathe a word of this to my mother when we go home. We will have to be extremely, economical, er … what was that phrase you used, Hennery?'

'Economical with the actualité. It was coined by Alan Clark a British politician. Coincidently he wrote a book about the fall of Crete.'

'Economical with the truth. Ma would be devastated if we told her everything. And she doesn't deserve to be yet another person who has been betrayed. There's been enough betrayal one way and another already.'

'What was he really like, your Grandfather?' asked Hennery

I had asked my Ma exactly that question after I had read the diary and a few nights before the trip.

'Difficult.' she had said. 'You know what he was like,'

'Fair comment,' agreed Hennery 'that's what I always thought. I'll admit I was wary of him when I was a kid, but he was old when I knew him and I suppose I took it for granted that old age had made him a cantankerous and bitter old man. Although, my Granpop wasn't at all like that at all. He was good as.'

'So, I asked my Ma, what he was like when he was young,' I continued.

'I can't say for sure,' she told me wrinkling her

forehead. 'I didn't see much of him when I was a kid. He was always working. He was a terrific businessman, you know that. He left you a healthy and successful vineyard. You have to admire him for that. He made clever and astute investments and the business grew steadily. He was well known for always striking a hard bargain. He earned a lot of money, you know. He was almost wealthy.'

'Frankly, I would say that he was bloody ruthless, man.' commented Hennery sourly. 'I heard that he hired and fired without compunction.'

Ma said he was a very hard taskmaster and that he was very demanding about everything. And never gave any praise or reward either. He forced people to obey him, and became very quickly angry and aggressive if they did not.

'I'll drink to that,' said Hennery staring at his glass, but leaving it on the table.

Fear drove people from him and it left him remote and isolated. But it got him what he wanted. Yes, he definitely used that fear to get what he wanted. And she says she was definitely frightened of him all her life.'

My mother had paused at that point and I could see that the memory, even after the passage of forty years, had upset her: she had bitten her lips and swallowed hard and she was blinking back the tears. I remembered her saying that Grandfather ordered her never to cry.

'Your poor Ma was really upset then?'

'Yes, so I dropped the subject. No use in distressing her.' Hennery poured me another glass of retsina.

'Ma told me that when my grandmother complained, and she often did, that she was short of money – apparently he never gave her enough of an allowance – there were terrible, violent rows, vicious words thrown about. He accused her of being extravagant – perhaps she was, I don't know – but he made her life hell. I think he was tight-fisted and mean where my Ma and granny were concerned.'

'Generous to a fault NOT' added Hennery. 'So we have

here a man who was quick to fury, blindingly self-centred, callous, unable to show emotion, demanding, and blunt. Almost the exact opposite of the hero of the diary.'

'My, Hennery, I did not know you were capable of such eloquence.'

At this Hennery laughed. 'Perhaps the diary's a work of fiction. He wanted to be a journalist originally, didn't he?' he joked, taking a gulp of beer.

'The problem I have is,' I continued, 'who was the real Lancaster? The young man in Crete or the person we knew in New Zealand?'

'So what was he really like and what changed him, you mean? Well it may interest you to know,' said Hennery leaning across to take a melon seed from the dish and splitting it between his thumb and forefinger,' that I trawled around the internet before I left God's Own and found a lot of interesting stuff about something called PTS or post traumatic syndrome.'

'What's that?'

'It's something a lot of soldiers suffered after the First Gulf War. I expect in many wars before that too, except that they didn't understand the symptoms before then.'

'Like in World War One when they suffered shell shock?'

'Pretty much the same thing. Well, according to the trusty internet, all the old man's negative characteristics are very similar to post traumatic war syndrome.'

I considered what Hennery had said and it threw a different light on Grandfather's behaviour.

'You know right at the start of this,' I said. 'I gave the diary to one of my secretaries to type up. She said:

'I really enjoyed this task, Alex. It was fascinating to read as I typed. Your grandfather seems like a really nice young man; brave honest, eager, hopeful. What he went through during that year hidden in Crete. It was frightening. Terrifying. I don't know how he coped. But I would love to have met some of those Cretan characters. So very courageous and so carefree. Though, of course,' she added hurriedly,' they were very serious about their resistance.'

I thought of the happy-go-lucky twenty-year-old rushing to volunteer to fight, full of eager anticipation, cherishing the romantic ideal of fighting for a just and honourable cause, with a Victorian sense of idealism in fighting for the right, valiant, daring and plucky. And I contrasted this with the taciturn old man holding rage at bay by virtue of a strong will, treating those around him with disdain, meanness, often cruelty and most of all betraying those who had given him their trust.

'It must have been the war,' opined Hennery, 'but not the war in Crete. It must have been what came after and we know nothing about that do we?'

'No, not much. After he escaped from Crete he was in Egypt, I believe, but I don't know what happened after that and like many man he never spoke of his war. He didn't experience a Gallipoli like our guys in World War One, he didn't see Belsen, he was not imprisoned in a Stalag, and he didn't endure the horrors of the Burma Railway.'

'Maybe not,' said Hennery, suddenly reasonable and for him sympathetic, 'but you cannot fathom what the experience of any form of war may do to a man.'

'I'll give you the diary to read, Hennery. You'll find a very different person depicted there. People liked him; he was popular; he made good friends with Wolf and the others who really respected him and wanted to be with him and wanted to help him. Elenitsa fell in love with him, after all. Nektarios thought so highly of him that he wanted to adopt him as his son. And these people lived with him day in and day out. How could he hide his true character from them? Yet he betrayed them just as Cooper betrayed him. He betrayed them all.'

'Look at JC, he was betrayed for 30 pieces of silver. If he couldn't have loyalty what hope if there for the rest of us?'

'Grandfather had a choice. One was easy; one was hard. He could have deserted from the army and stayed in Crete: that was the easy one, yet his sense of duty impelled him to try to escape from the island and rejoin his comrades: that was the hard one. If his sense of honour and obligation made him do the right thing then, why later didn't he return to Crete and do the right thing by Elenitsa? That was his greatest obligation. What changed him? What fatal flaw in his character, Hennery,' I continued, 'led to a failure of nerve and commitment? What happened to his sense of honour? We know he had one. Is this what war does to a man? Does it take away his moral sense? Does a perfectly reasonable, likeable, young man change so radically that he loses something of his essential personality? The admirable, upright, principled man turns into a controlling, ill-tempered, dictatorial despot who cared for nothing but making and keeping money – and a bigamist to boot. 'I found that I was shouting so I took a gulp of wine.

'Easy, man, easy you are being a bit harsh.'

'But I find it hard to forgive him, Hennery, I really do. I now realise why my mother showed no interest in the diary or the past. It was my grandfather's past she did not care about because he had not cared much for her or her Mother. Her instinct was correct. Maybe she was right and I should have let sleeping dogs lie. I cannot understand, can never understand, how he could have abandoned Elenitsa; she was so sweet and he betrayed her.'

'Blame war.' said Hennery flatly. 'War divided them. War changed him – bitter, bullet hard, ruthless war. It's the legacy of war. Alex. Any war. When the bullets start flying the soldiers get hardened to the violence around them. When some of them come home they unleash that destructive behaviour on those around them, especially their family.

'Think of this. The killed and wounded and maimed

aren't the only casualties in a war. No one emerges unscathed. The reality is that war can affect a man all his life and not just a man but his wife and children too even though they weren't anywhere near a battlefield. War is the evil genie of misery and injustice.

'That's the legacy of war. It betrayed them all.'

CHAPTER 21

2001

'The child?' Poppy asked. 'Did I not say?'

'No, Poppy, and we really need to know.' said Hennery who had been agitating to ask the question as soon as he saw Poppy.

'It was a handsome *Palikari*.'

'"Palikari" – what's that?' demanded Hennery.

'A brave young warrior.'

'So what are you telling us?' I asked.

'The child was a boy.' replied Poppy.

'A boy!' Hennery and I said together.

'No sweat!' added Hennery.

'Who looked after him?' I demanded. 'Who brought him up? Who was responsible for him?'

'Wolf was his godfather and it was our custom for the godfather to take responsibility for bringing up the child. Wolf went to see Nektarios.

'You have no woman of the house now,' he said. 'And the child has no mother or father. I have long wanted to marry Tonia. Give her to me now, if she consents, and we will raise the child as our own.'

So it was done.

A boy. A child who was half brother to my Mother and a half uncle to me. A child, of whom, for all this time, we had known nothing. An orphan child, growing up halfway across the world, unknown to us. A child we could have helped and supported.

My grandfather had never known that he had a son. Had he never suspected that Elenitsa might have been pregnant? Had the thought never crossed his mind in the years that followed that he could have fathered a child? Was it a thought that he suppressed?

And why had he never cared enough to find out after the war. I found it very difficult to put myself in his shoes and to understand him. I found it really hard to accept that he had left his life in Crete so deliberately, absolutely and completely behind. He had airbrushed away its existence and kept it a secret all his life. So many more questions....

'Poppy, is the child alive? He must be an adult. He must be – what – in his fifties now? Does he live here?'

'Yes he lives. Not here in Crete, but in Athens. You remember I mentioned my cousin who is a doctor? He is actually my nephew and he is a doctor in Athens'

'So he inherited Mama's love of *farmaka*. They always said she should have been a doctor.'

'How do you know this?'

'My grandfather writes of her skill in the diary. She saved his life remember.'

'*Alithea.*'

'Has my uncle family of his own?'

'*Malista*. He has a wife who is a notary and two children who are lawyers.'

'So, I have a ready-made family here in Greece. I would like very much to meet them. Can I meet them?'

'I will arrange it.' said Poppy decidedly as if the decision had been made long ago.

'I forgot. What is my uncle's name?

'Why Yanni, of course, what other name would Elenitsa have called her son?'

'Yanni.'

***

2001

The fear of a vendetta and the loss of family honour had meant that the secret of my grandfather's betrayal kept everyone silent and possibly in fear for years.

I flew to Crete with a simple agenda to find and thank the family mentioned in my grandfather's diary, the family who had hidden him for over a year and who helped him escape from the island. I had not expected to open up old and bitter wounds or to unravel a story of love and jealousy, intrigue and betrayal. I had not realised that my innocent quest had trampled on the deepest of feelings and ignited a profound fear that I had come simply for revenge or retribution.

Poppy, Fifi, Costa and Adoni had had every right to feel, just as my mother had said, that the past was the past and best forgotten.

But I had come along trampling clumsily and ignorantly, albeit innocently and with the best of motives, over the ghosts, souls and graves of a family wounded by the past.

I suppose that my obvious honesty of motive and my uncomplicated and straightforward interest in the past had led them to put aside their suspicions and finally to trust me. They had not perhaps expected that my detective work would be so thorough and although they threw up all sorts of understandable obstacles in my way, they finally understood that there was no malevolence or spite in my quest and that I had no intention of stirring up the past, or old enmities and unleashing – like Pandora – a load of secrets into a naughty world which would cause deep wounds and hurt.

'Awesome.' Hennery let out a loud breath when we entered Fifi's house once more through the courtyard a few days later. Eftiki or Young Felix as I still thought of him, stood beside the smoking barbecue – half an oil drum on metal legs – cigarette in hand with a group of friends, tossing steaks, chops and sausages. The scent of roasted meat mingled with the aroma of charcoal and cigarettes. Inside the house, two long tables were loaded with dishes, casseroles, plates and baskets. Hennery's eyes glinted with greed as he recognised the dishes he had come to love.

A roast leg of lamb with roast potatoes and a Pav is what we do in God's Own. The women bring the meringue Pavlovas, rich in cream and piled high with kiwi fruit and the men bring crates of tinnies. I always offer wine. My grandfather described many a Cretan feast in his diary but they were wartime feasts. He never experienced a monster feast arranged by Poppy and Fifi for my last weekend in Crete.

'Man, that's a two-foot pan of moussaka!' Hennery drooled, 'and, hey, look at that pile of *kalitsounias*!'

'Have a glass of raki.' said Fifi 'We always start with raki and nuts.'

I inspected a small round black morsel: 'Is it a prune?' I asked her.

'No. no, these are sweet pickled walnuts. Try one.'

Five large dishes of Cretan salad were set between the *kalitsounias* and the fennel pies. Huge plates of chicken and lamb chops, many different types of cheeses, boiled artichokes, chestnut *stifado* and octopus in red wine jostled for room on the table.

'I've died and gone to heaven,' breathed Hennery. 'I'm gonna eat the lot, man.' and he very nearly did.

The family gathered. Wolf came down to the plain from his mountain with his granddaughter, transformed from the simple girl I had first met to a gorgeous and glamorous young woman in high heels, smart dress, hair that fell in luxurious kinks down her back and enough make-up to stock an entire cosmetics department. Adoni arrived flashing gold teeth and tossing his worry beads from finger to finger. Fifi's extended family flooded in. Poppy gleamed with delight as she led us around introducing Hennery and me to my new family.

Finally, the bodies parted a little, the roar of voices died down to a murmur. Poppy and Fifi took one of my arms each and led me to a new arrival.

Silver hair flopped over the forehead of a stylish, tanned stranger. He was taller than the average Cretan. He wore expensive casual gear; open-necked Lacoste polo shirt and sand-coloured chinos. A golden cross hung on chain around his neck. Blue eyes, a distinctive long nose and a few wrinkles on a tanned face, a familiar face, my grandfather's face and, perhaps, my face.

'Alex,' said Poppy, 'we want you to meet Yanni – your uncle.'

'No sweat,' breathed Hennery.

We regarded each other intensely and then embraced. He spoke perfect English with hardly a trace of an accent. I can't remember what we said: the excitement and the emotion were too great. Hennery said later that we looked like father and son. Yanni told me that I looked very like his own son who was about ten years older than I.

Eftiki thrust glasses of the red family wine into our hands and as we drank each other's health. I thought of all those toasts in raki that my grandfather and Wolf and his brothers had drunk together in the war. Then we poured wine for everyone else and I went round clinking glasses with each new relative: cousin, uncle, aunt and I thought of those who were missing, especially Elenitsa.

'Stay here,' said my new uncle after I had met everyone.

'Stay. There is someone else you must meet.'

He left me for a moment and returned, ushering ahead of him an elderly, elegant, grey-haired, woman. She stood straight as a cypress and slender as a reed. Her grey hair was swept up and away from her face in a sophisticated chignon. Her eyebrows were a straight smudge of charcoal. The skin of her face was wrinkled, but the fine bone structure of her high cheekbones remained.

I sensed, no, I knew without a shadow of a doubt before he told me that this old, but beautiful woman was Elenitsa.

I am not emotional but I felt the hairs stand up in the back of my neck and even a small prickling behind the eyes.

'Elenitsa. You must be Elenitsa.' She inclined her head. 'I thought you were dead,' I blurted out gracelessly.' But I can't tell you how happy it makes me to meet you.' I added.

Behind me Hennery breathed: 'Awesome!'

I took Elenitsa's fragile hands and kissed them. The wedding ring on her left hand picked up the light.

She smiled gently.

'I am very much alive, as you see,' she said, stroking my cheek softly. Her large solemn eyes glistened with unshed tears but the expression in them was of intense warmth and love. I could see immediately what had enchanted my grandfather.

Time passed. We had much to say to each other. Later I asked: 'Didn't he ruin your life?'

'My life ruined? Why so? I found a great love. He was my soul. He gave me my son. A precious gift. I have him still beside me.'

'But he abandoned you. He left you alone forever. He betrayed you. Doesn't that make you angry?'

'Alone, yes. Angry, no. Very sad certainly and broken in my heart. But I had my beautiful son. Who was a great joy. I had my family to care for me, my parents at first and then my sisters and my work each day. You see, I had always hope. I did not know if he was dead or alive. None of us knew. Wolf asked everyone and so did Lucky, but no one knew nothing. Nothing at all. *Katholu*. Always, I looked for him to walk through the door. For many years I held hope in my heart. I prayed to the Holy Virgin Mother. I begged her to bring him back to me safely. But it was not to be. Simadis asked me many times to be his woman but I did not want to love another. Who could take the place of my Lancaster? So brave, so handsome.'

'But when you lost Lancaster, it changed your life.'

'I am a Cretan woman. My life is my husband and my son. My parents taught me to obey and accept what God sends. I had my work in the house and garden, my animals, my loom and this did not change until my son grew to be a man.

'By then the world was changing. We had cars, not donkeys. Electricity replaced the oil lamps, water was brought through pipes. I wanted the best for my son. He was a clever boy. He must have taken after his father. We sent him to Athens to study. I wanted him to have a good life. But when my son left me it was very hard. It was like losing Lancaster all over again. The he said to me 'Mama come to Athens also. Look after my house and look after me as you always did. My sisters said I must go. So I went at once. I closed the house in the village and travelled overnight by the ferry to Piraeus and then to Athens and there I stayed.'

'Did you or your son try to find Lancaster?'

'In Greece and Crete after the war life was very difficult. First there was civil war on the mainland and after that in the world there were many people looking for parents and children and husbands. Yes, it was difficult. We asked, but no one knew anything. And then again we did not know for certain whether Lancaster had been captured by the Germans and put in prison or even shot. We did not know if he had escaped and been killed in the fighting after. Also we knew so little about him: only his name and age, everything else was a military secret to protect him. And New Zealand is a big place, far away, no?'

I had to agree.

'But now,' she said gently, laying a thin hand on my arm, 'you have come from Lancaster. You are now family. You have found us and I have found you. I must go now, but tomorrow we will meet and you can tell me what you know of my wonderful Lancaster and his life and his work in New Zealand,'

This gracious forgiving lady, half a century on, showered me with trust and love and warmth. There was no anger, no resentment, no bitterness at my Grandfather's failure to honour his promises to her: just overwhelming goodness and acceptance.

I knew that when tomorrow came I would choose my words carefully. I would not destroy her image of my grandfather. The man I knew was not the man she had loved with absolute fidelity and deep devotion for over half a century. Her Lancaster was not my Grandfather. Her Lancaster was the plucky, happy-go-lucky boy aged just twenty who had volunteered to fight for a king and country far away. Her Lancaster was a brave, tough young soldier on the run from the enemy; a young man in a perilous world, fighting for survival, and living dangerously from day to day. Her Lancaster had loved her truly in that moment.

Would I reveal what we knew about Lancaster's character to Elenitsa?

No.

Tomorrow when I met Elenitsa I would choose my words carefully and coat the reality in Cretan honey.

END

Acknowledgements

This is a work of fiction. None of the characters existed except in my imagination.

The Battle for Crete did take place in late May 1941. It was a catastrophe for the Allies. Although the fighting was in the north, the Allied troops were ordered to retreat south across the waist of the island to a small bay called Hora Sfakion and to wait there to be rescued by the Royal Navy. They were under constant attack from German planes all the way and on the beach. Many soldiers had to be abandoned. Some were killed or wounded and were later captured and imprisoned by the German invaders. Others, including Australians and New Zealanders, escaped, wandered the island and were hidden in Crete by courageous Cretan families who took great risks to help them. Later, some were able to escape to Africa in small boats or caiques.

My first thanks go to all those who helped me in my research here in Crete. Their comments, contributions and practical help encouraged me enormously. They know who they are. Kind friends encouraged me and helped me to turn a manuscript into a book. I thank them from the bottom of my heart.

I found many books helpful in my research.

Any writing by the sublime Patrick Leigh Fermor is an inspiration and a pleasure. I recommend readers who love Greece and Crete to read his *Roumeli* and *Mani*. He knew Greece intimately and describes it sublimely and with great affection. Artemis Cooper, who knew him well, has written an excellent biography of him.

PLF was an SOE officer in Crete during World War 2 and orchestrated the kidnap of General Kreipe. These exploits are recounted in *Ill Met by Moonlight* by W. Stanley [Billy] Moss.

His great friend Xan Fielding also served in Crete in the SOE. His excellent book *The Stronghold* describes events in South West Crete later in the war. George Psychoundakis tells of messengers and missions and his astounding adventures in his autobiography *The Cretan Runner*.

For military and strategic background, I turned to Antony Beevor's excellent *Crete: the Wartime Resistance* which cannot be surpassed, although Alan Clark's *The Fall of Crete* comes close. Eyewitness accounts have been preserved in *Crete 1941: Eyewitnessed* by C Hadjipateras and M. Fafalios; there is archive film on You Tube.

Village life, customs and the rhythm of the seasons in Greece and Crete are described in *Portrait of a Greek Mountain Village* by Juliet du Boulay, George Apostolakis' *Traditional Cretan Wedding*, *Olives* by Mort Rosenblum and Mary Jacqueline Tyrwhitt's *Making a Garden on a Greek Hillside*.

John Pendlebury, the renowned archaeologist and assistant to Arthur Evans at the Minoan site at Knossos knew Crete intimately. He walked or climbed every mountain, knew every village and most of the inhabitants. He was immensely popular and respected and for that reason was killed, assassinated even, by the Germans in the early days of their Cretan campaign. There is an excellent biography of him called *The Rash Adventurer* by Imogen Grundon.

This book is dedicated to the generous, hospitable and, above all, courageous men, women and children who fought with such determination and bravery to keep Crete independent and free.